THE PALACE OF PLEASURE

AMALINA DALCA

· EPISODE 2 ·

C.L. HOLMES

BAD HOUND PRESS

The Amalina Dalca Series

Episode 1 · The Secrets of the Wailing Castle

Episode 2 · The Palace of Pleasure

Episode 3 · The Midnight Gift

Episode 4 · A Brocade Army

Episode 5 · The Silver Army

Episode 2

The Palace of Pleasure
Amalina Dalca, Episode 2
© 2019 C.L. Holmes

This text previously published as:

The Count at Play & Slaughter:
Episode 2: The Palace of Pleasure
© 2018 C.L. Holmes

Amalina and the Palace of Pleasure
Episode 2 in the Count at Play and Slaughter series
© 2019 C.L. Holmes

Bad Hound Press
A Division of Giant Dog Books
www.giantdogbooks.com
All rights reserved.

ISBN-13: 978-1-949043-44-0

Cover, design and layout by Dominic Wilde

THE
PALACE
OF
PLEASURE

Prologue

The Believers

Two travelers entered the inn. They shook the rain off at the door but kept their heavy cloaks on as they moved further into the crowded dining hall, pulling their damp, dark hoods tighter over themselves.

"You'll behave?" the short one rasped.

The taller one didn't answer, but by the sharp up-and-down movement at the shoulders might have given an annoyed shrug.

This made them a curiosity.

As the shrouded couple shuffled past the ranks of occupied tables, everyone's conversations resumed, but with voices lowered and their eyes tracking the new arrivals. And they paid little attention to what they themselves were saying, nor cared how well it fit with what was being discussed just seconds before, or whether they were making any sense at all.

Without looking up, the short one led the taller one to a corner table far from the fireplace.

"You'll stay here and behave," the rasp came again, after they'd rested a minute. "Just mind yourself and say nothing."

Odd accent. And a slight limp, it seemed. Yet the small one controlled the larger one, with the power to seat the larger one at a table and expect the larger one to remain quiet after it had gone away; which it did after delivering its instructions.

When the small, scratchy-voiced, limping one exited, the room's chatter dribbled to an end.

"You're going to do something about this, Brunhilde?" a patron whispered to the innkeep with a sly, baiting grin.

"Best to keep out of it," she said, toweling a table anxiously and eyeing the solitary figure.

"When have you ever?" whispered another. "You're the last to abide a mystery. Go do your job."

She nodded, now with a clever grin of her own.

"Who have we here?" barked Brunhilde, as she loudly dropped a flagon of something spicy and steaming onto the table in front of the remaining figure. Breaths were held as they waited to see what was to happen.

"I heard what he said," Brunhilde smiled broadly, with an almost jovial tone, "and I won't contradict your master's wishes. But I've a right to know who comes through my own door, don't I?"

The dark hood nodded.

"You thirsty?" she asked, pushing the flagon closer.

The hood shook side-to-side.

"A beer then? Make it real hot for your belly on a cold, wet night. Good and fortifying."

The hood shook again.

"You hungry? We've plenty to eat here, if you like."

Another shake.

"Can you speak?"

A shy nod.

"Hey, now. I can't hear you."

"I can speak," came a very light and soft voice, also with an odd accent. "Sorry, ma'am. I can speak, yes."

"Very polite. I can appreciate that. You hear that, you rude bastards?" she called humorously to everyone in the room, who were now openly staring. "A bit of politeness can teach you something."

Brunhilde returned her attention to the hooded figure. "That's a nice voice you got. Very pretty. But you're too big in body for such a small voice—that is, if you're to be a boy. You're a girl?"

"Y-yes, ma'am."

"Belong to that carriage outside? With those scary looking horses?"

"Y-yes, ma'am."

"Your master didn't even have them unharnessed. Or watered, or fed."

The figure did not offer comment.

"Not to pry too much more," Brunhilde said, "and respecting your master's wishes, but where do you come from?"

"Um …"

"What's that, girl?"

"Um …"

"Here, take off that hood so I can better hear you. It's all right. Let's just have a look at you and see who I'm talking to; and understand what you're mumbling anyway. I'm sure you are very pretty, the way your master has you all wrapped up."

The figure reached up and pulled back the hood.

"My!" cried Brunhilde with a beaming smile. "You are very pretty indeed! And young! But I was suspecting something like an abducted princess. Why, you're nothing more than a maid by the looks of you. But that couldn't be true. What's the story, then? Let's hear it: Where are you and your master from?"

"Ardeel." Shy, her eyes never left her lap.

"Never heard of it. And where are you going in that fancy carriage?"

"A-Antwerp ... I think."

"Antwerp? Well, isn't that interesting. And your master is out fetching our best tailor. He's got the dress of a princess he wants to mend and alter. What princess goes inside that dress? *Are* you just a servant girl? Or are you really a princess after all? But look at those hands of yours. So strong. They look to've seen more work than a royal daughter would see in a lifetime." The girl hid her hands in her sleeve. "Speak up, pretty one. Let's have your story then. Should I have bowed to the floor at your feet? I think it unlikely. Who are you two, and what are you up to?"

Now the girl looked up at Brunhilde with her large brown eyes.

"I ... " she began, but lost her voice, her face expressing a deepening worry.

"It's all right," Brunhilde encouraged, dropping her voice low, as if the conversation would be just between themselves and not heard by all the heads in the room; those heads leaning forward to soak up every word.

"Well ... " the girl started from a different angle into the conversation, but stopped again. "Um ... Can I ...? Can I *trust* you?"

"Oh, my dear! Yes you can rely on me! Of course! Just out with it and I will protect you! We all will! Are you in trouble, my innocent?"

Her eyes searched the faces staring at her. Her lower lip trembled. Her eye dropped a tear down her cheek. "I ... It might not seem believable. But it's true. You must hear me, please, I beg you. Listen to what I have to say and believe!"

"You have us worried." Brunhilde lowered closer, putting a fat hand on the girl's back to steady her, or to prod her into confession. "Do trust that we *will* believe you!"

"I can't say who I am," said the girl. "I'm sworn against it. But I must tell you everything: I'm in great danger. And the lives of everyone I love is under threat by..."

"Go on."

"You see, I was stolen away from my family, from my village, and kept prisoner in a castle high in the mountains of Ardeel, just outside of Netz."

"Oh!"

"I know it might seem unbelievable, and yet it's all true, I swear it. The one who kidnapped me ... he is a ... Well, he is an ancient monster ... A Strigoi ... I think ... if you know what a Strigoi is. Have you heard of a Strigoi? The one who's done this to me, he used to be a king or something hundreds of years ago. But now he says he is a count. He is very powerful, anyway. He can move at the speed of lightning, too, and he ... he's killed so many people. So many innocent people. I've seen it with my own eyes.

Almost ripping their heads off with his teeth and eating their blood. Why, he did it to a friend of mine, Lucinda—oh, but I can't say her name. I'm not supposed to say any of this. I can't, or he will kill my whole family. He told me so. He forces me to live with him in the castle. Cleaning it and getting it ready so he can … Oh, but I'm not supposed to really—oh, and I don't understand it all, anyway, but he's looking for a princess or some Lady of Title that might love him, I think. Yes, that's it. Or maybe, I don't really know. It's all very confusing and he is so monstrous. But I can't be released from his service unless I give him what he wants. Oh, it's so horrible!"

The dam had broke, she said it so fast, her words like surging water, flying in all directions without reason. And now that it was done she broke down crying. "He said never to tell anyone or my family would die! Why did I do it? Why did I tell you?" she blubbered into the fold of her arm.

"It's all right, little one," Brunhilde soothed with a voice now quiet, but with a troubled look in her eyes, and a tight expression around her lips. "That's a story that needed to come out, for sure. For sure! Too awful to keep it in. And know that none of us will tell a soul of what you said."

"But it isn't a story," she mumbled. "It's true. It's all true."

"Of course."

"Now I'm supposed to pretend I am his niece, and I will be presented at court. And I am to lure the princesses and ladies away to his castle."

"My …" Brunhilde exclaimed with less vigor than before. She looked haunted. The girl glanced up at her, and then swept her eyes around. Almost everyone had the same expression.

"You do believe me, don't you?"

"How can we not?" But … *was that a look of caution?* "You said to believe you, didn't you? You said we must."

"But *I* wouldn't," said she, becoming concerned. "If someone told me a tale like that a couple years ago, I'd think they were making it up, or were joking, or they were mad. I wouldn't believe them at all."

"How could we not believe you, little girl? Do you think we don't know about such things? You're so very young and we're much older than you."

This reminded the girl of something else, something she'd discovered after she'd witnessed Lucinda Skeldar's death and been taken by her monstrous murderer: most of the adults in her village—most of the adults in her country, in fact—not only knew of this monster and kept he and his crimes secret, had shielded his existence from their children and all outsiders, but they had for centuries allowed him to live unchecked. Left him at liberty to prey on the general population for fear he would kill them all if they should attempt to stand against him.

These people here in the dining hall were adults, too. And even if they didn't know of the Count, he being a monster in a far away country, they might have a monster of their own. Yes. She saw their looks and knew, even before Brunhilde said it:

"My uncle and three of my aunts were killed by a beast—a wolf that walked on hind legs and was as tall as a house."

"Oh, yes! And a fiery wraith," said a man just behind Brunhilde, his face pale and haunted, "ate of my neighbor's family. One by one, it did. And we could hear their screams when it done it. I cannot forget the racket. And it burned their whole house to the ground so that there was nothing left ... not even ashes!"

"Oh, yes! And something like a dragon mixed with a bird, and the bottom half a woman, naked as the morning," said another man, his body shaking, "has killed anyone travelling the southern pass at midnight, though we warn them against it. We can hear its mocking laugh every time someone sets out from the Briberg gate at sunset, though they just swear it's the singing of a nightjar."

"Hear, hear! And by the castle of the Koenig cliffs," announced a burgher, in the direst tone, "there is a lake in which dwells a creature no man has survived the sight of. But on certain days—not just by night!—it emerges, the size of an elephant, or extends itself from the cold, black waters, and reaches inside the castle to prey on whoever is foolish enough to live there. It has killed seven-score, leaving behind only a trail of slime, or the tell-tale prints of its feet—as large as an elephant, as I said!"

"Oh, yes! Hear, hear!" went up the chorus.

And it carried on from there, the girl's story having set fire to the room and spreading from one excited mouth to the next, building into something like an inferno, with the inn's patrons—though shivering in fear, as if experiencing the deepest, bone-chilling cold—throwing off their overcoats and jackets in the mounting excitement.

Almost every person took their turn, relating a terrifying story of a monster still more hideous, and more deadly, and more powerful than the last. Each defying credulity, but believable by the certainness of the moment and the brave candor of the speaker, the land seemingly bloated beyond capacity with creatures—though the girl did begin to wonder if everyone was telling the truth by the time some people rose from their chair to speak for a second time. They were like a mob, driven into a hushed fury; the excitement of a taboo to silence being shattered and their combined force of outrage concentrating into a critical mass.

In the end, all eyes returned to the girl in the corner of the room, who was now standing and looking ever more hopeful than before. She never thought she could be heard by anyone else and believed, much less driven into a passion for justice against the outrage of all the monsters of the world and their inhuman crimes; so that, to a person, they looked ready to declare open rebellion against those very creatures.

She had been so afraid to say anything. All the fears of the past year, during her stay in the Count's castle, in which she witnessed the further killing of people who she'd hoped would help her destroy the Count (or at least rescue her from his castle), and those fears bottled up and building pressure within her until she felt she could crack; not daring to crack out of fear for her family's life, yet now doing so. Revealing everything, and working what seemed a miracle. She could not believe it.

"And so you believe me," she said, nearly in tears again.

"Of course, little one!" cried Brunhilde. "Did you not just hear our confessions?"

"Then will you help me?" she cried in return.

A silence resounded in the room, more deafening than anything she had experienced before—and this girl had been trapped inside a castle during the winter with only two other people as company, which got very quiet indeed.

Only a snap of the fire in the fireplace impelled someone to mutter, "Uhhh … "

"How could we possibly help *you*?" said Brunhilde, dumfounded by the girl's expectation, almost looking offended by it.

"But my father and I need your help!" she cried pitiably, not understanding the innkeeper's sudden, cruel indifference. "I need to escape from the monster! Escape from him, or destroy him!"

At that moment the shorter one entered through the front door, bringing in a sweep of rain and a second figure who wore a tight-fitting leather smock. This was the village's tailor.

The short hooded figure froze at the door and surveyed the scene: every person on their feet, looking to have risen to—or been driven into—a high agitation; their complexions either ash grey, purple, or a mottled mix of the two. And there was the girl in the corner, hood off, looking guilty.

"What have you done, Amalina?" the short one demanded.

· · ·

Five days later, the old dress of an Ardeelian princess was restored and revivified into a (passable) modern shape, and the niece of Count Tepsji, Lady Princess Katarina Tepsji—pleasant and pretty, if shy and a little backwards; and strangely solid bodied, with her shape suspiciously more of a servant than a sovereign child, though her manners and artful language were exquisite—was introduced into the court of the highest Flemish nobility and royalty. She was inquisitive and made many fast friends. And then this happened several more times in the courts of Germania and elsewhere.

And then the mission was complete. Genadie, the small, raspy voiced man, pointed the carriage back to the high castle, taking Amalina Dalca, the imposter princess, with him.

PART ONE
THE CAGE

1

Reasonable Men

At about the same time Amalina Dalca was being introduced into the august home of Lady Princess Lisbet Spaarvierlet (who was all smiles to meet her new friend, whom she believed was the Countess Katarina Tepsji), the low constable of Tsobl, Attila Bronk, staggered into the palace of General Zsolt Marosh, under the thin-lipped scrutiny of the general's servants.

Held in the palace's plain, modest vestibule, Attila handed over his papers but introduced himself formally anyway, as they read what he'd handed them, the papers dripping.

"You're leaking," said Zsolt Marosh, when Attila stood before the old general minutes later in his less-than-modest sitting room.

"I'm sorry, your eminence, Lord General," he apologized, adjusting himself in his spot to minimize the puddle he would be forming. "I know this is no way to appear before you, sir. But I am—well, we all are, unfortunately—under a time constraint which forbids strict formality. I come as I am, at the tail end of a long pursuit through forests and mountains and streams and rivers and snowbanks. And mud. You see the evidence in the tears, cuts, and all around sogginess of my attire."

It was a bit of a dramatic delivery, but Attila Bronk's eyes were half-lowered, and he looked almost bored. The only tell-tale of his true internal agitation was that his right hand crept over to his twitching left hand, and then to steady it, clamped onto it.

Zsolt observed this without comment. He was a large man, with a block chin, blocky cheeks and squared forehead, so that his head looked like a solid chunk of wood that had its features chopped into it. His hair was thick and mostly grey, and shot out in massive plumes on every side of his head. For being as old as he was, he appeared still powerful, and cagey, and seemed to retain a youthful sense of humor.

"A pursuit," Zsolt smiled lightly at the corner of his lips. "Who are you chasing, low constable? And how might I help you? You know, no doubt, of my hunting talents."

Zsolt waved his arm toward the walls of his less than modest sitting room, with their rows upon rows of mounted antlers. There were so many, each wall looked like a densely packed thicket of thorns.

"The other way around, I'm afraid," Attila admitted, bowing his head. "I'm the one who is on the run."

Zsolt adjusted himself in his chair and brought his head forward so he could observe Attila more closely. His servants also shifted, their glowers heated and concentrated on him.

"From?" asked Zsolt.

"At the moment, from our government."

"You know my station in that government."

"Yes, your eminence."

"You *do* know how good a hunter I am; should I be given notice to track you down … which I haven't yet, at this moment."

"Your eminence: it is your legendary accomplishments as a fierce, unrelenting warrior for your country that made me decide to come here."

"Is that so? Doesn't seem like a bright idea."

"I appreciate your station, as it is, with the government in Tsobl. But I can also guess your opinion of that government, because of the people now controlling that government, and your loyalty to it. So it was a calculation, sir, and a gamble on my part."

"Bronk? That isn't an Ardeelian name. Attila Bronk. More like half-and-half. You're with *them*, aren't you?" 'Them' meant the new government and the people who run it, at which Zsolt sneered reflexively, revealing his true feelings on the matter, confirming Attila's suspicions. Zsolt, being a native Ardeelian, did not like the new government at all.

"Well," Attila looked grim, "To return to the point. As I said, time is not on our side. I was just giving you an explanation of my thought, but I will move on: You, and your father, and your father's father, and so on, have served this country nobly since time began. They were its knights and protectors, even through all its catastrophes and invasions."

"And new governments," Zsolt added wryly, smiling again.

"Yes, that too. And you and your family are original signatories to the ancient compact with the Knight of Ardeel. The Viscount."

Some of Zsolt's servants fell back a step. Zsolt flinched.

"What's that?"

"I saw your name written there, in the book, by your own hand."

He frowned now, but with his top lip drawn so far back in revulsion his teeth were visible through his mustache. He looked vicious.

"What are you talking about? Why are you saying this to me? What's this all about?"

Attila couldn't have looked any more bored. He reached into his jacket and pulled out a red book. Zsolt snarled in recognition. He almost came up off the chair.

"What!"

"This book, your eminence. I can show you your signature to the agreement with the Viscount."

"Don't you! How dare you! What are you doing with such a thing?"

"That is what I am here to tell you. Please allow me to live long enough to do so."

. . .

With the servants removed, and the book secured again in Attila's jacket, the audience resumed.

"I have come," Attila said, with his drowsy eyes, "more or less, straight from Tsobl. Where I was informed, by no less than the governor himself, and with the King's authority, that he has agreed to continue this relationship with the Knight—now referred to as the Count (or as I say, Viscount) of Ardeel—and under the same terms ratified by your forebears; which has continued unto this day even by you and your contemporaries. An evil and disagreeable compact allowing that monster to reside in these lands unchecked, and with the permission to kill, at will, any citizen he so wishes without retribution."

"If we had not agreed to it, he would have killed us all. Down to nothing."

"That may be—"

"That *is*, Bronk!" Zsolt shot in. "He killed armies. He's destroyed cities! Two of them! Wiped them from the map!"

"Is that so?"

"You'd never believe, but it's true."

"And so you signed your name to the agreement to permit him, at his leisure, to pluck innocents from our midst."

"How did you find that book? This is the very reason it was withheld from the general public. Nobody would believe."

"Outsiders, you mean. Not the public, but withheld from outsiders." Attila then added: "Your eminence."

"Outsiders, no outsiders," Zsolt muttered. "So what is this about? Come to the point."

"My point is this: the governor, and the entirety of the new government, upon the revelation of the agreement, followed suit and made peace with that monster, the Count—"

"Good."

"—and are willing to let the terms persist, in conflict with the laws of Heaven and reasonable men—"

"Good."

"—and remain in effect not for the purpose of keeping him from striking against the people of this country, or, as you claim, wiping from the mountains whole cities with his bare hands. No, that is not their reason at all. They are not afraid of him."

"Then they are fools."

"Your eminence, it is not within my power to fault you, a man of your great stature, even if I should want to. But I understand why you did it. It was not an unreasonable fear which caused you to sign your name to this agreement. No, it was not blind fear, because you have proven yourself again and again, demonstrated your courage and strength. Your fearlessness and skills as an Ardeelian knight and warrior are beyond questioning. And so why would you sign yourself to such an odious deal, an unrighteous deal, a sinful and ungodly deal?"

"A necessary one ..." Zsolt growled.

"Because you saw it necessary. You saw your father's name there, and your grand-father's name, and your entire lineage, written in their own hand, onto those perfidious sheets of paper. This was legacy. A dark one, but a necessary one. No doubt about it. You had inherited it, just as you did your abilities and brilliance as a general on the field of battle. You had no choice."

"True. No choice, Bronk."

"But the governor, and the king, and the new assembly, and all those new people, not originating from this land, not being bound to it by blood: they had a choice. A clear choice. They could have read that damnable contract and tore it up—"

"And died."

"No," Attila said with a patient shake of his head. "Because *now* is not *then*, your eminence. That beast has considerable power, it is undeniable. But all those accomplishments you speak of—the murdering of entire armies with his bare hands—that was in a much different time. Hundreds of years ago. The power of mankind has progressed. At the time, he had only to contend with barely trained peasants, and warriors weighed down by the very armor they hoped to protect them, making them as slow as turtles, and easy victims to a monster that can travel as fast as lightning, and with the strength of twenty men. He did not have to contend with modern cannon. Or muskets. Or pistols. Or even the latest crossbows and fine steel and military discipline, expertise and training. No, he was at home and in control as a predator in the old days. But these are no longer those days. Should a modern army somehow confront an army of that time, that ancient soldiery would be as helpless against our forces as they were against the slaughtering armies of the Khan; or the Count of Ardeel. Which means, we are at a match for him, at the very least."

Zsolt smirked, and scratched at the arm of his chair nervously, but did not raise his eyes to meet Attila's. He was thinking, and maybe becoming a bit alarmed, or embarrassed, or annoyed by the shameful truth of what he was being told.

"The governor, the King, and the assembly, they all know this. The governor himself told me to my face that they are confident we have the ability to stop that abomination in the mountains. But they have made a choice not to do so. And why is that, your eminence? In order to honor an agreement made by you and your valiant ancestors? No, they do no honor to you and your kind. They have seldom honored the people whose blood created these cities, this great country. They would rather spit on you and your people. You know that."

"And so why do they obey the agreement, if they have such contempt for us?"

"Their very contempt is the reason they maintain it. As the governor said to me with his own lips: 'while he is still alive, he is useful … and necessary.' Because, your eminence, if that creature were to be destroyed, he would lift a lid off the native people of this land. They would—you and your people would—no longer have this oppressive fear crushing you down, keeping you in place and passive."

"What nonsense," Zsolt scoffed. "We fought those western bastards and never feared them."

"Never feared them, but you lost. As you lost to, and were subjugated by, the Count. And, as the thought goes, should the Count be destroyed, you would not see it as a further demonstration of *our* superior strength, which could always be turned against you, but that that strength of ours—which defeated you, and something which has held you down for so long—just as *his* strength held you in check—can be defeated. His defeat would be taken as a positive example for you to defeat *them.*

"And even more," Attila went on, building in intensity, so that it seemed like he might drool—though, as ever, his expression was something like vague disinterest. "That monster is in a silent war with the Cardinal of Netz. That Cardinal wishes to grow his power, and he is actively consolidating it. But his movement is restricted by the Count and the Count's allies. Should the Cardinal leave the St. Grigori Cathedral for the day and not return by nightfall, the monster will find him and kill him. And so the Cardinal is a bit castrated, and cannot rise as a power—a native power of Ardeel, you understand, along with all its native peoples who would follow him, instead of obeying *the new government*—rise as a power and he, which means the people, which means *you* too, under him, reclaim the country in the name of God; and by doing so, claim it in the name of God's representative, which is he: the Cardinal of Netz."

Zsolt leaned back, and lifted his eyes to reappraise Attila.

"So what is it you want, Bronk? In the end, what are you suggesting here? Side with the Cardinal in a proper revolution against the government? Against *your* own government, Bronk?"

Attila shook his head, his eyes locked unflinchingly, though looking quite bored, on Zsolt's.

"I am, I was, and I have always been a man of the law. I want justice. Rightful justice, your eminence. And I care not about whose blood is superior to whose, or what people should control the other. I care nothing for that meaningless drek. Let revolutions come and go, I speak nothing on that. It is justice. It is all about justice. And that monster, that thing in the mountains, it has strutted with impunity for too long, thinking itself above retribution, when every living, sentient being on this earth must, in the end, suffer a reckoning for his injustices.

"Your eminence," Attila began his finale with a deep bow, "That creature, who has persisted for so long outside of proper law, and did so because he had too much power for us to enforce our will upon him, he has fallen within our ability to do so. We have advanced as a race to the point where we match him, and then, we outstrip him by our sheer numbers. We finally have the ability to bring him to justice, and right a wrong that has persisted like a shameful, self-inflicted pestilence for centuries. And even now, in this war with the Cardinal, he has grown so arrogant, or perhaps he is even now gaining a heightened power, that he has broken the contract, and he has violated sanctified ground, disregarding even that which was agreed upon, your eminence. And this means that, like it or not, a war is coming, and too much innocent blood will be shed unless something is quickly done about it.

"And that is why I have come, and put myself at your mercy, to appeal to a descendant of one of the first signatories to that terrible agreement, a man who is powerful and distinguished and brave and brilliant, and has reason to hate and loathe that creature, and has all the right in the world to prosecute him and judge him and destroy him in the name of all the righteous people he has destroyed."

"What a very unexpected thing you are," Zsolt said, himself looking sleepy, or deep in speculation of something almost pleasurable. "He's gaining power, you say?"

"Not too much yet, your eminence. But there are signs, most definitely."

"Do you know where he is?"

"I'd predict he's hiding in the high castle outside of Netz. It makes the most sense."

"And do you really suppose he can be killed now?"

"*They* think so. I agree. He's within our reach, General."

"And so you believe, actually believe, I can do it?"

"With all your forces, yes. And you have every right and reason to."

"To kill the Count of Ardeel? Really?" he paused " … Truly?"

"That was my gamble in coming here, to you, your eminence."

Zsolt Marosh closed his eyes. He leaned his chin on his hand. His mustache see-sawed above his murmuring mouth.

Eventually he came out of this state and said to Attila: "Get out of those clothes and clean yourself up, low constable. You'll have my best room tonight. Let me tell you: I am most pleased."

2

A Warm Breakfast

Attila woke to eager huffing, snuffling sounds, and a wet tongue on the back of his hand. His arm was thrown over the side of the mattress, and a hound was there at his hand, painting it with its cool, wet nose and slobbering tongue. Other hounds began pawing at his feet and legs, which were under the covers. Sitting up, he counted fifteen wolfhounds pacing around the floor of his room.

"Oh, very sorry, constable," Zsolt laughed heartily. "They're very good at locating fresh meat, I should have known they'd get up to this."

It was still dark outside, with just a touch of morning silver to the sky. Not yet dawn.

Attila said nothing, but looked inquiringly at his host, who stood in the doorway fully clothed in riding garb and beaming with a great humor to his face, regarding his pack of hunting dogs as he would his grandchildren.

"Well, you know me," his host said, lowering his voice to a considerate whisper. "The hunt is always on. Never a morning without one, even if it's for exercise. Now, come along and let us have something to eat before we head out."

Attila couldn't find a place to safely put his feet off the mattress for all the furry backs, wagging tails, and probing noses. Zsolt chortled as he watched the low constable stumble to the wash basin.

"You keep your hounds in the house?" Attila said, unable to restrain his curiosity. He was still very tired from his escape, from his long flight from his Tsobl pursuers, who'd driven him through every terrain imaginable; they always one step behind … and with their own hunting dogs. He'd grown naturally wary of the beasts.

"I indulge anyone I love," Zsolt admitted with a blush. "And I trust these children of the hunt more than any man. Anyway, don't mind them. They're just greeting their papa's new friend. I'll bring them out and you come down to the dining room. The kitchen staff aren't awake yet, they'll be busy tonight when the hunt is finished. But we'll find something good to eat."

Attila found his clothes folded on a dresser as Zsolt encouraged his dogs with pats and kisses to get out of the way. The clothes were stiff and streaked with mud.

"One more apology, Bronk," said Zsolt amiably. "The launderer was ill. We put 'em by the fire, though, so at least you won't be trailing water all over the house."

· · ·

By the time Attila got down to the dining room, feeling more comfortable now that he was in his old uniform no matter how soiled it was, he heard and saw the soldiers outside preparing their horses and equipment for the morning hunt. It was a bit of rustic charm which Attila, who was used to city life, smiled at. As if discovering something new yet somehow old and naturally comfortable. As if he had always been part of it.

"Ha, ha, there you are," Zsolt greeted him with open arms. He hugged Attila, patted him on the back, and then pointed him to a chair at the large dining table. It was laid out simply, thrown together by Zsolt himself. And it was meant for the two alone.

"The dogs?" Attila asked. But he could already hear them outside.

"Can't have them in here while we're eating. They're incurable scroungers and would have taken everything off the table before I got my hands on it. The master of the hounds is getting them ready. Here, Bronk, have a seat and let us get our stomachs set. It's going to be a long day. Some say you should go to a hunt hungry, as you will hunt more aggressively, more keenly. But those that believe so have a way of fainting halfway into one of my hunts. Have you ever been on a hunt, Bronk?"

"Well ..." Attila shrugged, not wanting to admit to his new friend he was not a salty man-of-the-earth, like the old Zsolt Marosh was.

"At least once in your life," Zsolt encouraged with a smile. "Your clothes didn't get that way by a stroll through the countryside. Oh, either side of the hunt counts, Bronk. I can tell you of many escapes I had to make during the war. Escaping from *your* side's forces. Nothing to be ashamed of. Although I do prefer to be the one doing the chasing."

"Well, I'm no expert," he said, tearing some pieces of bread to eat.

"You're a natural then by the way you kept off the Tsobl trackers. I heard the new ones are very keen. I'd love to challenge them to a hunt, side-by-side, see who comes out on top."

"I'd wager you would," Attila said, carefully chewing up hunks of dried meat. "You know this land better than any of them. Your family has lived here for centuries."

"Yes, that's true," Zsolt said, wolfing two sausages. He looked like a dog himself, tearing apart a piece of game. "That's very true. Still, I'm a sporting man. And I will give you a fighting chance."

Attila's bored eyes did not move up from the sampling his hands were making of the food on the table. But he paused to register the shift in the conversation.

"Did you hear me, Bronk? I will give you a good head start, as long as you're willing to play fair."

"Yes, I heard you." Attila now opened an orange. How had the general gotten a fresh fruit so early in the season?

"You're willing to play fair with me? As I hunt you down?"

"I got the point, General Marosh. Is there a reason you are going to put me to a hunt? I thought I was your friend."

"You are one of the greatest friends I ever had," said Zsolt, his voice loud but not so full of humor anymore. "You came to me—to me!—when you could have gone anywhere else. And you reminded me of who exactly I am: Zsolt Marosh, a grand knight of Ardeel, from a long line of knights, sworn to protect this precious land from its enemies. There've been too many of these futile, meaningless little farm hunts. I'd forgotten my true purpose."

"You'd thank your great friend by chasing him down?"

"If you weren't my friend we would not be having this meal, and you would not have been allowed in my best room for the night. You would have been executed by my lowest soldier, and I wouldn't even have been present as witness." Zsolt cleared his throat. "You showed courage, amazing courage, by coming to me, and telling me everything; telling me everything as it is and withholding nothing. You gambled that it would turn out in your favor. And for that, I award you with a gambler's chance. See if you can best me the way you did the Tsobl men."

Attila nodded, wondering if he should even look at Zsolt. It would probably be too much. So he settled on surveying the room, looking for escape routes; or if an escape was possible.

"Do you want to know why I'm doing this?" Zsolt asked him, as if Attila were being too slow, or had gone into shock.

"Simple enough. Corruption isn't a mystery. I had just thought that a man of the people would have remained so—as their true champion—but I was wrong."

"I remain a man of the people, Bronk. Don't get that wrong. I am a man of the Ardeelian people and its land."

"The governor, the King, the Tsobl assembly, none of them share your blood, General Marosh. None of their blood belongs to this land."

"When the land is rightly conquered, when treaties are signed and arms are laid down, then those native people must adhere to the new peace, and stand as one with the controlling body which bested it. Or they shouldn't have stopped fighting. Where you see corruption in my decision to abide by my agreements, low constable, you are very mistaken. You see dedication, honor and loyalty. Tsobl may come, Tsobl may go. I and my people and this land will always be here, and we will proudly serve those we've pledged ourselves to, given our word to, even if they were our conquerors."

Attila shrugged.

"Now pay attention, low constable. You thought you were being loyal when you came to me, but you were misguided. And in many senses *you* were disloyal. Disloyal to your kindred people, who are not of this land, and disloyal to the government you were pledged to serve. You believed you were serving a higher power. Being loyal to some principle, I can only guess."

"The good, and right, and lawful."

"Let's not argue about it. You have my mind on the matter. I'll leave you to eat in peace. When you are ready, let the guards at the door know and we will begin. You will be given a half hour's start."

Attila scratched his chin.

"Do you understand, low constable?"

"I understand." His eyes roamed the room again.

"Don't even think of escaping. If you do not follow the rules of the hunt, if you try to break early, the hunt will begin immediately. All the worse for you."

"So you will give me a fair chance, General?"

"As fair as can be. I will admit, having examined your clothes, I know your style and strategy to shake pursuit."

"And your hounds have been given my scent."

Zsolt chuckled guiltily.

"A half hour will buy you time. I'll give you one more hour here to prepare yourself and your soul. As I said, just let the guards know when you are ready. They are standing outside either door to prevent your being naughty … but I'd never assume you as a coward for the bravery you bared by coming here."

"And if you catch me, you will turn me over to the governor and his boys, or …?"

"I haven't decided yet. Maybe I will let you choose your fate. If you leave it to me, I can promise you a quick and painless death, anyway."

"And if I escape?"

"If you elude me what can I do? You are free, aren't you? And better, you can be assured I won't be bragging about my loss to anyone … so Tsobl will know nothing of your coming or going here. But I warn you again, Bronk: try to escape from here before we start properly, the hunt begins straight off. I trust you to keep your head."

Zsolt left. Two men armed with swords stood just outside the door as he closed it.

Attila finished the orange, his heavy-lidded eyes roamed the room for the third time.

Large windows along one wall faced out to a length of trimmed grass which ended in the distance at a wide stream. Oddly, no guards were outside. Attila tried the windows and found them locked and bolted. So he would have to break them if he wanted to leave quickly. And at the sound of shattering glass the guards in the hall would be on him in an instant.

Attila sat down again and ate some sausage, chomping heavily as he considered his circumstances.

Zsolt was probably hoping Attila would make for the windows. Even if he got out, he would logically head for the stream. Zsolt had already familiarized himself with Attila's tactics, and dropping into the nearest body of water—to throw off his scent—was one of them. So if Attila obliged Zsolt by jumping out the window, he'd be doing the old general a favor, giving him the excuse to start the hunt immediately, and then leaping straight into the most obvious route from the house and his howling hunting pack. The whole set up, with large windows peering onto an empty field, the guards posted outside the room and not inside, was deliberate and almost insulting temptation.

One more sausage and it was time to go, Attila decided.

He carefully and quietly pulled four chairs out from the table. The dining table had a deep underside, with thin panels that dropped on every side. Good enough, Attila thought. The remaining chairs he carefully and quietly pushed all the way in so the backs were up against the table's edge.

One by one he took the chairs he'd already removed and brought them to the doors. With the softest touch, he leaned and wedged each chair against the underside of a door handle. It was work to move as silently as he did, not alerting the guards outside, who were surely listening for any suspicious sounds of their prisoner inside the room, to what he was up to. He began to huff from exertion, and needed another couple minutes once he'd blocked the doors to the greater house and then the servant's doors to the kitchen; needed those minutes to compose himself for what was about to happen.

He took a tall candle stand, one of the napkins from the table, and one of his shoes, and went to a window. He wadded up the napkin, and then set that and the shoe on the frame of the window. Then, with a quick nod, he smashed the window with the stand. It only took several blows to clear out most of the glass. He then threw the napkin out the opening, and then, with extra care, launched his shoe as far as it would go.

The guards at either set of doors were already over the surprise at finding their entrance blocked, they were now shouting and ramming against them.

Attila scurried to the table, and after slipping under it, and slithering atop the chair seats there, he then wedged himself as far up under the lip of the table he could get. He sucked in a breath and held it when he heard the doors crash open. He tried to imagine himself as a thin piece of tapestry, so light and without need to breathe. Almost without substance, so that he would not be noticed.

"Look there! The window!" shouted a guard.

"Of course, you idiot! What do you think we heard? The fool blowing his nose? My god, he must be on the run."

"I don't even see him!"

"Made it to the river! Call out the alarm!"

"To hell with that! I'm going this way, through the window. The General said it's a gold coin for whoever catches him."

"Yeah! Me too!"

The guards who were greedy charged out the window. The guards who were loyal and stupid ran out the regular way, sending out a call of Attila's escape. Soon there were horns sounding. And a din of hounds on the hunt. And the shouts of men in a blood lust.

Attila crept out from under the table, dull eyes scanning for anyone who might have stayed behind. Out the windows, there was just the tail end of the hunting party swarming into the small river, heading downstream. He went through the doors to the kitchen.

The kitchen was empty. Who knows for how long? And it wouldn't be very long before Zsolt realized his mistake. Attila went to work.

He found a number of cheeses and meats wrapped in cloth. Except for one cheese, he dumped the contents of the cloth bags into the back of the brick oven, heaping the ashes over them to make sure they were hidden. After removing all of his clothes, he stuffed them into the largest of these emptied bags. Then he took the remaining cheese and rubbed it all over his body. On the shelves he found some pots of spices. The heaviest spice, one that made his nose burn, he put into one of the sacks, all the rest of the empty sacks going in after that. He found a sharp knife to swipe.

Then, after checking to make sure the grounds outside the kitchen were empty, though hoping there might be a horse he could borrow for himself, he let out one big sigh. And then, feeling the wind on his naked body, began his escape.

3

Welcome Back

As the carriage bounced along, Amalina's experiences in the western kingdoms danced like visions before her. It was almost like dreaming, except it was impossible to sleep with the sharp jolts of the cabin. One shock sent her tumbling forward off the padded bench.

"Genadie," she shouted out the window, "Do we really have to go so fast? Take it easy."

"Yes, we must!" Genadie blasted from the driver's seat. "We're going too slow as it is. Hyahh! Hyahh! Nk! Nk!"

The horses did not speed at his urging. It was a wonder they hadn't yet collapsed. Amalina heard their ragged breaths, and their groans of protest.

"I said slow down, Genadie!"

"Ah, Amalina, let's not forget ourselves. You are no longer the Princess Tepsji. You can't boss me around as you like."

"But still!" she shouted angrily. However there was nothing to be done about it, Genadie had returned to his role as slave to his master, the Count. And so she settled back into the cabin and wedged herself into the corner, hoping it would secure her from another fall.

"We must make the castle by today," Genadie continued, his voice wafting in through the window. "Or we'll have to stop for the night, and maybe lose maybe another day at that!"

"Today? Are we really that close?"

Amalina stuck her head out and saw the stony mountains rising like jagged fangs all around them.

Her heart beat faster. It seemed they'd only just left the Schiederburg gates yesterday and already they were home … well, at this point it felt like home: the Count's high castle. She could feel the nearness of Korr, her own village; saw in her mind the many roads linking the castle to her real home, connecting her to her father Dragomir, and the bakery, and her friend Cristine. She hadn't seen them in over a year. More dismaying, during her great tour of the western kingdoms she hadn't had any time to think of them at all.

Her mission (now completed) seemed almost like a dream. In the moment, from beginning to end, it felt hurried, tense, and stressful as Genadie rushed them from one city to the next, rehearsing her in the languages and the script she was to use to fool everyone. And then having to pull it off credibly, her heart pounding so hard, the sweat of fear—a fear that the charade would be discovered—pouring off her, soaking her dress, feeling she might faint.

But overwhelming as the experience was, it had certainly been worth the shock. Before she knew it she'd gone from being a reluctant participant, dragged into it, desperately trying to slip her shackles or bust through the eyebolt which secured her to the middle of the carriage floor, to being introduced into castles and palaces she'd only ever imagined. These majestic homes in cities she'd seen printed on maps but she'd never expected to visit in person; and being received as nothing less than a princess herself, someone of (almost) equal standing to these lofty nobles. And they believing her!

How easy it was to trick them. With just a ramshackle carriage, and little Genadie dressed up as a footman/valet/driver/guard, and—most importantly—with a letter of introduction from her 'uncle', the Count Tepsji of Ardeel, a man of great wealth. The wealth part opened the doors, as the parents of young, marriagable daughters clucked merrily over Amalina (or rather, clucked over 'Lady Princess Katarina Tepsji', the wealthy count's niece). And the excitement and novelty of an exotic princess from a little known land piqued the curiosity—and opened the hearts—of the daughters themselves.

She made friends with many of them, seemingly genuine friends. So warm and chatty and full of life. They weren't any different from anybody else, really—and that is what Genadie had kept assuring her, wasn't it? Only they were bound by manners and customs of the aristocracy. But deep down, stripped away from all the rituals, they scratched themselves, and had vicious senses of humor. So unlike a fairytale. Which tickled Amalina, and made her happy: to know there were other girls just like her out there in the world, but living in daydream settings; dressing in the finest clothes, eating exquisite foods, studying the most recent books, gossiping about the latest scandals, riding horses in hunting parties, dancing in lavish balls, and generally living a good life.

Only now and then did she feel bad that it was a bit of a hoax on her part. While she was genuine in what she said, and who she befriended as the 'Princess Katarina', she was, in the end, still just a baker's daughter, and her new friends would never have spoken a word to her in this life if they were to meet her as she truly was. Unless she had burnt a biscuit for their dinner— and then the interaction would have been a scolding, or thrashing, or to dismiss her from the house.

But it had been a marvelous adventure. To her inexperienced and fanciful mind what existed beyond the mountains had been a fantasyland of dragons and knights and maidens and castles. By experience, the cities of Germania and the Dutch were just larger, more colorful versions of her land's own. More people. Better fashion. Greater variety of foods. Their 'waltzes' were not as simple and matter-of-fact as what could be had in the festivals of Ardeel. More challenging and extravagant, but based on something common to them all. Not *much* difference then between Ardeel and the western kingdoms, everything being equal. The people on either side of the mountains were industrious, and serious-minded, and just a bit too dour sometimes in their devoutness.

Yes, most of all, she remembered and cherished her new friends. It was their faces she saw when she closed her eyes. And maybe some of their pretty horses.

But now that she knew that the carriage was approaching the castle, something snapped. Something brittle. Her memories became just that: light and meaningless against the waking moment. She was returning to another world; a whole other reality.

Just as much as she'd forgotten her village and her father and her best friend Cristine, she'd managed to forget the Count. Or, at least, forgotten his more dreadful aspects. As she delivered her rehearsed lines about the Count to the countless string of royals and nobility, and then embellished the stories when she felt comfortable or had grown bored by the repetition of it all, or sensed she needed to add something interesting for her friends, she'd also been convincing and fooling herself into believing the Count was exactly as she was portraying him: a member of the ancient royal family of Ardeel ... and nothing more. But, in reality, he was also a heartless, blood-eating monster; one who roamed the night seeking innocent victims for his savagery.

Even now, removed from it for so long, Amalina still remembered vividly the first time she saw him: he ripping the neck of Lucinda Skeldar, the poor girl's blood pooling between the bricks at her feet.

The violent image was just a flicker. A slight reminder that there was a duality to that man in the castle, and for her life there.

But later, as the castle came into view, she did not feel any sense of dread or apprehension, but was warmed by the sight. Such a fantastic castle, high up on a precipice, it was something from a storybook, indeed. And she was part of it. With its familiarity, she now felt a homelike relief and comfort, a swell in her chest. She remembered her room, high up in one of the towers. The view from it. The simple routine of her quiet life there with Genadie and his master, not the horrors she'd experienced—those things falling away easy enough. And there was the promise—the mystery—of what was to come if she stayed on.

"Genadie, look! The castle!"

"Yes, Ms. Dalca! Olympus reveals herself! Hyahh! Hyahh! Nk! Nk! We must get there by nightfall! Oh, Master, we are coming. We are almost there!"

"Never mind him. I'm starving. I'm going to make us a great meal. We still have those two ducks, don't we? And I'm going to put up some of those paintings. And that clock that Princess Derhovna gave me, too. And we'll go out and gather some flowers, if there are any late bloomers. We're going to get the castle into the best shape, won't we?"

"Yes, Ms. Dalca! Yes, indeed! You'll make some bread, too, won't you? I can't wait! Hyahh! Hyahh! And I will move my old bed from my cottage into the castle; make the room which Master kindly lent me really my own! What do you think of that, Ms. Dalca?"

"A brilliant idea! You know, I'm thinking of raising some bees. I read a book on it. I could tend them and we would have the best honey for our bread."

"That sounds wonderful. And I will repair our stables and the sties and the grain bins. We will have more stores to work with. And we will have the best looking castle than we ever saw on our trip!"

"And I hope the white horse—that wonderful, incorrigible horse, which I bragged of to all my new friends—is still in the stable! I will start riding him. I swear! I swear he'll mind me well now! And we will have many adventures!"

Now Amalina could not wait to get to the castle, all differences and doubts washed away by hope and a shared fantasy, and she wished the horses could be pushed even faster.

• • •

"Who are you?" said the grey looking man in the courtyard, as Genadie opened the front gate to allow the carriage inside. "What do you think you're doing there?"

Genadie, so surprised at the voice he nearly flew off his feet, whirled to face this man, his right hand throwing up the rear flap of his old jacket to reveal a knife tucked into the waist. "Who ... Who are you?!"

"I said 'Who are you?'" repeated the grey looking man, apparently unable to decide whether to look down his nose at Genadie or concentrate his glare at him.

"And I said 'Who are *you*?!" Genadie snarled more hotly than before.

"I am the one inside the castle, asking the one who has, without announcing his presence, or otherwise giving notification—with amazing audacity—opened the castle's gate as if presuming to enter."

"Where is Master?"

"What? And who is that with you?" the grey man looked even more upset by the appearance of Amalina, who was climbing out of the carriage. Amalina felt her stomach turn at the open hostility in his eyes.

With a growing upset at being challenged—by a total stranger—at the gate of her very own castle, she began: "I'm—"

"I said where is Master!" Genadie screamed. His hand, with its crooked little fingers, scrambled for the hilt of the knife. "What have you done with him?"

"Who is your master?"

"The one who lives here!"

"The only person who lives here is Count Tepsji."

"That's the one! He is my master." Then he added defensively: "He is *her* master. He is *your* master. He is the master of all who serve him, and all who do not *know* they serve him, and all that live upon this earth. That is Master. Now, where is he?"

"And who are you to speak to me this way?" bridled the grey man. He stepped forward in a menacing way. "I'm Count Tepsji's head of staff. Which follows: If he is your master, as he is mine, well, then, I am your master, too, aren't I?"

Genadie turned beet red.

"Head of staff? Since when? Let me tell you: I've lived in the Master's employ for over thirty years. And have lived in this very castle as its head of staff, as cook, as maid, as footman, as liveryman, as carpenter, as anything else you can name, for at least that time."

"That explains the state I found the castle when he hired me." At this, Genadie let out a shriek. "What's your name?"

"Genadie."

"Never heard of you."

"What's *your* name?" Genadie returned.

"That's none of your business."

"Master didn't mention me to you at all? Or her?" Genadie pointing to Amalina. "This is Ms. Dalca."

"He might have mentioned a word or two about some old servants. That they might return here at some point, on some day, or something like that. But nothing about another head of staff, or to expect someone rude enough not to announce their presence at the gates but to assault them right out."

"Assault them?"

"I see you've mistreated the Count's carriage if that is what it is, and left his horses on the point of death. You are a wonder, aren't you? Do you really expect me to believe you are not some scoundrels? looking to hide up here in a castle you thought abandoned?"

Genadie threw his hand in the air, announcing he'd had enough, and began to open the other door of the gate. "Stand aside," he told the man. "We'll see about this. Scoundrel, am I? I'll show you."

The grey man repositioned himself, looking like he might be amused to let the scene play out.

The carriage went into the forecourt, all the while Genadie mumbling about how he and Amalina had just returned from a very important mission in the name of the Count.

"Some mission he hasn't bothered to speak of … for months," the grey man muttered in return.

The carriage and horses squared away, Genadie held up a key, the one that went to the lock on the Castle's massive front doors.

"Look here!" he said.

Then he locked and unlocked the door for the grey man's benefit.

"Now," said Genadie haughtily, "where is Master?"

"If you know the Count as well as you say, you'd know where he is, wouldn't you? And where do you think you're going?"

Amalina had also had enough, feeling tired and annoyed, and wanting to lie down to sleep off the journey. Her legs still buzzed from the vibrations of the carriage. Now she went past him into the grand entrance hall and toward the stairs.

"I said: Where do you think you're going?"

"What's all this racket? What are you yelling about?" said a woman, as she charged down the staircase into the hall, blocking Amalina. "Who are these people, Georg?"

"They say they're the previous servants—"

"Previous!" Genadie howled. "You've no idea what you're talking about."

"Well, what's the problem?" the woman demanded, out of patience with everyone. "How dare you think you can disturb the peace of the high castle!"

Genadie looked apologetic at this.

"We're very sorry," Amalina said, not feeling very sorry at all. "We've just arrived and would like to go to our rooms to rest before Master … Um," she couldn't believe she'd said 'Master'. A word she had refused to ever bestow on the castle's resident monster. Genadie would have been beaming with pride and a sense of victory at having gotten her to admit it, if he wasn't currently at the point of murder. "I mean, before Count Tepsji rises for the night."

"What is your function in this house?" the woman asked, not very friendly.

"I'm, um—"

"'Um', what? Or aren't you bright? Is this one a little slow?" she asked Genadie.

"Not very," Genadie snarled.

"No need to be rude," said she. "So what are your functions *exactly* in Count Tepsji's house?"

The grey man said to the woman, "You wouldn't believe."

. . .

Eventually roles were sorted—not to anyone's satisfaction, as both sides felt the other was attempting to upstage them—and Amalina and Genadie went to their rooms. Only to receive the horrible surprise (separately) that their living quarters had been violated. Amalina's room had been turned over and redecorated. Her old clothes were thrown into a trunk, and from there into a service closet on another floor. That is, her *remaining* clothes, which hadn't been burnt.

"Burnt?!" Amalina cried.

"To prevent lice," explained the woman, whose name was Abraxa, and was, as it turned out, Georg's wife.

"There wasn't any lice! I don't have lice!"

"I said it was to *prevent* lice," Abraxa explained impatiently. "Who knows who the clothes belonged to? I didn't. And really, those clothes weren't something you'd actually want to wear in the Count's presence, would you?"

She didn't answer. One of the dresses had been Amalina's best dress, the one she'd worn before being abducted to the castle.

But Genadie's trouble was worse.

"Look, Ms. Dalca!" he said. "They threw out everything! Everything!"

"Who said you can live inside the castle?" said Georg, coldly.

"Master! Master did!"

"Well, the Count said nothing about it to me. We were instructed to prepare this house to receive royal families, not preserve its slovenliness and decay. For all I knew, by what I found in that room, I took it to be the spot to quarantine bodies of the plagued." Georg added with a brutal sneer: "It's all the better that we have you out of there. No sense quartering you directly inside. You can set yourself up in the back house, just outside the kitchen. You know what building I'm referring to, don't you?"

"I should have killed him straight away," said Genadie to Amalina, as they built a fire in the back house's hearth. The decaying little building had been Genadie's former home until the previous winter when, for the first time, the Count allowed him inside the castle. Genadie glowered in disbelief that he was here again. "I should have struck him down the second he challenged me at our gate."

"Genadie," said Amalina, "a large dog is bigger than you. You think you could hurt him? He's huge."

"It's my poor posture. But if I'd known he was there …" He tried to straighten himself taller.

"He's almost twice as tall and really twice as big. I wouldn't bother him if I were you. They aren't very friendly … a little vicious. But maybe we just scared them, you know? I can't believe someone could be so miserable, much less two. There must be a reason. We just need to get on their good side, the both of them, is all. If they have one."

"Hm," said Genadie, with a mischievous twinkle in his eye. "If they weren't expecting us but planning for the princesses to come, I should have said you are Princess Katarina, and I your driver. And then let's see how we would have been treated. Have them bowing to us, and scurrying after all our demands. And we could have made their lives something awful."

Genadie giggled at the thought of it.

"Until the Count showed. Then what would you say?"

"I'd have him kill those two!"

Genadie swatted his table. Then he kicked a chair.

"What's the matter with you?" said Amalina, trying to sound positive. "You've lived in this cottage for so long. You never thought you'd be permitted to so much as sleep inside the castle. Why does it bother you so much now?"

"Because, Ms. Dalca, I got myself into the castle! Master allowed it! He allowed it!"

"I know. And maybe he'll allow it again."

"Doubtful, if I have any sway in his thinking," Georg said sternly, he appearing from nowhere. "More like he will dismiss the both of you; you being the ones responsible for how we found his precious home. Who knows what further damage you might have caused if left on your own, and embarrassed our dear Count before his valued guests? No, you'd best prepare yourselves to leave and find new employment … with someone who would accept your low standards. If that's possible."

"We'll see about all that," Genadie said, with an amazingly smooth delivery; his dead-sure confidence winning the moment, "It'll be settled when our Master wakes tonight."

4

The Refreshing Air

"Your highness, I'm so glad to see you this evening and looking so refreshed," said Georg, jumping in front of Genadie and Amalina, and bowing his head to his knees. "The hours have been too long without your glorious presence."

"Your highness, likewise, sir," said Abraxa, throwing herself so hard to the floor that she and her dress became a pancake. "I was counting the hours until I could see your face again and attend to your needs. I was most lost without you. And while you were away I've washed the eastern wing thoroughly, not a spider remains I can assure you. You'll see how much better that is for your refined senses than all the rampant rodents, screeching and scratching about in the clutter and neglect—like before; before *we* came to your beautiful castle; so poorly managed, prior to your arranging *our* employment; positions for which we are grateful and ready to serve. But what do you wish of me now, sir, your gloriousness, now that you've risen, and I will do it straight away, as if I just woke from a long, restful sleep."

The count swerved around the two lumps on the floor and made straight for Amalina and Genadie; Genadie too overcome by the moment to drop as he usually did before his Master, but quaking. With tears raining off his cheeks.

"Ah! You've returned to me!" The Count's eyes glittered and a smile beamed under his long mustache. "Perfect! Perfect! Yes. Returned from your duties in the west. And so a plan comes together! Come, come. Come along with me and tell me all about it; what you saw and what you heard; and make this body happy."

Now standing with red faces, a throbbing vein in Abraxa's neck, and a throbbing vein on Georg's temple, the two watched as the Count—after having been reminded of Amalina and Genadie's shortcomings—greeted the long absent pair with the warmth reserved for dear old friends.

And with that, he embraced Amalina and Genadie and swept them into his private study. The door shut against Georg's and Abraxa's furious frowns.

. . .

"Lady Princess Derhovna was very nice," Amalina said, getting down to the part that most interested her employer. Though he was stretched out on the divan, and his eyes had been closed for most of her recollections—involving the architecture and innovations and food and the feasts and the waltzes, which had fascinated Amalina—imagining himself being in the scenery, he now leaned forward, his eyes open and hungry.

"The Princess Derhovna," the Count echoed, pulling on his mustache.

"Yes, she was very nice, indeed—"

"Genadie?" the Count said, prompting his servant, who seemed to have fallen asleep.

"Oh, yes, Master!" he said as he launched from his chair. "Who? Who was that again? I'm sorry, I didn't quite hear."

"Derhovna ..."

Genadie took a small, floppy piece of vellum, about the size of his palm, from the case beside him. He held it up to the Count's eyes.

"Hmm," the Count said appreciably. "Yes. The Princess Derhovna. Perfect. Continue, Ms. Dalca."

"You can call me Amalina, sir. You did call me by my name before, remember?"

"However ... didn't I dub you 'Mouse'?"

"Yes, that, too. But ... Well, I prefer Amalina."

"What more can you tell me about the Lady Princess Derhovna, other than that she is nice? I presume all of the princesses would be on their best behavior, and so 'nice' really means nothing at all, don't you think?"

"I wouldn't assume any such thing, sir."

"Oh?" the Count was even more intrigued, with a mischievous smile. "Some were *naughty*? How so? Tell me about *that* ... and *them*."

"What about Hansa?"

"Who? Was that one naughty, Ms. Dalca?"

"I mean, Princess Hansa Derhovna. I was speaking of her."

"She was or she wasn't, as you describe, naughty?"

"Well ... I don't know exactly ..."

"Get on with it," said the Count, impatiently. "What is your report?"

"Well, as I said, she was nice—"

"Yes! And?"

"Pretty, and ... Oh, I don't know what you want me to tell you, sir. You said nothing about making a report of it. All I knew—as I went into the whole thing—was what I was to say to those people I met ... and that's what I did. To tell you the truth I was very scared the whole time, trying to get everything right and to make sure that I did all that you wanted. I was so hard paying attention, and so worried I wasn't making a success of it, that it was hard to mind every detail. Any fine details, that is. Honestly, I can probably tell you who had dark hair, and who had light, who had curly hair and who had straight, who had blue eyes and who had brown, who had freckles—" *"Freckles ... "* the count cut in with a luxurious lick of his lips, as if tasting cinnamon, "—and who had none, who was dark complected and who was fair. But I might get them all mixed up just the same."

"I don't require your memory on such mundane things," he said. "But I see I should have instructed you more precisely on what I would have known about them in order to make the best decision."

"Yes, sir. What decision, sir?"

"Really, there was no reason to be nervous. You had all the lines down and were perfect for the part. No reason to be nervous at all."

"There was *so* much to be nervous about, sir. And not just my delivery. I had to make up so many lies just to patch up the holes in the story. And I think those lies covered so well only because they liked the idea of a foreign Lady of Title and wanted to have a look at me."

"What holes, Mouse?"

"Amalina, sir," Amalina reminded him.

For some reason, there in that room, she felt on equal terms with the ferocious Count. Was it because she had had the grand experience and he so much wanted to hear about it? So that she, owning the better part of this exchange, held an edge of power? Or was it because she stood above him, while he remained below her, spread out on the divan, prone and half wrapped in a blanket like it was a coccoon. It *was* a commanding position she held, even if he could take her apart with the slightest flick of his fingers.

"But for starters," continued Amalina, addressing his question now, "there was the dress. It was so old and out of fashion. And even the best of their tailors could only do so much with it. Genadie can tell you."

"My fault, Master," Genadie fell to the floor now, remembering his station finally. "I should have discovered that wrinkle earlier, knowing your timelessness and disregard for fashion—"

"I am interested in fashion," objected the Count.

"Yes, you are the study in fashion," he fawned. "You set the rules, Master."

"But it was so out of date," Amalina reminded them. "I tried to explain away the imperfections by telling them it was nothing more than the way we dress here. That was good enough of an excuse. But over there ... well, they're all expected to wear the proper clothes or they must pay a fine or be kicked out of court. And their styles keep changing. One moment, they are all choked up with ruffles around their necks, they look like peacocks. Then the next, it looks as if the clothes are falling off, and the bosoms are hoisted up into a box. Oh, and the under clothes: the corsets and skirts and petticoats. I'm surprised if they can get out of their bedrooms and into the fresh air by midday if they rise before the cock crows. It looks lovely, I was dazzled—and much ashamed that my own dress could not come close in grandeur, and that I only had one costume at that."

"You had access to all of Lady Flauna's wardrobe."

This sent a chill up Amalina's back. Yes, Lady Flauna's wardrobe. The wardrobe abandoned by the Lady once intended to play the Count's niece in the western kingdoms, before she flew from the castle in an attempt to escape the man who (she had discovered) was really a monster. He killed her, of course, and her servants Odetta and Kralov, and her lover Erik Kosche, in their failed flight. And in the end Lady Flauna's mission and wardrobe were turned over to Amalina. Well, Amalina could perform the mission, because she had no other choice but to do so. But:

"Do you think I could fit into any of her clothes?"

"Erik managed to get you into them just fine."

"You were too distracted in the moment, sir—with Erik trying to kill you—to notice that I wasn't as tall or as skinny for her clothes to fit properly. But I can tell you that the way the foreigners put such importance on what the other is wearing, especially the women, that I could never get away with a dress that did not fit. Their costumes fit so perfectly, it takes two or three other ladies to get them into a dress. Which brings up the next issue, sir: Nowadays, they all whirl around with a court of people whirling around them. Seems like they have a person for each of a body's requirements, and then sometimes a person for that person, and even then sometimes a person for that person's person. So when I arrived with just ... well, with just Genadie ..."

Amalina pointed at Genadie, who stood there in his tattered, dirty jacket, his body bent and greasy and with all the dirt on his skin shoved to his corners and margins, where it collected, he looking like an abandoned dog, and the meaning was obvious without having to make a face. The Count's expression didn't change, but his eyes seemed to nod.

She explained how they couldn't imagine a princess' safety was entrusted to just one man ... like Genadie. And that she not only didn't have a female attendant to see to her needs, but the male steward was also her driver and footman. And that man was ... Genadie.

"I see," said the Count.

"We hired two maids, who'd just lost their employment, to see to my needs, and anyway, make a show of it. And they did help me to remember names and to tell me certain secrets about the families I was going to meet; if they knew anything about them. They seemed to know a lot, but the secrets were always very dark, and mean, and sometimes I think they made stuff up just to see if I would believe them, or turn me against the people I was acquainting myself because they didn't like them, or maybe even to embarrass me. I don't know."

"Mm-hm. You did not bring the maids here to the castle with you?"

"They didn't wish to leave their country. I think they didn't believe I was a real princess … and I don't mean they didn't believe I was a royal princess by blood. They understood I was not that, but I was supposed to be a niece to a Count, so a countess, or lady, or lady princess, or a princess not-of-royal-blood (as confusing as all that is in their society and between the different kingdoms). But they believed none of it. And were wary we were charlatans, going to kidnap them when we offered to take them on permanently and bring them to Ardeel. And I don't think they liked Genadie all that much, either."

"Waste of money, Master. But Master, Ms. Dalca insisted."

"I trust she knew what she was doing, Genadie. I'm sure you both did well," a frown flickered on his face. "Now, Amalina, tell me what I want to hear."

Amalina nodded and told him what she knew of the ladies she'd met: The details she could best recall.

Princess Hansa Derhovna (a true princess of royal blood): Nice, cordial, with three younger sisters she doesn't quite get along with, but loves her parents, who are lenient, doting and permissive, and is seeking a life of adventure. Princess Rebekkah Gorjda (a 'lady princess' not of direct royal descent): Nice, friendly, with two brothers and one older sister she doesn't quite get along with, but is quite devoted to her parents, who are tough and strict (though fair), and wish to put off marriage until she decides if she prefers (or her parents prefer for her) a life in the church; and by the way, has a fine stable of excellent horses (where—*very exciting*—Amalina was trained to ride, and so able join in picnics in the king's reserve and gardens, etc.). Princess Dorothea Teerlinc: a bit of each of the previous two princesses. Princess Margaret van Henessen: likewise as the last. Princess Leni Verhult: the same. Princess Mary Peeters: the same. Princess Lisbet Spaarvierlet: the same. Princess Ursa Leyster: the same. Princess Greta Kampfen: the same. Princess Yudi Koos: the same. Princess Maria Blix: the same. Princess Almara Koenigsburgen: the same. Princess Johanna Der Grosse: the same. Princess Elaine Muskotte: the same.

So many princesses and lady princesses, and more.

And at the mention of each one, and during the recitation of her particulars, Amalina wracking her brains to remember the slightest bit of them, Genadie produced from his case another swatch of vellum and held it before his Master's eyes. The Count would stare at it for a while, occasionally adding a grin or a sneer, and then he would nod and the vellum would return to the case. Amalina became so intrigued by this, she tried to lean forward to see what was on those pieces of paper. But Genadie angled it just so that all she could see was the dirty back of his hand.

When the supply of princesses was exhausted, and so was Amalina, the Count lay back on the cushions and stared at the ceiling. He looked a bit unhappy that the recitation couldn't go on forever and he'd have to settle for what he could.

He reached a finger out towards the ceiling, as if he was touching something in front of his face.

"Verhult: Yes. Peeters: Yes, I think. Hmm. Koos: Definitely. I feel we should add Koenigsburgen and Spaarvierlet, as well. Yes. Yes, those will do for a start. But why so few from Germania, Amalina? You did visit all the cities I asked?"

"We went to many cities, sir," said Amalina. "Wherever Genadie took me. But it was much more difficult there, it is true."

"Because they turned you away, didn't they?"

"Not turned away, Master!" Genadie assured with a wavering cry. "Oh, no, no, no, Master. Not turned away. Never."

"Not so much turned away exactly," Amalina smirked as Genadie fell to his knees, his lips trembling, his eyes blinking franticly. "They just didn't have time for us at the moment."

"Yes, you were turned away," the Count growled hotly. "That's what they *would* do, wouldn't they?"

"Those confounded scoundrels!" Genadie started in.

The Count quieted him with a wave.

"It was expected," he told them. "Why would they honor someone of Ardeelian blood, when they think they have conquered us? How could we *think* to approach them? We are the peasant come begging at the gate; to be turned away. Naturally so. Well, they will get their turn. Now that I think about it, let us add Kampfen and Der Grosse, and I will decide what to do with *their* daughters. Did you get all that, Genadie?"

"Oh, yes, Master."

"Send notice today."

Genadie bowed.

"You are inviting them here, sir?" Amalina asked.

"It will be splendid to have them. But we must be ready. You two get to work immediately."

"You aren't inviting Hansa—Um, Princess Derhovna, that is?"

"Why her?"

"As I said, she is very nice."

The Count flicked his fingers at them, as if in profound irritation that they were still standing there wasting his time.

• • •

"Genadie, what've you got in your bag?" Amalina asked after they'd left the private study. "What were you showing him on those pieces of paper?"

"Oh, you mean this?" Genadie said, stopping and pulling one from his case.

He held it up in his palm. On the vellum was a small portrait of Yudi Koos. Amalina had not seen many paintings, and never one so small and not stuck in a frame. It was startling in its form and for its near perfect likeness.

"That's amazing," Amalina cooed, almost reaching out to touch it. Genadie fell back half a step to prevent such a thing. "Genadie, where did ... where did you get that?"

"I made it."

"What do you mean you made it? You?"

"Yes, Ms. Dalca." He didn't appear to be too overly proud of his work. She looked at his small, gnarled hands and could only doubt it was true.

"Really, Genadie? When did you make that?"

"I have a good eye," Genadie said, defensively. "And I had plenty of time waiting while you made your rounds. It was very important to Master to have these portraits to make his decision. Very important."

"Yes, I can see now. Yudi is very beautiful. You did her portrait very well."

Genadie shrugged and put the cloth back in the case.

"But Hansa's just as beautiful as she. Even more so, I think. Let me see Princess Derhovna, Genadie. Please."

Genadie fetched around until he found the one she wanted.

"Oh, Genadie, you got that one all wrong! She doesn't look like that!"

Genadie looked at the portrait and frowned.

"What's the matter with it?"

"You have her looking dull and unhappy. Look at the way you made her hair come down on her forehead, and her eyebrows are so thick and slanted and make her look cross. Why did you do that? She's nothing like that at all, but very nice and sweet. Didn't you like her, Genadie? Did you do that on purpose?"

"I did not like her or dislike her."

"You heard her maid tell me I needed a better looking valet, one who wasn't part animal. But that wasn't the princess who said it, and she reprimanded her maid after you'd gone. She was very nice and sweet and you shouldn't have done that. I would have liked to see her again."

"If you look at it, Ms. Dalca," Genadie said, squinting at the painting, and pointing at it with the tip of his crooked forefinger, "her eyebrows aren't like that on purpose. The paint was slashed a little, probably on account of it not being dried before I rolled it up. Takes a long while to dry. Probably not still all the way dry. And if I put them away too early, well …"

"Genadie, are you going to send out the invitations today?"

"Yes, Ms. Dalca, of course."

"Could you send an invitation to Princess Derhovna?"

"Master did not mention her name."

"But I'm asking you to. I'd like to have her come. And it really *is* unfair when he didn't see a proper picture of her."

"So you're planning to stay here until they arrive, Ms. Dalca?" he smiled brightly. "Before, you wanted to leave the Master's house as fast as you could. I'm so glad you've changed your mind."

Amalina gulped, and felt her face flush.

She *had* wanted to leave. To flee this castle. Desperately so, having once even thrown herself out a window. What had changed so that she no longer thought of escaping, but looked forward to a visit by Hansa Derhovna, as if this were her own home?

"Is *He* finished with you?" Georg asked loudly, startling them both.

"We've left Master in his quarters, if that's what you mean," Genadie said. "We've a lot to do for him today, the both of us, Ms. Dalca and I, and we've got to get to it. So stand out of our way."

"Yes, you mentioned you're to summon the princesses here to the high castle. An important assignment, indeed. I can't say I didn't wish his eminence had brought us on before he'd made his final selection for this task. Normally the head of staff has some sway in hiring. And well, I do know some excellent people …"

"Master is infallible!" Genadie barked. "Who he chooses to serve him is the ideal choice. Do not forget that!"

"And his highness chose me to be head of staff, Genadie. Don't you forget *that*."

"You can bet I won't," Genadie snarled. "That is something I will *never* forget."

"By my statement I didn't mean to hurt your feelings," said Georg, insincerely. "I just meant I know people who might have served him better toward that particular task. I'm sure you two are excellent in your devotion to our great knight. But I can only hope you are much better at selecting his new acquaintances than you are in properly maintaining a home, or it will be a loss all around for our eminence. Well," he added with a sniff, "We'll see."

Though the exchange made her nervous about doing so, later that evening Amalina insisted to Genadie: "Invite Hansa. I'm begging you."

5

Searchers in the Water

The soldiers were still on his trail. The low constable thought he'd lost them when he scrambled into the small river and floated down half a league before climbing onto the opposite bank. *Back into the water*, he noted glumly, as he back pedaled, and then was drifting along again.

The escape from Zsolt Marosh and his hunting party had been so much easier. He'd found a horse right outside the general's home and tore away through the fields, in a direct line away from the stream in which they were still searching, and lifted someone's old cloak hanging on a line to further cover his own scent. Not even old Zsolt had noticed the obvious signs that he'd faked his run for the water; so convinced they all were in the superiority of their trap, that Attila had fallen into it; believing that the low constable'd just gotten lucky with the speeding current, and that he may be an expert swimmer, and that it was just a matter of time before they caught up to him. Who knows when they realized their mistake? Or when they finally admitted it to their general.

Attila was not a good swimmer. He'd seen too many bodies pulled from the waterways around Tsobl: skin rotten; unnaturally blue and grotesquely bloated; eyes blank; tongue black and protruding from the mouth; the corpse bent into an unnatural, almost humiliating posture by the combined torture of sucking eddies and fallen tree limbs. It was a warning to never enter any liquid deeper than his ankles. And so he'd avoided it successfully until this month of pursuit: first ahead of Tsobl's trackers, then away from Zsolt and his army. Any route had been made acceptable to him, especially the most fearful of the mountain rivers, glutted and charged with late spring run-off. It was assumed—wrongly—that nobody would chance their life by throwing themselves into one. He'd already surrendered himself to two and come out alive, with his hunters gladly giving up the chase at the edge of the ferocious, bucking white waters.

But these new searchers seemed prepared to hound him to the ends of the earth. Even to the waters' edge. Where had they come from? How had they found him?

Likely by any one of the other knights he'd approached after Zsolt. Each and every one of these legendary Ardeelian warlords, who had warred with beast-like intensity against the western invaders—who were the proud sons of the country's old native royalty, the offspring of those men who'd originated the shameful compact for peace with the Count—had, like Zsolt, now given themselves over to their conquerors and sided with the newly-minted Tsobl government, acting like frightened children at the thought of betraying their foreign-blooded overseers. Or balked like nibble-nailed virgins at the prospect of taking advantage of the Count's moment of vulnerability, which they could do—and succeed at—by simply mounting an immediate attack on him ... and thereby remove the monster from the earth. Each and every one of these knights had turned Attila away (though without Zsolt's level of treachery, or his follow-up manhunt). No, they'd wished Attila well in his effort. Patted him on the back on his way out the door, and then dutifully reported to Tsobl and its legion of bounty hunters the whereabouts of their wayward low constable, Attila Bronk. Their *former* low constable, that is. And the chase was renewed.

Attila coughed out the water he was choking on. A horn sounded. They must have heard him. They couldn't see him at this point as they were riding outside the tree line, probably on a road that ran parallel to the river. They were close enough, though, he thought. They thought so, too. The horn sounded again, and he heard the beat of their hooves above the sound of the rushing water. They were very close, indeed. All they needed to do was find an access point through the woods that led down to the river and they would have him. After all, they'd already found his camp and captured his horse. Now it was time to override him and collect their bounty.

He paddled his hands quickly (but gently, so as not to splash), running with his legs below the surface on any ground he could manage, and hurried his body along the river as fast as it would go. And under his spluttering breath he cursed the native sons of Ardeel, who would rather resist him, feed him to the dogs and reward the corrupt power structure in Tsobl, than to take an action that would at once erase the embarrassment of their ancestors, vanquish a factotum of evil, and restore to their family names the dignity and power they once enjoyed. It was unthinkable to Attila. Here he was, the only man with courage in the country, half drowning, and fully freezing to death, in the gushing veins of the Ardeel mountain ranges.

The numbness in his hands was spreading up his arms. He felt it in his legs, too. His teeth were already chattering. Even though the day was summer-warm, some glacier's feeder stream had joined the river and dropped the water's temperature to something like ice. It felt as if his blood was slush crunching through his limbs. Attila knew he couldn't last much longer and would have to head for shore or succumb to the cold. And give these hunters a man-sized chunk of ice for a trophy.

Between the breaks in the trees, he saw the point of the lances. Then he saw the helmets. They were pushing inwards. And though the river's flow was picking up pace, it would not carry him fast enough away that his pursuers could not reach him if they wanted.

I won't give up, he thought.

Then he saw the soldier sitting atop the horse. He wore a helmet and a breastplate, and held a long spear with a shiny steel tip. He was downstream, where the river widened, and it was shallow enough that the rippling current only reached to his courser's belly.

"Ha, ha," the soldier said, catching sight of Attila. He barked it again, and loud enough to alert his friends. Their target was trapped.

Attila looked behind. The narrowness of the path delayed the others coming through the woods. They were a short ways off, lightly trotting along onto the narrow shoreline. They also began to laugh. No words to be said, apparently. Their mocking laughs were to provoke fear and panic in their quarry. Two emotions Attila was dedicated to never give anyone.

He flexed his fingers to get the senseless rubber out of them. It didn't work, but at least he could still move them. They were under his command. But the river was not. It only pulled him faster along.

"Ha, ha. Ha, ha."

Before him, the soldier on the horse had now lowered the spearhead and was swinging it back and forth, anticipating the spot where Attila would run into it.

Attila would be meeting that spear in seconds. There seemed nothing he could do about it.

Turning his head in every direction, he surveyed the scene one last time. On the right, and just behind, were the soldier's comrades, six of them, all in a line and observing the action, anticipating when they would be needed to break for him. The shoreline was relatively flat and narrow, with grass and a bed of tiny rocks that led into the river. An easy ramp in or out of the water.

Three seconds.

To the left was an impossibly high bank, the river beside it choked with weeds and long water-grasses; a place he could only tangle himself as he tried to climb onto the land. The fouled bank went on this way until the river bent out of view.

Two seconds.

"Ha, ha. Ha, ha."

The soldier ahead dipped forward in his saddle, lowering the glimmering spear tip into the water. Obscuring it. Allowing Attila to break his transfixation on it. To come to a decision on how to end this.

One second.

Attila plunged down into the river, the soldiers' cruel laughs becoming a garbled murmur as the bubbles and the churn pressed into his ears. He spun his body, shoving his feet and his hands into the rocks below, not so much to stop himself—impossible—but to buy time. The water was clear as glass, his eyes searched and found. Then it was one last turn. If he'd timed it right.

The spear tip found his chest, but now there was a flat rock between him and it. Attila really dug his heels in as best he could and pressed himself to the side, using the rock to guide the spear lengthwise across the front of the horse, like a fulcrum, bringing up the soldier out of his saddle as he tried to hold onto it.

But then Attila cannoned out of the water, screaming and flailing right at the courser's head, striking the stone at the horse's eye. Before he ran into it, the horse was up on its hind legs, blinking down in terror, a frightened whinny escaping its mouth. Attila grabbed hold the rein on this side and brought his full weight down again, yanking the courser's head hard to the side, twisting it, pulling it off balance. It could have flung him around like a toy if it wanted, but already off balance, perched on two unsure hooves, sliding on the uneven riverbed, with the surge of the current, and the shock of the attack, and the control of its head seized by a maniac, it toppled over, dropping onto the soldier and crushing him down.

The courser's weight served as an anchor, but they were sliding downstream. The soldier, his eyes wide with shock, tried to grab at Attila. But Attila already had a plan. He wrapped one leg around the soldier's neck, and while still holding the jerking rein with one hand, shoved the edge of the rock into the soldier's mouth, cracking the teeth, skinning the nose, poking into any soft socket he could. The eyes. Yes, the eyes. The soldier needed to scream. He needed to let out all his breath while he was still stuck under the horse, under the water, still unable to reach a weapon.

The soldier gouged at Attila's shins, and bit unsuccessfully at his thigh. There was pain, but not enough for Attila to let up. Attila's head was above water, he could breath. He was going to hold this position as long as he could, until he saw the bubbles rise from the soldier's mouth and hear the smothered shout. He sat down on the head, avoiding the courser's writhing body, and then stood, mashing his foot on the soldier's face. The soldier did not grab at Attila's ankles, as Attila worried he might, but in a panic, tried to right himself.

The courser's continued floundering and protesting whinnies had the other horses backing away from the river, no matter the urging of the men above them. Their riders cursed at them, spurred at their flanks, but they would only shuffle in place, dancing at the water's edge, not allowing one hoof to enter.

Good enough.

The sand worked up by the writhing of the horse looked like a brown mist blowing around the soldier's bloody, gasping head. He looked like a fish thrown onto dry land, mouth gaping, sucking at what it couldn't breathe. Attila shook his head in objection to the image, and made an agonized sound. He reached down into the water and pulled at the breastplate, trying to raise his opponent to the surface.

But the courser found its footing. It rose out of the water with a great crash of water, and bolted. Since Attila's arm was still wrapped in one of its reins, he was taken up on one of its mighty shoulders, and being torn free of the water, carried along for the ride.

The courser was still in a panic, and it charged senselessly in the first direction it pointed. This was going down stream. And for some reason it chose the left bank to summit.

Attila managed to straddle the courser in the meantime. The saddle was askew, and his feet could not find the stirrups. So he bent his knees and dug his heels into the sides of the horse, praying it would not fall back into the water and pin him down the way it had its previous rider.

Behind him the horses had given into the cursing and spurs and overcome their fear, maybe inspired by seeing the flight of their friend, and had come into the river. The soldiers were concentrated on Attila, but were moving slowly, cautiously.

The courser made it up onto the bank, and he encouraged it to keep up its pace, and head along the steep, narrow bank, hoping that once they were around the bend it would widen, he would find a gap in the trees to allow them to pass out somewhere, and safely and swiftly away from the fearless searchers.

He looked back again, hoping to see at least one of them had gotten down and were helping their friend up. The man hadn't come up on his own. He was too far gone and drowning in earnest, or the weight of the breastplate prevented him from rising.

The courser whinnied in fright again.

Around the bend, the bank turned to solid rock. Massive, jagged boulders that looked like they'd been cut to look like teeth. Helplessly plunging off the high bank and back into the water, Attila noted it was the same on the opposite side, too. The forest on either side of the river stopped abruptly at a length of rising stone. And very shortly after that, the river itself stopped. It ended in a rising column of mist, and the roar of tons of water rushing over a ledge and slamming onto something unseen far below.

The courser could not resist the rush of the current. It was being pulled toward the edge of the falls. Attila did as the soldiers had and kicked his heels hard into the courser's flanks, begging it to fight and push itself to the other side, where there was a chance of him climbing onto one of those rocks to avoid the uncertain drop. The courser was certain to go over, and maybe it understood this. It tried to make its way back upstream and toward the sloping right hand bank that it remembered. But the plunge was coming, and it was only a matter of how far it could get before that happened.

Attila stared at the coming rocks, trying to ignore the thunder of water and rising steam to his left, willing the courser to reach the bank of stone. Or at least get close enough that he could try to leap there.

If he fell in, he would be swept right over.

Nearing the right bank, he glanced upstream. Most of the soldiers, still atop their mounts, were gathered at the point along the shore where the grass gave way to the rocks. But two of their squad were in the water, their horses gamely fighting against the grip of the current, while they stared without expression at Attila.

He saw the puff of smoke rise from one of their shoulders.

He heard the buzz and felt the punch of the bullet before he heard the gunshot. He was shoved up and was almost thrown from the saddle. He gasped. The air went out, but it did not return to his lungs. There was a large knot behind his left shoulder blade, it pressed so heavily into his back he couldn't breathe. He tried to shrug off the weight. Pain surged through the cold-numbed flesh, feeling like lines of fire spreading in all directions.

The soldiers were staring at him. Not laughing. He couldn't see their expressions. His vision was blurring, and balls of light were beginning to whirl in front of his eyes.

He just had to get a breath in and he would be fine. Never mind reaching the other side of the river, just as long as he could inhale.

He felt the mist of the falls on his cheek. And just as his vision darkened, his brain was still working, noting that near the edge there was a deer standing on top of a jagged boulder watching him and the bucking horse, peacefully peering down at the scene, without expectation. He observed, too, there was still a good cover of foliage, even up to the rocks, the vibrant green canopy of the forest creating interesting shadows on the rocks and the water. And somewhere in the whirring processes, he also reconsidered the dress of the trackers, who displayed no markings of the Tsobl forces, or wore the heralds of a local knight, making them an unknown quantity. But also noted critically that it was stupid for them to have positioned that soldier ahead of him, in the middle of the river. What was the point of that? He might have just killed a man, killed *that* man—a terrible thought—when those unrelenting searchers could have kept together and formed a net behind him, and without suffering a loss simply advanced and pushed him off the cliff.

• • •

Two pairs of hands pulled the body out of the mud. The hands' owners didn't recognize who it was they were handling, because his face was battered and beaten and bloody, and his lips and eyelids were a dark blue, and the rest of his skin a disturbingly pale blue, where it wasn't caked in red. Unreal. Inhuman. Not someone they would know. But they recognized the value of his clothes, looked to be something fashioned in the capitol even. And they couldn't wait to see if the boots would fit, or could at least be sold at market.

"I'm looking for …" the body gargled through its blue lips, sending them screaming.

6

The Wrong Birds

Amalina found reasons during the day to seek Genadie out, and on every visit hounded him to write the invitation to Princess Derhovna. She asked to see the letters he'd already written, then demanded he write a new one. Write it just the same as the others, but addressing it this time to darling Hansa Derhovna. She'd gotten over pleading for the favor, but reminded him of all she'd done for him, and turned to making him worry he'd be an awful person for denying such an easy request. She felt a little ashamed knowing that writing so many letters with his crooked hand was painful, and adding another one would increase his agony. But still, the shame Amalina experienced was only a little.

When it was done, she helped him seal up the envelopes with the Count's wax seals, and tied them with lengths of silk ribbon, and then followed him to the process' final stage: the bird house.

"You're sending them out by bird?" Amalina said in wonder, looking dubiously at the three drab birds pecking around the room. They didn't look like they could carry more than a sliver of straw. And yet he expected them to fly half-way around the world? and deliver them to the proper recipient? To her mind, at this discovery, the chances of seeing Hansa again diminished greatly.

"No, no," Genadie murmured under his breath. "These are the wrong birds."

"I should think you're right," Amalina agreed, making faces at the scrawny things. "So now what?"

"Let's get out of here."

It wasn't a bad idea, she thought. The bird house was a gloomy grey room, with seemingly every surface littered with feathers, and worse. Whose air was close with the odor of a kind of nervous animal musk mixed with their stale excretions. The smell only lessened around the one wide, open window, but it wasn't enough to make her want to stay another minute.

Genadie meant they should leave the castle itself. In a half hour they were riding the two horse wagon to Netz, both of them blowing out sighs of relief.

"It's not fair the way they've taken over the castle," Amalina said, not needing to mention Georg and Abraxa by name.

"Nobody has taken over anything," Genadie replied in a sturdy but resigned rasp. "Master controls all."

"Admit it, the reason we're going to town is because you don't want to be there. Not with them."

"I want to be with Master, always."

"But he isn't the only one there. Not anymore. Those two …"

"All in his plan."

She could tell by his twitching eye that, even if he believed what he said, he still didn't like it.

• • •

"Where do you buy birds that will fly all the way to the western kingdoms?" Amalina asked him when they entered Netz. "And how do you know they will go where you want them to go? How will *they* know where you want them to go?"

Genadie didn't answer. He was turning his head this way and that, surveying the street. "Hmm," he said to himself.

"Is something wrong?"

Netz looked just like her own village, Korr. Or just about like any other large Ardeelian town. It was big enough to almost be called a proper city, and some people would try to claim it so. But the confines of the mountains, and the various waterways, conspired to constrict even the largest towns enough that they would not grow beyond a certain size, and discourage the creation of the much wider highways necessary to bring in the volume of trade needed to realize their city-wise ambitions. Netz itself was sandwiched between two mountains, which pinched closed on the village's south side, caging it into the long valley that, after turning like a dog leg for some miles, on its far northern end contained the high castle.

At this time of day, there should have been more people on the street. At least in Korr, that's the way it would be. Having traveled through the more populous cities of the continent, most Ardeelian villages now appeared (to Amalina) to be abandoned. Presently, her skewed perception made her unable to decide if something were truly amiss here in Netz.

Genadie didn't answer the question but kept flicking his eyes around the street, lips puckered.

"Here we are," he mumbled.

They went behind a building where stood long rows of wood cages, from which came the first real sounds emanating from within the town: the coos, flaps, scratching and warbles of birds. Hundreds of them.

A man came up a row, a large, square wood scoop in his hand. He wore all black, but his clothes displayed all the pieces of fluff and little white feathers that migrated into the air from his captives. His face was browned and dried by the sun, the skin drooped and sagged off his narrow, skull-like head, making his multi-ridged nose all the more prominent, look like a rough beak. His eyes were permanently slitted by a squint that thick eyebrows extended over like an awning. He came at them quickly, the scoop dribbling grains with each step.

No words passed between he and Genadie. The man simply joined up with them, and then they all, as a unit, traveled the lengths of the pens, with Amalina trailing curiously behind. Genadie stared into the dark cages, thumb and forefinger massaging his chin, lips still pursed, but in a shrewd way. Up and down they went, pausing every once in a while. After they returned to where they started, they began the circuit again, this time with Genadie pointing out the birds he favored. The man did not nod, but his eyes would hold on whichever bird was selected, until Genadie indicated another, or they moved on to a new cage.

"They're Tsobl," said the man finally, in a peculiar, high-pitched voice. It looked like he would have preferred not to say anything at all but he'd been forced to.

"Same price?" Genadie asked.

"Tsobl, though."

"I'll take them."

"So many for Tsobl," the man noted, but then seemed to regret having expressed this thought. He hurried away, saying, "Half an hour."

"I'll need traveling cages, too."

He halted, midflight.

"You aren't posting them from here?" Again, he winced and appeared to wish he hadn't said these words but had just gone along with what he'd been told. As if there were some discreet meaning to the process if the birds weren't dispatched directly from this station but taken somewhere else, and that it was unwise to possess such sensitive information.

Genadie clicked his crooked fingers, and whispered to Amalina: "Ms. Dalca, I've left the money in the wagon. Go fetch it while I help the master aviar prepare the transport cages. See if you can't also arrange for supplies." He gave her a quick rundown of grains, flour, cheeses, oils, wines, fabrics, etc., where she should find the particular shops, and ready all for pick-up when they were done here. He finished his flurry of directions with: "No need to haggle, agree to whatever they want."

"You want me to carry the money?"

"Of course. Pay as you go. Get receipts, though."

"But you never let me handle the money."

"When we were in foreign lands, Ms. Dalca, where we couldn't trust to our safety. There are cutpurses, robbers and thieves lurking everywhere in those places, who would take advantage of a newly arrived servant and his lady."

"There aren't robbers and thieves here?"

"Likely, but I wouldn't know it. We've nothing to bother about with that kind here in Netz. No. The safety of our persons and property is so much guaranteed, you see, that I forgot the bag on the riding bench. Now go and get things ready. I'd like to be home before midnight."

Amalina found the heavy leather bag sitting on the riding bench. She noticed several people on the street, standing at roughly the same distance from the cart, though at differing points of the compass. Turning her head, she saw them staring at her, the wagon and the horses. From the way she sensed it, the stares were not friendly ones.

She gripped the bag and walked up the street. The two Netzians ahead of her, on either side of the street, walked away. One went further along and out of sight, the other entered the building he'd been standing next to. From the way Genadie had put it, how he and she had nothing to fear of theft or harm from this village, she had thought he meant they were favored by the people. The way she understood it by this cool reception—and it was much more logical explanation now that she considered it—she and Genadie were simply too feared to be picked on.

She could smell baked goods ahead and figured that was the way to the central market square.

She read the signs hanging outside the buildings along the way, noting again how all the villages and towns *were* very much the same, just some in better repair than others. She felt a strange, unexpected pang of longing for the western cities. And the interesting people there. Not that the people were much different there, but they were different enough to make life more interesting and exciting. And maybe, she realized now, it was just that the business signs in those far off places, when they weren't displaying symbols for the illiterate, had been written in their particular languages, and so when looking at them it felt as if she had entered an exotic book, written in a foreign hand. In Netz it was as plain as an overly-familiar room.

As she closed in on the market square, the more people she saw the more they would turn and point, and find reasons to keep their distance. A few stayed rooted in place. They leaned to the walls to avoid her, and glared at her with some shred of hatred. Or was it defiance?

Instead of waiting to enter the first store she found on Genadie's list, she decided to be defiant herself, against the unwarranted enmity of the people here—what had she ever done against them?—and entered the first inviting door she found: one with glass panes, and with an ornate brass handle.

She found herself in a restaurant. She hadn't smelled any food, but inside the doors she smelled the combined fragrances of stews and stale beer. Her stomach growled.

"Hallo," said a man seated at a table. He looked very tired, and by the redness of his eyes, as if he might have just finished crying. "Have a seat. Not much on the menu for today, of course. But the stew is on. Hey, but, who're you, miss?"

He'd just noticed that she was a stranger. And strangers would be a rare thing in Netz.

"I'm—" then she remembered the Count preferred she remain anonymous to outsiders, at least inside the castle. How far did that prohibition extend? "I'm not from around here. I thought I smelled something cooking and I was hungry."

"No one with you?" he asked, sitting up. He meant, *you're a stranger here, and walking around unattended?*

"No," she said.

"You came in on the coach? I thought it didn't arrive until tomorrow."

"I came by myself. By wagon."

"Wagon?" he was more curious now. He eyed her closer, leaning forward to get her better in focus. She would not look like a farmer's daughter, or a miner's daughter, or a logger's daughter, not the way she was dressed. She could not be someone who would have wandered in from a field house. He studied her dress closer. And looked baffled by the mystery of her. So much, he didn't offer a seat anymore, but kept staring, trying to put the pieces together in his head. But he asked no more questions, as would usually be the case. Why not? Would asking questions be dangerous? Fear—or, at least caution—clouded his expression.

The door opened behind Amalina. She had to move to allow the door to open all the way.

"Oh, excuse me," she said.

The town's deputy sheriff, looking everything like the deputy sheriff of her own village, nodded to her courteously and with what looked to be a genuine smile.

"Hallo, Borga," the man at the table called to the deputy. "Just saying hello to this pretty young lady who's ridden into town in a wagon, it seems."

"Ah, yes," said the deputy his eyes hardening on Amalina. "You're with the little one from the castle."

The man at the table rapped his hand on it, the pieces of the puzzle had all fallen into place. He didn't looked pleased by the picture it made. His face hardened, too.

"I'm—is something wrong?" she asked them both.

"Never seen you before, miss. What are you doing with *that* one?" asked the deputy sourly. "He hasn't taken you as a bride, has he? He hasn't … taken you?"

"Um—well," she said. She wanted to protest. Felt like yelling at the top of her lungs that she definitely was *not* the little rat's wife! She felt her face go red. But what exactly was she allowed to say? And how could she ever possibly excuse herself for being associated with the Count—assuming these two men knew what most of the adult male population knew about the Count—had signed the agreement of peace with him in deference to his monstrous crimes. And even if they did know all that, the problem was she didn't know for sure what else they knew, or were allowed to know. Were they even aware that the Count was living in the high castle? Maybe they thought it was only Genadie, a measly caretaker, who lived there. There was no telling what they knew, and Genadie hadn't warned her one way or the other. So she had to be careful. "Taken me on," she told them presently. "They—I mean, *he*'s hired on some servants. To clean the place. Get it in order."

The deputy and the man traded looks.

"How many servants would that be, miss?"

"Oh, I don't know," Amalina said, biting her lip. "I don't know. Just got there. I saw two … besides Genadie."

"Genadie … " the deputy said. "That's his name?"

"Oh, uh … I suppose it is. That is what I was told."

"What else has he told you?"

"Oh, uh … not much. Not much at all, sir. Just that I would be working there for a little bit, and then I'd be able to go back home."

"You're from Ardeel," the deputy said. "Where? What's your name?"

"I—I don't know—"

"You don't know?"

"I don't know if I should say."

"Why shouldn't you say? I am a man of the law. You not only should say, you very well *must* say if I tell you to."

The deputy pressed his bulk against Amalina. She couldn't do much about it, as he had also taken her arm in one of his hands. His grip tightened. She wanted to pull away from him, to shake him off and run. She didn't like the look in either of the men's eyes.

"Of course, sir," she said. "My name is Hansa."

"Where are you from, Hansa? I don't recognize you."

"A small farming town. A little ways from Tsobl. You wouldn't know me, sir. But I think I should be leaving now, actually. I have a list of supplies. I'm supposed to be purchasing—"

"What are you supposed to be buying for that man, Hansa?" he squeezed her arm painfully. Maybe he wanted her to cry, but he didn't know the tortures the Count had already put her through. She easily pretended he hadn't done anything at all. But told him what she could remember from the list. He asked for the quantities. "Not much," he judged. "Especially if you're staffing up for a full house. Just enough for a handful. For how long?"

"I don't know," she said honestly. "I'm just doing as he asked."

"What's in the bag you're holding?"

She clutched it protectively to her waist.

He twisted her wrist and she dropped the heavy bag onto the floor. It clanked with coins. He motioned at it with his forehead. The man at the table nodded and picked up the bag. When he opened it his eyes went wide and he let go of it like it was on fire. Now it smacked the floor hard enough to let spill some of its contents.

"G-gold," the man said needlessly. "A fortune."

"I didn't know what was in the bag," Amalina told them. "I thought it was only just coins."

"They are coins!" exclaimed the man, as if she were an innocent bystander and needed matters clarified. "Gold coins!"

"Bold," summarized the deputy. "Thinks he can come here shaking it in our faces. Might as well have pulled down his trousers and shown us his hairy ass."

"What?" Amalina said, surprised by the sudden earthiness of the conversation.

The deputy was not apologetic, but smiled nastily down at her, trying to crush her arm with his grip.

"I don't understand," she said, thrusting out her jaw, acting ever more defiant despite the pain. "What's the matter here? We've just come into town to buy supplies. Is there something illegal in that, sir?"

"You've come at an interesting time, little Hansa," the deputy sneered (and Amalina suddenly wished she hadn't used her friend's name; to hear it said to her this way, with such hostility). "Do you know what has happened, girl? Happened last night?"

"No. But tell me, sir. There must be some reason you're this upset. All of you."

"The mayor's daughter disappeared out of her house. Ygardina. Most delightful young woman. Beloved by this city. And an obedient and god-fearing young woman, who would never abandon her family."

"Oh, that sounds so sad, and terrible." She saw now where this was leading—at least she assumed she did—the Count had been up to his bloody work—but couldn't let on she knew. "You don't know what's happened to her?"

"We haven't lost anyone in a very long time," the deputy said, continuing on in an accusatory tone. "And nobody ever *just* disappears. But Ygardina, pleasant and pious Ygardina, daughter of our mayor ..."

"That's very sad," Amalina said again, suddenly wondering how this related to her or Genadie. Unless they knew for certain she and he were servants of the Count himself. Why else would they act this way toward her, a stranger to them? As if she could be responsible for Ygardina's disappearance.

The deputy said pointedly: "We haven't seen much of the little man from the castle in a long time either—"

"Oh—" and she was going to say: *Oh, that's because we've been away in the west for months*. But she snapped that off quick, damning herself for even beginning the sentence without thinking first.

"'Oh'? 'Oh', what?" the deputy asked. "You've something to say about that?"

"I can't say," she said. "But as I just told you, he hired me out ... From near Tsobl, like I said ... and we just arrived at the castle yesterday. So he *must* have been away, you see ..."

"So you say. And just in time for Ygardina to be removed from her home ... and in the middle of the night. Haven't seen that little man for a long time, and now, the day after our most prized rose is plucked out in the middle of the night by unseen hands, he comes into town with a need of supplies, for the requirements of several bodies."

He needn't spell out the full accusation. It was written on his heated look, and sounded out on his grinding teeth.

"I don't know what you mean," Amalina protested, now trying to free her arm. But he did not surrender it. He pressed himself further into her, so that she might fall down. Him on top. "What does one have to do with the other? I'm the youngest up there. Everyone else is old. I've seen no mayor's daughter."

There came a cry outside. It was an awful sound. One of anger and grief and outrage. It was enough to turn the deputy's head, and then cause him to go to the window. They all did.

"Deputy!" went the cry. "Deputy! Come here! Come! See what's happened!"

Down the center of the street, a man in shabby clothes led a horse with a woman's body draped over it. The body was dressed in nightclothes, which were dyed red with blood. And its head and hair could not be clearly distinguished by the way the blood had covered it, beginning at the awful rend in its neck.

"Dear!" the deputy shouted. He dropped Amalina's arm and charged out the door. "Ygardina! Ygardina!"

The restaurant's owner rushed out, too, joining a crowd that was quickly gathering from all directions around Ygardina's body, as the horse traveled slowly toward the center of town. The man guiding the horse continued to shout, but now that the deputy sheriff was there, he switched: "Doctor! Doctor! Come out! Come see what has happened to Ygardina!"

Ygardina was a pathetic sight, and reminded Amalina of the horror of the first time she saw the Count, he tearing away Lucinda Skeldar's neck—the night he'd discovered Amalina at her open window witnessing his crime, and almost done the same to her. But instead he had thought of something better for her than become that evening's dessert.

The horror of what she'd returned to, the high castle and the monster that lived in it, Amalina suddenly realized in a sickening gasp. This! This tragic and pathetic sight, this town's outrageous tragedy, was Genadie's 'Master''s work. Her employer's work.

Oh, how she *had* wanted to leave! To flee the castle! Desperately so! Having once even thrown herself out a window! This was the reason! All those old feelings returned in force. Amalina couldn't believe she was here in the nightmare again. Again! After she had been free and clear of it. If only she had stayed in the western kingdoms. There must have been a way, even with the Count's threat to kill her family if she were to disobey him. There had to be a way. She was just too stupid to think of it.

And now she was back, back, back.

Her mind screamed. She had to find a way out!

That was all she wanted: a route—any route—to freedom.

If there was anything she could ask of life, escape was it.

· · ·

With all present concentrating on Ygardina, somehow they'd forgotten about Amalina: accomplice to their prime suspect. She expected them to turn, to point accusation at her. To strap her to a pole and burn her.

She ran to the door, remembered the bag of coins, grabbed it from the floor and tore into the street, running in the opposite direction. There would be no buying supplies today.

She was snared by very strong arms. At first, by the way the hands snatched her from either side, she thought it was a couple people. But it was only one man who'd seized her bodily just by grabbing her arms on both sides and lifting her off her feet; body, dress, bag of coins, and all.

Amalina let off a whoop of surprise, but she was already inside a building, and being dragged further in and up the stairs. She kicked and screamed. She swung the heavy leather bag at her abductor. But her arms were locked, and the bag smacked back into her, not coming close to its intended target.

"Oof!" Amalina said as the bag knocked the air out of her. She tried to catch her breath.

She understood she was being dragged up a small set of stairs, so narrow that her legs, still kicking, hit both sides.

Next thing she knew, she was on the ground, spilled out into the middle of a dark room. No sunlight. It could have been midnight by how dark it was. All the windows were sealed.

One candle was on a table, but the man who spoke to her was in the shadow of a side wall. She saw his stockinged legs extending from the shadow. His legs were large and strong, the stockings old and worn through in spots. She could only sense his eyes on her in the darkness.

"Well, well, what is this?" said the heavy voice. "What present have you brought me, Piotr? Why, I believe you've brought nothing more than a …why yes, look who it is, indeed. Greetings! Greetings, dear little, cute little, innocent little … 'Mouse'."

"Kralov?!"

7

The Undead

Kralov did not bring himself forward into the light, but by the large, bulky shadow, and the gentle low rumble of his voice, she knew it was him. Even if it was impossible.

"You remember me," said Kralov. "And by the look on your face, you are pleased to see me."

"I-I am!" Amalina nearly shouted, still reeling in disbelief. How could she not be pleased? Here was one of the party she'd once hoped would help her kill the Count; and then she had hoped would escape him when the plot didn't work out. But he hadn't escaped. No, he'd been caught. She had thought she'd never see him alive again.

Piotr, the one who had seized Amalina and was presently at her side, seemed to relax. Or rather untense, as Kralov made a subtle gesture. Glancing at him, she saw Piotr now held a long dagger, which presumably had been positioned much closer to her skin a moment ago. And, though no longer a direct threat, the weapon was still in his hand, and he was looking between Kralov and Amalina; one for instruction, the other to keep within reach.

Then she noticed another man in the room behind her, who had been standing in the dim rear corner. He looked so similar to Piotr he must be his twin. This one also had his knife drawn and only eased partially to match Piotr's watchful stance.

"Pleased you are, but confused …" Kralov corrected.

"Yes, I don't understand …"

"You thought I was dead, Mouse?"

"Yes! Of course! He came back and he had your hat … and there was blood on it. Blood all over him."

"And he told you he had killed me?"

"I think so. He must have."

"And so you see that among the monster's many crimes he is also a confounded liar." Kralov shifted again, as if sitting in one position for too long was uncomfortable. But he still did not enter the light fully, so that she could see him clearly.

"Maybe he didn't say it," she allowed. "I-I don't really remember now. It was so long ago."

"Making excuses for him, Mouse?" Fire in his words.

Quickly she assured him otherwise. Maybe she'd just assumed he'd told her Kralov was killed. With Kralov's hat in his hand and all … "but …" she finished up, becoming hopeful, "does that mean Odetta and Lady Flauna are also—?"

"They are quite dead." His voice dropped with each word, until he barely uttered the last, as if it were still too hard to voice something so painful, as if he must accept it by doing so. "Odetta … Katrina … gone. And I can only assume because the monster lived to find us that Erik also died. Unless he is keeping him in the castle as a prisoner?"

"No," she shook her head. "He died."

"As a hero," said Kralov. "But tell me what happened."

Amalina shivered. She didn't think she could.

But he ordered her. There was an edge of danger in his tone, a sharpening. He wasn't so delighted to see her as she was him. She was something to be appraised and evaluated, and then maybe let in. "You will explain to me what went wrong. Did all go as we'd planned? Or did you betray Erik … and betray us? Tell me now. And tell me the truth since you do not like to lie."

She nodded seeing there was a necessity, even if it would hurt her to relive that terrible moment. He couldn't be allowed to think she was responsible for Erik's death, that she had actually aided the Count in it. So after another shiver, she quietly recounted what had happened. How Erik had drugged her, and put her in Katrina Flauna's clothes, and hung her out a tower window. All as a ruse to make the Count believe the woman the Count was most interested in, Lady Katrina Flauna, was still inside the castle, and held in mortal peril, while the real Lady Flauna and her servants Odetta and Kralov fled, with Genadie as their captive, down the mountain towards the faraway town of Netz, and hopefully escape from Ardeel entirely. And the ruse had worked as well as it could have. While it was still daylight, the Count had been helpless about the situation, and he, the creature, confined to the castle. And the Count had believed, until the very last second of daylight, that Amalina was Katrina. But when the light closed off, the Count was free to do as he pleased. And while Amalina did not know what exactly had happened after that, because when the Count burst into the room to save her, Erik had dropped her out the window (and therefore the main act of violence out of sight), she knew, after waking later that night, somehow having survived the fall, that Erik was very much dead.

She felt her eyes tear up as she remembered the sight of him, just outside the castle gate, with the wolves still hovering over his torn body. And she shook violently again, at the memory of the wolf pack leader, a giant, vicious looking thing, composed of sharp red edges and black hair, that had come after her. And would have killed her, too, if she hadn't managed to, at the last moment, driven it howling away with a torch. She remembered its bloody fangs chomping at her, and its hot breath on her skin, and the fiery hate in its eyes. Yes, she could have ended just like Erik, ripped to shreds, guts spread out in the snow … never having seen the western kingdoms, or met her delightful new princess friends, or even known that Kralov had survived.

"Yes, that's right," Kralov was saying, lost in his own thoughts, "the creature arrived by nightfall, of course. The plan worked as best it ever could have, didn't it? We couldn't have done any better. We tried, Odetta," he murmured to a ghost, "Yes we did … It was worth a shot … Our only real chance …"

"But how did you … uh … ?" And now Amalina remembered how the Count had returned from that night with a limp. And how he would—when stiffly rising from a sitting position—hotly mutter Kralov's name, as if Flauna's old servant had been responsible for the injury. "How did you get away?"

Kralov shifted.

"We were too far away … from escaping the Count's little cage," Kralov growled in the shadows. "Too far away from Netz. The snow had hit us as we came down into the valley, and it was already too deep for the sleigh, anyway. We knew he was coming and that he would punish us for our betrayal. So we took our best chance for one of us to make it out. We each went our own way, and I sent the sleigh, with that creature's rat lashed to it, toward the lower river and rocks. I even cut Genadie, to leave a good trail of blood. I took my own direction, never looked back. The, uh … Their bodies were found by early summer, as you probably know. All the time I knew, though, that I was the only one to make it …"

The Count had been holding Kralov's hat, and cursing him for his limp. There had to be something more. She wanted there to be something more. That it was not only possible to escape the Count, but to do him harm. It was an exciting thought. "But how did you survive?"

"Mouse, I've told you all I have to say," his tone had grown colder now that he had relived his personal moment of terror and anguish. He and Amalina both were now agitated, and for some reason, at seeming cross purposes. Mostly, it was obvious, because he still could not fully trust her: "If you had not smiled when you saw me, Piotr would have slit your throat on my command, a command I would have gladly given him. Then we would have rounded up Genadie if we could, and I would have finished the job from that night. Because if you had not smiled, that would have meant you are the monster's accomplice, and guilty of all his crimes. But you are not really his prisoner, though, either, are you?"

"Well, not exactly …"

"Not exactly," he echoed with contempt. "Has he kept you prisoner this whole time and just let you free today?"

"No."

"Where have you been, then? Away? Serving him?"

Amalina nodded, her eyes on the floor, feeling the tears renewing in her eyes. She wiped them. She felt so guilty.

"Yes, serving him. You are not so innocent, Mouse. You knew what happened to us. You thought he'd killed me as well. But you continued on with him."

"You tried to kill me! Erik threw me out the window!"

"We didn't know who you served … but that doesn't really matter. We all played a part, and risked our lives so that one might survive. And so, here we are, Mouse: I am alive, and you are alive. We are the two survivors. Now: you are young, and you are scared, and you are naïve. But you do serve him, you understand. I do not. I live to destroy him. What do you think of that?"

Amalina nodded. Tears were still dropping from her face.

"We are enemies, Mouse."

Amalina shook her head. How could they be enemies? She'd once thought so fondly of him. She had mourned his death. And now, they both wanted the same thing.

"No?"

Amalina shook her head harder.

"But you aren't dead. And you still work for him."

"If I do not, he will kill my whole family."

"He killed mine, didn't he?"

"Yes, but …" she couldn't think of what to say to that. Then: "But mine are still alive. And I will do anything I can to save them. If I knew how to stop him, I would. I tried to do it, you know that. I told Erik about my plans, the ones that didn't work and the one I was working on when you arrived. But I never got the chance. I fought against him."

Kralov nodded slowly. "As long as you were telling Erik the truth."

"I warned you all about *what* he was. You never would have known if I hadn't warned you."

"Mm-hmm," he was sounding more satisfied. "Only you never needed to tell me. I suspected it the moment I saw him. I remembered him … from when I was a child and my parents brought me into Ardeel to play some towns … and he wore those very same clothes, and he looked that same way … I was sure of it then … If only I had seen him, seen who they were talking about, before I'd advised dear Katrina and Erik to play with him, and sent us all on this miserable, ill-fated course …"

"Commander," Piotr said after a moment of silence, to bring him back to the moment.

"Mouse," Kralov said, turning more fully towards her, but still remaining covered in shadow. "your master does not know if I am alive or dead. He does not know that I have built a rebellion against him, and that the day of his reckoning is coming. I am going to destroy that creature, and every last living piece of him. Now that you know this, the only way you and Genadie will be allowed to return to the castle, and not instead disappear entirely—in order to work the nerves of that disgusting spider, that leech on humanity—is if I know I am sending back to him a loyal spy for the cause."

Amalina looked up to him hopefully, nodding enthusiastically. "I can do whatever's needed. I promise."

"You will go there, and you will do as I say. Seek out anything I direct you to find. Even perform acts of sabotage, if so ordered."

"You injured him, didn't you?" she asked excitedly.

"You will even die, if need be. Promise me this, Mouse. Promise me you will do everything I require of you, even face death, and you leave this room alive. My soldier."

"I will do anything," Amalina said, for some reason sounding more frightened than excited.

"Tell me your name." Now he edged forward, the left side of his face coming into the light. His eye sparkled with something like anger. This would be a moment of victory over the Count, the theft of one of his pieces.

"Amalina, sir," she said immediately, knowing a moment of hesitation might just cost her her life. And she did not want to hesitate, in this charged atmosphere she wanted to do all she could to stop the Count's evil, and free herself from his bondage.

"Amalina, who?" Kralov prompted. "What is your *full* name? Where are you from? Who *are* you?"

"Oh, yes." She told him: "Amalina Dalca. From Korr, sir. My father runs the bakery there. We *both* do."

"Good," said Kralov. "I will verify this information. If it proves to be false, you understand the consequences. You will be destroyed alongside your master."

"He is not my master. And it's true, sir. All true. I swear it."

"And also understand, Mouse, that by telling me this, you have given me vital information. I have the same power over you as that creature in the high castle. If you should displease me, I can have done to your family what he promises to do to them: to kill them all, should you betray me."

Amalina gulped down a sudden rush of sick from her stomach. Why would he say such a thing? There was no need. She had always liked him and

Odetta and Erik ... even if she hadn't cared much for Lady Flauna, it didn't matter. She'd been so overjoyed to find Kralov alive.

The eye observing her was almost monstrous in its anger, in its desire for revenge. It did not recognize her beyond her familiar shape, or regard her as anything more than a piece on a chess board.

"Yes, sir."

. . .

After Kralov had given her her orders—instructions on her first moves against the Count—Piotr worked with the other man, the twinnish man, whose name was Roti, to guide her back to the streets. They were very careful about it, one running ahead of the next, checking around corners, winding her through halls and alleyways. She couldn't tell where they were headed. Piotr would warn her to keep quiet, and neither man relaxed until they wound up near the outer edge of the village.

"Not everyone is on our side here," Piotr explained in the end, his brother Roti disappearing wordlessly into a nearby alley. "They know nothing of the Commander, or that he is here. And it is best we keep it that way. You understand."

Piotr looked less severe than his 'Commander', and as if he might at least hesitate for a long second before killing her. He patted her shoulder. They were both soldiers in the war now, no matter how unlikely she was to be one. By the look in his eye, he might also be a little dismayed that she—a small girl—was a necessary part of it. What he wouldn't have given for another wide-shouldered young man with some fighting experience, the look seemed to say.

She heard the wagon and the horses before she saw them. They were clattering at such an incredible speed, reckless and dangerous in a village with narrow streets. It almost tipped over when it turned the corner and sped for the open road. Genadie was squatting, not sitting, at the front rail of the wagon. When he saw Amalina he shouted.

"Ms. Dalca! I can't stop! Grab here! Take my arms!"

Amalina wanted to run away from the charging horses and the rocketing piece of wood behind them. But she sensed she'd better do as he said, and at the last second, avoiding his gnarled hand, grabbed hold of the side of the wagon, and barely avoided the spinning wheels with her legs and long dress, as she pulled herself up and into it. She rolled over, running into the side of two cages, which squawked in protest. When she sat up she saw there were three such cages, a number of the birds he'd selected inside of them.

She also noticed rocks inside the bed of the wagon, and other bits of debris. A piece of masonry. Some vegetables. A broken and chipped newel post.

She climbed onto the bench beside Genadie, who was gape-eyed in terror as he hurried the horses up the road.

"What's happened?" she asked, holding onto the seat for fear of falling off with all the bumps.

"My heavens! Where were you, little one?" Genadie shouted. "I thought they'd killed you."

Amalina felt a nervous twitch, and a tug in her stomach. Did he know she'd been captured? That there was a rebellion forming? That Kralov was not only alive, but the revolution's head?

"What are you talking about?" she asked instead, not answering his question.

"Didn't you see? The mayor's daughter is dead! They think we killed her. They're out of their minds! My, oh, my, I thought they'd gotten you, for sure. But where were you, Amalina? I thought I'd never find you, I thought you were gone!"

He was so relieved to see her, and now she felt quite the same. Relieved to see Netz disappearing behind them. With a look over his shoulder, he then sat down on the bench, shaking his head.

"How did you pay for the birds?" she asked him.

"Where *were* you, Ms. Dalca?" He demanded again, and then looked at her empty hands. "And *what* did you do with the money?"

8

The Spy in the Palace

"**W**hat's happened?"

Genadie shut the gate, his bottom lip wiggling as if the lower half of his mouth, at least, wanted to say something. But his eyes were firmly on the ground, and he went through the motions of closing up the castle, removing the wagon to near the stables, and unharnessing the exhausted horses with the unconscious air of a sleepwalker.

Georg looked to Amalina, who kept close to Genadie—or rather, kept close to the crates with the birds in them. Despite all that had happened in the village, and her changed circumstances here, where she now felt like an intruder, an enemy, she still wanted to see how the big grey birds would be used to send the messages out. Maybe she also felt protected next to Genadie, although protected from whom or what was uncertain. It was good enough to know that at least one person in the castle was interested in her safety.

"What's happened, I ask you," Georg now demanded, lowering his top half over Genadie in a menacing way. "I can see there has been some trouble."

"What can you see, Georg?" said Genadie, looking untroubled by any physical threat. "I went to town for the birds, I return with the birds. As if it is any of your business."

"I see no supplies, cretin. You went to town for *supplies*. Unless you consider all this debris among the cages the fulfillment of our shopping list, you've not fulfilled your duties. Rocks, pieces of wood. Did they throw these items at you?"

Georg studied Amalina for her reaction. She must have looked guilty enough, he closed his eyes and nodded to himself.

"What do I care for your lists?" Genadie was saying, now using a pole to hook the crates out of the bed of the wagon. "Master needs his birds. I'm here for him, and not you and your wife. He needs nothing from your lists."

"Well, *you* do. See if you starve and still think the same." Genadie's stomach rumbled hungrily at Georg's reprimand. "You were frightened off, for some reason."

"Wasn't frightened off by anything."

"Then what's all this stuff? They did some business to his highness' wagon, too. Look here at these breaks and scratches."

"If you know so much, if you have spies down in the village telling you something happened, why don't you have them tell you everything, eh? Why bother me or Ms. Dalca? Yes, have them tell you everything, and leave us to our work."

"Well, if nothing out of the ordinary occurred, I can't see why you didn't purchase our supplies. I can only assume this attitude of yours means you are embarrassed that your brains are failing and you're trying to cover the unfortunate reality that you forgot your instructions."

Genadie threw a dismissive hand in the air, which Georg obeyed, returning to the castle, torch in hand, his head shaking back and forth.

"You think he's going to tell the Count?" Amalina asked.

"We'll see Master first, anyway. Let's get these birds out."

. . .

The Count appeared in the bird loft when they'd wrestled the last cage into it. As they set the cage down, with Genadie lowering it with his pole and Amalina guiding the box into a slotted spot on the counter, the Count leaned over and peered at the birds inside. Amalina, so concentrating on the arrangement, and with thoughts still darkened and distracted by earlier in the day, she leapt back.

"Yes, fine little flyers aren't you?" he said, not smiling, his lips turning downwards at the corner, almost mimicking the shape of the pigeons' beaks, and his eyes seeming to become smaller, almost beady and bird-like.

Genadie set the pole to the side and threw himself on the feather-and-dropping spattered floor, his shoulders quaking.

"Master, we've returned with what you requested. They are the biggest and strongest, and set for Tsobl."

"I could expect nothing more," the Count nodded. "But they will do. They will listen to me and obey."

"As we all do, Master," Genadie chimed, throwing himself on the floor again.

"Not everyone obeys. But everyone can be corrected, if need be."

"Oh, Master, it isn't our fault that we did not return with the supplies. We secured the pigeons first, because that is what you most wished for, and I am—we are—your abiding servants. I and Ms. Dalca, both. But before we could collect the rest, the villagers ... They turned on us, Master! The mayor's daughter was found dead, Master. They blamed us for it! They said we abducted and killed her! It made no sense, but that is what they did, and we just barely escaped with our lives. If they'd chosen to pursue us, we would have been dead, and not returned to serve you again. But I can make no sense of it."

"Yes," the Count purred, not taking his eyes off the new arrivals. "That explains *this*."

The Count pulled a small strip of curled paper from a pocket and dropped it in front of Genadie. He snatched it up and tried to read it in the dull light of one torch, which was stuck into the wall at the back of the room. He squinted and shook his head, unable to read it.

"Well, no matter," the Count said, beginning to fling open the cage doors. "I have other concerns, do I not? Are we ready, Genadie?"

Genadie sprung from the floor and went to the table closest the window. That is where he'd left the stack of envelopes. Tripping over them were now four scrawny, grimy looking pigeons. One more than was there earlier. He shoved them out of the way and began sorting the letters, and pulling to their full length the satin ribbons on each, as if in preparation.

"Ms. Dalca," Genadie said, "Bring that torch here by the window, I cannot see the writing very well."

Amalina did so, observing from the corner of her eyes the Count bending over the new pigeons, cooing and clucking at them in a sincere way. The birds were coming out of their cages and forming up in front of him, as if drawn to his chatter; like they understood what he was saying. He also used his hands to flit this way and that, like they were thin, featherless wings. She ran the head of the torch into Genadie.

"Ms. Dalca! Do pay attention! Let's not set the room on fire."

"Ms. Dalca," said the Count, his voice still caught up in its strange pigeon chirrup, but his head (and those beady eyes) turned toward her, "hoo-hmm, before we begin, hoo-hmm …"

And while he said this his left hand snuck out to snatch the first envelope from Genadie. His fingers now curled up in a way that reminded her of a bird's foot. The digits were thin and with large knuckles. The skin looked rough, with a bubbled texture. It even appeared as if he'd lost one of his fingers, and the remaining three were splayed out from a central location, instead of arranged across the back of a wide hand. As if he were turning into a bird!

"Ms. Dalca! The torch! Watch it!" cried Genadie again. He waved the flames away with the envelopes.

Seeing Amalina's frown and disquiet at his strange appearance, the Count shook his head and straightened himself up, looking amused but also apologetic. His voice returned to its customary deep rumble: "Ms. Dalca, before we begin, there is something I forgot to ask you when you delivered your report to me: Did you remember, when speaking to the gentle ladies of the western courts, to refer to the high castle as 'Count Tepsji's Palace of Pleasure'?"

Amalina still hadn't recovered at seeing his odd transformation and then retransformation—or distransformation—the quick return to his standard shape. She barely comprehended his words, as if he were still cooing like a pigeon. The Count repeated himself, pointing to the letter in his hand when he referred to the 'gentle ladies of the western courts'.

"Oh," she said. "Oh, yes. The Palace of Pleasure. Yes, sir. I remember now. I did call it that, sir."

"Very good." He drawled out his satisfaction, stretching it to seven syllables. *Vvehh-hhehh-rrr-hhyyy Goo-ooo-hhhddd.*

"At first," she added.

"Hm? What does that mean?"

Genadie turned in his spot, taking the torch away from Amalina, and dropping it close to her head, so her face could be seen better—at least by him. He pointed a worried look at her, too.

"Sometimes I'd say Palace of Pleasure, sir," she explained. "And often I did, at first. Only when their parents began asking what kind of 'pleasure', or what exactly 'pleasure' meant ... I wasn't good at providing answers." It was now her turn to look apologetic. The Count, and so in turn Genadie, was sorely disappointed. The Count's expression hardened and the envelope between his fingers began to crinkle and crack. "Now, it was a good question they had, sir. Really, if you think about it. I wasn't sure what it meant either. 'The Palace of Pleasure.' When I thought about it, Lady Flauna had said it during the rehearsals, when she was preparing for her role as Princess Tepsji, and she'd said it as a joke, really. Didn't she? It's just that you liked the sound of it. Remember? And it does sound nice. But there really wasn't a meaning behind it—"

"You won't use that name again in this house," he said looking slightly disgusted, the envelope bending in two, its wax seal chipping.

"Palace of Pleasure?"

"Katrina Flauna. Lady Flauna. The name ceases to exist this moment."

"Oh, yes, sir." She hadn't said her name aloud in more than half a year. Not until today that she could recall, when she mentioned Flauna to Kralov—the man who would avenge her. How strange the two reactions to a name. One evoking passion. The other, a monstrous creature turns into something small and brittle. And yet, the woman, whose name it belonged to, was long dead and beyond caring. This was a surprising, morbid thought to Amalina. Strangely dark. She wondered if it was her current circumstances changing her.

Meanwhile, the Count carried on, winding himself up and pivoting from his upset: "That name disappears for the rest of time ... Palace of Pleasure, on the other hand, shall flourish!"

He smacked the envelope in his hand, and with a great smile he flipped it around and read the wrinkled name on the back of it. "Princess DerGrosse. Yes. Pleasure awaits ..."

He tied the ribbon around the leg of one of the pigeons. Into this pigeon's ear—or rather to the side of its head, Amalina could only assume it had ears there—the Count muttered something, his wing-hand flittering at moments. He had it smell the envelope. The pigeon seemed to nod, and then it went where he directed it next to the open window.

Genadie handed him a new envelope. The Count was delighted all over again, picturing some new pleasure, apparently, with the name held up before him. He repeated the action of tying the envelope to another bird, making it take a whiff of its scent, and delivering his directions, and then the pigeon would obediently hobble off, dragging the small envelope behind it. This action happened many more times, and each one Amalina drew in a little closer, observing the Count's careful, gentle movements, and listening ever harder to what was coming out of his mouth. Sounds that made no sense to her, but the pigeons understood. One pigeon seemed to ask something back, as if it was having trouble fully grasping where he was supposed to be going. Without frustration, and with patience she hadn't yet seen from the Count, he persisted until the bird bobbed its head and joined the others at the sill.

"Derhovna?" The Count looked surprised and confused as he held the final envelope in his hand. "Genadie, what is this?"

"Oh, Master!" Genadie fell to the ground, conking his head on the side of the table in his haste to get there. "Ohh-ch!"

"I did not wish for Princess Derhovna to be invited here, did I?"

"Oh, no, Master! But Ms. Dalca asked me to write one out—I meant to throw it away, Master."

"Ms. Dalca?" the Count turned to Amalina, who took a step back. He held the envelope up, with the offending name pointed at her. "Care to explain to me?"

"Genadie's portrait made her look mean and ugly, sir. And that wasn't fair and she is really very beautiful and so very nice—"

"You established her nice-ness," the Count muttered. "Well established, yes. But whether it is her bedrock, and she is more charming than Cleopatra, I was content to leave her out."

"Why, sir?"

"It doesn't matter whether you know my reasons or not."

"Of course, Master!" Genadie sounded from the floor. "Amalina has unlearned her lessons!"

"But why not?" Amalina continued, sensing the Count's resolve in this instance rested only in his ability to easily crush the will of others. If she was going to be a spy and saboteur in the Count's house, she had to begin resisting somewhere. "Why are you inviting them here, sir? If there are so many who might come, what would be the problem with adding one more? If we are to have feasts, she's one more person to enjoy it. Reading, one more voice to speak … or sing! Dancing, one more partner to share the floor. Playing, one more mind to game against. The bigger the ball, the better, I heard it said. And so the more the company the merrier. Whether she pleases you more than all the others, she will at least provide variety and contrast to those you would prefer."

"The problem is not variety," said the Count, irritable all over again. "It is exclusivity. I don't know how you managed to go to the west, and yet find me a daughter of the east. Derhovna! She is Russian. Russian, you understand? Peter went to the west before he found the improvements he needed for his country, and still they lag behind. They are a backward people. And all of those westerners know it. And look down upon them. And if the Germans or the Flemish hear I've invited a backwards people into my court, they will just nod their heads and place any negative associations of them upon me. I tell you, I need new blood here, not old. Forward thought, not backward. The sun turns always to the west! And also: any association with the Derhovna's will threaten to bring up bad blood, because by their westward journeys to the westerly lands, they have traveled through or around Ardeel, and may have conflicts with me or my family I prefer not rekindled. That is why I have disallowed the very 'nice' Princess Derhovna."

"But it would make me happy to see Hansa again," Amalina said. "I would be so happy."

The Count stared at her, almost in disbelief. After so long with Georg and Abraxa swooning at his every word, her forwardness was probably a hard adjustment. But in a moment he turned from her, and fastened the envelope to the final pigeon, and he whispered something into its ears. It bobbed over to the window.

The pigeons, each attached by a ribbon to a small paper rectangle sealed with wax and pressed by the Count's signet, and addressed with a young princess' name, held their eyes on the Count; soundless. They were expectant of something from him. A final command. The Count raised his hand and pointed toward the window. As if his gesture became a hurricane that blew them from the room, the pigeon's flung themselves out the window. Genadie grabbed up the torch again and held it out the window, trying to catch them with the light to see where they flew.

Amalina watched as the Count turned from the window and looked to the loft's high, vaulted ceiling. Just as before with the pigeons, the Count's head reconfigured itself, rounding, darkening, looking more wrinkled, with a lip withdrawing over his upper teeth. His eyes were huge, but the black pupils spread out over the white, so that they were filled with darkness. He gazed up into the rafters, as his hands came together on his chest.

Genadie brought the torch up to light the ceiling. Gigantic bats hung from the beams, like tiny, furry, mirrored versions of the Count below them, peering down at the Count like the pigeons had done moments ago; waiting for something. The Count spoke to them in a greasy, spitting, squeaking language which excited them. When he pointed to the window, they poured through the window, their current catching the torch and the top of Genadie's head. The flame guttered, Genadie's hat shot off his hair, bounced off the window ledge and then out.

"They will make sure our messengers make it over the mountains and do not break from formation, or forget that Tsobl is no longer their destination."

· · ·

The Count may have granted Amalina's request to invite Princess Hansa Derhovna, but he made sure to reward her for this displeasure by having her clean the rookery. Though it had been a long day and evening, the Count did not recognize exhaustion—at least in a human way—and so she began immediately, with the understanding that if the job was not finished when he returned the next evening, she would have another punishing chore assigned to her.

Years of build-up clumped the floor. She'd never known the room existed for the entire year she lived there, and she was certain Genadie hadn't gone there to clean it in that time. Feathers of every size dusted the floor, and large pools of discolored bird- and bat-droppings stuck those feathers like a hard glue to the wood. The smell matched the mess. Genadie helpfully brought her three more torches, two buckets of hot soapy water and a rather worthless stick-broom.

There was no place comfortable to curl up and sleep, so she went to work. She would sleep well afterwards. If allowed.

Amalina found the curl of paper the Count had dropped in front of Genadie. It was on the floor, in the filth. She picked it up and brought it to a torch.

On it was a hastily scribbled message, the panic of the writer detectable in the misspelling and stretched, shaky, ink-splattered letters:

Troubl wit yor servints.
Lifes en dangr
right now!

Amalina cocked her head. Someone had sent a bird from the village with this message. Genadie had accused Georg of having spies down in Netz, but here was evidence the Count definitely did. Was it the man who'd sold Genadie the new pigeons? He had access to them. But the way he treated Genadie, it wasn't so certain he'd send warnings about Genadie's and Amalina's lives being at stake.

But whoever it might be, there was a spy. That is why Kralov had to be careful. Why he couldn't just openly recruit from the general populace for his revolt. The Count probably had spies everywhere in Ardeel. At least Kralov now had one of his own in the Count's castle.

When she thought of this she heard a flutter in the window. A new bird, as dark-feathered and grimy as the others she'd seen before. It bobbed back and forth on the table before the window. She saw a white band around one of its legs.

The pigeon looked so greasy, as if the dark patches in its feathers were made from rancid lard. And its expression was not the blank-eyed curiousness of a normal bird, but one of a sullen, suspicious nature. Something like a raven or crow. She didn't want to touch it. But the small paper scroll around its leg was a new message for the Count. One he had not seen yet, and if she read it, she would know something he did not. That made touching the bird, even receiving some pecks for it, worth the trouble.

It did not resist. When she leaned to it, cooing in an imitation of the Count, and reached out her hands for it, the pigeon lifted its leg to offer the message up to her. This was its job, of course. It couldn't tell from a spy.

She pulled the tiny scroll off its leg and opened it. The paper matched the one used in the other note, but the script was entirely different. It was controlled, with no flecks of ink. And the message made no sense. No, it could not be read at all. It was just a string of symbols and letters and numbers, and most of the symbols she had never seen before.

This was a secret message. A long one that stretched the length of the paper and ran for four lines. None of the characters were cramped in, though they were very small and the note packed to capacity, as if the entire missive had been pre-designed to fit the small space. The person who'd sent this message had regained control of him or herself, but had a lot of new information to deliver to the Count.

It must be important, she decided. It would have to be deciphered.

She stuck the two tiny scrolls in her blouse. And then she drove the new bird out of the loft, swinging a torch at it, making sure it understood it wasn't welcome back.

9

Troubl Wit Yor Servints.

Near dawn, Amalina sat up in bed, a victim of dream after horrible dream. One nightmare feeding into the next and never letting her wake, and not letting her rest either. She was hot, and exhausted, and her bedclothes and sheets were soaked.

The terrors had all been bad enough, but buffering between each new nightmare was the old dream come back to haunt her: Lucinda Skeldar skipping through the barley fields, with only her head and shoulders bobbing above the high feathery golden tops—wait, her head had never been found, had it?—and she staring directly—aimed directly—at Amalina, while whistling or singing gaily; the tune agitating Amalina's ears, the words to the lyrics frivolous, meaningless, but she understood there was another meaning behind them. *Find my killer!* Lucinda told her. *Take revenge for me! What are you waiting for?*

Lucinda never reached Amalina. When she got close enough her head would drop back down and then never come back up. Amalina would watch the barley, anticipating the reappearance of her head, dreading that what would rise next would be the shoulders alone, with a bloody stump between them.

Kralov's head popped up instead.

Amalina shivered.

Why this dream again? Why now?

And it seemed the power of it had only strengthened. As if Lucinda's lust for revenge only increased the more it remained unsatisfied.

And Amalina alone was in the position to satisfy her. She'd been the sole witness to the murder—at the hands (teeth) of the Count. So she knew Lucinda's killer, which was the first step. Now she simply had to act on the knowledge: To take revenge.

But that wasn't so simple was it? What could Amalina do that no king, no general, no holy man, no army had tried and succeeded?

Why this dream again? Was it because she was back in the castle, returned to the presence of the Count? Was it prompted by a subtle guilt, because she was not only employed by this foul criminal, but that she had basically accepted the position? enjoying the gold-plated trappings of the life in a castle, traveling abroad, meeting royalty, befriending princesses, never wanting for money, and ignoring her basic morality?

Or was it because there were so many concerns pressing down upon her, each one a secret to hold, each one an added weight: Her need to pose as a princess, to enact the count's plans. Her duty to play the part of a loyal servant, so that she could return to Korr and keep her father alive and well. Her requirement to serve as Kralov's spy, an invaluable pawn in the coming rebellion. And, yes, as always, to act as living vengeance for Lucinda, and all the innocents down through the ages who the Count has murdered; an achievement any being with a soul and a sense of *righteousness* should pursue.

And each and every one of those secret roles having balanced upon it not just Amalina's life but the threat of the destruction of her father, and perhaps even the lives of hundreds more if she should fail.

It was too much for her mind to handle at once, and so the stress manifested itself in the one nightmare that put a fine point on it: Find Lucinda's killer (who was the Count) and take revenge (Kill him!); which would also solve all the other problems at once (and she can retire in peace).

Kill the Count. Simple enough. And impossible.

Couldn't there be another way?

What if there was another way to reduce or to work out to everyone's satisfaction the troubles presented by the Count, while resisting the obvious (and impossible, and destructive, and suicidal) solution?

Well? What if there *was* a way?

She couldn't think of it right there in the bed, but the thought that there might be an alternate answer charged her body, and she quickly got into drier clothes and headed downstairs to prepare the morning meal.

. . .

"What happened to the dough?"

"Outside," barked Abraxa through her thin lips. She had her hair pulled back under her white cap, and she was briskly sweeping out the kitchen cabinets with a small hand broom, shaking her head at each puff of dust she sent into the air. With what she said, she might have been telling Amalina to leave the kitchen, but Amalina sensed she meant that that was where the dough was.

Just outside the door, on the stone tiles of the courtyard, lay a ragged whitish lump, as if the dough she'd left in the bowl on the counter the night before had not just been thrown out of the castle, but had been vindictively torn apart; savagely shredded by bony fingers, with broken fingernails.

"Why would you do that?" Amalina asked, trying not to sound too offended. She felt the heat on her cheeks and wiped them with the back of her hands.

"Doesn't belong in here."

"Bread doesn't belong in a kitchen?"

"Not '*a*' kitchen, our *lord*'s kitchen. The only thing that belongs in here are the foods and implements which serve him."

"He doesn't exactly eat, does he?" she said, snidely. But then she still didn't know how much Georg and Abraxa knew about the Count. She assumed they knew what he was—maybe even knew *more* about him than she did. Even knew the proper name for what kind of creature he was. Or maybe they even believed as Genadie did, that the Count was really *Zeus*, the king of the Greek pantheon of gods, come down in human form. What they knew, she hadn't established yet. But at the moment, with her hands clenching open and closed, she was too angry to pursue the subject.

"He doesn't starve, does he?" Abraxa countered nonsensically, but with a flash in her eye that she'd got in a good one. "And should he wish for something to eat, his wishes will not be impeded by any useless clutter. This kitchen provides for him and his guests and no one else. I don't care what you got up to before Georg was brought in to restore order, but Georg is here now and order will be observed. If you feel you need to make bread, you'll do so in the servant's house."

"Genadie's shack?"

"Whatever you want to call it."

"I'm a guest here. Doesn't that mean—?"

"Georg and I also have quarters within the castle, but we are not guests. It is only for efficiency's sake, and by our eminence's desire that we reside here, close at hand. But we, and *you*, are his servants, not guests. Do you understand?"

"It'd be easier if I used the oven here in the—"

"Genadie doesn't enter this castle unless he is bid inside. He eats outside, in his quarters. And so the easier and more efficient thing to do would be to do your cooking there. Now, do you understand me, Mouse?"

Amalina stammered, not believing she'd heard the Count's pet name for her come out of Abraxa's mouth. It offended her all the more. *Mouse?*

"Do you understand that I was making bread for everyone, not just Genadie and I? Wouldn't you like—?"

"No."

"You don't want any bread?"

"Georg and I don't need to eat. We are always at his highness' command."

"You don't eat?"

"Not at all."

Did that mean they were like the Count? But he ate just like anyone else. Only he subsisted on the lifeblood of others. They didn't eat at all? Really? They were so large, and though old, and their skin grey to pudding white, they looked healthy enough. Amalina suspected Abraxa was boldly lying here.

"You don't sleep, either, I suppose?"

"No."

"Then why did you say you and Georg have rooms? What do you need rooms for?"

There was a pause. Abraxa's thin lips pressed so hard together they disappeared behind her teeth.

"Because," she said, adding another pause again. "Because we change our clothes. And so we have somewhere to be when the lord of the castle does not require us. Now: *Do you understand?*"

"Why didn't you leave the dough in the bowl? It's ruined."

"The bowl belongs in my Master's kitchen. Use Genadie's pots."

"Well, you didn't need to tear it apart, anyway. That was very mean of you."

"You think I have time for something like that? One of your animals probably got loose—knowing how much attention you pay to them—and had itself a snack. Now go."

"And where to do you think you're going?" Georg said, coming up from behind, as Amalina turned.

"Taking the dough away."

"And why would you do that?" He glared. "Petty thievery won't be tolerated in this castle, do you hear me?"

"Thievery? I was just trying to bring it in!"

"You just told me you were taking it away." He stooped over her, to intimidate. "Lying will be even less tolerated and even more severely punished in this castle, do you hear me?"

Amalina pointed to Abraxa. But Abraxa was busy cleaning again, her mouth pinched and eyebrows cast downward, trying to ignore what was happening.

"What are you pointing at, child?" said Georg, testily. "This is your doing. And I can tell you now, it will be reported!"

"*She's* the one who threw it out," Amalina said, exasperated. "I was just trying to bring it back in. And then she told me to take it away, which is what I was doing. I didn't lie, and I wasn't stealing."

"Well, then what *are* you doing?"

"I was just trying to—I don't know anymore. Do you two want bread or not?" she asked.

Georg looked to Abraxa who put her head deep inside a cabinet and didn't answer. He turned back to Amalina. He stared at the dough in her hands.

"Are you trying to tell me," he said, sourly, "that you intend to feed us with *this*? Garbage? Little girl, look at the bits of leaves and dirt all over it. Is this some kind of rude joke? Or an attempt to poison us? It will be reported."

"Then I'm taking it away, like Abraxa told me to," Amalina said finally. After a thought: "Wait, Georg, did you say you punish lying more than stealing?"

"I have no time for idle chatter," he sniffed. "Get back to work."

• • •

Amalina went to the barn to comfort herself the animals were still there. She hadn't seen them in so many months (which means Georg or Abraxa had to've been tending to them or they were all dead). Also she wanted to discount Abraxa's accusation of them eating her dough. She assumed the woman was lying, and that she'd find the few animals (several chickens, a duck, two pigs, three goats, one sheep) as rotted skeletons, or alive and locked in their pens with no dough on their lips.

She then remembered the horse she'd been meaning to visit. Not Genadie's weird slave-horses that were left to roam the courtyard, but the one that Kralov and Lady Flauna had left behind. The marvelously large white courser, which she had tried to escape with once, but it hadn't let her ride. Well, she had spoken of it often to the princesses, feeling the need to match them pet for pet, and she had even given it a name: White Snow, after its remarkable color, and how it had helped cover her tracks in the courtyard during the tremendous snowstorm when she'd attempted her escape. It had been a recalcitrant, stubborn, frightened animal. But after all her stories to her friends, and after so much practice riding with them on horses from their vast stables, she had converted him in her mind into a great friend, and one she could easily conquer. She went to the stalls to find him.

Genadie caught her. He gave her a troubled look and she figured Georg must have given him some grief as Abraxa had her.

He brought her back up to the birdhouse. On their way she worried that she hadn't cleaned it well enough, and that she would be forced to scrub the place down again.

Then another concern rose: Had the fourth pigeon returned—and they knew there should have been a message attached?

Amalina began to sweat.

The bats had returned to the rafters. In the light of day, and bothering to look up, they were easy to spot. Spotting them didn't comfort her in any way. Then she saw the three pigeons clumped around a small bowl of grains, pecking at it. The fourth one, darker and greasier than the others, had not returned.

Genadie went to the long counter by the window and began moving the empty cages.

"Here, Ms. Dalca, have a look around if you could. I'm looking for the note Master handed me last night. I thought I had it on me, but I must have dropped it. Oh, stupid me."

From the random way he was shifting things, and looking in all directions, he'd probably been at it all morning and had covered the room a hundred times over.

"Did you see it, Ms. Dalca? When you were cleaning the loft, did you see it? Did you pick it up? You didn't accidentally throw it away, did you? No, you should know you never throw away even the smallest of scraps that belong to Master, unless he tells you to."

"I—" But then Amalina didn't know how to answer. He looked at her expectantly, his beady eyes wide with hope. He even pulled a lock of greasy hair behind an ear, preparing to hear the words he so wished to hear—this must be important. But the little message on the curled piece of paper, along with its cryptic follow up, were in her bedroom, hidden under her mattress. She couldn't tell him that. "I—I don't remember. I'm sorry."

"Oh, Ms. Dalca!" His lips turned down, almost comically, and the ends twitched, producing a white foam out of one. He blinked some tears, and steadied himself with a hand on the counter. "Oh, Ms. Dalca … "

"I'm sorry. Really. I just don't remember. I wasn't looking for it, you know." Amalina began circling the room, looking on the floor and under the counters. "Why didn't you tell me?"

"I'm so stupid …"

"Does it really matter? You read it didn't you? He read it, anyway. Why do you need it?"

"We never question the will of Zeus," he blubbered into his palm, looking helplessly. "Don't you understand that?"

Everyone asking if I 'understand', Amalina smirked. *None of them making any sense!*

She continued on with her false search, wondering how to get the slip of paper back out from her bedroom and over to the loft without being found out. It was small enough to hide in her hand, but how to explain needing to leave, and where would she suddenly 'find' it having gone over everything already? Or, despite Genadie's despair, was it even necessary to get it back to him, and into the Count's hands?

"Oh, Ms. Dalca, do try harder," he said.

"Why aren't you helping?"

"I looked already."

"Then what good is it if I do it? Maybe I did pick it up with all the dirt and it's not even here anymore."

"The midden! Or, where did you throw it? Show me where you put the clearings!" Genadie was already in the window, gaping at the grasses below, looking like he might fly out.

"Genadie!"

They left the castle walls and found the area under the loft's window. Sure enough there was a wide pile of feathers, fluff and grime, all sitting on top of Genadie's hat, which had flown out the window hours before them.

Genadie grabbed the hat, brushed it off, looked it over, inspected its insides, then, dissatisfied, he crushed it onto his head, sat down and started to search through the rest of the pile.

"It isn't in there," Amalina said pityingly. "You can see that."

"It might be," he said, crying again. "We can't give up hope."

"Maybe one of the bats made away with it."

"Maybe the bats made away with it," he growled with hostile sarcasm. "Maybe one of them ate it, eh?"

"Or maybe it blew away. Well, I don't see why it's so important. What did it say?"

He didn't answer, just chucked plumes of fluff into the breeze.

"What did the message say?"

Would he tell her?

"Genadie?"

"Leave me alone if you aren't going to help."

"I'll check the bucket and cleaning things," she said, testily, wanting to get away from him. "It could have stuck to the brush."

Maybe her tone was too negative, or he wasn't listening, but he didn't react as she left him.

• • •

Back in her room, she straightened out the strip of paper between her fingers, and studied its message:

Troubl wit yor servints.
Lifes en dangr
right now!

It wasn't a difficult message to interpret: the Count's servants were having trouble, and their lives were in danger, *right now!* A true enough statement at the time.

Or did it mean the Count's life was in danger, because of his servants?

Could it mean someone knew of Amalina's new link to Kralov and was warning of her coming treachery?

But it said *servants*, not *servant*. And Genadie was in no way a conspirator against his beloved Zeus. He wasn't created that way. And so the straightforward reading of its panicked strokes—that it warned of Genadie and Amalina in the hands of an angry mob—made the most sense, and so was the most logical reading.

And how could the Count's life be endangered by such a thing, anyway? How could his life be threatened at all? No, the reading was very clear after all: Genadie and Amalina were being attacked, their lives were in great peril.

So why would the Count want to have this scrap of paper back after he'd read it? His servants' lives weren't in danger anymore. *(No thanks to him.)* In truth: he'd gotten the pigeon post, then he'd sat back in the safety and darkness of his castle, unable to do anything under the burning sun, waiting to see if Genadie or Amalina returned. How weak he was, all things considered.

She read it again, thinking again: Why does he want to see this letter? It couldn't be any less important.

But the way Genadie was carrying on …

She took out the second curl of paper. Straightened out, it was still just a garble of glyphs and symbols. You'd think he'd want this one … That is, if he knew he'd received it.

Maybe this was some kind of test. Maybe he did know it had come. Knew it was being sent and he'd been waiting to receive it. Maybe Genadie'd seen it arrive, had been there, watching the whole scene, as Amalina took the note and drove away the bird.

Amalina shook her head. She was sure she would have seen Genadie, or smelled him, or otherwise noticed his presence. Maybe the Count? She would have felt him and his eyes. And this would be too round about of a way of confronting her. Why ask about the first message when he wanted the second?

She couldn't make sense of the cipher any better than before. On a second thought, she brought up the first note again, comparing the writing. She couldn't tell if it was the same hand. It looked like the same kind of paper, but it could just as easily be from a different source. Were these letters from two different people? Could the first message also be in code? With all the misspellings, maybe there was some other message hidden right before her eyes.

A quarter hour of searching for hidden patterns, and playing with variations on the letters themselves, she realized Genadie, or Georg, or

Abraxa, or even the Count, could enter her room at any moment. So she had to come to a decision on what to do with these messages.

She was sure that Kralov would appreciate getting hold of a secret correspondence between the Count and a confederate. Maybe he could recognize the writing or the poor spelling and identify who it was. Or decipher the code. It would be valuable. If for nothing else, it would prove to Kralov that she was working for him, and he would be less likely to think of hurting her father.

She couldn't just tell him what she'd read, either. He'd have to see the note, touch it, to know that it wasn't something she was making up.

Amalina nodded. She took up a piece of chalk and copied the message on the underside of her chair, same placement and exact misspelling. She could return to it later to see if it made any more sense, or could be broken down into a cleverly encrypted, more vital meaning. She started to copy the second message but abandoned it after the fourth character ... it would take too much time, making sure she didn't mess up the strange characters. And if anyone discovered the markings she would have a lot more explaining to do. She rubbed off the last bit and hid the second strip of paper under her mattress again.

The first message she lightly crumpled. Then she laid it on the floor. Then she stamped on it, and stamped on it, and kept stamping on it until she was satisfied.

. . .

"Oh, sir, I'm glad I found you," Amalina said, her heart beating loudly in her chest. With his acute senses, he could probably hear it.

The Count was at his desk in his private study. He wore a white, rough wool overshirt. Dressed down from his customary fashion. He was staying in tonight, she decided. He turned to her, his large eyes surveying her, but wore no expression.

"You have something for me?" he said.

"Yes," she said, unable to stop from gulping. "Uh, how did you know?"

"Why else would you invade my room and disturb my work?" he smiled politely.

"Oh, yes. Well, the door was unlocked. So I thought you might be in here."

"What is it? Is everything all right?"

"Oh, yes, sir." Amalina nodded. Then she kept making little nods, almost apologetically, as she crossed from the door to his chair. He watched her curiously. And held out his hand when she offered him the note.

"What is this?" He took the mashed and torn paper and unfolded it. "Ah! Here you are! I thought I would never see you again! Well, well! A little the worse for wear, but you've returned! Very good. Yes. Very good. Perfect."

He stood, admiring the little note caught up in his fingers. Long, thin, but powerful fingers which were whiter than the paper.

Absently, and still staring at it, unable to take his eyes from it, he began to amble toward the opposite wall. "Found it, did you?" he was saying. "Or was it Genadie, and he sent you here?"

"No, I found it. You'll never guess where."

"No, I probably couldn't."

"You'll never believe it."

"Yes, yes. Amazing. But you've been found, and I have you," he murmured sweetly to the scrap. "Yes, a little hard to look at. A little worse for wear. But you've returned. Very good. Yes. Very good. I am very glad, and Ms. Dalca has done me well again. Why shouldn't I be delighted?"

He had a way of talking inwardly. And frequently repeated himself. Amalina's heart stopped pounding, and she wanted to roll her eyes. She kept them in check.

The Count had gone to a tall cabinet, and without looking away from the paper, reached out his hand to near its top. Something made a loud wooden clack and the cabinet shifted awkwardly; suddenly, as if it popped off a mounting on the wall.

The Count spun toward Amalina, his eyes opened wide. It was the first time he was truly looking at her since she'd entered the room. Almost as if he was surprised to see her.

"Did you look at this note?"

"No. It was kind of mashed."

"But how did you know it was the letter I was looking for?"

"Oh, well …" Amalina bobbled. "I mean, I looked at it, of course, sir. I have eyes. And I opened it a little, just to have a peek. But it's not like I really read it. You know, it is yours, sir. I thought it might be private."

"So you did read some of it."

"I saw some of the words. I didn't read everything … I think."

"It's unimportant if you did," he said, now leaning against the cabinet. There was another loud wood clack, and the large cabinet popped back up to the wall. He brought his hand down, and trailed at his jawline with it. He might have pulled at his mustache in another time but the mustache was gone. He still looked handsome, but without the mustache it was a much plainer form of handsome. Like a wood chair without stain or varnish. "A message about my servants, and trouble."

"Well, like I said, I didn't read it all. Just enough to see it had some writing on it."

"You never need to be afraid, my little mouse," he said, forgetting the cabinet and walking slowly toward her. "Nobody in that town would hurt you. You understand that, don't you?"

"I wasn't worried, sir. They didn't come after us." Was he talking about the message now? Assuming she'd read it? And had understood its meaning?

"You are under my protection. These people, they would never think to touch a hair on your pretty head."

"Didn't you say that Neku killed one of your servants?"

The Count smiled viciously. "And he died, didn't he? You saw me do it. His is the example for those who would challenge me."

Amalina thought he was missing the point, but she wasn't going to correct him. She just wanted to leave the room without him asking more questions.

"If they had hurt you, they would have died. I would have found them out, to the last man, and made an example of them. Trust in me, little mouse, they would have regretted their action only long enough as was necessary, before they then experienced the most excruciating pain. Beyond any suffering they could imagine. Yes. You would have been avenged. I would have struck that vengeance, in your honor, against them!"

She began to feel drowsy. The whole room was taken up with his overly large brown eyes, his warm stare.

"Yes," she said, not knowing what she was agreeing to. She took a step back, thinking she should head for the door.

"You understand that, little mouse, don't you?"

"Yes ... sir."

"And you believe me."

"Yes."

"Amalina, I have lived a very long time. I know every man and woman and child in this country. I know their names, what family they belong to, who they love, who they hate, who they plot against. I have watched them be born. I have watched them die. I have kept track of them, every one of them, continuously. You understand that."

"You've lived for a very long time ..."

"And there is nothing someone can do that I won't find out. That I won't learn. That I won't mark down. And if they should offend me enough, I can remove them from that unending flow of history. Like a drop of water taken from a river. They will not be missed. Only I will know it happened, as only I know the course and shape of the river, because I am removed from it. I stand above it. I see it all. I watch it all. I can reach in and meddle with it. I can even, if I needed, bend its whole course to my will. But it is only I who can do such things."

"Yes."

"Your lives were not in any danger, little mouse. *They* know the consequences. Even now, the miscreants who frightened you, *they* will be made examples. I know the parties to strike, so that such a mistake does not happen again. And should harm *ever* befall you—and if you've stood with me, loyally—your name will never be forgotten. I can see to that."

"Thank you, sir."

"You've served me well. You may go."

She was in a slight daze. She turned to leave. And as she headed to the door, she heard that strange clack sound. Glancing over her shoulder she saw the Count had pulled the cabinet off the wall again. As he entered whatever lay beyond the entrance he'd just opened, he was staring fixedly, with a smile, at the scrap of paper.

• • •

"Master said you found the note, Ms. Dalca." Genadie's scratchy voice was breathy, as if he were on the verge of tears again. His knotty hands were clasped together prayer-like against his chin. He was already nodding at her, but he needed her to say it. To confirm what he'd heard.

"Yes, I did. And I figured he should have it right away, so—"

"So it's true?" he was quaking. "But I thought it was lost for good. I went and checked the buckets and the broom and the brushes. I couldn't find it anywhere. How did you find it?"

"You mean where?"

Genadie nodded, looking expectantly at her.

"I turned everything over and couldn't find it either. But I knew it couldn't just have disappeared, that it had to be somewhere. Maybe in a hallway, or blown into the forest."

"Yes, Ms. Dalca?"

"Can you guess where I found it, then?"

"Oh, please tell me."

"When I'd finally given up, thinking it was lost for good. I thought of the one place I hadn't looked." Amalina lifted her foot and pointed to the bottom of her shoe. "Right here! Stuck right on. I must've stepped on it last night. And I had it on me the whole time. Can you believe it?"

"Yes, yes, yes!"

Genadie looked so relieved. Knowing where the note had gone—and it being a logical explanation—made the impossibility of the message actually being recovered all the more real. He was no longer in trouble with his Master. He jumped for joy and danced around, the color flooding back into his face, the rare smile exposing his rotten, crooked teeth. He bounced merrily, belting out a happy tune, shaking his head from side to side, the embodiment of joy in mangled form.

Genadie was given to such flights of ecstasy, Amalina found him frequently entertaining, though she thought it was probably unkind to do so. Throwing another shadow over her thoughts was how much more unkind it will be when her silly friend learned she was a sworn enemy to the being he most loved. Which he would learn soon enough, now that she was free to begin revolutionary operations.

10

Amalina, Kralov's Secret Agent

From under the mattress Amalina pulled a small leather bag. From that she pulled her secrets: the scrap of paper with the coded message, and the small ceramic vial Kralov had given her with special instructions.

Amalina knew she had to do something today. No matter how difficult, she had to make some major stride as Kralov's agent. The message, with its mysterious code, promised only frustration. The little paper went back in the bag.

So: the vial.

She turned the vial in her hand. It was white with a small blue line around its slender belly. A ceramic stopper was sealed into its opening with wax. Amalina touched the stopper, testing how strong the seal was. It hadn't leaked its contents.

Should I open it? she wondered.

Kralov hadn't told her what was inside. He'd handed it to Piotr, who'd then placed it in Amalina's hands while the Commander explained the first of her missions.

"It's not much," Kralov had said of the item—or, more specifically, its contents—when he was done, "but it is enough. More than enough to allow for several attempts. But you shouldn't waste any. Nothing done frivolously. Do you understand?"

"What is it?"

"A liquid—harmless enough to you. There is nothing for you to fear of it. But you will find a way for the creature to come in contact with it. On the skin, or ingest it." He made a sound of appreciation. "Yes, to ingest it would be best."

"What will happen to him?"

"Do you understand what you're to do?"

"You know," she said, "I already made him drink wine infused with the root of—"

"Do you understand your orders?"

"Yes. It's just I already—"

"This is different. You will get it on him, or in him. If he does not die, you will report back and tell me his reaction, if any."

"What if he doesn't die but he finds out I tried to test him and—?"

"You'll have to be cautious and careful," answered Piotr; serious, kindly and full of comradeship. Roti nodded with a similarly commiserating, lightly grim *joie de guerre*.

"*'And'* what?" Kralov cut in on top of his sociable subordinates. "You will get me the information I need."

"But if he kills me …"

"Then at least we will know you've done your work, like a good soldier," Kralov grumbled with cold humor. Her safety was irrelevant.

It was entirely plausible he'd handed her nothing more than a poison, and Kralov reassured her it was safe only because he was willing to sacrifice her as a pawn so long as it took out his opponent, too.

A poison for the Count?

Without realizing it, she'd opened the vial. The stopper was in her fingers, little bits of white wax clung to it. The stopper's end which had rested inside the neck looked damp.

Amalina sniffed near the wet end. No odor. Cautiously, she sniffed several times, her nose crawling toward the opening of the small bottle. Nothing. She jiggled the bottle. From inside there was the bright, tickling noise of a liquid as light and quick as water. Did it have color? Should she have a look? Well, she couldn't just drop whatever was in there on him. She would need to know what she was working with if she was going to use it properly.

Just below the bed frame, with the bottom length of blanket in her hand, she carefully tipped the vial. A pellet of clear fluid dropped out. She made a little gasp as it splashed onto the stone floor. But then brought her eyes close. What started as a little drop quickly spread to leave just a dark spot on the stone. Swiping at it with the cloth, there was no effect. No smell. No obvious reaction. Just like water. Just water? It couldn't be. But it obviously wasn't an acid … or any of the nasty chemicals she'd seen used by Cristine's father, a businessman and owner of many mines (where those chemicals were employed), who demonstrated controlled burns and small explosions for the two excited young girls; to entertain or impress or scare them.

Kralov's gift was nothing so volatile or dramatic as those chemicals. Just thin, and clear, and with no smell …

Still, she wasn't going to touch it, or taste it, or swallow it. No.

Because it was a poison. It had to be.

But what poison could be so powerful that it would be effective on a creature such as the Count with just a drop or two?

Well, it was something she would have to work on: Getting the Count into position to receive a dose without realizing it, and without him suspecting Amalina if he should survive. It was a familiar feeling for her. Something she'd done before, setting the Count up for death but laying the foundation cautiously to avoid guilt (and the death part never quite coming off). In the meantime, she wasn't planning to stop at that. She was determined to impress Commander Kralov and her compatriots in the rebellion. Assuming Kralov's liquid would be as ineffective as the one in her previous effort to poison the Count (an embarrassing fiasco, so, so long ago), any report she gave them would be a disappointment if she didn't back it up with something, *anything* else. She had in mind her own private operation, which might yield even better results. How much more convinced would they be of her loyalty and commitment to the cause, and accept her, and withdraw any measures they were actively taking against her father, if she broke the Count's code? and his private network? or raided his most secret areas inside the castle?

There was a knock at her door. "Get to work," said Georg.

· · ·

Even when the Count wasn't within earshot, conversation in the castle was limited to, and singularly focused on, what extreme deeds of housework Georg and Abraxa could boast for themselves and deprive Genadie and Amalina. Their record of accomplishments was endless, and sometimes unbelievable. Had they really scrubbed out the privy chutes? Unheard of. One was left to wonder what new form of service could be found, invented, or dreamed. But whatever those two had gotten up to—while Amalina and Genadie were off sowing the Count's name in the western kingdoms—Georg and Abraxa hadn't much meddled in Amalina's old job: Cataloguing the books; the forest of books destined for the Count's Great Library.

"As you can see," Georg pouted maturely, lifting one hand in an outward arc as if lifting a heavy cover to expose a hidden surprise. "I relieved you of some of your burden."

"Yes, thank you, Georg," she said

The books Amalina had already entered into the catalogue and moved into the library before she'd left, Georg had dutifully placed some of them—in exact order of listing—onto the first wall of shelves. The rest sat in a neat order against the northern shelves, waiting to be put up. The ones yet to be logged he'd transferred from the Great Hall to the center of the library floor. From the looks of it, the piles had been moved precisely as they'd been stacked in the Great Hall. And if she wasn't mistaken, in the same relative positions to each other. There was something about Georg's meticulousness that was impressive and slightly disturbing to Amalina. The man paid attention. To everything. It was another point of pride, to sit alongside his status as an unequaled workhound.

"Better here than clogging the Great Hall," he said of the remaining stacks, in an effort to chastise her for having not finished her primary duty.

"Oh, yes, it'll be much better to work in here," Amalina agreed pleasantly. And it was true. The library's two-story wall of glass panes—something which looked modern and out of place—would be much easier for the eyes, as long as the drapes were open. A person could pour through books only so long in torch, candle or fire light before the eyes grew tired and the head ached.

"And so," Georg bowed and left.

He meant: "And so, *get to work.*"

Amalina picked up the library's catalogue. It was open to where she'd left off so many months ago. So remote a time, it seemed, that the hand—hers—which had written the name and subject of the books was not the same one now running over the page. At the time, she'd been planning the death of the Count. She had been afraid for her life, and the lives of Erik, Odetta and Kralov; and her father, should things not work out. At that time she hadn't been aware she was going to replace Lady Flauna in her mission to the west. That she would become a princess. The words had been written by someone born a baker's daughter, who knew nothing but the combining of ingredients, the recipes, memorized details of how to prepare an oven, and where to place a loaf and just how long to cook. She knew the drudgery of clearing shelves and cleaning cookware, battling the invasion of mice, and hawking to customers the last of an unwanted stock. She knew the routines of life in a mountain village somewhat separated from the rest of civilization.

The fingers now turning to the first page of the inventory, scanning down the entries, belonged to a young woman who had walked in palaces, knew the proper way to conduct herself in high society so as to win their favor; had gained the intimacy of nearly a dozen beautiful, charming princesses and their families, and savored the best prepared foods that the world had to offer. She'd seen what lay beyond the Ardeelian mountain ranges and she'd faced death very closely.

And she'd been sworn into a revolution.

It would be a bore but she had to review the list of books. All of them. There had to be one she could use. Her current mission: decoding the mysterious message. She didn't recall ever coming across a book on ciphering, but there had been so many books that—because ciphering was not interesting to her way back when—she might have blindly entered it and then forgotten it.

After an hour she was convinced she hadn't missed it.

She looked to the remaining books to be inventoried. Somewhere in there could be a book on how to create and solve secret codes. The library was so extensive, and the breadth of the Count's acquisitions so wide, it was very possible to be sitting within the room. But if so …

The temptation was to rush through, reading the titles off their spines. But some books didn't have cover titles, and some titles wouldn't reveal the complete nature of what was contained within. Patience, and being methodical would reward. She had to sit down and carry out the cataloguing process: pick up a book, open it, page through it, write it into the inventory, and then move to the next book.

Still exhausted from cleaning the bird house, and with months of riding around in carriages having softened her, her back and arms and knees ached. Old people in her village would talk for hours about such pains, and now she knew what they were worked up over. She looked at the stacks of books, turned her head from one end of the room to the other, and sighed. She felt both tired *and* restless. So she left.

There was always time to crack the code of the Count's secret message. There were other ways to serve the rebellion; to root out the Count's secrets, to prepare the critical infrastructure within the castle for the working of subordination and sabotage. And then there was Kralov's very specific assignments. She didn't know where to begin.

Where to begin? she thought. Where to begin? The restlessness and indecision was like a surrounding wall, too high to scale, too thick to break through. Let's have fun, she thought, and the wall might disappear.

She decided for a quick ride on White Snow. That seemed a pleasant idea. Amalina found him in a stall, and he looked very hot and was nickering disagreeably. She led him out and he seemed to cheer up, and he even allowed her to pet him and brush him and put on a saddle and harness. She remembered all the fun the first time she'd finally gotten atop a horse and guided it out onto the fields and roads. Carrying on light conversation with this princess or that one, her watchful parents riding just ahead, and thrilling over being in command of something so large and strong. She recalled the gentle rocking of the saddle, the undulating forward movement, and could not wait to feel the freedom of doing this on her own, in her own home, through her own territory, upon her own horse. It felt so empowering.

Though she'd grown a little, White Snow was still too tall for her. She had to use the stirrup and a bit of strength to haul herself on top. White Snow wagged his head and began a trot. The clopping of his hooves in the stone courtyard worried Amalina it would bring Georg or Abraxa out of the main building to scold her for her indolence. But the real trouble came at the gate, on the castle's threshold and looking out onto the approach road: White Snow froze and refused to budge. Then he bucked Amalina off.

Amalina didn't bother to remove the saddle, her hands stinging from her landing on the stones, and just returned White Snow to the stall. The ride—

or even the fall—hadn't cleared her mind. But in the meantime, she thought of something better to do.

"Genadie, where do those ugly pigeons come from?" asked Amalina breezily, while rubbing her raw palms together. "You know, the ones hanging around in the loft?"

"Why?" He was distracted, disassembling the last few pieces of scientific equipment to be transferred to the Count's laboratory.

"I was just wondering."

"But why would you wonder something like that? Don't you have work to do, Ms. Dalca? Best not to let Georg catch you here asking worthless questions. Georg *or* his pet lizard." He whispered the last part, and spun his eyes around suspiciously, as if he thought either one of them might appear at the uttering of the insult.

"You won't tell me?"

"They belong to the castle. That is why they are here."

"But they deliver the messages *to* the Count—"

"—to Master—"

"—from somewhere else, right?"

"But they come from here, they are the Master's pigeons," he said.

"How do they know they need to go out and collect a message? How do they know there's one waiting to be picked up?"

"It doesn't happen that way, Ms. Dalca. But why do you care? Forget about all that, just get to your books. Master will be most displeased if we are not ready to receive the princesses when they come."

Since Amalina didn't immediately leave, he now glanced at her with suspicion. She worried she'd better start covering her tracks.

"But if I could send a message to Korr, to my father," she said, slipping into a prodding voice and a pleading expression. "Would that be possible?"

"Ah, I see!" Genadie grinned triumphantly. "I know what you're after! But you know the rules, Amalina. There is to be no contact with your father until your work is done here."

"But it's been so long," she whined. Since there was some truth in it, her whine became a bit more real than expected.

"It will seem much longer if you think about it too much. And it will be longer ... if you don't get back to work."

"Well, I tried."

She suddenly felt a genuine quiver of defeat—the second that morning—and pouted and shrugged and turned to leave.

"Don't let me catch you in that birdhouse, Ms. Dalca," he said with a gentle but warning tone. "Those pigeons are ugly and dirty and nothing for you to be messing about with: they are Master's alone."

• • •

Amalina closed her eyes and thought: When the Count had taken the slip of paper from her hand, almost unconsciously he had gone to the cabinet and … and what? … it was like he was opening a doorway to which the cabinet sat in front.

The cabinet was a door in disguise.

Erik Kosche had predicted there would be such a thing in this castle. That the Count seemed to move through the walls by using an existing network of hidden passageways. And while the Count had the ability to move instantly from one place to another—flying through walls, it seemed— because of an incredible speed and perhaps an ability to dematerialize himself, Amalina did know of at least one true secret passage. It was below the castle and led to a hidden room. One which contained a woman bound to a giant turning wheel. That poor woman was still there (now that Amalina remembered it). Amalina had been the one to set the chain across her mouth, to prevent her from crying out in the night and disturbing the peace of the castle.

So there was a secret passage, and that weird wheel room at the end of it. Logically there would be other secret passages. She was sure of it.

How many doors appear and disappear in this castle, from one day to the next? Amalina had noticed them. One moment there, then gone. No seeming reason.

But now here was a new *secret* doorway she knew of, behind that cabinet. And it would always be there, and not likely disappear behind stone. Otherwise, why hide it behind a piece of furniture?

Eyes still closed, Amalina angled her head and thought about it some more.

Inside the Count's study, at its far end, there was a plain door. One that was always locked. She had suspected it led to the Count's private quarters where he slept—perhaps slept in a coffin. That is, if he was a strigoi and the book describing the habits of such creatures was accurate.

Her thought turned a corner: She now considered the matter of the strigoi.

The Count had disproven several times that he was a strigoi. And still, he was *some* kind of monster, even if he could not be found among the many creatures documented in books on such subjects. And so he *might* sleep in a coffin—or something else—behind that locked door; and was vulnerable to attack.

Or was his actual place of rest behind the tall cabinet? The study's locked door might have been there as a piece of misdirection, no? His real sanctuary, behind the cabinet perhaps, well hidden from intruders and would-be assassins.

Well, anyway, something was behind the large cabinet, and the Count had been drawn to it while still in a reverie about the message. He'd only caught himself when he remembered that Amalina was in the room with him. And he couldn't stop himself from running straight to it once she was on her way out.

Something was there, something important. Something she had to see and maybe report to Kralov if it panned out.

Or, if she discovered something vital to the Count, maybe she could take immediate action: to end the suspense and the multiple threats to her and her family. To wreak havoc on the creature and relieve the world.

But to find out she would have to get behind that cabinet. That was what she had to do, and must do. Which meant getting into the Count's private study.

• • •

"Excuse me, Georg," she said, almost apologetically, when she located him in the entrance hall. Her mincing voice made it sound like she was afraid of him. She didn't like it. She straightened herself and spoke from deeper in her chest to sound in charge. "Georg, your Master gave me a key to his private study."

"*My* master?" he sneered with disapproval. He continued sweeping the floor, though there didn't seem to be any dirt moving. The room shimmered with a cleanliness that felt unnatural. Modern castle halls were known to be littered with straw and stray bits of garbage, or hadn't he heard?

"The key to Count Tepsji's study was in my possessions," said Amalina. "Now I can't find it. Did you—Or was it Abraxa?—throw it out with my clothes? Tell me that didn't happen."

"I have it," he said.

"You took it from me?" she accused.

"I removed it from the room," he answered coolly. "I gathered all the house keys so that I knew where they were. It wasn't going to be used by anyone else but me, anyway, since there was no one else here but Abraxa and I. Does this not make sense to you? What is that look on your face?"

She asked for the key back. "Now that I'm here, it is mine, and I should have it. Please."

"I don't see that as the case."

"First, you had no reason to throw out my dresses—"

"—that was Abraxa's rightful decision, she is the house maid—"

"—and you had no right to take my key."

"*My* key," he sneered again. "It was *your* key when it was Genadie and you alone in the castle. Now that I am the head of the staff, I am in charge. And I say which key belongs to whom. Your duties lie in the library now, and that does not require your possession of any key at all. That is all I have to say about it, little lady."

"Yes, I understand," Amalina smiled and bowed, swallowing her anger and frustration. "I hadn't considered it that way. It is the Count's decision above all else, in any matters. Then it is yours, then mine. I should get the key back only if the Count requires it for me. Thank you, Georg. And I want to say, I really like your jacket. It's prettier than any of the ones on a head of staff I saw in Antwerp."

Unready for the compliment, his reflexive offended-glower tangled with a well-flattered smile. His confusion was hardly a victory though, she thought, without coming away with the key to the Count's private study.

. . .

Amalina knew she only had to enter the kitchen to summon Abraxa.

To make the trick work, she went around the outside of the main building and to the rear entrance, where Genadie's 'servant's quarters' was, and the access door to the castle's kitchens. She made some loud fumbling sounds at the door, and then came through, carrying a loaf of bread, still steaming.

Abraxa showed.

"What's that doing in here?" her face and her posture hard.

"Well, Abraxa, if you don't mind—"

"Just break the bread with your hands if you don't have knives out there in the shed. You think we have them in here? There isn't anything sharper than a ball of yarn in the whole building. More items you and the rat could have gotten us when you bungled your trip to Netz and ignored the provisions list."

As she had with Georg, Amalina swallowed down her anger. But much more quickly, so that she could smile and pass over the offense and move into what she'd come for.

"I know," she said sweetly, apology written on her smile. "Next time we must get everything on the list. But I wasn't looking for a knife at all. What I was going to say was, if you don't mind, that I baked this bread for you. You can say you don't eat, and maybe you don't, but I used to be a baker's daughter, and our bakery made the finest bread in the land. And so ... well, I couldn't think of anything better to give you as a gift. Here have a whiff, doesn't it smell good?"

At first Abraxa had the same confused look as her husband. After a grumble from her stomach, her mouth shifted. Almost beyond her control she leaned forward, placed her pointy nose over the bread, and sniffed. Her stomach growled again.

"That was kind of you" Abraxa straightened, trying to harden the parts on her that had apparently come loose. "Why?"

"Because I thought you and your husband would like it. And I think, for the Count's peace of mind, we should all be friendly and kindly to one another so that we can work all the more closely."

Abraxa's eyes flicked up and down, as if to announce that what she just heard was impossible and couldn't believe her ears for it. Amalina might have been a fish come out of the water to discuss land rights with a goat.

"We really don't know how long you'll remain here," Abraxa smirked.

A hard one, all right, thought Amalina as she maintained the smile. She pushed the bread at Abraxa again. "While we're here, anyway. Would you like to try a bite? It's fresh."

Amalina tore a corner off. Its flesh was perfectly soft and tan, and inside was airy and white, with curls of aromatic steam coming off of it. She held the piece out for Abraxa, until the woman's right arm melted and took it. Under her patient watch, Abraxa gave the piece another sniff, and then she slipped it through the slot in her face. She began to chew.

"Very good … Mouse."

"Thank you." She held out another piece, which Abraxa could not prevent her body from snatching away and consuming.

"And there's another thing," Amalina said, softer now.

Abraxa stiffened, stopped mid chew.

"I think I need a favor," said Amalina. "No, I mean: I do need a favor. From you."

"If you have some problem, it's yours, to be sure. I have more than enough chores of my own—well more than enough—than to be looking after yours, too."

"No, it's not that *I* have a problem, Abraxa. It's more like I'm afraid Georg might have one—that he might have made a mistake."

Abraxa's eyes burned. "Unlikely. What are you trying to do here? To poison our highness' opinion of Georg with cheap perjury?"

"In the name of our friendship, Abraxa, you are mistaken. I am looking out for him. Count Tepsji is still unaware, but I'm afraid the problem might come to light. I shouldn't wish to see Georg suffer for it, if he doesn't have to. I've seen the Count punish people—punish Genadie—and he can be cruel."

"He is most fair."

"Fair in judgement," Amalina nodded. "But cruel in punishment. Believe me."

"Genadie deserved it." brayed Abraxa, though she hadn't seen it. Amalina shuddered inwardly as she recalled Genadie's body twisted and tearing apart in the Count's grasp, blood spilling out of the rend. It had taken months for him to recover.

"We aren't talking about Genadie now," said Amalina pointedly. "Now will you help me?"

Abraxa held up a finger and made a tour of the kitchen to make sure Georg wasn't there.

"Why are you coming to me?" she asked. "Why not Georg?"

"It is a favor, as I said." Amalina paused, for suspense. When Abraxa cocked her head, she continued: "Georg has very high standards. He is precise and demands perfection. The simplest mistake is below him."

"Of course."

"And yet, everyone is human, aren't they? Well, everyone is entitled to an error."

"What's happened?" Abraxa was worried.

"But if I went to him, and I asked him, he might be angry with himself to learn what he'd done. If we can clear things up without him knowing, I think it would be all the better. He would be left undisturbed."

"What are you accusing him of? What do you think he's done wrong?"

"He put the books onto the shelves in the Count's Great Library, no? Following the order of the inventory. I thought he did it perfectly, only …"

"Only …?"

"Two books are missing."

· · ·

In the library, Amalina pointed into the catalogue, and then went along the shelf, naming out the books. Then she stopped. She tapped one book then the next book, then tapped on the second book's name in the catalogue, two entries down from where it should be.

Abraxa's eyes were a little unfocused, her mouth slack. Unsure.

"You see what I mean, don't you?"

"I—are you sure?"

"Just look here: *Von Gier und Der Welt*," she pointed at the first book she'd stopped at on the shelf. Then pointed to the next book over: "*Physiolog, Theolog* by Larimus. Yes? But there should be these other two books in between. See, here in the list: *Der Buche Uberwelte* and *Minos* by Hegolus"

"I—but are you sure?"

"What do you mean? Don't you see?"

"I—" Her eyes darted between the page of the inventory and the books on the shelf, looking even more confused; somehow blank, focusing above the titles and not on them.

"You can't read."

"I can't be expected to," she said crossly. "That isn't my job."

"No. But you see—or, I mean … So the books should be here, but they aren't. Every other book is in its place but those two." She gathered herself, readying to present the drama: "Think if the Count should come to this library, wishing to read one of those two books—or both!—and he can't find them. He can't find *either one!* Think of the *inconvenience* to him. Think how *mad* he would be."

"It was your fault," hissed Abraxa. "It was your job."

"He knows everything, Abraxa," she replied with a confiding and anxious voice, rather than a pitying one. "You think you can fool him? He knows I was away when these books were put on the wall. He will know it was Georg's mistake. That *your husband* lost the books."

Abraxa looked at all the piles of books in the center of the room.

"They aren't here?"

"No, Abraxa. No." Amalina poured on the sympathetic tone. "I searched, but …"

"But how could he have lost them?"

"There still might be a chance I'm wrong."

"You are?" Abraxa said hopefully.

"Maybe something else happened, I mean. It's possible the Count came here and took the books after they were put on the shelves. If that is so, then Georg has nothing to worry about. The problem is, I don't think it's likely. Look how close the books are packed onto the shelves. If the Count had taken them, there should be an open space, shouldn't there? Since there isn't, it would mean the Count pressed the rest of the books together to fill the space. But why would he go to that trouble? Especially if he'd just have to open a hole in the row again to put the books back in. And why would he want to read *Der Buch Uberwelte* and *Minos* at the same time? One has nothing to do with the other. It is very unlikely. Very unlikely."

Amalina heaved a big, sad sigh. She looked consolingly at Abraxa, who was still dazed and unsure.

"It is *very* unlikely, Abraxa. But it is our only hope. Maybe the Count took them. We need to find out."

"I will ask Georg to find out."

"You can't ask Georg! As soon as you do, he'll wonder why you are asking. Then what'll you say? The best that could happen is that the Count *did* take the books—which is unlikely—and you simply revealed to him that I thought he might have made a mistake. But if the Count didn't take them—

which is very likely—then Georg will discover his error, and the whole point will be lost. Don't you understand?"

"What are we to do?"

"The Count reads in certain rooms of the house. We search there for the books, see if they aren't there. If they are, Georg is off the hook. But it will have to be a thorough search, you understand?"

"I will look everywhere."

"You won't look anywhere," Amalina countered.

"I *will*, you snot!"

"I mean you can't!" Amalina said with frustration. "What would you be looking for? You don't know how to tell one book from another! You don't know how to read!"

Abraxa quaked.

"We have to do this as quickly as we can and as secretly as we can. And we can't have the Count or Georg know what is happening."

"I—I suppose."

"Do you want to help Georg? Do you want to make sure that he is clear of blame? Do you want to know for sure whether he will need to be protected from the Count's rightful anger, Abraxa?"

"He will get what he deserves if he is to blame," she said. Then, with concern: "But I must know."

"What you'll do is you will provide me the keys to certain rooms when I ask. No room that I haven't been permitted entrance before, so I won't be violating the Master's trust. And I will see if the books are there."

"Oh ... But what if he doesn't? What if Georg has somehow failed our highness?"

"At least you can plan and pray the Count is merciful. And if he is cruel, then thank every day he let pass before making the discovery and commencing punishment."

Abraxa said nothing but nodded slowly. Anger and bitterness lay behind her eyes. She hated Amalina for this news, but could only be grateful for having received the information, and was indebted for the help in locating the books.

"When the time is right, I will ask for a key, or keys, and you will find a way to get them from Georg."

"I will tell him I'm cleaning, and I will take you to the room with me."

"You will say anything you like *but* that. There mustn't be any way Georg can find out about this. You will get the key to me, and while I do my search, you will keep Georg distracted. Then I will return the key to you. Hopefully it won't take long. Maybe they will be in the very first room I go to."

"Could our lord really be so mad for so little a thing?"

"Think how mad Georg would be if Genadie or I had made such an error."

Abraxa nodded at that unfortunate truth.

"So you will get me the keys? when I need them?"

"Of course, Ms. Dalca."

"Call me 'Mouse', or Georg will know something's happened."

"Yes. Of course … Mouse."

"We'll start with the Count's private study. If I can't get in there beforehand, by the Count's request, then you will get me the key and I will have a look. That is the best place to begin: the Count's private study."

Abraxa was agreed and all was set. Now the only thing Amalina needed to do was make sure not to be invited into the salon—the private study—beforehand, which would negate (for Abraxa) Amalina's need to snoop; as she needed to get in the room alone, without the Count inside, and with the two heads of staff distracted. And with enough time to open the concealed door and see what was behind it.

Amalina felt a rush of excitement having set a plot of her own in motion. The secret agent finally at work.

How have I become so sneaky? she wondered with a pang of guilt. It certainly wasn't by being a baker's apprentice.

11

The Corpse and the Pawns

The corpse's position on the floor, with its reaching, outstretched hand, spoke of a man who was desperately trying to get to his bed. He must have known he was dying, or was at least suddenly very ill when he went for the bed.

"Poor Popov," the Mayor said. "Never made it."

"Turn him over," said Rosczy.

"What are you doing here?"

There was a gathering of five of the top citizens of Netz. The Mayor. The Physician. The Sheriff. Rosellier the Miller. And the Undertaker. All summoned to the room by Popov's daughter, who had found him this way. Nobody had called for Rosczy, who had appeared and started giving orders.

Rosczy stared down at Popov and said: "The Cardinal will be arriving soon to observe the handling of the body. But turn the body over."

"What difference does it make?" the Physician complained, unhappy to take orders from the Cardinal's lackey.

"When the Cardinal arrives, his eminence will deal with Popov's front; and not his back."

When they turned Popov over—his arm frozen into a permanent grasp for the mattress—there was a combined gasp. Seven knife holes were opened above Popov's heart. His shirt was lightly stained with blood around them.

"He's been killed!" Rosczy exclaimed for everyone's benefit. Then he shut up—as the Cardinal had instructed—and let the leading men of Netz boil in confusion and fear.

"I know I shouldn't say these things," said the Sheriff, "but Popov might have met with a deserving fate."

"How so?" asked the Mayor.

"He took the ancient Secret History of the Sheriff of Netz. I caught him returning it. I asked him why he'd taken it and what he was doing with it, and he didn't answer well." The Sheriff eyed everyone gravely. "There are new elements in this town. Foreigners being harbored here. I know where some are, others are being sheltered by our own. One of my deputies saw Popov talking to a man. A large, old man who wears a fur cap."

A couple men stirred, reacting as if they recognized the description.

"Yes," Rosczy said. "I believe I saw Popov meet with this man, too."

"When?" demanded the Mayor.

"And how?" asked the Physician. "You are always in the church beside your master."

"Not always," Rosczy countered. "And anyway, twice I saw him from the cathedral grounds. I observe many people who don't suspect they can be seen from there."

The Sheriff scowled at Rosczy, then continued with his own thoughts: "I asked Popov about this information, and he denied it. But would someone collaborating with outsiders admit such a thing? I think not."

"I've seen Popov speaking to many people," the Physician said. "He was a gregarious sort, wasn't he? So who's to say whoever he was talking to, especially a foreign element, he gave the old History to?"

"What do you mean by that?" Rosczy said.

"I've seen Popov talking to you. And I've seen him talking to your master, the Cardinal." At this he shot a side glance to the Mayor. Then back to Rosczy: "Who's to say he didn't show *you* the book?"

"But we already know about the book, the history and the compact and have signed it," Rosczy said. "Who else would need to see it but someone who'd never seen it before? A foreigner."

The men mumbled in agreement. The Physician nodded it was a fair point.

"And still one doesn't equal the other," mused the Physician. "If he showed the History to an outsider ... well, that's one thing. And if he was guilty of that, it would be on his head, wouldn't it? But that doesn't reason why the man he revealed our secret to would then murder him."

"To cover up the crime," said Rosczy, with a sober nod.

"When did you say the Cardinal will be coming?" asked the Mayor. "Is there a reason you are here other than to announce his plans to arrive at some point?"

Rosczy bowed his head. "He should be coming any moment. As you know, he has many pressing matters."

"Busier than his boss in Rome," Rosellier guffawed, needing to get a word into the scene. Rosczy bowed his head again, allowing for the disparaging remark to also be very true. "Or is it really because early dawn is still too close to night and he doesn't want to leave the cathedral to join us until the sun is safely overhead?"

At last the Cardinal entered. Everyone, even the Mayor bowed their heads to him.

"It is true," the Cardinal said as he gazed sadly down upon Popov. "He has died. Too young, too young."

"Well, your eminence," the Mayor said, letting a snide tone slide into his mourning. "The Sheriff was telling us how he might have been up to something with a foreign element within the village. And Simon"—the Physician—"has said he's seen our Popov meeting with many people in this village, and within the St. Grigori grounds, besides strangers. But, hold now, it seems you haven't observed what is very clearly before your eyes, Cardinal: the wounds on his chest. And the blood. Popov has been murdered."

"Yes, oh, yes," the Cardinal said, his eyes rounding in horror at the relatively simple gore. "I wasn't … I didn't know. But my grief was such that I didn't notice such an obvious—but, then, a very unnatural—thing." He sent up calls to heaven and invoked the supreme deity and his son and the holy spirit, he cursed the evil-doers who had caused such a thing to happen to a good family man.

"Someone didn't see it the same as you," the Mayor said with a note of sarcasm. "They thought he *deserved* to die. While I loved Popov, his treachery against our order might have led to what at first seems to be a crime, yet was fate declaring justice."

"You have an idea who it was?" asked the Cardinal, looking slightly offended by any implications the Mayor might have been making.

"Popov's daughter said he was feeling ill after returning from a service at St. Grigori," said the Mayor, pointedly. "We had assumed it was a sudden illness. Not uncommon to certain people who visit your church. Until we discovered the wounds."

"You seem to be implying something of a criminal nature about me," the Cardinal sneered. "Am I not a member of this community in good standing?"

"I imply nothing, Cardinal."

"Or does your wife have influence on you, and you still think I have the power to send bodies out of the grave to attack her?" He chortled at his reference to an embarrassing incident from the previous year, mocking the mayor's wife who was humiliated after making the claim.

"She's a good woman!" The Mayor threw a punch at the Cardinal. The other four men caught him before it could land, and the Cardinal easily backed away. "You say nothing about her, Cardinal! I will beat you for it."

"Am I to stand here and be insulted by you, Mayor? I only wished to remind you reason should influence your thinking, not emotion. Though, now that I think of it, you are permitted some degree of emotion, it is true, due to your recent, tragic loss."

The Cardinal thought he might say something more cleverly forward and vindictive; about how this current misfortune might be all too provocative for the mayor's sensibilities: Popov's daughter losing a father so soon after the mayor had lost his own daughter, Ygardina. And both in bloody fashion. But he held back, and just let the petty cruelty glimmer in his eye.

"I asked Rosczy this, and I now ask you: Why are you here? You could have sent anyone along to attend as you usually do. But why now? Why for Popov?"

"The same reason we are all here," the Cardinal answered coolly. "He is one of the better men of the community. I wished to show him respect."

"He was my close friend," said the Mayor. "Closer to me than any of you. And I know where that places him with *you*, Cardinal. And you can't deny he's had words with you. Not just met with you, but had open disagreements, despite your level *greatness*."

"I was trying to be discreet in what I said," the Physician said apologetically. "But it's true, there were disagreements between you and him."

"Popov was an honest man, never afraid to speak his mind."

"Or do as he pleases," said the Cardinal with a raised nostril. "Like revealing our sworn secrets to those who are off limits."

"You knew of this?" said the Mayor with little surprise.

"People confess everything. It is not my place to act."

"I won't accuse you—" the Mayor began.

"Yes," the Cardinal nodded as he cut the Mayor off. "And this is just what I imagined would be the result. Popov, a man too young to die, does so suddenly. And like so many rumors that run through the mountains: There was a sudden illness after visiting my cathedral. And, as the rumor goes, the fault rests with the Cardinal, who has some mysterious powers to fell those who displease him. As ridiculous as the story of rising corpses. But it is believed ... until reason steps in."

All five pillars of the community were mollified. The Cardinal took this as an opportunity to cement his innocence.

"Reason says he was killed. And not by mysterious means, but by a dagger. Do we all agree?"

"His daughter said he came home ill," Simon said. "She did not hear a struggle at all. Which one would expect from a violent attack. For him to call out at least."

"Yes," Rosellier put in.

"Not if the assailant was waiting for Popov behind the door," the Cardinal explained. He walked to the position next to the door, and then mimed the following action: "Then he stepped forward as our poor Popov walked in, put one hand around his mouth, and with his other hand, plunged the weapon repeatedly into his chest."

"How did he get out without being seen?" the Undertaker asked. "His daughter was close by. At the hearth."

"I would ask you: how did he get *in*?" the Cardinal countered. "Because the criminal must have. The wounds are evident, are they not? Popov didn't die of anything but these terrible wounds, inflicted by a mad man."

There was an agreeable murmur.

"And he must have died on his way to the bed, as you observe, which would put it at a time when I was in St. Grigori, along with all my men."

"Nobody is accusing you," said the Physician.

"Well, I'm telling you," said the Cardinal. "I didn't do it. And I couldn't have done it. And no one under my command had a hand in his death. It was done by someone who was desperate to close Popov's mouth, and has the lowest of morals."

They were looking at him for an answer. The way the Cardinal was winding up, it seemed sure that he was leading somewhere. It was so like one of his sermons.

He crouched now, and extended an arm out, almost duplicating Popov, but pointing his finger.

"Now, here," the Cardinal hummed dramatically, his eyes becoming shrewd slits. "Look at Popov's hand. He seems to be reaching out, doesn't he?"

"For the bed," Rosellier said helpfully.

"Yes, that is what it looks like. For the bed. Yes. But to get to it? Or was it for some other purpose?"

Even the Mayor was caught up—the Cardinal's slight against his wife forgotten, his grief at Ygardina's murder put on hold—as he waited, without breathing, for the conclusion.

"Rosczy," the Cardinal said, maintaining his stance, "Go to the bed, which Popov was striving to reach as he died, when the killer left him for dead. Go and search it. Throw off the covers. Now throw off the mattress!"

Rosczy threw up the floppy end of the feather mattress, and below it, resting on the leather netting beneath it, was a fur cap.

. . .

"Damn you," the Cardinal swore at Rosczy as they left the small home. "Why didn't you put the holes in Popov's back?"

"You said you wanted them on his underside."

"Which would be his back!"

"But he was lying on his chest, Cardinal. I made sure of it. He was face down so that they couldn't see the holes."

"Then why was he facing up when I arrived?"

"Well," Rosczy murmured, full of apology. "It seemed they were going to overlook the wounds—"

"But that was the point, Rosczy." The Cardinal's fingers stabbed the air in front of him emphatically as his voice hissed. "They were supposed to come to their conclusions on their own. Their rash conclusions, blaming me, as I knew they would. Popov poisoned! The Cardinal the criminal. Then I would arrive, we'd have our dispute, and then you'd roll him over to reveal that he'd been murdered by means of physical brute force, not by poison, as they thought and they were accusing. And then, when they were reeling from that, I would deliver the *coup de gras*, and discover the stranger's hat."

"It went well enough, your grace. It worked."

"You might as well have pointed out there should have been more blood, and how you got through the window before his body was discovered," the Cardinal groused.

"All is well, your grace."

. . .

Kralov didn't know what was happening, but felt himself being pulled through the air. He could not find a proper footing and stumbled as his body continued to move forward. Was this a dream? He was bouncing in all directions. Off of walls. At first he thought he was in his grandmother's house. Then he thought he was in the Grand Palace in Pest.

Then he realized he was in a narrow hallway inside of a home in Netz. Piotr was shoving him along.

"They're coming," Piotr said. "We have no time. We have to get to Archim's cellar, you will be safe there."

"Who's coming?"

"Something's happened. The mob again. But they are looking for you. I heard them. We're in danger, Commander."

They stopped in a long corridor that stretched from one end of the house to the other. On either end was a door. Kralov rubbed his eyes as they waited beside the door, breathing heavily, listening for voices and the march of so many stomping leather shoes. Piotr stood next to him. On the other end of the hall, it was Roti, Piotr's brother.

"Here," whispered Roti. "They're coming this way."

"No, here," said Piotr. "I hear them."

"They're surrounding us," Kralov said. "Can we get anyone else to help?"

"Not this quickly," Piotr said. "Not now."

"What do we do?" Roti said. "We have to do something now before they have us."

"There's no choice," Piotr said. "We have to run."

"Which way?" asked Roti. He asked his brother, not Kralov. Their Commander had become their burden, like a sack of bad potatoes.

"One goes first, draws them off. Then the next. Then the Commander, when there's nobody looking."

"Right," said Roti. "Let's go."

"Wait," Piotr said. "Who first?"

"Me."

"No, me."

"What stupidity is this?" Kralov growled hotly.

"I know," said Piotr. "Fingers. I take even."

They both started shaking their fists in the air, preparing to throw out a finger or two.

Piotr counted them down excitedly, bracing himself to fling open the door and run if he got the winning score. Roti doing the same on the other side, looking to Kralov like a mirror image.

Kralov felt a horrible pang in his chest. What was it? Guilt, of course. Here were these two innocent boys he'd pulled into a game of revenge against the Count. It wasn't any different than when he'd advised Katrina Flauna and Erik to pursue a bold, treacherous scheme against a rich mark, who turned out to be the Count of nightmares. He'd gotten them and his adored Odetta killed because of it. And now here he was again, instead of leaving well enough alone; having pulled more people into his folly, about to get more innocents killed.

Piotr and Roti were looking excited, as if they were having the time of their lives.

"Three."

"Two."

"One …!"

12

The Remarkable Woman

He remembered his mother's comforting caress. Her finger sliding gently down his round cheek, and she cooing to him with a look of tenderness that matched the warmth of the sun. Then he remembered he did not have a mother. He had had a woman who tended to him so his mother could be elsewhere; attending to more important things than him. Not a sad point, because if it wasn't for his mother's indifference, and unconventional idoling of the world more than her own child, Attila would not have been who he was.

The remarkable woman who *had* accepted his mother's position, unlike his mother—and perhaps leading to the key difference in his upbringing and instruction—this woman hadn't been imported from western civilization along with the rest of the Bronk household, but was recruited from the supply of cheap Ardeelian laborers. She bore no bitterness (for some reason) toward the invaders of her homeland, and did everything she could to make little Attila feel welcome in the world. Her magnanimity towards her people's oppressors in that she would lavish her charge with such attention, might be explained by a need to have a substitute for her young brother, who she'd lost to the war. At times she fancied her mistress' baby possessed by her lost brother's soul. Attila could not be certain this was true. But she'd given him her brother's name, Attila, and *that* part of her brother had stuck, anyway.

Vedya was her name. The first he remembered seeing her, he was on his back, bathed in a column of light streaming in through the window, wishing he could lie there all day. She stood above him, smiling, then sent her finger over his cheek, her eyes warm, and a little sad. She would indulge him, but she would also teach him, and guide him, and fill him with all her fears and cleverness, so that her brother's spirit would have an easier way of it now that he had been given a second chance. The last he remembered of her, she was in bed enveloped in shadow, barely able to breathe, but finding enough air and energy through the cruel illness to remind him that he was a creature of purity, and righteousness, and was dedicated on this earth to steadying the hand of justice, so that it would not allow injustice to reign, or another innocent to suffer or to die unfairly as her brother had.

At this memory, Attila shrugged.

He could shrug. This was new. He could feel his shoulders, and his torso. He squirmed his tongue and noted the rancid flavor of his mouth. His body felt wet and cold. He opened his eyes. The lids would only come up half way. He remembered that was normal, too.

. . .

"God has shown favor on you," said the woman. She had pale blond hair, with blond eyelashes and eyebrows, and blue eyes so light and fair it was like the winter cover-ice on Lake Tsobl. "You should be dead."

"I'm not," he said, and found it painful to speak. A throb worked his right shoulder blade, he saw colors before long. "What's the damage?"

He'd been shot, but it had been a glancing blow. The bullet had smashed into his back and then bounded away, leaving behind a torn cloak, coat, and shirt, broken bones, ripped and burnt flesh, and a shallow, oblong hole with rucked up skin on either side, which had sealed over with a black crust. The hole he could not see. But he felt it when he breathed. He'd also been smashed on rocks and tree branches. Wide bruises and long, scabbed over lacerations decorated his skin; on legs, arms and face. These wounds radiated their own separate lines of agony, pulsing lightly whether he was breathing or not. Breathing, he judged, was probably the better option. Because he'd also been half-drowned his lungs still felt ragged. He coughed several times in a row, which brought phlegm and blood. It felt more like shard ice and razors as it came up.

He was still wearing clothes, and the clothes were still lightly damp. He was freezing. He must have been laying there for days, but no one had bothered to remove his clothes or do much else for his comfort after carrying his body to the barn. He didn't remember being fed. They had basically just waited to see if he would die. And prayed over him; to nudge him onto the side of the ledger with the living, or the other.

"How long?" he said.

"A few days. Who are you?"

"It doesn't matter. Did anyone come looking for me?"

"That depends," she said.

"Depends on what?"

"On who you are."

Attila raised his eyes to her. She wasn't being ironic or sarcastic. He looked away.

"Who all is here? On this farm?"

"The children and I. I have two children, sir. They pulled you from the river. It was a dangerous thing for them to do. But they did it."

"I thank them."

"They're silly and foolish. And my husband. He's here, too. There are four of us."

Attila was undecided whether she was lying about the husband. It was something to tell a strange man, to warn him that there was another *friendly* man about. Even when that stranger was shot, damaged and drowned. You could never be too careful with men these days. You could never be too careful with anyone, period. It's something Vedya would have cautioned Attila on. Lying is a sin, of course. But one should never offer to someone who might harm you information they can act on. And it was permissible to allude to a greater threat if in one's own defense.

Attila shrugged at the woman's possible lie, then was stung by his constellation of holes and tears. His skin shook at all the trauma. He coughed and spat.

"Did you lose someone?" she said. "Was someone with you in the river?"

Attila shook his head. His neck was stiff. He continued shaking his head, to loosen the tightness.

"In your sleep you kept saying you were looking for someone."

"I was looking for someone when I fell into the river. I still am. Where am I, may I ask, ma'am?"

There was no need to be gentle with her, or polite. She was the wife of a peasant. He was a man of some authority. Even stripped of his rank, he had the right name—the elevated lineage—to place him well above her. But there was no call to be rude, either. So he proceeded gently. She looked surprised, but also appreciative he'd called her *'ma'am'*. Peasant as she was, she was probably used to worse. It was tough to be a peasant. But to be an Ardeelian mountain peasant ... ? His courtesy was notable and could buy him favor.

A loud sound broke the silence like a rifle shot. Attila twisted around, sending bolts of pain throughout his body. Out on the far side of the yard, where the farmhouse stood, a young blond man had chopped clean through a log. He was shirtless, and his body was massive with slabs of muscle. His face, from this distance, looked empty and gentle, and serenely concentrated on his work at hand. Cutting firewood was a hard business, but this young man was enjoying himself, and looked like he could be at it all day without care. He was one of the many simple workmen, born to labor and sweat, and grateful for the few pleasures life afforded to his kind, and careless of the pleasures heartlessly withheld for the likes of him.

He appeared very young. He could possibly be her son. But the way she regarded him, then fixed Attila with vague look of relief and victory, the man was, instead, her husband. She *was* protected, the expression said. *Here was the proof.* Being not much above the mentality of a prize-winning ox, he may not be someone to be proud of for a chess match, or economic ambition, but she could rely on him for her physical comforts, satisfaction, and safety.

"Your husband," Attila said needlessly. She didn't even answer, but continued her self-satisfied smile.

She shut the door on the yard. The young man didn't even look up as she did so, he was entranced by the logs he was splitting; nothing else mattered, the world shut out. Door closed, Attila wondered if he was being kept as a secret from her husband. But why?

"Does he know I'm here, ma'am?"

"Why wouldn't he? He's my husband."

"Why close the door?"

"He's got a lot of work to do today," she said. *He doesn't need to be distracted*, was what she meant. She was not only his wife, she was her prize ox's eternal guide. "I'm safe enough, aren't I? Or does the door need be open? Or should I call him?"

Attila shook his head.

"But I was asking, ma'am … Where am I? Where am I, then?"

"Where are you… ?" She looked a little lost. Like it should be obvious that he was in a small barn. Or maybe that she didn't know what he meant by the question. How could someone be so lost that they didn't know where they were?

"Whose territory is it?" Attila explained.

"I don't know, sir."

"You don't know where we are … at all?"

"This is a farm."

"Who owns it?"

"My husband."

Attila nodded patiently.

"But who does your husband rent the land from?"

"No one. This is our land."

He looked at her clothes. They were old and worn through, with some patches sewn in with thick thread. Her hair was loose under her dirty hat, falling in greasy yellow locks on either side of her mouth. Her hands were large and rough and speckled with chips of wood and mud. From what he'd seen of her young husband, who, by the sound of it, was still cracking through logs like a machine, he wore only a grubby pair of leather pants, holes sewn over. His hair was not only greasy, but clodded through with bits of mud and dirt. His skin was tan as dark wood, telling of a life dedicated to labor outdoors. Both of them were not the pictures of land ownership.

Attila understood: This land was not theirs. Or rather, this was property nobody wanted, and they had wandered onto it and claimed it, and worked the soil so that they could eat. If it turned out the land was worth anything, it would be confiscated soon enough by investors who could afford it. So it was theirs, but only temporarily. He didn't say this aloud, but she probably knew it. There was at least some reason her voice was beginning to sound defiant.

Attila nodded and smiled. Even his lips hurt. They felt tight, and like there was only one layer of skin left on them.

"Is this the Baibay Valley?" he said, not knowing, in her simple mind, whether she'd know this much. If she answered, it would at least give him some bearings. He couldn't have gone too far down the river after the falls. He felt he could still hear the roar in the distance. Or was that his ears malfunctioning? Toyed with by the splitting of the logs?

"Yes," she said as she nodded, "this is Baibay Valley. Just along the river."

"Just after the falls."

She nodded again.

"Well, I *am* looking for someone," he said. "But first, one more thing: have you seen men on horses, with amber and black clothes and metal armor? Have any of them been through here?"

"They came. Asked if we'd seen a man or a horse wash up. They stayed for a day, but then they left. They ate a lot of our week's vegetables."

"And they didn't pay you for your produce, I gather?"

She shook her head.

"You didn't give me to them."

"They said they were looking for a traitor and a criminal. Are you?"

"Depends on how you look at it. In Tsobl and with the current government I suppose some of them might rightly call me a traitor. But only a traitor to *them*. And I suppose, along the way, I've had to resort to theft to eat, or gain a piece of clothing or two. Which makes me a criminal."

"If it is to save your life it is not a crime," she said, looking into his eyes; more defiant, challenging, and not ashamed. "We've been called the same and worse. It means nothing when you are just trying to survive."

"I'm glad we agree."

"Who are you searching for, sir?"

"I need to find a knight. I heard he became a lord in this area, relocated from his ancestral territory after the war. And before these men with the armor caught up to me, I'd hoped to reach him and sue for his protection. Let me tell you, I've had a very hard time of it this past month. And to my displeasure have found that all the old true knights of Ardeel have given their allegiance over to the foreigners in Tsobl. They would not hear my call to arms, or even protect me from unjust treatment by their old enemy, those foreigners in Tsobl."

"I'm sorry, sir."

"Every noble knight has turned me out of their houses, and off their lands. So that this man I'm looking for, he was the last one for whom I held out hope. His family was a great family, known to be one of the strongest Ardeelian roots, and would never back down from a fight; would stand courageously against any invader, and defy even the Tsobl assembly of outsiders. He is the man I seek, oh, yes."

Attila's speech took away the pain and worked up his energy. He began to feel hope again.

"I don't know of any knights," she said. "I don't know of many people around here. There are very few, sir. The ground is too hard, and the winters terrify even the wolves; more than in other places. Not many people here at all, sir, besides us."

"The family name is Vogoneyevic. Hak Vogoneyevic is his full name—"

"Hak?" she said, interrupting him. There was a strange look on her face. "Hak?"

"Yes, Hak Vogoneyevic. Do you know him?"

"No," she said. Only she added, suspiciously: "What do you want with him?"

"You *do* know him then?"

"No," she said again, shaking her head a little, looking him too steadily in the eye. "Never heard of him before. Hak. *Hak.* No."

"But that's papa's name," said one of the children from just outside the door. One of their eyes looked through a break in the wood. "You remember, don't you mama?"

Her eyes flashed angrily at the child's eye, so that it tumbled away from the hole. Her face alternated between red and white until, turning back to Attila, it was a dead grey, and she looked as if she might kill him.

"Ma'am ... Hak Vogoneyevic ..."—*that burly, wood-splitting oaf?* Attila marveled but did not add—"... is your husband?"

13

The Increasing Solutions

Walking slowly down the hallway, lazily careening from wall to wall, the cool stones tickling her bare feet, Amalina considered the many flaws in her plan.

The biggest flaw: in order to access the secret door, the Count had to be out of the castle and yet his exact whereabouts known. It wasn't his habit to report his schedule to Amalina or anyone else. And because he was not like a normal lord and didn't require constant attention—the fitting of handsome clothes, the serving of favorite meals, the lavishment of compliments, which Amalina had observed as a necessity in the royalty of the western kingdoms—nor did he need horses and carriages prepared for travel, she never knew where he was or what he was up to, unless he announced it; which wasn't his inclination.

As she'd learned during last year's winter, when she had been so bored she'd taken to noting every little detail of the castle and its routines, she knew when the Count had left the castle during the night, or when he was returning, by the sound of various animal calls in the surrounding forests and mountains. But, she recalled with pursed lips, she could never guarantee, when alerted by these alarums, just how long he intended to be gone. And time would be crucial here. She'd need plenty of it to discover how to work the locks on the secret door. And then to search whatever lay beyond. Who knows what surprises the other side of the cabinet held? If it was anything like the network of sewer passages she'd already encountered below the castle, there might be miles to survey before she found what she was looking for—or, that is: discover the thing she didn't even know she was looking for.

To add to the trouble of timing, before she even began the expedition, she didn't know how long it would take for Abraxa to get the key from her husband and to sneak it to her. She wouldn't know when her moment of opportunity had arrived until she heard the howl of the wolves, or the screech of the bats, or the hooting of the owls as the Count flew from the castle. And if Abraxa wasn't cooperative, or it took too long to coax the key from Georg, then she might hear the cries again, announcing the Count's return, before Amalina reached the study's door. And then it would be over.

She only had one shot at this, realistically. So she would have to make certain she had enough time to allow for all the uncertainties when she set her plan in motion.

As if by thinking about him, the Count was summoned. With a breath of wind he was before her. Her cheeks flushed guiltily, afraid he had been listening to her thoughts and she'd been found out.

"I think I have solved our problem," he said.

"What problem?"

He took her to the series of rooms packed with equipment which served as his laboratory. The odd bulbs of glass stuck in the complex body of thin wires and tubes were now alive with bubbling liquids, squat oil lamps burning under some. The room smelled strongly of anise.

"Yes," he said appreciably to himself, as he went to a tray at one of the benches. The tray contained roughly rounded bits of dull glass. Or, what appeared to be dull glass. He held one up, studying it. "Yessss."

Amalina wished she was wearing one of her dresses with handy pockets and that she'd snuck the vial into it. This might have been the moment she needed to test the liquid on the Count. Instead she stood there mute, thinking it best to not to say anything or ask anything while the Count was absorbed in fondling the curious ball. A dull, apple-red piece of glass. Best not to act too curious, she thought. Not when it wasn't necessary and might look out of place. Kralov's anger would be volcanic if she gave away the game—that she was a spy on the prowl for information—to the Count prematurely. She kept her head straight, and used only her eyes to scan the room and take in any detail that might be helpful.

It was surprising how preoccupied the Count was with alchemy and its science, the many hours he devoted to it. How often she'd seen him hunched over books or tinkering with the equipment over last winter. And now that the lab was fully installed, who knows how many days and nights he was in here, working up something.

The current something he held between his fingers, the product of his devotions to science, he brought down to Amalina's face, and she leaned forward to have a better look at it. But she mistook what he was up to.

"Oh!" the Count exclaimed as the ball ran into her closed lips and bounced out of his hand. There was a whir, and he held it again—before it had a chance to hit the floor. His catch was too hard, or the ball couldn't handle the resistance of her teeth. There was a crack in it. The Count threw it against the wall so that it shattered.

Amalina rubbed her bruised lips, and squinted with tears at the fading pain, as the Count leaned over an open book and changed a number with a pencil. Then he presented her another ball from the tray.

"I meant you to eat it, Mouse, not look at it."

"You should have told me. You can't just throw something like that in a person's—uh—I'm supposed to eat it?"

"Yes."

"What is it?"

"You could say it is a medicine. A cure."

"A cure for what?"

"We'll see, Mouse. We've only to try."

"I'm not sick."

"Everyone is sick, believe me. But you might say this is—if it works—a preventative cure."

"What's it made out of? It looks like glass."

"I don't think you'd understand what it is made from. This has taken me a year's study, after decades of education."

"But I can't eat glass."

"It isn't glass. It is translucent, yes, and with a natural, pleasant discoloration. To add to its charm, I have introduced some herbs and spices to make the taste pleasant for you."

"Have you tried it, sir?"

"I don't need the medicine. It's just for you."

"How do you know what it tastes like?"

"I know the flavor of herbs and spices. I've been around a while. Now open your mouth, Ms. Dalca."

"I think it's too big. I could never swallow it."

"It will dissolve in time. Now open your mouth and don't delay my experiment anymore."

He brought the ball to her face, pausing only to make sure her jaw was open this time. Then he deposited it into her mouth. The skin of his hand was cold against her smarting lips. She smelled him—a smell that reminded her vaguely of rodent fur—before the taste of the lozenge took over her senses.

The hard bead of medicine was tacky, like frozen syrup. Her tongue manipulated it, circled it around her mouth, clacked it on her teeth, scraped it with them, sent it from one cheek to the other. The flavor was anise and gave the sensation of needles on her tongue. She wanted to swallow but it was too big for that. The juices flowed, and she could tell the ball's size was reducing, though not as fast as she'd like. The spicy flavor died quickly. It had been pasted to the surface. She was left sucking on an increasingly bitter substance. The needle effect strengthened. She made a face.

"Finish it," he said, his face lowered to hers, his eyes studying her reactions.

"The good taste went away," she told him awkwardly from around the lozenge.

"Don't speak. Just keep going. Swallow it when you can, but don't spit it out. Do you understand?"

Amalina nodded and rolled her eyes, trying to ignore the cringe-signals from her mouth. At least the bitterness had leveled off so that it was tolerable. Still, she sucked and stirred it around as hard as she could, willing it away. As she did this, the Count spoke to her.

"Georg came to me," he said. "He isn't satisfied with your service. You are neglectful of your duties within the castle, and you and Genadie are rebellious to his command."

Amalina frowned, made a noise and shook her head.

"I had to remind him that I am the only force in this house. But you understand that, Ms. Dalca, don't you? Of course you do. You know more than most about me. And you appreciate my power and my will, and how far it extends. You would never disobey *me*. No, no. Nobody would think to disobey. Nobody would think to rebel. Everyone within my reach is under my command."

Amalina began to worry his speech had something to do with the cure rattling around in her mouth. Its bitterness increased sharply. Or was she imagining that? She nodded, hoping he'd be satisfied and stop staring.

"Georg thinks I should punish you ... the both of you." If the Count still had his mustache, he would have been pulling on it. Instead his fingers tickled their tips together beside his broad, flat cheek. "But I think that unnecessary, little mouse. For all that you've done for me. It really wasn't your fault you failed to bring what the castle requires. Genadie had his priorities set, and he has only a mind for me. And you ..."

His eyes flicked up and down, taking her whole body in.

"How is the flavor, Mouse?"

She shook her head, hummed disapproval.

"But not so bad. Not that you wouldn't finish it if I asked?"

She nodded and winked.

"You were just scared," the Count continued from where he left off. "The townsfolk had forgotten their hospitality. Lost their minds from the sudden, personal tragedy they experienced, to be sure. But every day is a new day, is it not? And today, when the sun rises, you and Genadie will go back down there to collect the supplies you were supposed to."

She nodded.

"Do you know why, Mouse?"

She shook her head.

"Because those people need to see how this castle handles rebellion, and how it deals with the few who forget their place under its command."

The ball had gotten small and soft enough, with all her nervous energy she crunched it to pieces in her mouth.

The Count flinched at the unexpected sound. But then Amalina flinched at his flinching, and slipped, and wound up on the floor.

"You will go to the village, then. Tomorrow."

. . .

Even on the way down to Netz she worried how she would handle a meeting with Kralov or one of his associates. With nothing to report, it was too soon for a rendezvous. And any attempt by them to contact her would only chance the discovery—by the Count's spy—of her link to the fomenting rebellion. It felt so real to her, this discovery, she was glad she hadn't taken the curl of coded message with her, if by chance she were caught with it. Her fretting went unnoticed by Genadie, who was wrapped up in his own concerns. His brow was knitted together. And those greasy caterpillars above his eyes shoved further into each other as the cart neared Netz.

"What's the matter, Genadie?" she asked.

"You take Georg's list and arrange the supplies, Ms. Dalca," he instructed, his eye winking nervously.

"You aren't afraid to do it yourself, are you?" she said, suddenly fearing for her own life if Genadie was uneasy about it. "Afraid they're going to try to grab us again?"

"What are you talking about, Ms. Dalca? Never mind the villagers. All is well, you'll see."

"Then why do you look like you ate too much porridge?"

"Maybe because I ate too much porridge."

"You didn't eat anything. I'd prefer we stick together this time."

"We aren't sticking together. You get the supplies." He paused. Then: "I need to speak with someone. Alone."

"Why alone?"

"It's none of your business."

"What's the matter?"

"It's none of your business."

"I thought we were a team Genadie. Why are you keeping secrets from me?"

"Secrets?"

"Tell me we aren't going to keep secrets now. Tell me we aren't going to divide ourselves, when it's us against Georg and Abraxa; that dreadful duo."

"Dreadful duo, eh?" he smiled and tamped his dirty hat onto his head. "More like the prickly pair."

"Poisonous pair."

"Cranky couple."

They settled down.

"One of the pigeons came back," Genadie confided softly, sounding concerned. "Didn't have a note."

Amalina gulped. But then made a face and pretended it was the bad taste from the medicine. "So what's the matter with that?"

"Who knows? Who knows?" he said, his brow easing a little. "Could be anything. Might have just escaped its cage, you know. Yeah, that's probably what happened."

She was so distracted by what Genadie might suspect about that pigeon and its lost note. What he might learn from the person he was to meet in the village. Find out the bird *did* have a message meant for the Count, and that someone *must* have intercepted it. So distracted was she that, as she wandered the streets on her own, all the while trying to keep track of the direction in which Genadie was furtively shuffling, she didn't notice Piotr slip to her side. Until he'd grabbed her, and pulled her into some anonymous room; his knife to her throat.

• • •

Piotr growled angrily into Amalina's ear: "You've nothing to tell me? You've no new information at all?"

"The secret message—"

"Some worthless message? You think we don't know he has spies all around us?" His grasp tightened around her chest, his knife pressed against her throat. "We need actionable intelligence, *little mouse*. You think you can convince the Commander of your commitment by throwing at us meaningless trifles? By not conducting your assignments as ordered?"

"There wasn't enough time," Amalina pleaded. "I didn't even mean to come here. He sent us down—"

"Why?"

"To get the supplies we didn't—"

"To show your faces. To let us see how bold you are now, and how cowed the people of Netz are to your Count. And by doing so, frighten our order. That's why you came, and you did not seek out our Commander, but snuck around like a—"

"No! It isn't true!"

But it was true—if spied from a perspective of mistrust. She had been sneaking around the village (after Genadie), and hadn't gone directly to find the Commander—or Piotr or Roti.

"Where's Kralov?" she asked.

He snarled at her familiar use of his name.

"Where's the Commander?" she corrected.

"Wouldn't you like to know? But you never will. The Count will know nothing unless it is in our interest he do so." Amalina decided not to tell him that the Count knows everything. Or he claimed to, anyway. He knew *most* everything pretty well.

"But I'm still with our Commander," she protested. "I'm with you all, I swear. But—"

"We should kill your family," he snarled savagely, "just to set an example. But then there'd be nothing left to hold over you except your own worthless life, would there?"

"Why are you so mad? Leave me be!"

She tried shoving away from the knife, but it dug in dangerously below her jawline.

"Should I?" Piotr hissed. "Do I let you go? Or do I set you up on the other end of town?"

"Let me go."

"Or do I set you up on the other end of town?" he repeated. He said it like it had some important meaning she should understand.

"What are you talking about?"

"You don't know? You haven't seen?"

"Please, Piotr, let me go."

His arm loosened. Then it relaxed and the blade fell away. Gently, Amalina pushed herself free.

"Don't return until you have followed his orders; when you have done something useful for the Commander. When you've decided whose side you're really on. But understand: There's an army coming. The people are rising. When they finally arrive, all who stand against us will die."

"Are you all right, Piotr?"

Then he added with a soft voice: "And others will die, too. We have verified everything about you. And we've positioned men around your father, baker's daughter."

She wanted to run.

"Please continue your day," he said, gesturing toward the street, "to serve the monster. But before you return to his castle, why don't you visit the southern gate—the highway out to Kirgyl—and *see* why you are safe to walk these streets, when before you would have burned at the post, taken by the fury of the mob. Go and look, and know what has preserved you ... You will see."

14

The Southern Gate

It wasn't that they were friendly, but the people of Netz were definitely no longer throwing bricks and crying for Amalina's death. And they appeared to recognize her, and greeted her, and said familiar things that would indicate she was on good terms with them. Or, at least, they were on good terms with her because of who she knew, whom they feared. Nobody inquired if the Count was living in the castle, or whether it was just her and Genadie tending to his property. She thought it curious that they wouldn't ask after him, since *he* was behind every one of their smiles. She would have asked if she were in their shoes, she thought.

When Genadie hadn't returned to the cart, she considered walking to the other end of town, along the road that led out on to the highway to Kirgyl. But on a second thought, she left the cart—holding the newest bag of gold coins—and went to see if Genadie was with the bird keep, who she assumed he was meeting (and who she assumed was the Count's spy).

Genadie wasn't there. But the keeper was, and cocked his head at her curiously when she entered the maze of coops. He walked towards her, one halting step after the next. His head turning this way and that, as if one eye worked at a time. His draping skin shook with each darting move.

"Has Genadie been here?"

His head cocked.

"You remember me? and the man who I was with?" Amalina lifted a hand to show the height of Genadie, and then adjusted her hand when she remembered how short Genadie was. "Bought seven birds."

"Yes."

"Has he been here?"

"No."

Amalina nodded. He imitated her nod like he couldn't control himself from doing so. His wattle shimmied. Feeling shy and awkward, she scratched the ground with her toe, knowing what she should be asking, but afraid to.

"Are all these your birds?" she asked.

"No."

"Who do the others belong to?"

"Many people."

"Could I buy one?"

"You are staying in the castle?"

"Yes."

"And where would you want it to go?"

Where would *she want it to go?*

"Where *can* they go? Anywhere? You just tell them where to go, and they go?"

His tiny downturned lips lit upwards. The sudden smile looked unusual on his face.

"That's not the way it works. They have to be set for somewhere."

"How do you set them?" She remembered the Count half-turning into a pigeon and giving them directions in their language. The bird keep couldn't mean that.

He shook his head: "Rather, they are *from* somewhere. They know where their home is. You just take them away from their home, and when you want to send a message, you let them go. As long as you keep the cage closed, they will return home once it is opened."

"Return with the message."

"With anything they can carry."

"So you couldn't take a Netz bird and send it to Tsobl."

"No. But if you want to send something to Tsobl, I still have more than a few birds that you can use. Most of them in here are for Tsobl."

"Oh, really? Why is that?"

"Why would you send a message anywhere else?" his question seemed more like a statement. Anything of importance came or went to Tsobl.

"But how can you be sure when the bird gets to where it is set for, the message will go where you want it to?"

"We are messengers, girl. It is a service, after all. When the message arrives, we know where to direct it. Or who to call."

"But, I mean," she said, "what happens if the bird wanders away?"

"Doesn't happen."

"Or gets eaten, or shot out of the sky."

"I haven't heard of it. But I'm sure it happens in war. Nothing is for certain."

"What happens if you receive a bird, but there's no note on it. What would explain that?"

"The bird got out of its cage."

"But say you know there's supposed to be a note on him... If I put the note on the bird, and then it arrived where it was sent, but the note was gone" Amalina realized she was talking a little too much. A little too directly. It was still possible he was the man whose cipher she'd intercepted. "Uhm, what I mean is … is it possible the bird might lose it, somehow? How do you know it won't just fall off? Could it just fall off … somehow?"

His head cocked to the other side, and he stared. His smile shrank, and then returned to its normal upside-down v.

"Anything can happen," the keeper allowed. "But I've never heard of such a thing. Not in my experience."

Before she left she couldn't help but ask: "Do you have any birds that are set for Korr?"

She'd never heard of this pigeon system, and was sure there couldn't be a bird keeper in her home town. She would have known of it, as it's such a remarkable thing. But if there was … if there was, maybe she could send a note to her father.

But the bird keeper looked astounded: "Why would you send a message there?"

• • •

When the sun began to arc downward towards the mountains in the west, and Amalina began to worry they would be travelling after nightfall, Genadie appeared. She paid off and dismissed the laborers, who loaded the cart with the castle's supplies and were hanging around silently but obediently to see if there was anything else they might get paid for.

"You look tired," she told Genadie. He always looked tired, even when bursting with great spirit, but she figured it was a good bet. He'd been troubled earlier, which can sink a person's energy. "Can I coach the horses?"

"You know how to drive this wagon, Ms. Dalca?"

"I've watched you enough. I want to try." Then she reminded him: "And you look tired."

"Well, I'm not."

Amalina already had the reins in her hand, so she tugged them the way she'd seen him do it, and made the sounds with her mouth. *Nk! Nk!* The horses began to move.

"*Multo buono*, my pupil," he said in Italian. *Very good*. Her language lessons—another pre-expedition holdover; now concentrating on Italian and French—would continue in their proper hours. This hour was apparently Italian. His tiredness dissipated a fraction and he grinned at her new accomplishment.

Driving the cart was easy enough, it seemed, though much different than riding a horse. It required a good deal of strength, holding her arms out in front and keeping the reins in her hands as the horses jostled against them. In this moment though, driving the cart wasn't so much an accomplishment as it was a necessity.

And she also needed to distract Genadie.

"Did you meet the man you were supposed to?" she asked him.

"Yes."

"Did it go all right?"

"As well as it could."

"It took you a long time."

"Did you make sure to get everything on the list?"

Amalina ran down the list from memory, while Genadie verified it was in the wagon.

"Ms. Dalca, why are we going this way?"

"Which way?" she asked innocently.

"We want to go the other direction. Toward the castle."

"Oh, right. I thought this was the way. Well, we'll have to find a good place to turn around."

She continued on the main street, shooing Genadie's hands away at every intersection, telling him she didn't think it was safe to turn around here.

"You don't know *how* to turn this wagon, do you?" he accused with a grin.

She didn't answer, but kept the wagon moving until they reached the far end of Netz.

"Here," he said helpfully. "Let me have the reins and I'll show you how to do it. You've done well so far. We haven't foundered."

Amalina yanked hard on the leather straps, bringing the cart to a dead halt, almost sending them both off the bench.

At the end of town, just off the highway, a cage was hung from a pole. Inside the cage was Roti. Roti's body. The cage was tall and so narrow that the body (slumped over) was still essentially standing. The cheeks were light purple, the entire body held a green tint. He was very much dead, of course. And so Piotr's upset was explained.

"Excuse me," Amalina called to a child throwing rocks at the body. "Who is that?"

"Ygardina's killer," the boy said, throwing another rock. "I bet I can make him pop."

"He killed the mayor's daughter?" she asked. "Are you sure?"

"Yes! Or he wouldn't be rotting out here."

"Let's go," Genadie said to Amalina, trying to grab the reins again.

"But you thought someone else killed her the other day." Amalina felt a rising outrage. "Going to put *them* to the torch. How do you know this one did it?"

"'Cause he said he did it," the boy said, becoming outraged in return. He pivoted and began clacking stones together in his hand, like he might be lining up a shot at a new target. He pointed to Genadie. "And *you* said you didn't do it. I remember the both of you. You were the ones."

"Well, we didn't do it. When did he say he did it?"

"Wrote it all down," the boy said. "Right here. Wrote it all down before he swallowed some poison. Why would he write out a confession and kill himself if he didn't do it? What would be the point?"

Amalina handed Genadie the reins and came off the wagon.

Up close, Roti's color looked much worse. His eyes bulged against the lids, parting them. They looked dry and vacant. He was beginning to smell like bad meat.

Hung from the bottom of the cage was a plaque with a piece of paper shellacked to it. The note read:

I killd beautiful Ygard
becase she lofd anothr.

There was also a drawing of Ygardina next to the note. It was difficult to tell if this portrait was drawn by Roti, or drawn by someone else and just meant to remind everyone who the letter was referring to.

A larger sign was hung off of an upright arm on the cage's side, so it could be read clearly from anyone entering from the highway. It read:

Strangers and Foreigners
Bewar!

From what Piotr had said to Amalina, he considered this grotesque display a warning to anyone entering Netz. An example of what sort of welcome outsiders coming off the highway (and perhaps joining the approach to the Count's high castle) could expect. And so when he threatened to put Amalina *'on the other end of town'*, he must have meant staking her body at Netz's entrance from the northerly high castle road, alerting the Count and all his associates the penalty, in-kind, if *they* should dare to come to town.

The atmosphere was warming.

15

Prove Her Worth

Amalina put the reins in Genadie's hands, telling him to not speed the horses because she felt queasy and too much shaking would make things worse. Because she did this, and Genadie offered no complaint, along the slow, winding trip back to the castle, she was free to think.

Foremost on her mind was not poor Roti's sullen corpse, which was haunting enough. Instead, she was thinking: An army is on its way.

Or so Piotr had growled into her ear.

It could have been a bluff. But one meant to impress her—or scare her—to keep her on Kralov's side? Or did they still suspect she was an agent against them, and they assume this disinformation would reach the Count; the news of the rebellion's approach a different, subtler way to intimidate their enemy? intended to rock him back on his heels, to flush him from the castle?

But if an army really was coming, and the rebellion really was about to happen, that meant time was running out for her. Just how much time did she have to prove herself? To aid them in their cause? Because she was on Kralov's side, wasn't she? She had to be.

She had to be, unless … unless she joined Kralov, and then his army turned out to be just as many lambs to the Count's wolf, as all who'd fallen before. That would be a disaster. What made Kralov think an army had any chance against the monster? Had he even read the secret history of the region, which detailed the fall of whole armies at the hands of the Count? Maybe not. He wasn't from Ardeel. He was an outsider. A Muscovite, from what the Count had said. He knew of the Count only what he had experienced personally: seeing him as a child, and then encountering him again in old age—with the Count impossibly unchanged, and displaying a strength and speed beyond all belief. So did he understand the Count's full power? Or had he just convinced himself it was simply more men he needed to tackle this entity? If that was the case, his mistake would be fatal.

Then again, Amalina remembered, Kralov had escaped the Count. Kralov had injured him; so that the Count would wince and limp and curse Kralov's name. The Commander knew *something*, then, that Amalina had not discovered on her own: how to damage this monster. There was that to consider.

Anyway, she had to do something, to try something, to prove she was capable and valuable and on Kralov's side. No reason to hesitate now. What happened to the days when she was willing to risk her life just to make an attempt on the Count, not knowing how it would turn out? Yes, she had to act as fearlessly as she once would have. Time was growing short.

And yet, another voice in her head spoke out (a voice that sounded very reasonable and not at all cowardly), *it wouldn't do to make any move that would positively mark you out either way*. In the end, she could always claim allegiance to either side, depending how the luck played out, and cry innocence and ignorance to the victor for why she hadn't been as helpful as she could have been. She thanked providence that she was still just a girl, and young, which provided her cover.

Remembering the cold of Piotr's knife against her neck, she understood that ruse was limited. That for the Commander and his army, her innocence would only get her so far. At least she knew that the Count was a little more credulous toward her. In her experience, maybe even fond of her. Though it was hard to tell with his self-admiring, and rampant narcissism. He was fond of himself most of all. Who knows how much anyone else *really* mattered to him. But maybe his self-involvement could also be used against him, to blind him and trick him …

At the churning of her cold calculations—with enemies becoming allies, and friends converted into pawns—for the second time in so many days, Amalina wondered, with regret, how she had become such a sneak and conniver.

Necessity, she guessed.

With Roti's dead eyes returning to mind—joining the many dry, dusty gazes she'd seen in the age of war and plague—Amalina felt sorry for him. And, as well, bit her lip with the keen desire to not end up joining him as a pitiable focal point for children's stones.

She'd have to be careful, whatever she did. It was her duty to return home to her father.

Yes, that was her priority.

… Wasn't it?

The churn, threatening to begin another cycle, was interrupted.

Genadie was singing an old romantic folk ballad. She'd never heard him do that before, only belting out scraps of merry nonsense when dancing a jig. With his scratchy voice, she was surprised he could carry a tune so well. Well, it was more humming than singing … but it was on key, and to a pleasant, easing rhythm. His eyes were focused into the distance, not on the castle. It was not in sight yet. Who knows what he was staring at inside his head? With the song, he seemed to be calming himself.

Even though she wanted to ask him what he had learned about the fourth bird and the missing message—wanted to ask him desperately so—she didn't disturb him.

. . .

Telling them she was not feeling very well and needed to rest, Amalina excused herself from the unloading of the wagon. Abraxa snorted contemptuously and bragged that she was five times as old as Amalina, had bad knees and aching hips, and a raging ache in the head, and then demonstrated her superiority by hefting a large, heavy box of flour. Amalina went upstairs anyway.

Saying she was sick was just an easy way to get alone and give her more time to think and plot. But then on the stairs, she began to wonder.

Her whole body buzzed, but that was to be expected at the end of a long ride. She was also lightheaded and slightly nauseous, but it had been a long, stressful day, and she'd only eaten in the morning before she'd left the castle. There was an acidity in her mouth, too. But that was left over from last night, when the Count had fed her that strange medicine. The aftertaste had lingered.

She threw herself out on her mattress and lay there for only a minute. Why had she wanted to get upstairs? To get away from them? She'd already had enough time to think on the trip back, she didn't want to think anymore. But sleep wasn't going to happen. Nervous energy was pushing at her, seeking an outlet. Which was not easy to do with the bitter taste of the medicine still curling her tongue, and still tickling her imagination of what it was meant to do to her. Maybe the little red ball was the reason for the nervous energy; the unsettled feeling that was causing such mental turmoil.

She considered the ball the Count had shoved into her mouth. She didn't know its purpose. Was it meant to poison her? Something slow acting? What would be the point of letting it run on for so long without affecting her? Give her time to go down to Netz? ... to allow Genadie to observe her from a distance ... in case she was contacted by the rebels?—*because the Count knew she was working with them!* Wasn't that what he was intimating with his curious monologue, when she was sucking on the medicine, that he knew she was with Kralov? *Because he knows everything that happens!*

Amalina became dizzy. She remembered the drug Erik had given her when he'd wanted to knock her out, and she began to feel the symptoms again. The heavy limbs, the cold sweat. The bitterness in her mouth grew stronger. Maybe it was the same poison Roti had taken—or he was forced to take! Yes, it was a slow-acting poison. It had given her time to contact the rebels, and then see what had happened to Roti. And now she would suffer his fate!

But in a minute, she knew it wasn't true. She steadied herself. It was just her swirling, chaotic thoughts overwhelming her. This manic situation, with plots and more plots, and constant danger, and all of it transforming her innocent life into something constantly secretive and mean and increasingly paranoid. She began to cry.

She closed her eyes, and there in the distance Lucinda's head bounced above the barley. Enough!

Amalina wasn't going to be able to rest.

She tried to take stock of her situation one last time:

She was the assistant to the Count. If she refused, she (and maybe her father) would die (*he* as a consequence of her disloyalty). So then she had no real control, or any choice in the matter. She would be his assistant.

She was an operative in Kralov's operation against the Count. If she refused, she (and maybe her father) would die (*he* as a consequence of her betrayal). In this, she had no real control or any choice in the matter, either. She would be an operative.

To serve the Count, she had only to do as he said, and ignore his crimes, and she would tour the western kingdoms, live like a princess for a time, and return home safely—unless Kralov has his way.

To aid Kralov in his just campaign against the monster, she had only to carry out her given assignments, dangerous as they were, and the world would be rid of a dangerous, inhuman creature, and she would be able to return home safely—unless the Count won out in the end and had *his* way.

No, thinking about it didn't help much. She just had to think smaller, more directly. One step after the next. Making decisions as she needed, at critical moments, and see herself through safely.

But she knew whose side she was on: Commander Kralov's. So her priority was there. She *should* get his liquid to—on or into—the Count. Nothing else mattered at the moment, even if by accomplishing the task she should make herself the Count's open enemy and die. This was simply the next step for her, everything else forgotten.

Knowing that coming to her bedroom had done little to improve the situation, she went back downstairs, small vial tucked into her pocket, hoping the cart hadn't been fully unloaded yet. So she could prove her worth to Georg and Abraxa.

16

Contact

> Governor,
> I pray I have not caused any irreparable harm to any of the
> pursuers you sent after me. If I have, I will dedicate my life
> to repairing the damage I inflicted on the families so injured.
> But I am sure that I have not. I pray that I have not …

Attila scratched it out. And then he tore off the top of the paper, shrinking the sheet by a quarter. It was the only paper on the farm, and the ink he was having to sustain with his spit, so he had to be more careful. There was no need to trouble—or reveal—in the letter his fear that he'd killed the soldier in the river. Though the image of the man's desperate, gasping face, and the remembered sensations—radiating up from the bottom of Attila's foot and up his leg—of the crunch of his nose and his frantic gurgles, haunted him every unguarded moment; the knowledge that he might have murdered this man; that the man who caused those sensations, alive in that terrifying moment, was now silent, and empty, and as clay, was his fault. And what a terrible thing if that were true. Attila could barely resist the guilt, and the fear for his own soul. But he had to coldly quash it.

Better to focus on his mission. And when he addressed the governor, it was best not to let his personal troubles bleed into it. It could only make him appear weak, when he had to not only appear strong, but in command. In some *form* of command, anyway … lying in a bed of straw, huddled in a farm house, his body still wracked with pains. His brain was still active, and his thoughts could be fashioned into weapons.

He wrote again:

> Governor,
> Let us declare a truce. Our interests are not so far divided
> that we need to wage war against each other. In the end, we
> wish for a peaceful, lawful society.
>
> Whether you will grant this truce, because you are better
> seated to survive our differences, in this letter I will seek to
> better your position by improving your understanding of

what you are up against. I have already shared some of my understandings with the high constable, and perhaps he has passed them on to you. By studying the histories, and the records that still exist from the earlier days of this country, I believe that this so-called Count, or Knight, is of the family Teppes; specifically the former Voivod, the King, Vlad Teppes, whose bloodthirstiness and inhumanity matches the humour of this creature of the castles and mountains. To compound the coincidence of evils: from the reported accounts, he bears a strong physical resemblance to the man. He rescued the body of the Teppes queen from her mausoleum in the Netz graveyard—a curious thing to do for someone without a tie to that family. And the timing of the Voivod's disappearance, and then the appearance of this creature, is curious, if not convincing.

What does it matter whether this creature is the former Voivod of the 14th Century? He is what he is now, no? Yes, he is a representative and embodiment of evil, and deserves to be destroyed. This is true.

But if he is this person, then you understand better who you are conducting an alliance with. This is the man that drove a foreign empire out of his lands, with no respect toward the dignity of human life and morality. He bides his time until he can do the same to us. And what do you conceive you might gain by delaying his destruction—while we possess the technology and capability to destroy him—other than allowing him to strengthen himself and perfect himself, and guarantee he will come at us at a time of his choosing, when he knows he has surpassed our powers again, and he can deliver profound and outrageous suffering on you and your family and your friends and their families, and all who cannot claim a relation to this land, but stepped on it as temporary conquerors? You will know his vengeance.

In your future dealings with him, I suggest you determine if my suspicions are warranted. If he won't speak readily on these matters, or you are too timid to ask directly, you should address him as Viscount and not the proper title he has chosen for himself. Viscount is merely an empty, honorary title. If he challenges this change, because he is proud on top of his other offences, you will offer to restore him to his status of a true Count if he should formally identify himself and his family line. A simple thing.

And then you will know what future awaits, if you do not start seeing things my way.

Your loyal subject,
No more

"What does it say?" asked Hak's wife, holding one long blond lock back so she could look at it clearly with both eyes.

"You don't know how to read?"

"No."

Attila explained it was a private correspondence, and it would have no negative repercussions for her or her family. Conversely, if she posted the letter to where he asked, there might be a return of money for her. This seemed to improve her attitude towards it, and she handled it like she would a note-of-lending from the King. She even looked nervous as he folded it up to place in a hand-made envelope, as if he might lose her a fortune if he bent it the wrong way or created a tear. Attila addressed the envelope: Private: Governor Schluckgeld, from Low Constable Attila Bronk.

She was eager to get it to the nearest town, and from there off to Tsobl. So was Attila.

. . .

Attila was forbidden to go near the farmhouse. "You will not speak to my husband or I will kill you," Hak's wife had threatened, fully meaning it. "Just get well and then you go." And by his wife's constant chores and scolding looks, Hak was kept well away from the sidehouse where Attila was recovering. She was a force keeping the two apart. The two, Attila and Hak, were men of honor and obeyed and respected the woman who cared for them. So their intention, no matter how curious they might be about each other, was never to meet if she forbade it strongly.

But it was no matter. Understanding that their mother had left for the nearest town, and that it was their mother's will for the two men to be kept separate, the children's immediate purpose was to introduce Hak to Attila, or Attila to Hak; just to see what would happen.

Life in the Baibay Valley was slow and boring.

In the stretch of ground between the two houses there came a scream. It was high-pitched and drew Attila's curiosity. A second scream joined the first, and the combination was enough to get Attila out of the straw and to the door.

The little girl ran in circles, gripping the wrist of her left hand, which she waved in the air. Where her thumb should have been was a red streak. Her brother chased after her, whooping and crying, somewhere between trying to catch her and alerting their father what had happened.

At the center of their circular path was a stump with a hatchet buried into it, and flopping next to it in the grass was a headless chicken. The chicken somersaulted in place, flicking blood in all directions. Attila couldn't see it, but presumably lying next to the hatchet, on the stump, right beside the head of the chicken, was Hak's daughter's thumb.

Hak charged up from the river path with a small smirk, but curiously untroubled eyes.

"Hey, what's happened, Lija?"

Lija did not stop running but kept making loops in the grass, shoving her left hand more dramatically in the air and increasing the hysterics. Her brother also built onto the commotion, waving his arms and encouraging his father to hurry.

"I told her not to!" the boy shouted.

Hak saw the stump, the headless chicken, the ax. His mouth made a small o of surprise. He joined his son in trying to capture Lija.

"Come, Lija! Come!" he shouted in a low, tender voice. "Show me!"

But Attila already understood what was happening, and without much concern from Lija, he lurched from the door of the sidehouse. Not that he needed to: Hak's children increased the measure of the circles, widening and shifting them away from the stump and toward Attila. If the girl had really removed her finger, no matter how crazed by the pain or just the idea of it, she would have run straight into the arms of her father. Even now, as she led her father closer and closer toward the wounded stranger, her eyes kept darting to Attila. And her small smile grew ever wider.

When Hak grabbed hold of his child, scooped her up into his arms and took hold of her wounded hand, her thumb—covered in chicken blood—popped into the air. And now her father stood next to Attila.

"Oh, Lija!" her father scolded with his smile as big as hers. "Now, why would you scare your papa like that? What a naughty girl you are. Did your brother put you up to it?"

"No, papa!" the boy said. "It was her idea!"

"How could you think of such a thing to do?" he set the girl, who'd begun to squirm in his arms, down on the ground and patted her head. His chin came up and he looked in dull surprise at Attila. "Oh! Well ... hello."

"Good afternoon," said Attila. He bowed, but did not append a grander title, like 'my lord', to the greeting. He still wasn't sure this man was the true heir of the Vogoneyevic line. "Your name is Hak, sir?"

"My, uh, my wife said I shouldn't talk to you."

"No? Did she say why?"

"She said you wanted to speak with me and you were dangerous. She said you were shot by a pistol."

"I was shot by a fiend holding a pistol," Attila corrected, his expression even. "But I don't see how I'd pose much of a threat to someone as well-bodied as you. If I should even wish to. Which I don't. But your wife has been kind, and she has healed me, and I can't fault her for looking out for you and your family. Where is she now?"

"She's … gone visiting," he said slowly. It seemed the slowness was not intentional but rather a consequence of living out in the countryside, where there were no demands of time; or much of any reason to quicken a conversation. He didn't even bother to elaborate on *where* she'd gone visiting, as if the statement were good enough.

Which it was. It explained everything to Attila. Mama had gone away from the farm—she'd gone to post a letter, but no need to correct him on that point. And she'd cleverly sent her husband off to the river, to make sure he was away from the home while she was gone. To prevent Attila from talking to her husband while she wasn't around.

The quick children had understood this, and devised their scheme accordingly. And now, with their mother gone, the dust of her departing barely settled on the trail, papa has met the stranger. They were smiling brightly and mischievously in their sunburnt faces, with a front row view.

"Your wife, the kind woman, told you nothing else about me?"

"Uh, no." The man shifted his weight slowly and had a look of apprehension.

Well, maybe there was something more to the man's slowness, Attila now observed. More than just a victim of idleness. His wife did the thinking, and she'd told him the stranger was off-limits. There would be a reason she ran the house and not him, after all.

"My name is Attila Bronk," with a second, shorter bow. "I'm from Tsobl. A former constable there. And I've come here looking for Hak Vogoneyevic. Am I to understand that is you, sir?"

"Vogoneyevic." He nodded slowly. "Uh, yes, Vogoneyevic. That is my family name. But I … Nobody calls me that. I am Hak, if you need to, sir."

It offended Attila to hear Hak call him 'sir', and say it with a deferential tone. Hak's eyes dropped with a subservience, too, when he said it. It would have been too much if he'd kept looking at his feet. But to Attila's relief, Hak had enough confidence to look him in the eye; and with a soft, gentle, interested gaze.

"Your family was a great family."

"But I shouldn't be talking to you." He said this, but he didn't walk away. There was some life in him, Attila assessed.

"I can't see any harm in it. Can you?"

"Uh … no." he shook his head. "I … don't know."

"I am well pleased to meet you, Hak Vogoneyevic," said Attila, seizing the moment. "I had hoped to meet you. Because, of any knighted family, to my mind, yours was the greatest: Powerful and bold and courageous."

Hak glanced at the starved, scrubby children dressed in rags, then he looked at the farmhouse that was ill-created and in disrepair and leaning as if it wanted to sit down.

Hoping to keep him from dwelling on these things, Attila said: "You must be very proud. Yours is the finest blood of Ardeel."

"You want to tell me something, Mr. Bronk?"

"Yes, I came to this valley in search of you, with the firm intent of imparting to the legitimate heir of Vogoneyevic, which apparently is you, sir, a matter of great importance. His legacy. But if we could speak privately. Away from the children. This is a matter for men alone."

Hak waved a large, browned hand and the children took several steps back. He waved again, this time with a nod toward their house. The two obeyed dutifully. They took spots against the wall, but leaned forward and stuck out their ears.

"They're gone," said Hak. "What do you have to say?"

"I can see you are a very good father. That you love and care for your children."

"Doesn't everyone?"

"Because you do you will want to hear me out. This involves their safety."

"Tell me." His eyes narrowed, his head pitched to the side. He was paying attention the way a large, dumb animal would. Attila's fervor was flattened a little more.

"The Knight of Ardeel is at a moment of crisis," he said. "His powers are growing, he is beginning to stretch out into the world again. But in this *moment*, he is still vulnerable. It is still possible to launch an attack on him, and hope to remove him from the face the earth."

"Remove him from the face of the earth?" Hak said, trying to keep pace. "You mean … kill him?"

"That is, sir," began Attila, looking bored, but hoping the enthusiasm in his voice would catch on—or the promise of violence would excite his warrior spirit, "*exactly* what I mean. Kill him."

"Hm." Hak nodded gravely, the magnitude of the information sinking in. But then, just as grave: "Who is he?"

"The Knight of Ardeel," prompted Attila. "The monster ruling these mountains for centuries unchecked. The dread reason why hundreds of our innocent women and children die every year. The reason for our night curfews, and the bolting of the windows, and the wreaths at our doors. The thing who your great ancestor began a shameful pact with, to establish a one-sided, unfair peace with him. A contract which you signed with your own hand."

"Did I?" Hak seemed lost. All the words Attila threw at him just confused him more.

"You can't tell me you don't know the creature I'm talking about, I saw your name on the contract. You signed it, sir. Or … but no. Tell me this isn't a new sign of cowardice."

"No." Then: "What do you mean?"

"Admit you know who I'm talking about. Do this at least, sir. And admit you signed the contract—which I have read, sir, and seen your signature in it, sir. At least admit that, before you continue this degradation of your name and soul."

"My wife says I'm not stupid."

"I never said you were. I told you not to deny what you've done."

"I didn't sign such a thing, Mr. Bronk."

"You did. I'm telling you, sir, I saw your signature set down on the page. It's how I know you exist."

"I deny it."

"You can't."

"But I *can* deny it," he said, not getting angry, but almost becoming amused, a gentle smile touching his mouth at the corners. "I will deny it, too, Mr. Bronk. I can't sign anything. I don't know how to write."

Attila considered Hak. The man's smile was beyond gentle and benign, it was simple. And he was happy to have proven himself right to the stranger. The kids had snuck toward them, eager to know the results of their trick. They saw Attila's ambivalent expression and took two more steps, trying to see their father's, hoping there was something fun to hold onto.

"Someone signed your name to the contract?" asked Attila.

"It must be." He guessed: "My father. He knows how to write."

"Did he tell you he signed your name to this agreement?"

"I don't think I ever spoke to him in my life, Mr. Bronk. Only once, when he told me to leave his house when I told him I didn't want to marry the girl he wanted me to."

Attila considered this some more. Just how much did Hak know or didn't know?

"How much do you know of your father? your family?"

"We had a big house," he remembered fondly. "Lots of people stayed with us, and visited. But we don't need a house like that. Gug and I. This is much better. Small and easy, here. It's a nice life." Sadly: "I miss mama."

"You board your windows at night," he observed. "You don't walk in the darkness. You hang the garlands."

"Yes, Mr. Bronk."

"Do you know why?"

"To be safe."

"Safe from what?"

"Monsters?" it was a guess.

"Any one in particular?"

"No. I don't know." He was apologetic. "I think I forgot ... But I don't forget to do it, Mr. Bronk!"

He smiled proudly at this fact.

"Very good," said Attila. "Let's start with monsters, then. One particularly."

But when he began to tell Hak Vogoneyevic why it was he and his family took the specific precautions of sealing the windows, and keeping indoors at nightfall, and setting out the garlic wreaths, and what specific creature he was keeping from his wife and children, a new scream burst out.

Hak's wife, knife raised high in her hand, came around the side of the house, from the direction of the forest road, screaming: "I told you I'd kill you! Kill you!"

The children's eyes lit up at the new entertainment about to begin.

17

The Second Ball

A couple months passed, the remaining books were inventoried and then packed into the Great Library's shelves. Strangely, with so much effort to create and ready this room, on its completion the Count did not visit to admire it, to appraise it, or to judge it. Its doors were closed unceremoniously, and Genadie informed Amalina that their language lessons (concentrating on Italian and French) would be extended to fill the empty hours while they waited. Georg also filled it with meaningless chores which he could then complain weren't done right, or if done correctly had been misinterpreted and shouldn't have been done at all, and so had to be undone. And for her part, Amalina tried to fill it with as many rides on White Snow as she could sneak in. The results of which were bruised arms, legs and head after so many tumbles to the ground, the horse refusing to leave the castle doors. He pitched himself into unexpected fits at other times, which could only be brought under control by Genadie (for some reason), who was unfazed at sliding himself underneath wheeling hooves. The horse never softened to her. Never succumbed to bribes of sweet hay in her hands. After the latest battle, White Snow backed himself into his stall, nickering defiantly. He spread his hooves to the sides of the stall and bowed his head as if to head-butt her, challenging Amalina to dare try to take him out again.

"What are we waiting for?" Amalina complained to Genadie, a cold cloth on her head.

"For the princesses to arrive."

"Can I go home now?" she asked hopefully.

"Not while we wait. They might come at any moment."

"Any moment," she scoffed. "But isn't my work done here?"

"We've yet to visit Italy or France, to meet with *their* lovely prospects," Genadie reminded her in his raspy voice. "And I thought you wanted to stay on, Ms. Dalca. Didn't you say that? I was looking forward to you keeping on with us. Wasn't that your intention, to stay with us and see your friends again? Don't let that horse get you down."

"You just want me here to even the odds against *the pair*."

"Even the odds?" Genadie was surprised. "You staying helps boost our faction in the castle against Georg and Abraxa, it's true. But the sides are already beyond even. I am on Master's side, *He* is on my side, and that makes us even against the world! Doesn't it?"

"I haven't seen him in weeks. Where is he?"

"It isn't our business, but to serve him."

"Of course," Amalina said. "But without him here, then it's just you against them."

Genadie frowned.

"Abraxa has been nice to you, I've noticed," he was trying not to sound jealous, but regarded her suspiciously. "You're friends now?"

Of course she couldn't tell him why Abraxa's attitude had improved toward her.

"Really, they aren't so bad anymore," she said. "Don't you think? They've been very polite, even if they're annoying."

"Don't trust her," Genadie cautioned Amalina with a squint, and touched her arm with one of his crooked hands. "You know, Georg has sent me on so many false errands now. She can only be up to something, too."

I need to trust her, she thought.

"My little mouse," the Count's baritone rumbled through her body.

He stood in the doorway. The fire from Genadie's hearth lit him weakly, but she could see his posture was slumped, and his large eyes were half-closed, as if drowsy. His mouth was slack.

"Master!" Genadie exclaimed, wriggling off the bench and throwing himself on the floor. By the relief in his voice, Genadie hadn't seen him in a long time.

"My little mouse," he repeated. "Come."

His movement was slow and elegant, and it did not show the limp he'd had for months. Had the damage healed? But his skin was not as fresh. Though the wrinkles were few, the energy was depleted underneath so that it hung. And when they arrived at his lab, she realized they had walked the entire distance, where she could have expected him to sweep her there in a stomach flipping flash of black.

He motioned her to the table occupied by books and equipment. There were no fires or bubbling liquids. One of the glass bulbs was more than three-quarters full with a dark brown liquid. The rooms smelled of something sour.

The tray of colored balls was also on the table. Now they had the shade of stained wood. His hand came out of his cloak, took one of the balls, and swept in a wide arc toward Amalina's mouth. She was ready for it this time.

By the smell of the room, she braced herself for a wince at the sour flavor. Instead of sour, it tasted like honey and rose.

"Different," she said around the ball.

"No," he murmured in his heavy voice. "It is the same as before, little mouse."

"I meant the flavor."

"Oh, yes." He passed a hand over his weary face, then leaned forward to stare closely at her. "Better?"

"I like honey," she said. He said nothing to this. A glum statue. To fill the time, and cover the sound of sucking and clicking against her teeth, she continued: "I thought of raising bees. I've studied a book on the subject."

"They are lower than worms," was his opinion. "Buzzing maggots of the air."

She didn't know what to say to that. She'd always enjoyed the sound and sight of bees. And the honey. They were her favorite of all the earthly creatures.

The ball was only partially dissolved. It seemed to be taking much longer on this try. And it would feel even longer if he remained in this foul mood. She wanted to throw the tray across the room to relieve the tension. At least the honey-rose was continuing strong and not becoming bitter or sour. An improvement she could concentrate on.

"Honey is delicious," she said in defense of the bees.

"A surprising byproduct of a loathsome pest."

"Where did you get the honey?" she asked idly.

"Tsobl market."

"You've been to Tsobl, sir?"

"I'm everywhere I need to be."

Not even halfway through.

Maybe just shutting up and ignoring him would be the best method, she thought. She tried to work the ball faster. It was still too large to get between her molars to end the scene with a quick crunch, as she had last time.

She loathed the silence. He breathed, but somehow he didn't make a sound. Even that unnerved her.

"Is it working?" she asked.

"I think so. Yesss. But I will see … In time. Just finish it all."

"What's it supposed to do?"

"I already told you, girl. It will solve our problem."

"*Our* problem? Or *my* problem?"

He wiped his face again.

"You look tired," she said.

"I don't tire," he muttered. "But I can be drawn out to an unbearable length—by what does not comply to my will, and lies beyond my control yet."

Amalina's eyebrows flew up. She almost gulped the medicine ball, and instead gagged.

Beyond his control?

He has a limit.

This was information.

"What lies beyond your control, sir?"

"Your *nice* friends," he grumbled. "They do not respond to my invitation. How wearing that is on my infinite patience."

"It is still too soon, sir. Who knows how long it takes for the birds to reach them? I don't know why you didn't send the letters out by messenger on a good fast horse."

"One of my birds, under my command and flying without rest, can travel in one day what it takes a good fast messenger to travel in three, at least."

"Oh … well … if they don't get lost or killed, you mean. And how do they know where to—?"

"The recipients received my letters long ago. And they have had months to decide and to make their plans." He looked despondent. Wounded emotions in the Count, something she'd never expected to see.

"But then their family has to post an answer, don't they? No, they're so very far away. It's still too soon to think—"

"If they don't respond before long, it will be too late. The winter will hold them off until next year."

"If it bothers you so much, why don't you go to them, sir? I think you'd enjoy Antwerp."

Life sprung into his face. But it was not the kind of life she wanted. His eyes flared at her, his face twisted with disbelief and anger.

"Aren't you done with it yet?" he complained.

"No." She slowed her sucking on it. "What's the matter?"

"You know very well I *cannot* go to them." Now he was offended by having to explain a matter that bothered or embarrassed him. But he continued: "If I could go there, I wouldn't have needed your assistance in drawing them to me, would I?"

"You are so powerful, sir," she said. "Why can't you?"

"The medicine is still in your mouth?"

"Yes … Why can't you, sir?"

"The burning hours have become too much for me. I could not withstand the exposure required for such a journey."

"You don't have to travel during the day."

"Just to leave this damned infernal cage I would need to. With these mountains I can only fly so far, I can't outrace the sun before it will rise again, and I haven't a safe place to land and rest anywhere. I've scouted all the routes, let me assure you. I've had plenty of time for that. But there's no path that will allow me to escape beyond the perimeter of these mountains. No, not in time."

Amalina didn't quite understand what he was saying.

"You can't prepare secure locations? You know, one after the next? Which would allow you to jump every night a little further along? I don't understand."

"If I could reach beyond the frontier, to Germania, I could do it. I could move from one city to the next, as free as I wish, as long as I had arranged for adequate lodging. But the mountains—the mountains!—separate Ardeel from the nearest town on any of our borders. It is too wide a gap for me, before sunrise comes. No. I cannot."

"You can travel by carriage. You can seal it—"

The Count was already shaking his head, an annoyed sneer carving the sags in his face. "Carriage, cart. No, never."

"But you seal it up—"

"And what happens when the horses go wild? Or a wheel or an axle breaks, and the whole thing tumbles over?"

"It wouldn't matter if you were in a coffin."

"I already told you I'm not a strigoi," fumed the Count. "I do not live in a grave, and I won't start. And even if I did, or I would, how would it help me if I were in so much as a hardy iron box when the carriage flies apart, or is taken over by highway men? I need my room to maneuver, and I can't have that if I'm trapped. I'm sure that Genadie—and you—and anyone I trust, would do their best to see me through any difficulty. But I can't trust my safe passage to anyone else but myself. For all the living are prone to failure, even if they should try their hardest. I cannot afford to gamble. Not in that way. Oh, I can just picture it, stuck in a carriage in a ravine, my rescuers opening the box's doors in my aid; the fools only destroying me."

The way the Count spoke, and by his tone, he was more annoyed by her, and dismissive of her, than he was an outright coward. But the content told another story. He reminded Amalina of a child frightened of a simple rainstorm, giving all kinds of excuses for why he was agitated other than that he was simply afraid of it.

But maybe he had a better knowledge of his vulnerabilities.

Amalina was stunned by how easy the Count described his destruction. Or rather, how easy it was to destroy him. *Could it really be that simple?*

She needed to pump him for more information. Any weaknesses and fears she or Kralov could exploit. It seemed a mean thing to do, but in his state, he was handing her weapons. Just keep him talking.

In her excitement she forgot herself, and with the crack of a rifle, the ball of medicine exploded between her teeth.

· · ·

The Count's irritability continued on. And it was more visible than before. He swept through the Castle regularly, muttering loudly to himself or grinding his teeth, blind to whoever was in the room. Sometimes he'd be speaking in languages she did not know. For the previous weeks she couldn't be sure he was in the building, now he was a constant presence, prowling and frightening even Genadie with his abrupt appearances. Though this behavior was entirely opposite than before, just as before, enacting any of her plans was impossible. Where for one golden moment the Count had promised to be a fount of new information, carelessly revealing his inner fears, which would be as valuable as diamonds, she'd blown it by finishing the medicine. She was shown the door without another word. And now this.

I feel useless, she pouted.

Without information, without *enough* information, she didn't feel safe— or comfortable—making an attempt at testing Kralov's liquid on the moody, petulant, and unpredictable Count.

At least gathering intelligence would be doing *something*. Getting out of the room and moving around, it couldn't be said she was intentionally procrastinating. If teasing information from the Count was impossible, she might get it from other places. She still didn't know how much the prickly pair knew about him. She could speak to Abraxa and find out. Or at least test her.

Where to start?

The castle held at least one prisoner that Amalina knew of. The strange woman hidden underneath the castle, who was fastened to a constantly turning wheel and who had filled the castle with her sorry wails; until Amalina had helped the Count silence her. She was gagged now, unheard from, but still spinning below their feet.

Did *they* know?

While there were two ways to access the hidden room, the direct route was a network of corridors that stemmed from the lower cellars and dungeons, just down from the kitchen. Amalina took a torch and went to the cellar where the Count had shown her the door in the wall, a door that hadn't been there whenever she'd been cleaning, but it appeared when he wanted it to be there. Would it be there now?

No.

As before, she faced a solid wall. She ran her fingers over the cracks between the large, cool, grey blocks. The seams seemed painted on. Were impenetrable. Did the door only appear when the Count was there? Was that possible? The count wasn't a sorcerer, was he? There was some method to open the wall, to reveal Castle door and passage.

She placed the torch in the wall mount, took up the broom and began to sweep. It took an hour before Abraxa was roused. The old woman came at

Amalina, trying to snatch the broom away and thundering objection to having her domain being invaded by the Mouse. While Amalina protested that she was just trying to help, she watched Abraxa's eyes, to see if she would glance at the false wall. There'd be no reason to look there unless she knew something important lay beyond it. Amalina took several innocent steps backward, toward the wall, and where the opening should be, to see if she would look.

Abraxa was focused on the small pile of dirt Amalina had managed to scrape up. And once she had the broom in her hands, she went to gathering clouds in the center of the room. She didn't care where Amalina was, and didn't give her a second look. She was scrambling to rearrange the mess so that she could claim the cleaning of the cellar was all her doing when she brought the dirt back together and finally removed it.

As she watched Abraxa's single-minded effort, Amalina concluded she most likely didn't know about the hidden door. Which meant she didn't know about the spinning woman.

Most likely. But not certain. Not yet.

"I've been working my fingers bloody," said Abraxa, "to clean this castle for our Master and the day his guests arrive. And here you go looking for the deepest corner you can find, just to prove my unworthiness. Who else would go down here with the rats? A frightening place if I've ever seen one. No reason to come down here but to deliberately go out of your way to find some trivial waste to point the blame at me. Think you're going to make me look bad before our master? Georg wasn't enough for you?"

"I didn't make Georg look bad."

"That's your plan."

"My plan is to make sure he's all right. Or let you know if he isn't. That's all."

"Taking your time about it. Oh, I know what you're up to. I remember everything you hold over him, don't you worry! Don't you worry!"

"Wait!" Amalina said, holding a silencing finger in the air. She cocked her head and spun it around. "Do you hear something, Abraxa?"

The old woman's eyes goggled, and she clutched the broom to her chest. Her eyes went for the door leading upstairs.

"What?" she asked in a quavering voice. "It's him? Is it him?"

The old woman threw herself flat onto the stones in the anticipation of the Count's arrival.

"No, no. Listen. Like a moan. You don't hear it?"

Abraxa lifted her head. "What are you talking about?"

"I thought I heard a moan. A woman's moan."

Abraxa held her ear to the air. Then she shook her head. She got to her feet and began to sweep in slow arcs on the floor, her eyes fearfully aimed at the open doorway. Not even a glance to the concealed door.

"It's me," she scolded Amalina. "You scared the soul right out of me. Making me think *He* was upon us; that he'd learn of this untidiness, and my oversight. You set my innards to moaning and groaning, and I'll be lucky they don't just give up on me."

"I meant to help, Abraxa," she said, full of apology. It was certain now: the old woman didn't know of the hidden passages or the tragic wailer.

"No threat could have been worse or more effective," Abraxa told Amalina, almost weeping. "In this time of uncertainty and woe, and our lives held on a razor's edge with his eminence in a dark humor? It was cruel to do. And nothing I'd have expected from you."

• • •

Amalina couldn't hope to speak to Abraxa after that—at least for several days. Or to try Georg, which would only compound suspicion that she was up to something. So she decided to tour the castle as she had last winter; as she, in her despairing boredom at the time, sought to explore and document the layout as best she could. She had recovered her old dress with the hidden map written into it. She would add to it today. On went the room with the bats and the grimy messenger pigeons. Then, a more important addition ...

In Erik Kosche's scheme to kill the Count, he'd used the Count's aversion to the sun to his advantage. At the time, Amalina understood that open sunlight was somewhat debilitating to him. He was sensitive to it, he wished to avoid exposure. But the way the Count worried so openly now, it was much more dangerous than a simple sensitivity. Why else would he chew his lips and wring his hands at the idea of traveling by carriage—refusing to entrust his safety to such a fragile (rather, sturdy) apparatus, even with Genadie to assist him—even if by rejecting it meant denying himself glorious liberty on the continent; and the ability to meet the women he so desperately wanted to meet, and to visit the wonders of the advancing world personally? Why else would he instead confine himself to the certainty of a massive and sturdy building, constructed of stone, and set permanently onto a mountain?

She reasoned: Having lived so long, everything else in the world must seem impermanent to him, even trees. It was only the mountains and the sun that remained fixed in time. And if one of those eternal things could destroy him (the sun), he could only trust the other for protection (the mountains). All else was as comforting as a passing mist.

And so that was a weakness. He trusted his stony castles. Nothing else.

Amalina made her tour of the castle—at least the places that were accessible to her—but regarded it with a new eye. She noted every spot where the sun penetrated, or could be opened to it. In the old parts, the windows had been constructed with sieges in mind. The windows were tall, but mostly narrow. Only the higher windows in the towers were as wide as a man's shoulders.

Besides the laboratory—equipped with a ceiling port to allow for venting—and the bird loft with its generous egress, the Great Library, with its newly installed windows, two stories high and wide as a house, was the point of greatest vulnerability. It had been part of Erik's original plan to distract the Count, and maybe it would have been better if the Count could have been pinned there, somehow, with the drapes pulled open to let in the light during what he called, tellingly now, "the burning hours".

She continued on, noting every window, no matter how small or well-sealed, and every door, too. If she couldn't think of how to use them, maybe Kralov would.

She was in the middle of chalking in the windows on her map, when she heard the loud, mad cackle. It seemed to come from everywhere, but its source was the Count. Amalina stuffed the dress under the mattress, and returned the chalk to its drawer. With the insanity of the laughter's pitch, she imagined him tearing through her door at any second, as he had done more than once before.

When he didn't, but the laughter continued, she took a candle and went looking for him.

He was in *l'entrée grande*. He stepped in an odd, almost comical way, with a jerking gait and his head tossing this way and that. His face was a mask of blood, with strands of hair caught in his teeth, and chunks of skin and tissue stuck to his cloak. He was no longer the thin, hollowed out man, but engorged with blood, his eyes poking out of their sockets with veins as thick as strands of yarn. Genadie was waving his arms in the air, a great smile on his face, matching the delight of his master. Georg and Abraxa stood at the edges of the room, near the fireplace, looking polite and terrified.

It seemed like the Count was in some manic delirium, marching with the oddest steps she'd ever seen. When she reached Genadie's side, and heard the tune he was moaning joyfully, and reconsidered the way the little rat's arms were flitting in the air as if he were conducting a symphony, she realized what the Count was up to.

"A waltz?" asked Amalina, hoping her question would stop his nerve jarring laughter.

"Will you join me, Lady Princess Tepsji?" he commanded rather than asked.

She scratched her head and then entered the floor, as if part of a line of dancers advancing to meet him in the middle. She tried to instruct his movements, modeling for him the correct and precise motions she'd learned at court. Her arms and legs moved slow and gracefully, as he, with his large, observing eyes, bobbed and leapt at her. It was his rendition of a waltz, which Genadie must have taught him, and which he was going to demand Amalina imitate instead of the other way around. She began to lift up and down on her feet, feeling somewhat ridiculous.

"Do you like dancing?" she asked as they met.

"I couldn't expect them all," whispered the Count, resentfully, as he turned to be at her side, and they march-hopped toward the petrified, pusillanimous pair, Georg and Abraxa, the conversation now being shared between themselves alone. "But *not one*, little mouse! It is an insult. Have they conspired among themselves to shun their eastern cousins?"

It sounded all very sad for him.

"Conspiracy? Why would they do such a thing? And we were up and down the country, those many cities. They couldn't—not every one of them—know each other, much less conspire, sir."

"It would be better if it were a conspiracy," he snarled. "It would be less of an insult than being rejected by all, individually. To think this great house can be spurned so easily. That they esteem us so little. I would tear them all to pieces and burn their palaces to the ground if I had the chance."

"You can have the chance to do anything you like if you just *went* to them," she said, reminding him of his fear and his fault. "But then you could just dance their dances, and partake of their feasts, and join the men's talk in their parlors. Think of all you are missing."

He hissed through his teeth. "Don't try to make me feel bad. It is their fault, not mine. Where is their curiosity, and their kindness?"

"No, sir. I mean, yes, sir."

"It was I—me!—who took the blow of the Ottomans, and broke the Asian spear that would have stabbed right through their ribs. But they forget. Only *I* remember."

"There are many noble and royal families right here in Ardeel, sir. If you want to have a dance, if you want to meet princesses, why not invite some of our own people here? I'm sure they are just as much fun as—"

"But I already told you, little mouse. I know them. I know them all, and all their secrets. Even you, I knew of. And you were no more than a peasant when I found you. I want someone I don't know. Someone I've never seen and whose name I never heard. Someone that knows things and has seen things that I have not. I want someone who can teach me, who is exciting, who will give me a challenge. I need fresh blood ... yesss, fresh blood ...

"How long I have waited for this," he continued. "And planned for it, once I learned what it was I wanted in the world. All the centuries I've passed feel like a single breath, matched against this lifetime of waiting on disappointing, untrustworthy, disease-ridden *mongrels!*"

"That doesn't make them sound so exciting or interesting. And it isn't true. They are very nice people."

"*Nice*," he scoffed. Then he turned his blood caked face to her, the several long, thick auburn hairs hanging off his lower lip lashing out and falling on Amalina's shoulder. "All my work for nothing. You should be just as mad as I am."

Those auburn hairs could have been Lucinda Skeldar's own. Lucinda's face flashed before Amalina's eyes, her mouth silent but hanging open, blood rushing from the ragged hole in her neck. Amalina suddenly wished for Kralov's little ampule—which was now sitting in her pocket—so she could throw its contents on him, whatever the consequences.

To do just that, she tried to subtly turn her wrist. To free her hand from the Count's unmindfully powerful—quite impossible—grip.

18

The Interview

Somewhere in the night, Amalina's anger turned to inspiration. She leapt from her bed with a positive energy, her toes flexing and curling. The answer to all her challenges had come at once—and though she didn't remember her dream which accomplished this miracle, she suspected it featured Lucinda's head and that the girl's gore-sodden lips had *told* her something.

How thankful Amalina was that during last night's midnight waltz with the Count she hadn't been able to ferret out the vial, to make the attempt; to risk her life.

And she never need try again!

There was no need to serve as Kralov's operative.

There was no need to remain an accomplice to the Count, the embodiment of evil, either.

These were not her *only* options.

There were *always* other options, weren't there? Amalina glowed brightly. She thought of the countless ways her father had experimented with making their bread: the mix of ingredients, the length of leavening, the intensity of the fire, the nearness of the bread to the fire, and the timing of a loaf's stay in the oven. Even the Count would understand, wouldn't he? Being a pursuer of alchemy. She'd seen the hours, days, and weeks he devoted to studying, and running trial after trial on mysterious liquids. Who knows how long he'd taken in arranging then rearranging the components, and perfecting the sequence of production, to make his honey-rose medicine balls. And hadn't the medicine begun as an unpalatable anise-bitterness?

There are always more solutions! Often better ones.

It was late morning, and she hoped the Count wouldn't be hid away as he usually was at this time of the day, especially after an evening when he'd taken a new victim. Unfortunately, he wasn't in the common areas, and the laboratory was locked and nobody responded to her knocks at the door. Which left Amalina only the private study, a room she could not afford to enter before having gotten the key from Abraxa and, knowing the count wasn't in it, searched behind the cabinet.

But don't you have the solution? mocked a small voice in her head. *You don't need to see beyond his secret door anymore. Or don't you* trust—?

"Oh, shut up," Amalina said impatiently, and aloud. She couldn't waste time on contradictory thoughts, not while she had hold of this burst of positive energy ... like a ray of sunlight pouring down on her, and through her.

But she couldn't become *overconfident*, she reminded herself. Shouldn't make one bad decision due to a sudden euphoria and cut off her *other* options, should they be needed.

Amalina could tell there was only so much of this feeling within her, and like the logs in a fire, it would only burn for so long before the enthusiasm crested, and her opportunity, like those logs, dwindled to cool ash. She couldn't wait until night ... or the next day, or the next week, before she saw him again.

"*Professore*," Amalina said to Genadie, during their Italian lesson, "*Sai dov e il Conte? Ho bisogno di parlare con lui.*"

"Are you really asking me this, *mi studente*, or are you just practicing?"

"I need to see him, Genadie. Do you know where he is? It's very important. Could you ring for him?"

"Ring for him?" Genadie looked taken aback.

Amalina and Genadie once had bells to summon the Count when they needed him. Genadie seemed to have a whole series of different bells, which spoke to different reasons or levels of importance. But their bells had been confiscated when Georg and Abraxa had cleared their rooms. Only an old iron one was left, which Genadie found in a pile of straw in his hovel. He hadn't had a reason to sound it since they'd returned. And now he tapped his fingers nervously, and ducked his head, looking shy and reluctant. As if he were saving the bell for the right occasion.

"We're in the middle of class," he reminded her.

"Aren't you worried about him?" she asked, she touched his fidgeting hands. "What happened last night ... He even scared the terrible two how he behaved ... He even scared *me*."

"Nothing to be scared about," Genadie said defensively. "He was just having some fun, learning to turn the figures to dances he will have with the ladies."

"Don't you see it? He's sad, Genadie. And lonely. He's feeling very down, and I'm starting to worry about him."

"Zeus is infinity. He is in command. There is no reason to worry, but for your place in his glory."

"He likes people to pray to him, and for them to make sacrifices," she said. "So he must have some measure of feelings."

"Zeus only cares that his subjects show him respect."

"If he cares, he has feelings," she persisted. "If he has feelings, well ... Feelings go up and down."

Genadie grimaced like a parent watching her child crying. The kind of parent who was helpless to do anything but shrug, feebly.

"We won't give up on him," said Amalina, "Not before Georg and Abraxa do, will we?"

"Are they leaving?" he asked, suddenly brightening.

"What I mean is, they only do what he says. They don't look out for him. Not really. Not like *we* do. You know what I mean?" she nudged him. "We're smarter than them, and we *really* look out for him. And we won't ignore when he is having trouble."

His internal pain increased.

"I need to speak to him, Genadie. Bring him here, right now. So I can talk to him before he does something crazy."

"What are you going to say?"

"I don't want to tell you. It has to be private or he might not want to listen."

"But what can you tell Master that he doesn't already know? A creation cannot instruct a creator, Ms. Dalca."

And yet there was a look of hope and expectation in his squint. The corner on one side of his mouth trembled upward.

"Genadie, I am going to pray to him."

He nearly fell off his chair.

"Pray? Ms. Dalca! I'll—No … Let's go to his study right now, Ms. Dalca. Let us both—"

"Give me your bell. Ring him here to me. Right here. If I go to him, it will seem unnatural. Like I was dragged there. It must be here, right now, in *this* room. Does that make sense?"

It didn't make a lick of sense. But Genadie was so excited he swallowed the whole shiny, unbaited hook. Nodding and running right out the door.

Pray to him?

Amalina got down on her knees and prayed her apologies to heaven, if saying something like that was considered a blasphemy—besides being an outright lie, of course. She prayed very loudly within her thoughts, thinking it would speed the word along.

Then she jumped to her feet to get the room prepared. This was the Great Library, with the massive windows, and the giant shaft of light filling the room almost to the walls.

Amalina closed the thick drapes over them. With the fire mostly embers in the fireplace, the library felt like deep midnight.

Opportunity? Trap? Gathering information? This moment could be anything, but it was happening now, and her heart beat faster.

She went to the wall, and with her familiarity with the catalogue, she quickly found the thin book she wanted: *Demonalogae: Monsters In Our Lands And How To Destroy Them.*

. . .

The Count poked his hooded head in, then seeing the drapes were closed, he casually stepped inside and closed the door. Amalina glimpsed Genadie out in the hall before the door shut, his expression ecstatic—but upon seeing her, suddenly became confused and nervous.

The Count moved to the middle of the library, observing Amalina with his large eyes. His face was no longer caked with blood, but was clean and radiant.

He came all the way to her, even knowing his protection from a flood of destructive sunlight hung heavily on thin wood hooks before the window. Just a light tug would bring it down, wouldn't it?

He trusted her. At least somewhat.

That was information.

"That book," the Count said, absently straightening his old, velvet, crimson tunic under its broad, black leather belt, "again?"

Amalina set the book on the side arm of the chair.

"I was just re-reading it. For ideas."

"Genadie tells me you think I am Zeus. I expected some kind of prepared sacrifice."

"What are you planning to do with the princesses, when they come here?"

"Are they coming to me?" he said peevishly. "I haven't heard. At this point, if it were just one, I would be pleased."

"What are you planning to do with them?"

"I already told you. I'll enjoy their company and partake in the modern joys of this world."

"You aren't planning to kill them. To rip out their throats."

As always, when she brought up the subject, he pursed his lips and looked like the subject was far below him.

"Well, sir, are you?"

"There isn't to be a sacrifice for me, then?" he muttered sarcastically, looking about the room. "You're lucky my mood has improved."

"Are you going to stack their bodies up like cord wood? Or do you plan to begin a boarding house? You have something in mind."

"I will hold court, and entertain them after the fashion, and maybe have a ball if I can. I will enjoy myself, as is my stated pursuit. But they won't come to any harm, if you are really concerned about such a thing happening."

"Do you plan to scare them?"

"Only with pleasure. This is to be Count Tepsji's *Palace of Pleasure*. And if they are frightened because of their delicate upbringing, they will soon get over it, and be laughing at their once childish ways."

"But what happened last night, sir. That wasn't a proper waltz, if you think it was."

"I will hire musicians."

"That's good," Amalina said. "You might also try washing the blood off your face. And taking your victims' hair out of your mouth. And changing into clothes that aren't pasted over with gore ... sir."

The Count looked himself over and touched his cheeks, making sure he was clean.

"What I'm saying is, sir: If you don't want to scare them away, and enrage their parents—which would not stand in service to bringing more of them here, remember—you'll need to hide just what you are."

Amalina touched her finger to the book.

"We've already been over what I am not," he said testily. "That book is worthless rubbish and I should strike it from the library if it is going to give little girls bad ideas. Strigoi, strigoi, strigoi ... Will I never hear the end of it? I am not strigoi."

"If you continue to behave the way you are—the way you really are—then they will suspect you are *something*. And something, moreover, to be scared of. I know—well, just about *everyone* in Ardeel knows your power, and they are afraid of you. But that doesn't make them want to come up and stay with you. So far you just have Genadie, Georg, and Abraxa. You can't count me, because I was taken here against my will. And, anyway, none of us are beautiful princesses, with powerful families, who have the ability to come and go as they please. They will not stay for a horror show."

"I have lived in civilization. I can be discreet. Just ask Erik and Lady Flauna, they never suspected."

"Until they came to your castle," Amalina said. "Then they knew. Erik and Lady Flauna and Odetta and Kralov. All of them knew there was something wrong. And that is what I am talking about, sir. Everyone else will cower before you, but the ladies you've invited here will not stay long if you don't learn how to mask yourself properly."

The Count sat down. "I've lived for a very long time—"

"I know, sir."

He smirked. Then he motioned for her to continue.

"So I don't know what you are. And you don't really know what you are."

"I am not a 'what', I am a 'who'. And I know exactly *who* I am."

"You need blood. You need it to survive. Or to give you energy. Or … ?"

"Blood brings me power." His eyes were level on her, with a small spark of interest—of course he was interested, they were discussing *him*—but also with a bit of caution, as if he'd never spoken on a subject that could be dangerous. "A lot of power."

"How often do you need it?'

"I cannot say. I do not need it unless I want to thrive, to do things. Then, what I require is how much I will expend. Or the other way round. Everything needs power to go. I can do many things, many extraordinary things. But then I need power."

"So you don't know, say, how much you require. How long have you gone without it?"

He shook his head. "I've never needed to go without."

"You've never tried?"

"I don't know a man who has gone without food if he can afford it, or it doesn't sicken him."

"It doesn't sicken—uh, it doesn't bother you that you kill people?"

"They will die without me. Everyone on this plane dies … except me." He sounded a bit saddened at the concept. "It is what I need to do. I can't help it."

"But you haven't tried?"

He shook his head.

"Why don't you?" she asked. "Just as an experiment."

"Is this some method to kill me? No, I don't think you're trying for that. You're really trying to … to help me in some way?"

"Yes."

"I don't need it."

"You should at least try."

"Why?"

"I already explained. What blood do you need? Just women's?"

"I prefer the female. Their essence is richer, it seems to have more energy—more vitality to it. The male is weaker, and leaves an unpleasant aftertaste which lasts."

"But you can use men."

"In a pinch."

"How young and how old?"

"I cannot stomach children. The old are too thin."

"Too thin?"

"Not as much energy for me."

"But you can stomach them."

"The female preferred," he reminded her. He was enjoying himself again. He sat forward.

"Yes, the female preferred. But you can stomach them: the old. Don't you think it might be more tolerable ... or less frightening ... or less objectionable, anyway, if you would use the blood of the aged, those who are near death, than the young? Some might even—or *you* might even—consider it a service to help those who are suffering to reach heaven quicker."

"Or hell, and the King would pay me a coin for every body I retired from his prisons," he said, sarcasm returning. "No, even when I was removing the dreaded Ottomans, I was considered too much—a step too far away from their god. I would be despised all the same. Believe me, I provide services, more than anyone would admit, and I am the eternal monster for all the petty monsters that rise anew in the next spring of generations. And besides, for my history they would have me the first executed."

"But they can't have you executed, because, first off, you wouldn't allow it," she explained. "And so they would still prefer if you'd take those of us who've lived a full life, or a loathsome and condemned life, than rob the ones just beginning it. You understand that, don't you?"

"The way things are is best. I've lived a long life, and the patterns and habits I developed aren't by caprice, but have formed naturally. It's the way nature and providence deemed it to be, and who am I to argue?"

She argued it was his own best interest to try everything he could to understand who he was, and his limits. And to take advantage of anything that would make peace with the rest of the world.

"I *am* at peace with the world."

"You're at a truce," Amalina argued. "And I can tell you it makes nobody happy. And if they find some way to kill you, they'll do it gladly. And if they can make your life unhappy, and stand in your way any way they can, they will do that, too. Up to the point of letting you know they're doing it and you come after them. Wouldn't it be better if everyone were really, truly happy? and satisfied?"

"That never happens."

"Well, you aren't very happy now, are you? You want all the pretty princesses to visit, don't you? And you don't want them to run off the second they find out you are a despised monster."

There was a gasp outside the library door. Then a thud. Amalina had been talking too loud, Genadie had not only heard her not giving reverence to his beloved Zeus, but called him a monster to his face.

"He didn't know I was going to say all this," Amalina said with a concerned look. "He thought I was just going to pray to you."

The Count didn't know what she was talking about. He was staring, his mind actively contemplating a new way of life.

"Besides humans," she continued, ignoring Genadie to pursue a purpose the Count was warming to, "what about the blood of animals?"

The Count almost came out of his chair. He lurched forward and his hands snarled together like the legs of a dying insect. "No ... No, no, no, no, no, no, no," he said. "No. One thousand times, *no*. We are incompatible. Mortal blood is necessary—"

"Would animal blood harm you if you ate it?"

"It would disgust me. Like the many other things I won't speak of here. I could drink it. I could drink piss. Both would be as harmful as they would be satisfying. No. Listen: Human blood. Feminine. Move on."

"And it's strictly the blood you consume from your ... uh, from the, uh ..." she didn't want to say victim again. "Nothing else but the blood is what you want. You don't need the skin or the muscle, or anything else from us?"

The Count resettled. He nodded slowly, steepling his fingertips underneath his chin.

"All right, blood," she said. "But must you drink it *all*? Couldn't you just take a little, enough to restore you, but not drain a fair soul completely? so that they don't die?"

The Count did not answer, but his lips shifted against themselves, not deciding on a final shape. She couldn't interpret it.

"Have you ever done that? Just taken what you strictly need?"

"I am a creature of instinct," he said at length. "I am drawn to the hunt. And the kill."

"I thought you were drawn to the blood."

"In the moment it becomes ... out of my control."

"You can't put it under your control, sir? You've never tried, sir?"

He shook his head.

"You see the advantage, though. The loss of our people is what upsets us most. If you weren't killing us ... and so many of us ... and so many innocents ..."

"Do you intend to change my nature?"

"That's not the right way to look at it, sir. Don't say it's your nature. You see? It looks like you've just accepted your curse instead of putting up resistance to it," she groused in frustration. "How do you expect to hide this curse of yours from the princesses, should they come? Unless you *plan* to scare them away."

"I find it curious you refer to my heightened senses, my unmatchable speed, and my strength, which is enough to lift the world upon my shoulders, a curse."

"Well, it isn't doing you any good if ..." No, that line of attack wasn't going to work. But she had to say something: "Now, sir, you've told me yourself—remember that talk you had with me last winter?—you grew up with power, and all you understood was power. And it was your royal upbringing and education to take land and destroy your enemies. And this *gift* you have, all it did was allow you to do all that. But never mind that *I'd* consider it a curse. Because along with your abilities the sunlight will wilt you like a fragile little flower. And it has you scared half to death to escape your nation's physical boundaries to enjoy the rest of the world the way you'd like. Never mind all that. It's a curse because all your advantages played into what you were taught, and never gave you a reason to think in any other way. You hunt, you kill, you threaten good people with destruction just to get your way. And because you're stronger than anyone else, you can get away with it. But there is also the advantage of being subtle, and restraining yourself. Maybe by withholding your powers you don't get everything as perfectly and as fast as you want it, but you have all the time you want, so speed means nothing. You don't even get perfection as it is now, you just get what you can get, and upset everyone around you by the way you go about doing it. If you tried something different, if you'd test yourself like in one of your scientific experiments, you may discover an advantage in doing things a little differently."

Amalina took in a big breath, and then let it all out in a sigh.

"You are saying," said the Count, "it is both a gift *and* a curse."

"I'm saying your truce could be made into a better *peace*," she hoped she wasn't coming off like she was pleading, but confident and serious, and convincing. That he would accept what she was saying like an intriguing line of reason in some scientific text he'd read, and not someone—a little girl— simply trying to counter his will. "I'm saying maybe you don't have to outright kill people to get your blood. That maybe death isn't necessary. What do you think?"

"Some of them are," he said cryptically. "But it *could* be a start. Perhaps. I do see that. Yesss."

"Good. Well, there's one last thing, then, sir. And since we still have the whole afternoon to plan, you'll be able to begin your greatest challenge when night comes!"

"Challenge?'

"And if you succeed, you'll be free." To sell it: "You *do* want to be free, sir, don't you?"

19

The Hidden Room

The map he pulled off the shelf was old. Its paper crackled and dropped off in amber chips when it was unfolded. She readied the quill and ink (which were still in the library, next to her inventory). It took an hour for him to add to the map all the villages and towns, the roads and highways, that had sprouted and grown in Ardeel over the centuries. It might have been the spidery way the Count drew the ink across the page, but it struck Amalina that the activity of humanity within the mountains resembled the network of veins in the body, with the villages and towns like clots forming in nooks and pockets. Also, she noticed the names of the towns weren't quite how she knew them to be: Korr—which was her village and which she would naturally look for first—was Korgzi; Netz—where they were nearest, presently—was written as Agnetz; Kirgyl was Amroszji; and Tsobl was Tosjosiblivscu. Placed near every large town was a little claw-like symbol she assumed to denote a castle.

"You only trust castles to your safety," said Amalina, more confirming than inquiring.

"I never said that."

"You don't trust carriages."

"I don't trust anything that can crash, break down, fall apart, be shot to pieces, burn up, and doesn't allow me room to move." He looked down his nose at her, impatiently, as if to say *is that good enough for you?*

"But, anyway, you don't need roads the way you travel."

"Roads only slow me down."

"Do you … can I ask you, sir? Do you … change yourself? Do you become an animal? Like one of those pigeons? Or bats?"

"Or owls, or wolves, or centipedes, or a cloud if I feel like it. Many different things. Most things. Anything."

"Can you become a star in the sky?" It would be too much for Amalina if he said yes. She held her breath and her skin tingled.

"No."

"What's the fastest creature you can be?" she said quickly, to hide her relief. "A falcon?"

"If you're asking me how far I can travel over a given length of time," he supposed, and then he put his thumb and forefinger onto the map, sizing and resizing the distance between them over different pieces of terrain. She couldn't tell if he wanted to hurry things along or he wanted to preserve some of his trade secrets. But he was giving her this much. "Depending on the wind, and just how high I have to go to summit a mountain, and the energy I have within me … I can go about *this* far on an average night. Shorter on summer nights, and much farther on the longest winter night. But winter also has the cold and the elements that might work against me. So, let's say *this* far, as an average. Do you know what I mean by an 'average'?"

"Yes."

"Yes, of course you do," he smiled admiringly, almost with pride. "You are Dragomir Dalca's daughter, after all. My golden find."

She let the comment pass. He needed to get out of the castle at sundown.

"So," said Amalina, "where is the closest town outside of Ardeel that lay beyond your reach?"

He nodded, studied the map with a quick glance over, like he was just verifying that his first assessment had been correct.

"Of course, yes; easy enough," he said in a low rumble. He pointed to an area to the north of the Ardeelian mountain ranges, where there was a small town icon. "That is my gate to the west." Then he drew his finger in a gently sloping southwesterly direction, and stopped in a fold of mountain which had a grouping of odd scratches and squiggles. "My hidden castle is near here. This is the narrowest point between Ardeel and a viable path out of it. Near the Borgo Pass. Starting from the pass …"

He pushed his finger back and forth, his nail scraping the map's brittle surface. His gaze was heavy-lidded and seemed to suggest frustration, or sorrow, at his inability to travel such a small distance. A distance his fingertips could traverse in seconds.

"How far is that?" she asked.

"You can see it on the map," he tapped the map to help her.

"But how far, exactly?"

"What's the difference? It's too far. It exceeds my range."

"How do you know this for a fact? Have you tried it?"

The Count shook his head. Then shrugged, and added tartly that he didn't have a taste to go all the way to his hidden castle just to disappoint himself.

"What's the farthest you've gotten at any one time?"

"When I was chasing the sultan's grandson and his army." He played his fingers on the southern edges of the map. "But those were the days when the sun wasn't as heavy against me, and I just lay in a well when it reached noon-time and I felt I needed a rest. If I tried that again …" His lips became small and turned downward. "My Queen … She said I would be safer to keep within my territories. She might have been right then. Maybe. She didn't know it, but she trapped me here ... in this damned *squash*; its walls too thick to ever leave. And sometimes I think she did it on purpose. So I couldn't leave *her*."

Amalina used the feather of her pen to measure the distance between the Borgo Pass and the unnamed town outside the mountains. Then she found a small talon shape near Netz, which she figured demarked the high castle— or was it the *Palace of Pleasure*?—and then turned the feather in all directions, almost like a broom, with one eye shut, the other scouting sharply. She spotted another talon shape at almost the very edge of the feather. Several rows of squiggles—mountain ranges—stood between the one point and the next.

"What's this here?" she said. "A castle? Is it yours?"

"It's nobody's," he said. "It was destroyed."

"Could you hide yourself in there?"

"I don't hide," he muttered heavily.

"I mean, if you go there can you stay out of the sunlight during the day?"

"It isn't complete rubble. But there are other castles of my own that are along that line, if you can see."

"But they simply aren't far enough, sir. You need to reach this one. You see, if you can make it there—and right now isn't even the season of long nights—you could reach that outside town up *here*, couldn't you, if you use the Borg pass?" She tapped the talon with the brush of the feather: "This will be your test. You can try tonight. If you don't think you can make it, then there are your other castles en route you can leave off. But you *must* do it."

"Why tonight?"

"What else are you going to do?"

"Hunt."

"You had your blood last night, sir. Or was it the night before? But, no matter, you do it now while you have nothing else preventing you, and you can concentrate on that alone. It'll take your mind off your wait for the princesses. Even if we heard from them today, they couldn't be coming before a month or so, when all the arrangements and details are accepted and confirmed. You only have to race as fast as you can tonight, and then return tomorrow night. And you will have your answer."

The Count stared at the map, excitement and temptation causing him to tug at a mustache that wasn't there.

• • •

Before Amalina could find Abraxa, the old woman was on her: "Why did you bring his eminence in there? Huh? Did you show him Georg's mistake?"

"No," she said, trying to calm her down. "That isn't it at all."

"I don't know where the little rat dug up that bell, but I should have known you were behind it. And what do you do but lead him into this room. And for what? For what mischief, I ask you?"

"Count Tepsji planned to make a tour of the library, to see for himself that everything was in order before his guests arrive. I just thought I'd get him in here during the day, when he isn't at the height of his powers. And I made sure to steer him away from Georg's missing books. That's what I did."

Abraxa came to a full stop. Her eyes widened, as if Amalina had suddenly been lit up by an angelic beam from the sky.

"And now I'm going to need that key. He mentioned he might be traveling tonight, and if he does, this is our moment. Now go and get it for me. And make sure Geor—um, your husband—doesn't suspect what we really plan to do with it."

"If our eminence is leaving for the night," Abraxa whispered greedily, "and you know it's true, let's use all the keys we can, just to make sure and get it all over at once."

"*Perfect*," Amalina said, taking Abraxa's quick switch of emotions in stride. Then felt dismay at having used one of the monster's pet words. Perfect! To get his echoing voice out of her head, she added: "Even better."

• • •

The Count left the high castle not long after sundown. Amalina knew it was so when she heard the screech of hundreds of bats, first circling the upper floors of the main building, then floating off into the sky. It was probably the earliest she'd ever known him to leave the castle—except the evening he killed Erik and went after Katrina Flauna, Odetta and Kralov. On that occasion, the last spark of light had just died at the crest of the mountain, parts of the sky still a pure blue. She would never forget it. It was one of the last things she'd seen as she plunged out of the tower, helplessly strapped to a chair, down toward the courtyard stones below.

Abraxa met Amalina in a hall, and handed her a roll of leather cloth that was hard and clanked a little when it hit her palm. The keys to the high castle. She couldn't believe it was this easy.

"Let's go," said Abraxa. She was still holding one end of the key-roll.

"No, you have to go keep Georg busy. Or at least out of my way."

"He won't bother us. And, anyway, if he catches us—"

"—He will—"

"—I'll just tell him you're helping me clean."

"But we've been over this before, Abraxa. Nothing must look out of place. When would I help you with cleaning? When would you let me? *Never* is the answer."

"You were pretty good about it down in the cellars," she smiled sharply. "Didn't you? I told him all about it. Then I told him I was taking you as my apprentice. So there you are. Let's go."

"Wait," Amalina put a hand on her arm to stop her. "We aren't going to do it now. Not yet."

"Isn't our *grand royale* gone for the night? He instructed Georg he was leaving for a day or so. There's nothing to worry about while we have the time."

"Just because he said one thing doesn't mean it's true, or he meant it. He could have forgotten something and turn back at any minute."

"So what? We're just cleaning, little mouse. Aren't we?" the faintest, half-hearted smile flashed for an uneasy second. "What are you worrying about?"

Amalina gritted her teeth, knowing it was of primary importance to get into the private study alone. Abraxa would never let her open the secret door, much less let her into a secret room, or passage, or whatever lay behind it.

"We do have to be quick about it," Amalina agreed, tugging the roll from Abraxa's controlling fingers.

She opened the leather and looked at all the keys there. More than she'd ever seen Genadie carry. She couldn't imagine where they all led to. And though she saw that there was a variation in their lengths and teeth, they all looked the same to her. The private study's key would be impossible to pick out. She shifted them hopelessly and the fragrance of oil wafted up.

"Oh," Amalina said, sounding overwhelmed. "So many. What we should do is split them, you take half and I'll take half."

"No. I'm with you. We're together."

"But it'll be much faster if we split them."

"But the cleaning will go quicker with an apprentice in tow," Abraxa said in return, licking her non-existent lips nervously.

Whatever her reason, it was obvious Abraxa didn't want to let Amalina out of her sight. She still hadn't established any lasting trust. There had to be a way to do it, even with a woman who was dedicated to her husband. In the way Sadra, the minister's wife, could ply away a wife from her spouse and make her drop any kind of secret, just by appealing to the hidden strings that connected all of womankind—as thick metal chains seemed to hold the men in their bonded brotherhood. Amalina had watched Sadra work her near-mystical powers on many women in the side rooms of their church, getting them to admit to the most embarrassing marriage troubles, even with three or four other wives standing witness.

Amalina was too young at the time. She hadn't paid enough attention; she hadn't taken the lesson. It was beyond her ability to pry as Sadra could, and she wasn't going to be able to learn it now—or fake it.

"Maybe we can make this faster than it looks. He'd only have the books in some of the rooms. Let's go through them. Which one does this belong to?"

"I thought you said you used these keys!"

"I said I'd only go into the rooms I've already been in. But I wouldn't recognize a key to a certain room if I saw it."

But as she said it, she spotted the one to the Count's private study. The large, looping head of it was distinctive, and she remembered the feel of it in her hand. She grabbed that one first.

"The study. That's the most likely. Now what are these others?"

It was painful counting through the rest, knowing the one she wanted she already had. She knew it would be best to pay attention, though, because she might learn of other rooms she hadn't been into or seen. But it turned out there wasn't one place in the entire pile of keys that she hadn't been—even the Great Library and the bird loft. And the only one restricted at present was the private study, which she was holding in her hand. So Georg hadn't given Abraxa *all* the keys. He couldn't have. There had to be so many more. There were still locked doors she hadn't been through, which would presumably have keys.

Or had the Count not fully come to trust Georg, and hadn't given *him* all the keys. An odd relationship for the head of staff, not to have the head of the household's complete confidence.

"Wait!" Amalina held her finger up in the air as she'd done in the cellar. And she turned her head, eyes looking from one ceiling corner to the other. Abraxa shrunk, her shoulders touching her ears.

"I don't hear anything," she said.

"You know ... *he* could come back any time he wants. There's no saying that he's actually going to be gone as long as he said. It might even be a test, and he will return no sooner than we've started. And in a place he didn't wish us to clean. He might like our tidiness, but he might also get suspicious. We can't have that."

Now Abraxa's eyes pinched, but they radiated her anger and frustration well enough.

"Not to worry, my dear." Amalina paused, wondering what had caused her to express that term of affection, 'my dear.' Even Abraxa blinked at it. "We'll get to every one of them, I promise, as long as we know we're safe."

"How can we be any safer from discovery than at our Master's just departing on a long voyage?"

"The middle of that voyage. When we know he's already gone, and how long it will take for him to get back. If he doesn't return tonight, it means he will be gone for the whole day, and won't return, at the very least, until the night. So we just have to wait until tomorrow morning."

Abraxa nodded. *That* made sense. Even if sneaking around behind Georg and *his majesty*'s back still troubled her. With their new plan established, and rendezvous times and locations arranged, they both headed off for some sleep.

• • •

Just after midnight, Amalina entered the Count's private study. The flaming head of the torch she held low, causing flickering shadows to crawl up and along the walls. She closed and locked the door behind her.

But for the whispering hiss and crackle of the torch, it was as if the darkness sucked all the other sounds out of the air. She couldn't hear her breath, or beating heart. She listened for the Count, for movement, for Abraxa outside the door. For any warning against doing what she was about to do.

The images of Lucinda and Kralov appeared on either side of the room, stuck in bracketing corners, one smiling and excited, the other frowning with arms folded across his massive chest. They did not urge her, but she understood their meaning. She only had to blink to remove them, but was left with equal parts thrill and sense of seriousness of purpose.

For one brief moment, silly as it was, Amalina's eyes scanned the Count's desk for the library's missing books. Of course they wouldn't be there. But it was as if she need to look there just so she could tell Abraxa that she'd done so, and so not come off as a complete liar.

The cabinet was much taller than Amalina. She tried pushing its side at an angle away from the wall, the way she'd seen it opened when the Count had done it. It didn't budge. She pulled a chair over to reach the top of it, for what she assumed was some latch or other device to unlock the cabinet from the wall. It wasn't hard to find. A large block ran along the inside of a groove there. She felt it. She poked at it. She tried pushing it inward. Then sliding it from side to side. She stopped when it let off a loud *clack* and the cabinet shifted.

Amalina got off the chair, kicking it aside so quickly the legs skidded loudly and it almost tipped over. She begged it not to fall, waving at it, trying to catch it with her free hand. It came down on all fours and stayed.

She pushed against the cabinet. She thought it would swing aside like a door, the way it had done for the Count. But it must've weighed more than a horse. It was like trying to pull or push White Snow out of his stall. It did not open, even when she pivoted and braced her back against it and shoved with all her strength. Her feet slipped on the stone floor as she tried again and again.

It had opened so easily for the Count. But he was very strong, and capable of almost any feat. Even throwing aside a massive cabinet with the flick of his finger. No matter she'd gotten the latch open, the cabinet was an impossible obstruction in and of itself.

She slumped onto the chair and stared fixedly at the problem. No answers came to mind besides fire and explosives. But there would be no hiding what she'd done if she tried that route. Maybe she could knock out the back of the cabinet to get what was behind it? She opened its doors. Inside the cabinet were many smaller shelves, all of them dedicated to rolls of fine fabrics and gowns. She would have to pull everything out, knock out the shelves along with the backboard if she wanted through it. Something to do if she had no other choice.

She attacked the side of the cabinet, running at it and ramming full into it, and coming at it at an angle to push it out and swing it away—as it had swung open at the gentlest pressure by the Count! It seemed to move. But looking to where it met the wall, the wood was still flush with the stone. The stone here was perfectly flat, not permitting her to dig her fingernails in, or insert the edge of a fireplace's andirons (all of which had been blunted, so that the irons were as dull and almost as thick as a thumb). Without something narrow and sharp, she couldn't work or wedge anything between the wood and the wall.

Well, what was she to do? Bring a horse in to budge it open? White Snow couldn't be trusted.

It *wouldn't* take a horse to do it. She was sure just one more person would do.

Genadie?

Could she ask him to help her do such a thing? To invade the hidden inner-workings of the castle? Did he know about the cabinet's secret entrance and what it concealed? Would he be curious enough to help her get inside and not tell the Count?

Whatever they found on the other side, he wouldn't let her touch, or take anything, or stay too long to learn anything of importance. He'd see it as a violation of Zeus' privacy. And without a reason for breaking it, it would be a criminal act, no doubt. Something he'd be too guilty to hold as a secret for long. If he didn't just report it outright as the regular squealer he was. He couldn't help himself around his beloved.

She charged the cabinet. From the pain and sound, her shoulder popped its socket.

. . .

Abraxa was ready early, already knocking discreetly at Amalina's door before the sun was above the mountain's shoulder. They sat quietly and watched from the window as the purple sky turned to pink and then to blue.

"He didn't come in the night," Abraxa said eagerly. "I'm sure of it."

There hadn't been any warning sounds from the animals of his return. Not that Amalina had heard, anyway. So she could only agree.

"We have all day then," the old woman said with the body shaking impatience of a child, "But let's get it over with. Go down there now and look."

Amalina rubbed her sore shoulder and nodded.

"He isn't up yet." Abraxa meant her husband. "I can wait outside his room while you do it. Get him to help me with starting the fires if he wakes."

Amalina nodded.

"Is something wrong, Mouse?"

Amalina shook her head, rubbing her shoulder again, wincing at the pain.

"You've hurt yourself? What's the matter?" Abraxa came close and gently touched around Amalina's arm, seeking where she was sore.

"I was just being silly and banged myself. It's nothing, really. Let's get on with it."

It didn't take very long to go down to the room. Abraxa sped off in her own direction while Amalina took the study. With a sigh she pressed herself to the cabinet. For a brief second she thought the big box would obey. She would feel it give.

Then she sat back down on the chair, as she had last night, and stared lightning bolts, while rubbing her shoulder and thinking angry thoughts.

Right on the other side of the cabinet: a treasure of new information. But she could not reach it. Not alone. If Kralov were there, that giant could help her throw it aside. But the only people she had close to her were fawning subjects of the Count. Not one of them a likely candidate for the revolutionaries.

Amalina sat up straight. She snapped her finger and ran from the room.

"Just be quiet," she said as she reentered the Count's private study, pulling Abraxa along with her.

"But I still don't understand."

"I thought you wanted to come with me, so what's the matter now?"

Abraxa stood inside the door, unable to bring herself fully into the room. But her eyes were wide, and they flicked around, searching in the dark for anything that looked book-shaped. "Over there? What about over there?"

"I already looked. It's not a book." Amalina took her arm and guided her into the room. "That's not why I needed you, Abraxa. I just completely forgot that I'd need your help with this."

Amalina positioned the old woman on the side of the cabinet, and demonstrated what she wanted her to do: they would both push against it.

"What are we doing?"

"We're opening the door."

"What door?"

"This."

"This isn't a door, it's a large cabinet. And the doors are in the front."

"But it's also a door," Amalina said, pretending it should have been obvious. "Wait, you didn't know that?"

"Know what?"

"That this is a secret door."

"No. What's behind it?"

Amalina felt a light sweat burst on her forehead. Her cheeks must have gone red, too: her natural response to lying, and a sure giveaway to anyone who could read the signal. Amalina decided to hide it by huffing and puffing and pushing against the cabinet.

"Come, Abraxa," she grunted. "Help me."

"But where does it lead?"

"If you don't know," she said, "then how could I tell you, in all good conscience?"

"You don't know." Abraxa narrowed her grey eyes with suspicion. "I think you don't."

Amalina protested. "What do you mean? Of course I know."

"I think you don't know, and you're just trying to snoop around."

"What's the matter with you, Abraxa?" Amalina cried, giving up on pushing the cabinet on her own. Maybe even with Abraxa it wouldn't move, she thought. "Of course I'm trying to snoop around! To help you and Georg! It isn't anywhere I haven't been before, you know, but I need to get inside to look. I didn't realize Count Tepsji would close it up when he left."

"So you've seen it open?"

"Of course. It's almost always open when I'm in here with him. If you're saying it isn't open when you're in here, well, what does it say about how much he trusts you?"

Abraxa shook her head, a shamed expression spreading. But Amalina knew she couldn't let her have any more air to make a counter-attack. She had to press while she had the advantage.

"If you're worried because I called it a secret entrance," Amalina chided, "it doesn't mean it's secret for me. If it was supposed to be off limits to me, how would I even know about it? It's just I don't have the strength to open it on my own. You know how the Count is, he could probably lift a mountain. I'm a little girl. Now help me."

"Not so little," said Abraxa, still wary, but joined now in the effort against the cabinet.

The cabinet bucked over a stopping point. And then, grudgingly, it slid outward and at an angle, as if on a hinge. Amalina and Abraxa had to press, and push, and rock together against the wood, straining to move it a quarter inch at a time. Amalina had positioned herself on the inside, and she greedily kept ducking her head to the opening. But there was no light inside and she could see nothing through the widening crack. There was a small breeze, with an herbal, moldy smell carried on it.

Abraxa fell to the ground gasping. They'd gotten it open only a foot or so wide. Amalina got the torch and thrust it into the opening. Sticking her head in, she found a long room crammed with shelves and several tall desks.

"All right, I think I can get in," Amalina told Abraxa. "You go back to Georg and keep him away until I come and get you. Just make sure he doesn't come in here."

"Why don't I wait for you?" she said, panting. Her eyebrow cocked over her left eye. The woman was an addict to suspicion. "Pop in, Mouse, and have a look."

"I can't just pop in. And it might take a little. You have no idea how big this place is, do you? Well, I can't tell you if Count Tepsji doesn't trust you. And it's bad enough I let you know about it. As a matter of fact, you'd better never tell Georg a thing about this—absolutely not, for any reason—because he'll know the consequences for learning something forbidden ... and that's assuming he even knows about this door and what's beyond it. I'd be surprised if he didn't, but since you weren't let in on it, there's no telling that he was, either. Trust me, though, I won't say anything to Count Tepsji about it. I'm on your side, remember. I wouldn't want to see either of you hurt for something as meaningless as his truest allies learning a little confidential nothing. Anyway, keep quiet and wait for me to come get you, so we can close the door."

Abraxa nodded her head; the old woman abjectly warned and admonished. She slunk from the room like a wounded cat, tail between the legs, with just a quick look of embarrassment over her shoulder before she closed the door.

Amalina locked it immediately. Then she entered the hidden room.

20

The Counting House

Once inside, the room was more massive than she'd been able to see by her brief glance. It was a vast vault, with shelves that reached the ceiling along every wall. The room wasn't as big as the Great Library, but it was impressive. In the middle, the floor descended by several stairs, making the far side of the room that much deeper. The shelves were almost entirely occupied by cloth bags, whose contents were (uniformly) square and solid. She prodded one of these bags with her finger. The contents were solid as wood. A small chest? A stack of books? She was tempted to take one down and open it.

She had hours to search. So long as Genadie or Georg didn't begin asking where she was. Or they and Abraxa grew impatient and came looking for her. Or the Count impossibly returned while the sun was still in the sky. This meant she actually had all day long—literally, until sunset—to investigate.

She tried to lift a sack. It stuck to the shelf as if it were part of it. As usual, this castle was made for and revolved around the Count, and so many of the items inside it were fitting only for his extreme abilities. He could open the weighty cabinet like a normal door, and lift one of these bags between two fingers no doubt.

Bags were meant to be opened. Amalina leaned down to one on a lower shelf, holding the torch as close as she could without setting fire to everything. And with one hand loosened a string knot and tugged the top of the sack loose. Its insides glittered. Whatever was there, it was cool to the touch. Sticking her head between the racks, the torch closer still, she saw the blocks of gold. One stacked upon another in ranks, filling the bag to capacity. Not books after all, this was the Count's treasury. She poked the neighboring bags in every direction and they were the same. Bags upon bags of gold.

Spinning in place to take it all in, to estimate its worth, this room's contents was the boundless horde of a dragon. Impossible to conceive in scale, much less calculate. The only difference was that the Count was a real being, and a creature of order, and had bound it all up neatly and shelved it. He could purchase the whole continent with such a fortune, and turn it into one giant castle—if he wanted.

The closest desk had a book, an ornate quill, a glass of ink, and a small oil lamp on it. The book was bound in a soft, cheap looking leather, stuffed thick with pages, longer than it was tall. Amalina could guess what was inside before she flipped it open: it was a ledger. An account of all the money contained here within. The only surprise for Amalina was that it began messily, with little thought to proper organization. The entries were not only weights of gold, but lands and their dimensions, homes, buildings, and castles and their dimensions. Numbers and properties were written in and then scratched out. Debts written in and then their payments recorded. Cross-outs were circumnavigated by their corrections. By the dates, it was begun nearly a century ago.

Jumping to the last used page, marked off by a leather strap, the entire process of the book had changed. Now there were organized columns, distinguished by well-ruled lines. But what was written in were not numbers, but letters she was unfamiliar with. And even the descriptions of the transactions were written in characters she'd never seen before. It wasn't the glyphs from the cryptic pigeon message, and could be understood as a definite language. However, it was a language alien to her. She couldn't tell what the final tally of numbers were. By the length of the string of letters, a nonsensical sentence, she could assume the amount was beyond belief.

The other desk, several steps away along the long wall, was set up for a different kind of industry. There was a square stone pedestal beside it, looking like a tall, hollow mortar. In its deep cup were ashes. Small fires had frequently been set inside it. On the desk were metal cups and clamps and tools she could not interpret their use. The surface of the wood was burnt and charred in places, describing round and squared shapes. A thick set of leather gloves hung off a hook, and from several other hooks were leather bags. She recognized these bags. They were the same color and roughness, and with the same leather ties, of the coin purses Genadie brought along on the trip to the western kingdoms, as well as the excursions to Netz to make their purchases. Moving a couple iron blocks around, she found the circular depressions in them, with images in relief at the bottom. These were molds. This desk was the Count's foundry, where he melted the gold down and used the iron block charges to forge his coins.

Amalina observed the room again in whole. So it was all just blocks of gold? No jewels? No rings? No necklaces? No crowns? No pearl inlaid chalices? Not so much a dragon's horde. So unlike the castle treasuries recounted in fables and romances. The organization was not romantic in the least. It was cold and industrious, and lacked all human charm. It stopped feeling like anything really valuable to Amalina. They could have been walls of lead blanks and it would be the same.

Still, she had to recognize that there was an untold fortune here, enough to incite the greed and launch a king's army to get at it. And it was all being guarded by some old stone walls manned by a young girl, a crooked little wreck, and a pair of ancient grovelers. In other words, it was for the taking. As long as someone knew where to look for it.

She moved to the end of the room just to poke a few more bags, to confirm all was what it seemed. Her breath caught in her mouth as she discovered, near the end of the room, that the shelving on the left wall quit before the corner. There was a new door, or a passage. She hurried to it. And then she gasped.

What lay past this recessed entrance was a room almost five times the size as the counting house, the treasury, perhaps more than that of the Great Library. The torchlight barely reached the far wall, and it faltered at the floor and the ceiling. A set of stone stairs descended some yards below. This room was lined with shelving, just as the treasury and library, but also boasted a central row of large but somewhat shorter shelves. One could see over them, from front to back of the room, from the stairs. And where the shelves in the counting house and library were packed full and neatly arranged, the shelves here felt alive. They were bursting with disorganization, with all kinds of papers and books and scrolls and whatever else shoved into it. No flashes of metal bars or coins. It was a storehouse of papers.

Block letters were cut and painted into the front of the shelves. Names. Names of towns, names of cities. The largest section of shelves it seemed was devoted to Tsobl. Logical enough.

She had passed by a tall desk at the foot of the stairs, now she returned to it. On it was a large, leather-bound book that was flipped open to the middle. Pasted onto its pages were bits of paper she recognized immediately. They were the messages carried by the pigeons. The last one pasted into it was the one she'd seen already, the one Genadie and the Count had feared lost. It had been smoothed out and glued in to fit into the mosaic. *'Troubl wit yer servants …'* it read. Looking around to the other strips, she saw the mysterious characters. All of them had it. Which meant this last one *had* been written in haste—as the splattering, scrawling nature of the text had suggested—with no time for the writer to transcribe it into the proper secret code.

A sentence in the margin below it, written by the count, said as much: *Precautions forgotten in haste.*

Amalina turned to the first leaf of the book, and saw that the first page of messages were written in her native language. It was a different hand than the one that had written the last entry. Flipping back and forth, she also noted that the Count had set a date down below the last one: the day it was received in the castle. The first page did not have any markings around the messages, but they had been simply stuck in somewhat haphazard. They told of movements of names she didn't recognize. Where they'd been last seen. Where it was thought so-and-so was headed. How large a force was.

What kind of weaponry could be expected. What arms were being manufactured by the blacksmiths. They were brief flashes of urgent information, trapped on a wide, stiff, yellow rectangle of vellum. The count didn't begin dating the entries until the seventh page. Just like the ledger in the treasury, it began little over a century before. So these messages were beyond ancient. From a time before her grandfather's father. Twenty more pages past that, the messages changed to the weird characters used in the later ones. In the remaining she scanned, she only spotted one or two that had proper language: *"They're coming now"*; *"Sundown comes early she said. Check the clouds, though. Maybe earlier then."*. Flipping back and forth, she noted that his secret writing began only a little over twenty years ago. She closed the book and saw a title pressed onto the leather: *"Warnings."*

She left the book open to the page as she'd found it. She studied the desk. There was a small pot of paste. A horse-hair brush caked with glue set on top of it. There was a covered cup of ink, a miniature blade for trimming nibs, a blackened blotting cloth, and a long, beautiful quill fashioned from the feather of a bird she'd never seen before. Its plume was large and colorful. Along the top ledge of the desk was written an alphabet. Something like she'd seen in a book of instruction, but it repeated several times from one edge of the desk to the other. She opened the desk's thin drawer and its contents rattled. Inside were long strips of wood, and a set of five keys.

Amalina noticed the weight of the torch. She'd been holding it for too long, her injured shoulder began to throb. There was a stand for a torch nearby. She used it.

Fishing her hands into the drawer, she brought some of the wooden sticks into the light. On several sides were hieroglyphs, similar to the strange shapes she'd seen on the message she'd taken, but not exactly so. This was it! The solution to his code! Or was it? She shoved the stick below the strip of alphabet running along the top of the desk. The separate sets of characters were spaced the same. Placing the stick's edge before the A, the odd characters finished at the end of the alphabet.

Yes. He'd developed his own code!

Some of the sticks had the same characters, but their order was changed. Others had a new kind of code altogether, with weird loops and symbols. On the ends of several of the sticks were letters, or numbers. Something to differentiate one from the other. She didn't find any stick with characters matching the one on the message hidden upstairs in her bedroom. Its characters were most peculiar, and she was sure she would recognize it if she saw it. She bit her lip. So frustrating to know one half the solution, but not the other.

Maybe just knowing this would help.

Five keys in the drawer. They were organized from large to small. They were plain iron, thick and sturdy. Nothing delicate. What she'd imagine for a dungeon, or the locks for shackles.

She put the sticks back in the drawer and shut it.

This room was a crush of intelligence, and she had no time to go through it. Even if she grabbed something at random off the shelf and got it to Kralov, Amalina doubted he'd appreciate it. He'd be just as frustrated knowing there was still a mountain more material hidden from him. If only she could bring him here, or one of his agents, and she could guarantee him enough time. They might find something useful to exploit.

She roamed the room. This time she paid attention to the organization of the shelves. They weren't in alphabetical order, or numerical order, but seemingly at random. Like he'd just chosen the shelf closest the desk and just started tossing stuff in. And when something else came in of interest from a different area of Ardeel, he would mark it down on a new shelf and begin stocking it there. Maybe there was an order and she couldn't figure it out just yet. She'd have to think about it. But would it really matter? Would it be significant?

Villages, towns, cities. All of them represented, it seemed. Packed with every manner of paper, some in books, some in canisters, some in envelopes, some wrapped, some just loose. They were thrown in carelessly it seemed, like the leftovers of a feast swept as a jumble into the corners to await the next layer. She wanted to take one piece off a shelf. A book, a missive, a scroll, any of them. To see what they were. But now she feared there was some kind of organization she couldn't tell, but the Count would notice immediately if it had been interfered with. The temptation was all the worse at the shelf emblazoned with 'Netz'. This shelf wasn't as large as most of the others, but there was a good buildup. There was more space devoted to her village, Korr, than to Kirgyl. And what of the towns that had been erased from the Ardeelian history—or so the Count had claimed to her, boasting he'd razed them to the ground and eradicated them from the common memory of the people? What of them? There were no shelves dedicated to *them*. There weren't even shelves that had the lettering burned out, the way it was in the Secret History of the Sheriff of Korr.

Maybe the Count's story of razed cities wasn't so true, after all.

On her third tour she noticed, pushed back into the furthest corner, a large trunk. A lock box. And it was locked shut. Amalina measured the size of the key that would open it. Then she nodded.

The largest key from the desk turned its locks and the lid came up. But inside was another, smaller box. Amalina smirked. She struggled and removed it from the trunk. Another lock box. Amalina took the next smaller key from the desk and opened this chest, wondering why something would need to be doubly secured, only to find another chest fitted into it. This was a game. She retrieved the last three keys from the drawer, assuming all would be needed. But what could be inside that was worth this level of security? It couldn't be too valuable, considering that it couldn't be too large, or too heavy. Even with the example of gold in the other room, Amalina was still too young to consider anything small as truly valuable. The trunks took effort to lift out, but it wasn't impossible. Whatever was so painstakingly locked away, it was relatively light.

Another box inside. Of course. She just hauled that one out, easier than the last. Something shifted inside. She used the second-to-last key.

Inside this chest was, as expected, the smallest lockbox yet. But there were also several books inside. She pulled out the books. The writing was unfamiliar. It looked pretty, and flowed laterally in a right to left manner, and was decorated with dots and flourishes. There were illustrations, with figures dancing with oddly stoic expressions, wearing fantastic outfits, their skin dark and bearing oriental features. She touched the lettering. It was Arabic. The language of the Count's most hated enemies. Maybe these were the histories of the Ottomans. She couldn't tell. She couldn't read any of it. It was pitiable she couldn't. And she took to wandering the pages, enjoying the gorgeously intricate illustrations, highlighted with vibrant colors, even in the dim light. When the torch crackled, she remembered the dangers of a stray spark—how the one stray spark had once saved her life by blinding the wolf that was biting at her throat—how much more disastrous one chance bit of fire would be in a room filled with wood and paper. She returned the books, but noticed one had modern roman lettering stamped into it. What was that one? She couldn't understand the title.

But how long had she already been inside the secret rooms now? It couldn't be more than midday. And while she was confident the Count would not suddenly appear (arrived during the daylight; or having never left, but waiting close by for intruders, to surprise them), she couldn't be sure that Abraxa or Georg or Genadie wouldn't come looking. How long could Abraxa really keep her husband occupied? Or keep her own anxiousness and curiosity at bay before she demanded to enter the study to see if the books had been found?

Amalina hurried onto the final box. She pulled the small chest out. It was so small, her father could hold it in the palm of his hand. The key, as small as it was, looked ridiculously large for such a tiny thing. She inserted it into the keyhole, turned it, and opened the lid.

She didn't understand what she was looking at. A tiny broken bracelet? The inside of the miniature chest was lined with red velvet, with an oblong circle of shiny metal nestled in the bottom. The metal was a perfect oblong loop except where a chunk had been broken from it. There were bits of the loop—some bits that had broken off—scattered around. She touched the piece, wondering if she shouldn't have her skin protected in some way. Something this hidden, to this degree, at the center of five locked boxes, must be dangerous, mustn't it?

But it felt like metal. Normal steely metal. If a bit cool.

Amalina took the oblong loop out of the box and brought it close to her eyes before she understood what had excited her and had caused her to do so. The metal was much brighter than ordinary steel. And its shape recalled a memory. It seemed so long ago, when measured against her adventures in the western kingdoms. But really was a handful of months ago, when the Count had brought her into that room underneath the castle, and she'd encountered the reason the Count's high castle was haunted by an unending wail during the night. The source of the wail itself: a withered woman chained to an ever-turning wheel, the chain binding her in place; the wheel's spin keeping her from finding her bearings. It was a torture that no living human could survive. She wasn't a living human, after all. And the chain that bound her to the ever-turning wheel, kept her still and, now gagging her, quiet: it was made of this same metal. What Amalina held in her hand, what the Count had hidden away inside five lockboxes, in the furthest, darkest corner of his counting house, was a link from that very chain.

21

The Delivery

Count Tepsji did not return by next morning. Only Genadie, who claimed the Count had visited him before leaving and had casually mentioned they "might never see each other again", and who was now crying in his little hovel at daybreak, was plainly troubled. For everyone else, his failure to appear wound their feelings into confusion: If he'd come back, so their thoughts went, then they'd know where he was and the order of their world was restored. But while he was away ... for Georg: while the Count was out, he wielded the authority of his master, an intoxicating and seductive power. For Abraxa: her husband was spared from punishment; because Amalina had not found the books, and so her husband *had* erred during his arrangement of the Great Library. Every rising dawn without the Count meant another day Abraxa could serve beside her husband Georg without immediate fear for his life. For Amalina: There was the chance the monster had escaped his boundaries, found a safe route to the west, and Ardeel would be free of him. And he could do whatever horrible thing he wanted elsewhere, like the terror of an angry hornet now unleashed into the wide world, instead of being locked inside the small room with you. Or there was the other possibility: That he might not have overcome the distance. That he'd been caught in flight, unable to locate a suitable place to hide himself as the sun rose. And he'd been driven into the ground, either weakened and injured, or actually burned into a charred lump. In any case, no longer a threat.

For Amalina, a third positive of the Count not arriving in the night, one more realistic and appealed to her pragmatic side: It gave her another day to search the hidden room.

"But why *again?*" Abraxa questioned, her eyes studying Amalina sharply, and with a wince, like the young girl was tearing at a not-yet-healed wound.

"I only brought a candle in—"

"You had a torch," Abraxa corrected.

"Well, yes. But once inside I lit a candle, you see, and it wasn't very bright, I think. And I was in such a rush. It really is a big—uh, well, I still can't tell you what's inside. But there is a lot of room to search where the books could be. I looked in the obvious spots, but I didn't think to see where they might have been stored, or covered, or hidden in some way. You see what I mean, Abraxa. There's still more to look."

"You had quite a long time, I don't see why you didn't think of it then."

"What's the matter with doing it again? I still have the key."

"I was hoping to get it back this morning. And we already closed the door. It wasn't easy getting it open or closed, remember? But if you think you *must*."

"*If there's still a chance*, shouldn't you say?" she reminded Abraxa.

The old woman's thin lips slanted off to the side, and she wondered quietly if Amalina was absolutely and completely *certain* His Eminence did not come during the night.

"You know as well as I do, he didn't."

"How would I know it? I don't know anything anymore." Abraxa hurried away with bursts of angry movement. It seemed she was resentful at having to believe in Amalina's possible lies, because she couldn't understand a reason for her to lie. So they might not be lies even if they sounded like them. And if Amalina was instead telling the truth, it could only be in the services of her husband, so she must obey. Amalina started after her, but then stopped, unsure if she was supposed to stay close behind or wait. She didn't know where Abraxa was going.

An hour later she found Abraxa in the kitchen with Georg. She didn't look up from the grains she was cracking in a mortar, but her pounding and crushing intensified when Amalina entered. She was not going to be rousted from her work.

"Excuse me," Amalina began softly.

"And have you seen the courtyard?" Abraxa snarled to Georg. "I suppose appearances don't matter when our lordship is away. Standards fall, I suppose. I could expect it from the rat. But also from the mouse?"

Georg's left eyebrow raised, and the eye below it fell onto Amalina. He frowned.

"You'd think a mouse would know by now," the old woman sneered over the surrendering grains, "the most dangerous place in a house for her is the kitchen."

So Abraxa had made up her mind and was back on the attack, when yesterday she was grateful to Amalina (even if sad that Georg hadn't been exonerated). How many times had it been this way? No matter how much ground gained toward making the old woman a friend, upon the morning it was back to the old hatred, the enmity reset during the night. Maybe instead of sleeping, the terrible two work themselves up with kindred loathing of the Count's other servants, sharpening their thoughts for use as offense and defense. And the negativity carried successfully into the next day.

For the rest of the day, Abraxa made herself inaccessible. Not avoiding Amalina, but intentionally placing herself near Georg, and conspicuously dedicated to some task from which she couldn't be called away.

. . .

The cabinet would remain shut, no matter how long Amalina stared at it. No matter how many times she battered it with her body. She needed Abraxa's help—anyone's help—to force it from the wall. She was just glad she hadn't handed over the room's key, after they'd both groaned and heaved at the door to shut it, or it would have been that much harder to get inside again. The old maid would never lend her the key now, judging by how she was avoiding Amalina.

But Amalina ached to get back in. For at least one more look. The whole night she'd tossed and turned, half listening for the Count's arrival, dreading her entrance into the hidden rooms would be discovered, half chiding herself for having been too afraid to explore more than she had. In her wandering imagination, she pictured opening the series of trunks and finding new items of interest. Pistols that would shoot a spear through the Count. Acids bottled up in the same kind of ceramic vial Kralov had given her. Yes, anything the Count had put inside those chests he'd wanted well secured—and maybe not just secured from potential invaders of his castle, but as protection for himself. Items that were dangerous to him.

At least she'd been smart enough to grab the broken chain link. She had that bit of metal, if nothing more.

But she wanted more. It felt like she was wasting the hours of daylight when she knew it was hers to use as she chose. However, there were language lessons.

Genadie had decided to conduct class in his shack. His opinion was now set: if Georg and his wife controlled the main body of the castle, his undisputed domain was the remaining portion that surrounded it: the walls, the interior side buildings (like his hovel, the barn and animal pen, and the vehicle shed), and the courtyard itself. No longer considering it a demotion—because he'd never been allowed to really live inside the main building during the decades before his injury—he was proud of the territory ceded to him by the head of staff, and cheerfully tended to the small bit of livestock. Even parading White Snow in a display of occupation, circling him around the main building, before Georg slyly convinced Amalina to try to sit on the horse, which she couldn't help but want to do, and White Snow bucked her off and Genadie was forced to put it away.

But because the Count hadn't returned, Genadie was still in a tragic condition: teary-eyed and groaning pitiably when he thought nobody was looking. She didn't see how she could recruit him, much less convince him to help her open the secret door in the Count's private study.

"Genadie," she began, deciding she should just start talking, hoping some strategy would come to mind and the words to come along with it.

"*Pourqoi pas 'Professeur'?*" Genadie reminding her he was still her instructor, and that she was still in study.

"*Pardonne.* That woman … under the castle …"

"What woman under the castle?" he asked as if he had no idea.

"The one on the wheel. Who used to cry out all night long?"

Genadie said nothing now. His eyebrows raised, his mouth drooped, and he looked at the floor to avoid her gaze.

"You remember her, Genadie."

He shrugged.

"I keep wondering what kind of metal that bind-chain holding her is made of."

Amalina was surprised by her own question. This had nothing to do with getting into the secret room. Still, she waited for the answer.

He tottered his head this way and that, and pulled off his hat and scratched his greasy hair.

"It wasn't iron," she pressed, having decided she should just go in the direction she'd begun. "And it couldn't be steel. It didn't look like steel, exactly."

He shook his head, his mouth puckery, like someone was squeezing his face together at the cheeks.

Amalina sat for a few more minutes in unsatisfied silence. She couldn't understand why that question was the one she'd asked, instead of anything else. Something closer to getting back in that room! She couldn't even think how to turn the conversation in that direction. Instead, realizing the path there was broken and had to be abandoned, she pouted at his pucker.

And that night, for a third anxious watch for them all, the Count did not return. Nor on the next night. Or the night after that.

Oddly, Genadie's distress leveled out to an almost benighted sort of serenity. She found him on the fifth morning, whistling a tune (!), expertly so (!!), his eyes closed, his body swaying, while he milked the goat (!!!). His opinion was that, though such a long absence after a dire farewell was unheard of, it could only mean good things. Zeus was at work! Or he'd ascended to the heavens! Whatever the case, there was no need to worry unless one was unfaithful and doubtful of His omnipotence. Though his master was gone, conversely his master was all the more present within the castle, watching from on high, or from within, observing and delighting in Genadie's calm piety.

"He knows who his staunch servants are," Genadie winked at her. "And who he will have to *punish*."

Amalina shivered, wondering if it could be true. That the count had the ability to see what was happening within the castle while he was away.

"What's that supposed to mean?" she asked Genadie. "And why are you grinning like that?"

He laughed scornfully: "Just you have a look at *the Pair*."

. . .

"What are you doing?" Amalina asked Abraxa. "The both of you."

"Doing what any sensible person would do," the old woman said, setting her small bag onto a pile of cases and boxes beside the front door, which Georg was organizing. "Prepare ourselves for our next situation. Our great personage has gone and forsaken us. It is important we move on."

Amalina stared in disbelief at Abraxa. Had she just said they were giving up on the Count?

"He hasn't been here for days, with not so much as a posted instruction. What is any reasonable person to think, than we've been abandoned?"

A horse whinnied loudly, as hooves clattered to a stop outside in the courtyard.

Abraxa's eyes went wide as plates. Georg gasped (though somehow keeping his face as straight, sour, and grey as it always was). They both looked to the door, then grabbed what pieces of luggage they could from the pile and fled the grand entrance hall. Leaving Amalina to see who was outside.

"Hello?" boomed a voice that was not the Count's.

Amalina pushed open the door and saw two riders coming off their horses. They were dressed in clothes much newer, cleaner, and more fashionable than anyone from Ardeel. They reminded her of another place altogether, which brought along with it the memories of late spring and early summer and the experiences of foreign lands.

Riders from the western kingdoms! Servants of some kind. Couriers, from the look of it. Yes, that made sense. The horses had large orange silks over their necks, and large drapes on their backs, with a saddle and bulging saddlebags attached. Couriers with a delivery!

"Hello," she called to them.

They tilted their hats down as they approached. The lead man held up a large square envelope which was sealed with a pretty ribbon and a thick splotch of colored wax.

A reply post from a princess? Amalina was already light-headed from the pleasant flash-back memories of her foreign trip, now she became giddy.

This letter was the hand of one of her friends reaching out to her ... or reaching out to Count Tepsji, anyway.

"Who is this?" Amalina cried happily. "Who has written us?"

"*Us?*" The lead man lifted his head to reveal his face—when it was counter-custom for a servant to gaze directly upon a titled personage—insolence aimed to provoke, both with his question and his savage grin. And when she saw his face she recognized him, but could not place from whose court he—

Piotr!

Amalina blinked.

"'*Us*', little mouse?" he repeated, his grin radiating menace, his eyes pinning her as a confirmed traitor to the cause and a personal foe.

Amalina glanced over her shoulder, and then to both sides of the courtyard. They were alone yet. She rushed forward and tried to grab the envelope, while whispering quickly. Her face now as serious as two intimate comrades sharing a knowing look when awaiting the first wave of an enemy onslaught.

"What else should I say when I'm here in the castle?" said Amalina in a low breath. "Piotr, what's happening? What are you doing here?"

"Delivering a letter to the Count, Lord Tepsji," he answered loudly, filling the courtyard with his voice. He kept the letter out of her hands, and then swept it behind his back. "Not to a silly little girl ... who doesn't know her true place."

"Hallo, hallo," Genadie's scratchy voice called from the far end of the courtyard as he rounded the side of the main building. He was waving his hat, but his face was screwed up with concern and suspicion.

There was a sound behind them. And with a glimpse of a terrified Abraxa snatching away several more cases inside the doorway, Georg stepped out, his head held high so that he looked down, almost contemptuously at the couriers.

Genadie sped up when he saw Georg. Georg sped up when he saw Genadie. There would be a foot race, and then a tug of war in a minute.

"Idiot," whispered Amalina to Piotr crossly, feeling her cheeks flush. She had only seconds before Georg was at her side. "If you're supposed to be from a princess, tell these people you have a private message for her friend, Lady Katarina Tepsji. Tell them this, and then *meet with me*."

She flashed her eyes angrily, trying to will her comrade to obey.

Then she spun, and with a worried look at Georg, mouthed to him, "I need to dress. I need to change!"

22

Piotr

Amalina kept Piotr waiting for almost an hour. When she met him in the Great Library he was standing in the middle of the room, turning from one wall to the other, searching the countless books blindly, his lips turned downward.

Georg announced Amalina before she entered, but it sounded more like he was asking a question: "The Princess Katarina Tepsji."

Piotr bowed.

Amalina moved quickly toward him, with the enthusiasm of a young Lady eager to hear from a close friend. She waved one hand back at Georg.

"You may leave, Georg," she told him. "See the horses are tended to."

"That is Genadie's service, milady," Georg reminded her with a sniff.

"*See* that Genadie *does* his service, Georg," she spun away from Piotr while pronouncing the anger of a true princess indeed. Only with her back turned to the courier, she smiled at Georg with all her teeth, letting him know how much she enjoyed this new rearrangement in the house order. "And close the door behind you. And have Abraxa ready the ovens, and I'll let you know when dinner should be prepared and who will be my guests."

"Princess Katarina Tepsji," Piotr said, still bowed, even when the door closed. "What would you have of me?"

Amalina tapped him on the shoulder. "Get up. Tell me what you're doing here." Then, with her back to the door, she motioned discreetly to it, and kept her voice low, in case Georg might be deliberately disobeying her, and that if he or anyone else was at the keyhole, they wouldn't be able to tell what was being said. "Was that really a note from one of the princesses?"

"Where is your uncle?" said Piotr loud enough for someone standing in the courtyard to hear, and stood up fully, squaring his shoulders. The coat he wore looked uncomfortable, too small for him. The seams creaked. The pants stopped too high, above his knees. These weren't his clothes. His hand pulled the coat over his hip aside, and there it touched the hilt of a knife. All of this would have looked wrong and sounded outrageously impertinent coming from a servant. Amalina moved to block as much of Piotr she could from potentially spying eyes.

"He isn't here. He hasn't been here for almost a week."

"That's what we've been told," Piotr mumbled.

"How did Georg explain it?"

"Georg? Oh, you mean the houseman? He didn't say anything. Other than the Count is expected to return soon, and that his niece would be willing to speak with me in the library. Did you have something to say to me? Or is this really about wanting to hear idle words from your foreign friends?"

Unfortunately, she *did* want to know if the letter was real and who it was from and what she had to say—always holding out hope it was the delightful Princess Derhovna telling her she was coming to visit. But Amalina knew Piotr wouldn't be too pleased if she answered along those lines.

"I have a lot to say to you," she answered. "I have information, and more." Amalina squatted, making it look like an odd curtsy, and took her old dark dress out from between her legs, which she'd been holding there uncomfortably since the trip from her room. Unfurled between them, she pointed to the chalk markings on it. "Here is something I made. This is the layout of the castle. All that I know of it. Get it to Kralov. He will remember most of it from before, but I've added to it since."

Piotr nodded, studying the markings.

"Are you going to tell me why you're here?" she said. "It wasn't to see me."

"Since our spy wasn't delivering information to us, we needed to get inside to see what was happening. Perhaps she had sacrificed herself in the line of duty, was one thought. Which has proved to be untrue." He smirked at her. "Anyway, we heard the Count wasn't in the castle anymore—"

"Who told you that?"

"Informants."

"Who?"

"Are you kidding me, girl?"

But what informants could he be talking about? Surely not Genadie. Or Georg or Abraxa. Unless he was bluffing it must mean they had very perceptive lookouts somewhere in the mountains. Or … there were farms between the castle and Netz. Maybe one or more of them had sided with the revolt, and they were as familiar with the animal warnings of the Count emerging from his castle as she was. The close-by farmers would know more keenly about it because the sound was a warning against their own lives, as on those evenings when the Count left the castle he was headed their way. Nearly a week ago they must have heard the alarms of his leaving, but had yet to hear the call of his return.

"We took the opportunity to get in close," Piotr was saying. "See for ourselves. I've got men in the treeline right now, ready to come with the charges."

"Charges?"

"Some are on the horses we brought in. At this point, we've enough powder we can take down a wall."

"What good is taking down a wall?"

"Think of it as a practice run," he said, looking annoyed at having to explain anything to her. "Now what else can you tell me? I suppose you haven't used the bottle on him yet?"

"There hasn't been a chance. I swear! But I've been doing what I can." But Amalina was still curious: "Where did you get the letter, though? Is it real?"

Piotr told her who it was from, and her heart didn't dance like it should have. It wasn't from Princess Derhovna, after all. Apparently whoever else, no matter how much she liked them, wouldn't satisfy her as much.

"We caught her post coming through Netz. They stopped to refresh their horses and get breakfast. We got to them before they could make themselves known in the village. Who knows how the princess and her retinue will take it when her couriers don't return."

"What did you do with them?" she asked after this ominous statement.

Piotr snapped his finger to get her attention.

"Why isn't the Count here?" Piotr demanded, his right hand gripping the hilt of his knife. "Where has he gone?"

"He could be anywhere," Amalina said soberly. "He might even be dead."

Piotr's head jerked. He searched her eyes for confirmation it was true. She explained, altering the story a fraction so that it came out that she'd challenged the Count to give up eating blood, and dared him to simply try to outrace the sun. She didn't want Piotr knowing he might have actually broken free of the Ardeelian borders and might actually be loose in the western kingdoms; just that he might have mended his ways or was possibly dead.

"But that means he could be anywhere," Piotr said, following the details to their logical conclusion. "He might have even left Ardeel."

Amalina nodded, somewhat embarrassed.

"What good is that to us?"

"It means we're safe, doesn't it?"

"It only means someone else has to deal with him. It means he lives another day. Our purpose is to kill him. He must be stopped. He must pay for his crimes, not be modified in habit or location to please us."

Amalina nodded again, an expression of apology appearing without her calling it up. She was relieved she didn't always have to act around Piotr, her expressions occasionally natural, even if they didn't suit her.

"So this is all your fault," he said.

"My fault?" she gaped.

But it was true. She couldn't look any sorrier about it, so she didn't. What could she have done otherwise? She didn't have the means to kill the Count. Softening some of his aspects, or getting him safely out of her life had seemed good enough. So she'd acted. She hadn't really thought it *would* work, just that it might. And in any case, even if it didn't, she'd wanted to buy herself some time to get behind the secret door. That was all. If anything positive came from it, all the better.

"There doesn't seem to be too many people here," said Piotr, moving on. "Just the servants?"

"The head of staff, the maid, Genadie and I."

"Only the four of you?" he was astonished.

"Yes."

"The two old straw bags, the rat and the mouse are what's left to defend the body of this structure? You understand, I have men outside, inside the forest, waiting to take this place down."

"But you won't?" she asked, seeing the strange look on his face and in the exasperated tone which he'd pronounced the fact.

"What's the use, you fool, when you've sent away the bulls-eye of our target? It's almost like you knew we were preparing for a raid ... oh, wait, you did know, didn't you?"

Amalina was startled by the accusation.

"You think I sent him away ... to *save* him from you?" Then she remembered she shouldn't get too agitated, for the benefit of her possible audience in the hallway.

Piotr rubbed the hilt of his knife while contemplating her and his next action.

"There's a secret room here," announced Amalina, to stop the dangerous silence, pointing to the map. "I've just discovered it."

"Where he sleeps?"

"No. Less important, but more interesting. It's where he keeps his money. And where he keeps his communications."

"Communications with his agents? Who does he talk to, little mouse? Where?"

"A lot of people. Everywhere."

Piotr's stance shifted, almost coming up on the balls of his feet, with a newfound energy. He looked at the map. "Where?"

"There's a door here—"

"You're taking me to it." He took hold of Amalina's hand and they were already out in the hall before she regained her footing and could protest.

"Careful!" Her eyes looked every which way for Georg or Abraxa. "They could be anywhere."

Strangely, the couple weren't anywhere. She'd expected at least one of them to be spying at the keyhole. They either weren't spying, or whichever one had been there was very fast and was soundless in escaping. When they reached the entrance hall, she saw the pile of Georg's and Abraxa's belongings—their preparations for departure—had been further reduced. The pair were busy removing the evidence.

"Which way?" asked Piotr.

She pointed to the door that led to the private study.

He turned in the opposite direction and ran.

In the courtyard, next to the water-trough Genadie had set up, the second courier—with the look and build of an Ardeelian warrior itching for battle, who'd been stuffed inside the clothes of a tiny, slightly effeminate horse handler—was patting down their rides, and fumbling with the saddlebags containing the explosive charges. By the time Amalina caught up to him, Piotr was already at the man's side, handing over Amalina's folded dress-map and quickly relaying instructions.

But the second courier held a strange impatience as Piotr spoke. His eyes blinked, his head nodded too quickly, his jaw ground back and forth. Piotr noticed.

"Is there a problem?"

The man glanced down at Amalina. Piotr gave a dismissive wave.

"She's ours," he muttered quickly.

"Well, uh," the man said, still uncomfortable. Then he looked at the top of the outer wall. "We aren't bringing in the other charges, sir. No, I don't think so."

"Why the hell not?"

"Listen yourself." He nodded his chin at the wall.

Past the sound of the breeze, and the stir of the horses' hooves scraping on the stone, there were men's shouts, and inhuman growls and howls. Wolves. Wolves battling men. Amalina remembered the great black wolf, with its fiery eyes and deadly fangs chomping toward her soft neck. Though she'd wounded the black wolf that night, and driven it and its pack out of the castle grounds, they were still lurking the neighboring forest. That beast and his friends were out there right now, tearing into Kralov's rebels.

"What the hell is that?" But then Piotr swore, knowing full well what he was hearing.

The second man pointed discreetly. Genadie was up on the wall, staring over the barrier into the forest, his hat off, scratching at his head.

Piotr leaned to his comrade's ear and rattled off some new orders, his forefinger stabbing the air to emphasize his seriousness. The second courier nodded gravely. When he was done he turned to Amalina: "Now, Princess Tepsji, if you'll be so kind, take me to his money."

. . .

"You'll need a torch," Amalina told him, suddenly hoping it would delay Piotr, or stop him, and he'd have time to cool off and rethink whatever he had in his head to do.

"Gladly," he said as he grabbed a torch off its post.

As they headed into the private study, with Georg and Abraxa still nowhere to be seen, she wondered why she wasn't trying harder to stop him, but going along, removing obstacles for him. As she unlocked the door, with no idea how she would explain their entering the study, she felt that part of her wanted to see what was going to happen—thrilled at it—almost feeling like she was witnessing vengeance at work. Part of her predicting just what he would do: set fire to the treasury and all the letters and messages tucked away there.

She shut the door and locked it behind them.

"Where?" he asked, already heading for the door at the back of the room.

"No," she said, pointing to the cabinet. "Here."

He looked confused.

But she had already taken the chair and dragged it over. She worked the latch until she heard the familiar clack and the weight of the cabinet shifted. He joined her and they swung the heavy piece aside. But only a little faster and a little farther on each shove than when Abraxa had helped. That was demoralizing to Amalina, who'd just assumed Piotr, who was young and strong, could open it on his own and with little effort—like the Count.

Piotr drew his dagger and rushed inside, holding the torch in front of him. He didn't stop. He just swung his head around as he pounded through the counting house and then, finding a new threshold, moved down into the larger chamber of the message archive. Amalina followed him quickly, keeping within the light of the torch, and watched as he circled the high shelves, looking for more passages or doorways. When he didn't, he came to a halt and stood there panting.

"The gold is back up there," she said, pointing at the stairs behind her.

"Gold?"

"He turns it into coins," she explained.

Piotr turned in place, gaping in confusion at the shelves around him. When he noticed the large trunk in the far corner, he lunged the torch at it.

"What is that? Is that where he sleeps?"

"No," Amalina said, starting to worry his overexcitement was a break into madness. She went for the desk. "It's just a trunk."

"Just a trunk?" he thrust his knife forward, and crept toward it like a cat testing a rival. "Like a cabinet is just a cabinet and not a secret door? What are you doing now? What's in there?"

With a loud sigh meant to quiet him, Amalina brought the keys from the desk, passed him right by. Only after the first trunk lid was opened, and she wrestled out the next chest to work on that one, Piotr flipped his knife back through his belt, put the torch in the stand and came to help.

"What's inside?" he asked.

"Nothing much," she said.

"What do you mean?"

"Nothing that can help, anyway. Why don't you calm down, Piotr? I can hear your heart beating."

His eyes were large, the white all around the irises. He was panting. Beads of sweat were all over his face like small blisters. The way he was, so youthful, somewhat handsome, a body much larger and stronger than hers and yet his fear conquering him, he was, Amalina thought, like Erik Kosche. Swaggering one moment, nervous to quaking the next. Piotr hadn't had the stage-training to control his body, to hide the fear as well as Erik had. She could see him shaking, and he didn't even give the sense that it was something to hide. It made him seem even younger, like an Erik who had just one more year before schooling began. So much for the cool ruffian he'd been in Netz with his knife at her throat.

"What?" he asked, questioning her stare.

She shrugged. "I'm only doing this so you'll see he isn't hiding inside."

"It's too small for him to hide inside."

"Well," she said, debating if she should tell him. "I'm pretty sure he can change into other things. Even something this small."

His eyes rounded at the next box as they hauled it up. He was obviously trying to picture the Count, transformed into a new entity, something tiny but ferocious, crouched inside ready to spring. It almost made Amalina nervous.

But she *was* nervous. They were inside the hidden room, with the secret door standing open. And Abraxa and Georg free to break into the study to see where Amalina and the courier had gone, and what was happening inside. They didn't have much time to waste, and this was definitely wasting time. She shrugged again as she opened the next to final lid.

Piotr grabbed up the books inside.

"What are these?" he asked, paging through them quickly.

"Don't get them dirty," she cautioned. "Don't smudge them with your hands, be careful."

"You said there was nothing in here—"

"Nothing useful."

"What are these books, that he'd lock them this deep? They must be something."

"They're books from the Ottomans. The Count hated the sultan—"

Piotr spit heavily on the ground.

"What are you doing!" cried Amalina. "You can't spit there! Wipe it up! Do you want him to know you've been here?"

He rubbed out the phlegm on the floor, more spreading the thick puddle than drying it.

"If he hates the Ottoman, maybe he isn't all bad." Piotr flipped through the books. "But what are they? What are they meant for?"

"I don't know," she shook her head. "I can't read them at all."

"It's the writing of the heathens, you *shouldn't* read them at all."

"You aren't making any sense."

"What about this one?" he asked, holding up the last one, written in Latin. "I recognize the letters, but what does it say?"

"You don't know Latin?"

"I barely know our language."

"The title is: 'On Burning Glass'. Whatever that means." But as soon as she'd said it, her mind went on alert. She tried to take it from him, but he shouldered her away, turning open the pages, looking for who knows what. "Hey, you don't even know how to read!"

But the illustrations inside said all they needed to. This was a book, from what Amalina could glimpse, on the subject of a new kind of destructive power. Black blocks, some with curves cut out, had lines tracing from them. And at the lines' thin ends were small mounds of fire. And from what she could tell, the sun, which was shone on nearly every diagram, held the force these devices used.

Erik—no, Piotr—slammed the leaves shut. He stared at her. She couldn't tell what he was thinking.

"Well, what do you want to do?" she asked him. "Take it?"

"You said the sun can wound him. Look what's going on in this book!"

"Yes, I understand," she said, catching on. "But we can't take it out of here."

"Why not?"

Yes, why not? She'd already taken the chain's link. The Count would notice that was missing. And it would be easy for him to discover someone had entered the hidden rooms, gone through his private things, and stolen some of his valuables, when he saw the spit mark on the floor near the trunk, then growing suspicious, looked inside. Things were getting out of control.

"He'll notice," she told him.

"How often could he look inside these chests if these are books he's all but banished? I suppose he hasn't been inside one in years." *Maybe even hundreds of years*, Amalina thought. "It's mine now."

"I wish you wouldn't."

"Who do you work for, Princess Tepsji?"

Amalina smirked.

"I don't expect to have to remind you again," he said.

He threw the other books back into the chest, and pointed to the smallest box.

"It's empty," she said before he could ask.

He eyed her and she sighed again. And taking the smallest key she opened it for him.

"But that's not why we're here," she told him as she began closing up the boxes and chests and trunks—while feeling they'd wasted too much time already. "You wanted to see these rooms for yourself, look around. And there on the desk, here are the messages, sent by pigeons, to warn him if there's trouble."

They closed up the trunk and she returned the keys to the desk, but then plucked out several of the code sticks.

"And these are what really matters: This is his secret language. If we knew how it worked, we could find out everything he knows, and who his people are, and where they are. Here, if we just get some paper I can copy this down, and copy the alphabet track, and you can take it to the Commander and—"

"And what? Send the Count messages of our own?"

"It'd be good to have," she protested, but realized he was right. What good was it to Kralov without the messages to decode? It's not like he was living inside the castle, with access to the secret room. This was non-actionable intelligence. "Well, here, let's get up to the office and let me copy these out so *I* can have them."

"Are you sure there aren't any other doors in here? They could be hidden behind the shelves."

"We only have so much time," she hissed. "Help me with this."

She held up the handful of sticks, grabbed the torch and ran up the stairs.

Piotr cursed in the darkness behind her.

She didn't have time to worry. If Piotr and his raiding party weren't going to be tearing the castle down today, she knew this was vital. Amalina sat at the count's desk and began copying out the strange characters on the cipher sticks. It was odd to be holding the Count's fancy quill. To transcribe onto his private stock of vellum paper his secret code using the ink from his gold capped reservoir. The ink was smooth and shiny, and so deep and rich, even when it dried it held its weight and luster. As usual, the Count's refinement and tastes were evident in the items he owned and collected. It would have been just as fun writing meaningless words as it was transcribing the means to spy on and sabotage him, using this exquisite equipage—

Oops! A splatter.

She dabbed at it with her sleeve—Oops, again! Why did she use her sleeve? What awkward questions would be asked? *What had she been writing while in this dress?* She'd have to avoid wearing the dress again inside the castle, to keep from having to come up with answers.

"Gold? Gold? All of this is gold?" came Piotr's voice.

"Yes," she said.

"I didn't think there was this much gold in all the world."

Piotr emerged from the hidden room, a heavy bag caught up in his arms along with the book.

"You must thank your uncle, Count Tepsji, for his generosity," Piotr said without a smile. "Tell him Commander Kralov will spend it wisely."

"What are you doing?" she asked. "You think he won't notice a bag is missing?"

"Not when I took it from the back of a shelf. And I rearranged the bags. He'd never really know unless he decided to do a complete inventory ... or somebody told him."

"You can't keep treating me like the enemy," Amalina said crossly as she almost blew the glyph she was copying. She hurried on, trying to ignore the circling and prying Piotr, time seeming to press in so that it felt like a physical pressure on her body. Piotr was opening drawers, then he was moving furniture, then he was knocking and testing doorknobs. She blew a sigh and moved onto the next stick.

"What's through this door?" The door at the back of the study.

"I don't know."

"Where he sleeps. His coffin."

"Maybe. But he isn't in there right now, and I don't have the key."

Piotr tested his knife on it, picking at the keyhole.

A bell rang. A weight dropped into Amalina's stomach.

"What's that?"

"I don't know." Amalina rushed the last few glyphs, grabbed the torch and returned the sticks to the desk, arranging them as well as she could. When she ran back upstairs, the bell was still sounding, and seemed to be getting louder. Closer.

Piotr had his ear to the door.

"Help me," Amalina called to him. "Hurry. We have to get this closed before they find us."

"Princess Tepsji?" Georg and Abraxa chorused. "Princess Tepsji?"

"Oh, no," she said, her pulse racing. "They're coming. Shut the door! I'll try to stop them before they get here. Hurry!"

Piotr seemed unsure, not used to taking commands from a subordinate—and one who also happened to be under suspicion.

A moan escaped her as she fumbled with the study key and raced to throw the lock, to get outside the room before they arrived. "Hurry!" she said.

The last she saw of Piotr, as she shut the door, he had given up the book and the bag of gold and had begun shoving at the cabinet in earnest. It scooted an inch.

"Ms. Dal—ah, I mean, Katarin—ah, milady," Abraxa said coming at her from the opposite door in the antechamber. "Where were you? What are you doing there?"

"Well, I'm here aren't I?" Amalina said calmly, probably not looking it. She patted down her dress.

"But what *are* you doing there? You were inside our eminence's private quarters? Don't lie to me, I saw you!"

"I don't understand," Amalina said crossing the room toward the ringing bell, which sounded to be inside the entrance hall. "What's the matter?"

"What's the matter?" Abraxa hooked Amalina's arm to stop her. "You disappeared from the library didn't you?"

"I didn't disappear—"

"And the couriers left."

"Have they?"

Abraxa explained how both of the courier's horses were gone from the courtyard, and Amalina wasn't in the library, or in her room, or anywhere she might be expected to be, which suggested the couriers had taken her with them.

"What does that have to do with me? My horse isn't gone, is it?"

"*Your* horse?"

"Yes, my horse. Snowy. So why would you think they took me if my horse is still here?" inquired Amalina, with a not-putting-up-with-this-nonsense tone, and trying to head for the entrance hall again.

"Because we couldn't find you anywhere!" she said, stopping her again. "Your horse not taken? They'd prefer you on one of their horses, of course. It is much easier to ride off with someone tied-up in front of you on a saddle, than expecting a victim—whether bound or willing—to come along on another horse. You can ride much faster that way and be sure the person is always with you. Just leave the victim's horse behind is how it's done."

Abraxa had made it very plain the innerworking of her thought process. How suspicious and calculating she was. Amalina looked surprised.

"But it's a silly thing to think," Amalina scolded, "considering it didn't happen, since I'm right here in front of you."

The wrinkles tightened around Abraxa's mouth, her cheeks flushed. Amalina took advantage of this victory and darted into *l'entrée grande*.

"Oh, there you are," Georg said, annoyance bowing his left eyebrow into an angry checkmark. He let the large bell fall into the palm of his free hand like it was a blunt weapon. "Thought you'd been kidnapped."

"Kidnapped?" Amalina began, revving up to scold him, too.

"Never you mind," Abraxa yelled at Georg, before Amalina could also make him look ridiculous, which caused his mouth to become a small stunned o. "I'll see she's punished for giving us a scare. You clear the rest of the belongings while there's time."

"Of course," Georg said, almost timidly, looking back to the remaining cases by the door.

Abraxa took Amalina's arm forcefully and nearly threw her back into the antechamber. "We still have your mess to clean. Go on, Georg, I have her!"

Abraxa didn't let go, but marched Amalina straight for the private study.

"Now what's the matter?" asked Amalina, as she wriggled in her grasp.

"Nothing's changed. You still haven't answered my question: What were you doing in that room?"

"What do you mean?" Amalina decided to keep answering Abraxa's questions with more questions, until she could formulate a good answer. Right now her thoughts were clanging inside her head without clarity.

But instead of asking another question, Abraxa threw open the study door.

A gasp caught in Amalina's throat, she expecting Piotr to be standing there with a bag of gold in his hands. But the room was empty. That didn't stop Abraxa from pulling her inside and closing it.

Amalina's eyes darted all around the room, trying to figure out where the tall young man could possibly hide. The cabinet was closed. There were only so many places he could compact himself to make himself invisible. Behind the divan? No.

"Don't pretend you weren't in here," Abraxa was saying, her eyes surveying the room as intensely as Amalina.

"Why would I?"

"See the torch!" she cried, accusingly. "I didn't bring it in. Which means you had to've."

"I meant: why would I pretend I wasn't in here? Of course I was. You saw me coming out."

"I caught you, you mean."

"Caught me doing what? What do I have to hide?"

"You still haven't told me what you were doing in here. Answer me now!"

"What could I have been doing you'd act this way to me? What do you think I was doing?"

"I can't imagine. First we thought you'd been taken by criminal imposters, then you show up here."

"I wrote a reply to the princess," she said, finally. "A letter for the courier to pass to her."

"Why?"

"Well, why not? She's my friend. He would see her before I do next. It's a strange thing to wonder about. I suppose you have friends you correspond with, don't you?"

"*Princess*," she scoffed. "A *princess* you are. And corresponding with a *true* princess."

"Is that what's bothering you? That I actually have a princess as a friend and you don't?" That didn't seem to be the real issue. "Better get used to it."

"And you needed to compose your letter in here? There's ink and paper in the library."

"That's true."

"So you needn't really write in here. If that *is* what you did."

"You don't believe I actually wrote her a letter?" Amalina asked in a bemused form of offended innocence. She lifted her arms to display the fresh ink stains on her sleeve. "See?"

Abraxa wandered toward the desk, nodding vaguely, her eyes still slitted and roaming.

"But why here? Why in *here*?"

"The reason I came to this room, Abraxa, if it is any of your business—no, wait," she made her voice calm, "if it will put your mind at ease, kind woman—was to use the Count's wax and seal for the envelope. So that the courier would be less likely to open it, and the princess could be assured the message was from this house."

"And where is the courier now?"

"I don't know. I thought you said they left." Her eyes darted around the room again, making sure he wasn't there. But also wondering where he could have gone. Did he pick the lock on the door on the back wall? "I just came back to return the seal—I was still holding it, so you understand—when I noticed the bell."

Amalina felt the weight in her stomach disappear. She nearly floated when the logical explanation appeared, like a miracle, from her mouth. Of course! It all made sense!

Abraxa's eyes ticked back and forth, her lips in a sour wriggle, as she sought for Amalina's lies in the excuse.

"I don't know why you're acting so suspicious," said Amalina with genuine hurt. Why was *was* the old grouch still persisting they be enemies?

"Wait," Abraxa said, pointing a finger of accusation toward the cabinet. "What's going on *here*?"

The cabinet was still open. It wasn't obvious at first, but coming to the side where it opened, it was all too clear. Piotr had only gotten it partially closed. There was enough room left that—

Piotr must have panicked. He couldn't close the secret door in time, or so he thought, and so he'd slid himself—impossibly by that narrow space— back inside the counting room.

"Hm," Amalina said. "That's strange. It must have come open."

"You needed my help to open it. So how could it just come open on its own?"

"I don't know. But I couldn't open it by myself, could I?"

"No, you couldn't."

"The courier was in the library," explained Amalina, sounding reasonable. "And now he's gone. And I'd never bring him in here. This is the Count's private study. Never, without his permission."

Abraxa measured the space of the opening with her eyes—just barely enough room to allow Piotr to squeeze through. He must have skinned part of his chest doing it, even without the jacket. Maybe he was able to find a way to pull on the cabinet from the inside, to close it just a little more before hiding himself. Now Abraxa put her ear to the space and listened.

"I don't think you should be looking," Amalina said with concern. "*You* aren't supposed to know what's in there."

"I'm listening."

"Well stop listening and get away. It's off limits."

Abraxa nodded, looking sheepish at having been so bold.

"I'm not sure how it got open," said Amalina. "I guess because I didn't secure the lock. Well, I'm glad you noticed before the Count returned."

"Yes," Abraxa agreed. "Where are you going?"

"Let's get back out before Georg comes looking for us."

"But we have to close the door."

"Oh, yes. That's true." Amalina swallowed. *How do I talk my way out of doing that?*

Amalina pretended to engage in a groaning, limb-shaking struggle to push the cabinet closed, while not putting in any real effort. Maybe Abraxa wouldn't be able to do it on her own and be forced to give up. But the cabinet crept and ground by pieces of an inch, with Abraxa huffing and puffing and turning red; Amalina feeling the heat and dampness coming off the old woman until she could smell her. Then it shut.

"Well, good," said Amalina, inwardly cursing, as she patted her hands together. Now what was Piotr going to do? He was stuck inside that room without even a light! She bent over and blew out a breath, in imitation of Abraxa. Then she stood up, grabbed the woman's hand and headed for the door. "Better get back before Georg misses us."

"One more thing," said Abraxa, as she gasped for breath. She pointed. "Don't forget the latch."

"Oh." Now Amalina was really cursing; so much that her face glowed as red as Abraxa's. *Why did Piotr—the fool!—hide in there?* Now what could she possibly do to avoid locking him in? She pulled the chair up, intending on fumbling at the device and feign locking it closed.

Abraxa jumped up on the chair and her hand went right to the spot. She must have minded Amalina carefully last time. Her fingers scrambled for just a second, her eyes rolling upward, the tip of her tongue appearing at the outer edge of her non-existent lips. Then, to announce with finality to anyone on either side of the door that the latch had fallen securely into place:

Clack.

23

The Whirlwind

Amalina's night was punctuated by a fit of passion. She touched the sheets, swam her body on them, and then finally tore at them. She thrilled to the sensation of the textured linen, her sensitive skin, the heat of the room, her sweat, its smell, and the lingering fire. And her thoughts wandered violently to areas that were strange and so nonsensical they made her want to laugh, or shudder in disgust—how often it wrapped into its scandalous, pyrotechnic folds people she hadn't thought of in ages, or others she would be shocked to find in her dreams, like the rat Genadie, or the Count himself, wearing someone else's blood on his face. Tonight it was princesses, and marzipan, and handsome princes and kings on pale white stallions dressed in lurid silks, and Piotr with his knife at her throat, and … oh!—and while afterwards she was often left confused, this time, like most, she ended refreshed, positive, and energized. These bouts weren't a frequent occurrence, but they were regular enough, and becoming more regular as she got older. And these bouts almost always preceded the taxing event in her body, the one she found most annoying about being a female. Only, she realized now, this 'taxing event' hadn't happened for some time. For too long. Was this a sign of trouble? But who could she ask about it? Abraxa? When she lived in Korr it had always been Sadra, the minister's wife, who supplied the answers to the mysteries of the feminine. But Sadra, as helpful (admittedly) as she was in those moments, was nowhere nearby. *Should she return to Korr to speak with her? Or have a doctor called?*

The enjoyable spell and its many confusions withdrew slowly. One after the next. Until she was left wondering just what exactly was bothering her: Was it the amount of time that had passed since her last menstruation? Or was it the simple curiousness of the sensual pleasures of her body and how it made her shake and turn, so like a fever? Or was it a concern over who, or what, encouraged these fits within her? or was it that she had nobody to confide in?—what was bothering her, when all that mattered was Piotr was locked inside the Count's most sensitive area of the castle!

She sat up. Why was she lying in bed? What had possessed her to do something like that, when he was trapped below?

Oh, right: Abraxa.

After they'd closed the door, the old woman did not take the study key from Amalina. Which was curious. By all rights she could have demanded it back. However, though Amalina still had the key, Abraxa had stuck to *l'entrée grande* from that point on, sweeping, stoking the fire, polishing armor, dusting the dull cup, sweeping again, as if she was resolved not to leave. Sneaking past her and to the Count's private study was impossible. But Amalina had to get in there. If the Count returned, Piotr would be found and killed. And Amalina's aid in getting him inside would be exposed, certainly. And what punishment would the Count reserve for her?

It was still night. The sky was deep black but she sensed it was now on the other side of midnight—her endless dreams suggested many hours had passed—and so dawn was coming. With the sensual heat of her body tingling in her limbs, she lit a candle and climbed down from the tower. Abraxa was no longer in the entrance hall. Amalina breathed a sigh and moved quickly into the next room, the antechamber, and then toward the study's door.

"What are you doing here?" cried Abraxa. Amalina spun and saw the old woman coming at her from the rear corner of the room, her finger waving. Her eyes were red, with dark circles under them—the new brown puffy bags being the only color on her blanched skin. No candle or torch, she'd been sitting there all night, in the dark, lying in wait for Amalina.

"What are you doing here?" Amalina asked in return. "You scared me."

"I *knew* you were up to something in the study. What was it?"

"Why do you keep treating me like an enemy, Abraxa? Haven't I proven again and again that we're friends?"

"Friends?" Abraxa huffed. "When you went out of your way to find fault with Georg? And then to hold it over us, like the ambitious, scheming, lying, treacherous blackmailer that you are?"

Amalina fell back, her mouth hung open, honestly shocked by the accusation. Only one or two of those things were true, and those being necessary tools for her own survival.

"Well, why are you here?" Abraxa demanded. "What could be your excuse this time?"

"I had to see," she said, amazed at the speed of the lie that was coming, "I thought I heard the Count."

Now it was Abraxa's turn to look shocked. Her face couldn't turn any whiter, but her head spun toward the door to the private study as her eyes saucered and the skin wobbled back and forth underneath her pointy chin. Fear permeated her whole expression for a second, and then her face fell neutral, and hardened. She tilted her head, listening.

"I didn't hear anything. But is it true?" she whispered. "His eminence…?"

She took Amalina's hand (the one holding the candle) and ushered them both toward the study.

"What did you hear? Exactly?"

"The owls. Sometimes they make a noise outside my window when he returns. There was one standing in my window, and I thought—"

Abraxa shushed her. She put her ear to the door.

"Nothing. I don't hear anything, girl. Were you trying to scare me?"

"You're the one who scared me," Amalina reminded her. "I didn't know you were here. I was just coming to check … should I use the key?"

"What are you two doing?" Georg's voice rumbled behind them.

Amalina leapt and Abraxa screamed.

He stood in the far door. He was fully dressed and holding a small candle.

"My god, Georg! How could you scare me like that?" cried Abraxa, clutching her chest.

"What are you two doing?"

"Who, us?" Abraxa asked, shooting a strange, guilty look between Amalina and her husband. "Well, don't you worry. You've got nothing to worry about from *her*."

"Why should I think I had anything to worry about from the mouse?" he asked in a rising tone, like a twittering bird coming alert. "What *is* going on here? Ms. Dalca, explain yourself."

"I thought I heard the Count."

Georg shook, but not as profoundly as Abraxa had. He went paler than grey, smirked and gave a slight nod.

"Yes, I thought I heard him, too," he said.

Now it was Amalina's turn to lose the blood in her face. Her gut knotted.

"Where?" Amalina asked.

"It turned out to be you two," he said, dryly. "But I thought I heard his voice. At first within the grounds. I didn't know where. But you know how his voice carries. From everywhere it carries. I dressed and came down. Which is more than I can say for you both. You expected to greet him on his return, after so long away, dressed in your sleeping clothes?"

"I'm not in my sleeping clothes," Abraxa argued.

"You look terrible," he told her. "Unattended to. It's just as appalling."

"And you're the king's portrait?" she huffed back.

"Well is he here or isn't he?" Amalina asked.

Georg nodded grimly. "I heard his voice. I know I did. But, outside then … ?"

He turned back towards the entrance.

"You go that way," Abraxa told him. "We'll check in here."

He didn't argue but waved at them, as if they'd annoyed him long enough with their distraction, and hurried away.

"Shouldn't you get dressed?" Abraxa told Amalina.

No! No matter what excuse they'd have to resort to, if Piotr was found within the castle, as long as he wasn't discovered inside the hidden rooms there was a chance of surviving the Count's unexpected return. She had to get into the study, and get Piotr out. Now.

"You'll learn soon enough he doesn't care how anyone is dressed," said Amalina non-chalantly. "If you want to make yourself up, go right ahead. I'm going in."

Abraxa paused, but when Amalina took out the key, she bustled away. "Hold on," she whispered over her shoulder, "Wait till I've gone and he doesn't see me."

As her key touched the metal hole, there was a loud shriek, and the key dropped out of Amalina's hand. It was Abraxa, and she was crying and blubbering as if death itself had landed on her. She'd gone out the door and just entered *l'entrée grande*. Georg's reedy rumble was heard under her cries.

Amalina took up the key from the floor. Peeking outside, she saw.

The Count stood above Georg and Abraxa, though some yards away, in the open doorway.

He was much thinner, and tinier, reminding Amalina of the days when Genadie lay near death in the castle closet, and the Count seemed to shrink to a size almost as small as she. His large eyes regarded them with a gaze too steady, too unblinking for something living.

"Your lordship," Abraxa was crying, flattened on the ground just behind her husband. "Your eminence, your highness, your grandiosity, my beloved Count and King, you've returned!"

"We've kept your home as faithfully as if you'd been here every second," Georg groaned alongside her, matching her cries in volume. "Where others would have faltered in their devotion, to have lost faith in the absence of their lord, become mutinous while the captain was ashore and thought to leave or escape, we were the solid foundation of the castle itself."

"If you would but compare our service to how poorly the animals have fared, the neglect they have suffered in Genadie's careless hands, and which is not at all our sphere of employment, but his ..." Abraxa began anew. And the two carried on this way for some minutes, heaping as much derision as was possible on Genadie and Amalina's performance while he was gone. To Amalina it was infuriating, and eye-opening, to learn their tainted view of her. Just how awful her conduct could be reinterpreted and misrepresented, to make her appear as the laziest and worthless and untrustworthy of servants.

At least they don't know about Piotr, Amalina swallowed guiltily.

"Who is that?" the Count's basso voice rumbled from the doorway. "Ms. Dalca? Mouse, are you hiding from me back there?" He crossed the entrance hall, stepping right over his head-of-staff and maid. With reddened faces and throbbing veins in Abraxa's neck and on Georg's temple, the prickly pair watched as the Count, for the second time since Amalina had returned—after having been briefed on her many shortcomings—greeted her with the warmth reserved for old friends.

"I apologize for the girl's poor appearance at your reception this evening," Georg called after the Count, hopefully, "and her absolutely inexcusable and inappropriate clothing. If you've noticed them, your grace."

• • •

The Count went right for the cabinet. Amalina gulped as she shut the door to the study, wondering if she should keep it open in case she needed to run. This was it. Piotr would be found. She or her father, or both, would be executed—either by him or Kralov; whomever took the most offense at the bungled foray.

The Count opened the cabinet doors—the cabinet's real ones, in the front—and pulled out the map from the Great Library: The old, brittle map. He laid it open on his desk and pointed impatiently for Amalina to get closer with the candle.

As he spoke, his arm moved smoothly but very quick. He dropped his pen into the ink and then began placing more symbols onto the map, first in one direction, and then another, following odd trails that only he could see. He would make small circles, or small crosses, or a circle and a cross.

"The land has changed," he told her. "Much has changed. And this I knew. I know everything that happens here. But you were right. I haven't pushed the boundaries, I haven't bothered to really *pay attention*—no, not for a long time—to what I have at my disposal. Why assume I am trapped? It was my own mind that kept me here. When the sultan came for me, and I still had the capacity to resist the sun, my beloved counseled me not to leave. That I couldn't trust foreign lands for my safety, as I had never trusted them before. Why should they treat me any kinder than I treated them? she said. But had I run when the moment was there, I would have gotten past the mountains, and I would have been free. One should not always take the advice offered by loved ones. Because even though they may love you, and you them, they don't fully understand you. No."

The Count itched at his nose. He regarded the map, which now had farms promoted to hamlets, hamlets promoted to villages, villages promoted to towns, and some foreign villages and cities were added and placed just outside the mountains. He itched his nose again. He looked at the cabinet. Then he gazed sullenly down upon the map once more.

"Here it is, little mouse. My cage. All that lies within it is mine, and under my watch and control. Everything outside of this cage is the life I could have had, had I not listened to her. But here I am."

He itched his nose again, and glanced around the room as if looking for something, then waved at the map.

Amalina pretended to stare at the map. Inside she was crawling with the suspicion, with all his itching and looking about, he must be sensing Piotr.

How to get the Count to leave this room so she could get Piotr out? And get him safely away, at that?

"I took your advice, Ms. Dalca, and despite some minor alterations, my circumstances have not changed one whit. I am caught here. At the mercy of the fates."

"Not completely."

He itched his nose, starting to look irritated. "What do you mean?"

"Did you try eating blood other than human blood? Did you try to be delicate, and choose those who would celebrate the leaving of life? Did you attempt to take only the barest essence of what you require, and not just kill someone?"

"We're talking about this nonsense again? When it was settled that escaping this infernal cage is my only *realistic* course of action?"

"It wasn't settled. And you only know what is real when you've tried *everything*, sir. And that means trying *less* sometimes."

"I suppose you'll be happy to know that while I was out doing … *this* … I was too busy to see to my needs," he muttered resentfully. "I can hardly stand, let me tell you. But I devoted my entire effort into my project, only to see it shattered by damned reality. Now, you can either help me here or you can go to bed right now."

"All I was saying," she began firmly, "All I've *been* saying, is that it looks, to me, like you've accepted your curse instead of resisting it." He did not appear to understand, distracted by an itch to his nose, and it was left at that. He turned to face the cabinet, looking at it a little too long.

"You flew as far as you could?" she asked, returning his attention to her.

"Every route possible that I knew. Not all of it is as simple as you think, Ms. Dalca. The world curves at the horizon. The sun can spring from behind ridges suddenly. One has to take the highest precautions."

"You could not reach any of these cities across the border?" she asked, pointing to the marks that were still drying or he was absently blotting.

"I learned they were there. Never saw them. As it happens, I just tried for one. The closest. Couldn't make it. My castles are too far away."

Amalina suggested that if he would trust to something besides his castles—

"That's not how one survives," he said, scratching his nose and looking more agitated by the minute.

"Well then, why don't you just *move* one closer," Amalina returned, just as irritably.

The Count laughed. "But Amalina, you've got it. Yes. Yesss. Just as I thought you would. You've seen through my problem and solved it."

"Move your castle?" She pictured the high castle growing legs and walking down the valley and into the countryside. Or it riding on the back of the cart it took one thousand horses to pull, with Genadie up in a tower shaking the reins. She rubbed her face, she was getting tired.

Don't forget Piotr.

"Look, clever mouse. You see the solution, but you don't understand it yet," he pointed at the map with one thin, sickly looking finger, while he scratched his nose with the other. She wondered just how weak he might be. He hadn't fed in days. It was the longest he'd ever gone without nourishment, as far as she knew. Maybe if he opened the door to the hidden rooms, Piotr could actually beat him in the fight. Maybe keeping him away from the cabinet wasn't her concern after all. Maybe she should lead him through it. "Now I tell you, I can't make it to these cities, but that is because they are too far away from my castles. But why can't I just build a castle within my range, one that will allow me access to them come the longer nights? All I have to do is build the castles I need. Do you smell something?"

"Can you afford it?" Amalina asked. "It must be very expensive. To build it with stone as you say you must, in order to trust it for your protection? Do you have enough money anymore?"

"Money is of no concern. It will only cost me time, which would normally mean nothing to me, except now that I know I have the solution, it will take too long. How long must I wait to locate the perfect land, and to contract with the right sources, and to construct it to fit my requirements? You might not live long enough to see our project completed." His dismay turned to irritation again, as he itched his nose and looked around the room. "But I say, do you *smell* something?"

"No," she said, wondering if maybe … maybe she should point him to the cabinet. Maybe he wasn't so strong at all. Piotr had his dagger. As long as he hit hard, or could cut off his head before the Count could stop him. But Amalina felt a chill. A sweat grew on her. And she felt guilty for even thinking something so violent, and towards someone she was talking to. It seemed unnatural. "I don't smell anything."

The Count backed into the room, then circled it, sniffing. "Have I been gone so long?" sniff. "That I don't remember?" sniff, sniff. "It couldn't be." sniff, sniff, sniff. "But I don't recognize—there is a strange smell, and it seems to permeate the castle. An odor that doesn't belong."

Without a thought, the count lifted the divan with one hand. He pushed aside the desk and a bureau as if they were made of feathers. Though he looked drained, and shrunken, his might was tremendous. He went to the cabinet, and standing on his toes, worked the locking mechanism, and then he opened the impossibly heavy secret door with the effort of waving a hand through a mote of dust.

If Piotr jumps out right now, she thought, he will die.

"Oh, sir, I know what it must be," she said snapping her fingers, stopping him in the doorway. He closed the door with a gentle movement, looking at her suspiciously, and with a slight worry that by opening the secret door he'd absent-mindedly shown her something she wasn't supposed to know about. "The couriers. When they came—"

"Couriers?" he said, closing the door completely. *Clack.* "Whose couriers? They entered the castle? On whose orders? Not mine. Why weren't they stopped?"

"They were *couriers*, sir," said Amalina, questioning his objection. "And I wanted to talk to them—but, sir, you would *want* them here, sir. Of course, sir. They were delivering a message—"

"From who?" Shouting, his deep basso voice beat hard on her chest. It wasn't so much that he was frightened by the news, but that he wanted the answer quickly. Apparently he didn't like surprises. There should be no surprises in a world he controlled.

"From … From the princess, sir."

"Princ—" Then it came: his dawning realization! His eyebrows lifted to the middle of his forehead. "Princess? There's been a reply from the west? Where is it?"

His hands grasped at her greedily. Almost manic.

"I don't know, sir. Georg had it—"

"Georg!" The castle shook. But then his body shook, as if readying for something. There was a burst of air and he was gone, blown right through the door.

Something clattered outside the study door. Abraxa's legs were sprawled and kicking around on the floor outside. She must have been at the keyhole and the Count had bowled her over when he'd smashed through.

"Georg!" the Count's voice quaked through the castle. Georg's high-pitched scream followed.

Amalina took a step for the cabinet.

Then came the laugh, the Count's booming laugh of victory (that she'd heard all too often). It normally was the aftermath of a killing, and the prelude to her wishing she hadn't seen him again, his body and clothes painted with fresh blood—reminding her of the horrific creature he really was.

He was in the room again, the gust of air that followed him pushed Amalina into the wall.

"She's come. Yes, she's come," he growled merrily, waving the letter at her. Now his lips were pulled impossibly high on either side. The largest smile she'd ever seen in her life. "You thought they'd abandoned me, but I have *one*!"

"Yes," Amalina said. His happiness felt dangerous to be too close to, even in his depleted state. She retreated from the cabinet. Circling toward the door where Abraxa was still recovering and trying to get off her knees. "I thought at least one would answer, sir."

"Tell me about her," he said with the look of a child imagining a fresh pie. "Tell me about her again."

"Well," Amalina said. "She's nice—"

"Bah!"

With the feeling of a punch to her stomach, Amalina was suddenly in her room, thrown out onto her mattress.

"Pack your clothes," the Count said over her, smelling the paper he held, its colorful ribbon flapping at his eager breaths. "It's time for my Princess Tepsji to ready herself, to meet her good friend. It seems she values your friendship. Splendid. She trusts us. We must keep her pleased and amused. You must keep her pleased and amused until all is prepared for her entrance."

Amalina got off the bed, her head in a whirl.

The Count's eyes flicked toward the window. The stars were gone. The sky along the mountain ridge was purple. He frowned.

"Genadie will have everything ready and will take you to the black castle. You will meet with her in Tsobl, where she is waiting for you."

"N-not here?" Amalina stammered, feeling nauseous.

"Only when all is in its proper order and she's ready. Yes. The plan is coming together, isn't it, Ms. Dalca? Isn't it exciting?"

"Oh, uh-huh."

"Get moving, Mouse! It's almost sunrise!"

Only after she'd packed half her trunk (which had cracked up the middle when he threw it, with so much impatience, into the room) did she recover her wits. "What does the sunrise matter to me?" She shook her head and moved at the speed most appropriate, hoping to avoid seeing him again. Emptying her drawers methodically, on a quick thought she took the vial and the papers with the ciphers written on them. Everything secret had to come with, she guessed with a shrug. Part of her was simply observing what her body was doing and throwing in comments along the way. It seemed so unreal what was happening, the decisions that were being made. Too quick. Everything spinning like a top.

"Aren't you ready?" the Count groused from the doorway, his eyes on the dangerous red bloom along the eastern sky.

"Yes, I just—"

Wham!

Amalina was in the carriage. She heard the trunk land on top. She hoped it was closed.

The early morning air was cold and passed easily through her night clothes. She shivered. At least the cold tempered the nausea from the explosive trip down from the tower.

In the window, the Count's face appeared. He was holding his cloak over his head to block the growing light.

"I see you look cold, I will get you a blanket," he told her. "But tell me something, Ms. Dalca ... How long has it been since your body has had its last crisis?"

She didn't understand him, then she saw the look on his face and understood completely.

For some reason the question didn't make her skin crawl, but it felt like a relief. She'd been thinking of it just this morning, hadn't she? A fear and a question. A matter she'd only have confided to Sadra, and now it was a subject that was out in the open, regardless how disconcerting the circumstances. He'd asked about it plainly enough.

"It's been a long time," she said, leaning forward, speaking confidentially, and with a light worry, and a hope that he might have some answer. "No blood at all. For some time. For too long."

The Count gave a subtle smile of triumph, the happiness more in his eyes and his growl, than on his lips.

"Yesss. Perfect." He dumped a tin box onto her lap. It rattled. When she opened it, the round honey candies were inside. "You will continue to eat them. Not too often. But you will introduce them to our dear Princess when you meet her. Tell her they are your favorite if you have to, and insist she eat them. Let me know when she has done so. The timing of this must be right, so I don't have her visit spoiled for me. But you know what I mean."

A blanket appeared in her lap. Then Genadie shouted and the carriage tore out of the castle and onto the road.

It took a moment for Amalina to steady herself and catch up to the moment.

What was he talking about?

He's poisoned me, she thought angrily, feeling the tin rattling in her hands. No, that wasn't it. He'd altered her with these bits of medicine. Changed her chemistry to his preference and his advantage. He'd *cured* her, was how he probably looked at it, in his typical inward, selfish reasoning.

And, frankly—so it seemed to Amalina as she settled under the blanket, and sunk into the familiar jolting of the compartment, like she was nestled in swaying arms—it relieved her. Not only was an answer put to the fright she'd had in the morning, as to why she hadn't had to deal with the annoying pains, and the consequent care, maintenance and cleaning up—such a messy ordeal at times—of her body's cycle, but it was a decisive answer to the problem altogether. His feeding her the candies felt less like an invasion than a miracle he'd performed. She'd never have to bother with that issue again, and the trade-off was sucking on a honey-flavored lozenge? Thank you.

The entrepreneur in her, a calculating mindset germinated and cultivated in her by her father and the running of the family bakery, considered these honey drops a product that might be marketable. Every woman would want to buy it. She rattled the box in her hand.

No doubt the men of god would find something unnatural about it, she smirked. Considering its source, they would be right, of course.

Well, she wouldn't tell the princess what they were for, but let her have one to taste. She'll like it and not know the difference. And probably would be relieved at the side-effects. If she ever became worried, and confided to Amalina that her body was misbehaving in some way, Amalina would just reassure her it was the water or the mountain air. Everything will be all right when she got home.

She noticed the carriage had slowed. Looking outside, she saw that they were passing through Netz.

The carriage jolted as they turned out onto the highway, and launched toward Kirgyl and then on to Tsobl. Who knows how long or short that would take, considering the unnatural speeds Genadie could work the horses up to when required.

Glancing back towards Netz, she saw the iron basket with Roti's body inside. Roti looking bored and rotting. And on the board the warning to outsiders.

Poor Roti, she thought.

Stunned, Amalina realized that in the chaos and confusion of the Count's arrival and then her rushed departure, she'd left Piotr locked inside the castle.

Part Two
Count Tepsji's
Palace of Pleasure

24

Spaarvierlet

The Count's castle near Tsobl, known as the Black Castle, was tucked high up in the mountains and at the end of a narrow winding road that was so overgrown the carriage had to be stopped, forcing Amalina and Genadie to walk the last three uphill miles. Panting and shaking, and wishing they'd brought more food with them, they arrived at the gates. The reason for the Black Castle's name was instantly obvious. Its blocky high walls were dark as smoke, like the stonework along the upper lip of a fireplace, though the color was uniform and not an uneven cloudy stain. Amalina wondered if it had been painted that way. The building was impressive and imposing in its size, but in daylight it wasn't as frightening as it could have been. Its color made it appear more like a derelict vessel which had sat too long under the sun and had burnt out; become carbonized, not haunted. And the high hour made the whole setting seem alive and benign. Even the birds were chirping brightly, as if in greeting. As if delighted to have them there.

Genadie's legs were kicking around on top of the wall before she'd realized he'd begun climbing the rough outer barrier. She suspected there must be some hidden hand and footholds for him to climb so quickly. His legs worked like a frog until he'd shimmied over the ledge and fell in.

"Genadie?" she called. He didn't answer.

The sound of his pattering feet echoed from above, so she shrugged and surveyed the wilderness around them. The mountain wasn't as tall as some of the others. The Black Castle was below the treeline and the woods pressed up right against it, with trees so tall their green shade covered the lower half of the castle. There wasn't even a moat to separate the fortress from the outside world. Maybe one of the reasons the Count did not stay there, he not trusting locations that were in the least bit vulnerable. The woods would hide the approach of an army, and could be burnt to try to smoke him out, or spread the fire to the castle. Maybe that is what had happened at some point—some great conflagration—which had given the deathly color to the castle's stone. It had to've happened very long ago, though, maybe centuries, for the forest to have regrown so high and thick.

Amalina spotted a grouping of blue flowers. She picked them and set them by the gate. A touch of pretty color. Then she found a pocket of strangely colored flowers with large petals. Purple with deep red spots, like a purple cloth spotted with blood. The stems were tall and thick, and she gathered almost an armful because there were still dozens upon dozens more stretching off like a stream into the forest.

The gate creaked open, sending the echoes of woody pops and metallic screeches through the valley below. Amalina stepped in only to have Genadie shoo her back out. With a shake of a head and a scowl on his lips, he quietly indicated that there was no reason for them to enter.

"What's the matter?"

"Twenty or forty …" he mumbled in his scratchy voice.

"Twenty or forty what?" she asked.

"I don't know how I'll find twenty or forty men to clear this out." On their way back down he assessed the road's overgrowth and kept adding. "Fifty. No, sixty. At the very least."

When she threw the flowers into the cramped interior of the carriage, she saw a bush of wild berries through the window. She yelped, catching Genadie off guard, and ran to them, her stomach growling.

"Berries! Berries!" she cried, as she grabbed them and threw them in her mouth. They were more tart than sweet, but with her hunger they were delicious.

Genadie leapt off the driver's bench and pulled her back.

"No, Ms. Dalca! Stay away from those!"

"Have some Genadie. I know you're starving. Here, there are so many. Don't be like that."

"No, no," he said, dragging her back to the carriage.

"But why not? What's the matter?"

"Can't have you staining your face and fingers with those berries, Ms. Dalca. Just think of it! No, you get in and get changed into your good dress on our way to the city. As it is, if we don't hurry, we'll be too late to meet the princess."

• • •

Princess Lisbet Spaarvierlet. The most striking feature about her was her bulk of thick blond hair (blond hair, as Amalina understood it, normally being very thin) which puffed out like a bale of straw on all sides of her head, so that it was difficult for her to wear a hat, and it needed to be gathered in a blue ribbon almost as wide as a bolt of fabric at the back of her slender white neck. This made her head appear unnaturally large, and seemed to create a yellow glow around her, especially when the sun was behind her. The rest of her was thin, tall and creamy pale, so that at a great distance she might look like someone was standing there holding up a tall, white painted oar, with its yellow-painted head stuck in the air. Her features were smooth and delicate, with round eyes whose color was as blue as berries; with triangles of lighter blue within those eyes, making it look like there was a core fire of ice crystals inside. She had a long, straight nose that ended with two little smooth shells of flesh on either side. And below that, a pleasantly shaped mouth with pale pink lips. Her lips were almost always touched with a slight smile, and her head tilted in a way that made it seem she was bashful, or maybe embarrassed by her height and elegant beauty. Or as though maybe her hair was too much to hold up by her thin neck but she was gamely trying. Her long, delicate fingers, sporting rings of gold with emeralds and sapphires inlaid, were crossed together in front of her at all times. Unless she was reaching out to clasp the hands of a friend, which she was partial to doing because, above all else, Princess Lisbet Spaarvierlet was nice.

Which saddened and troubled Amalina, because she felt nothing but what a fraud she was herself, misleading Lisbet into thinking she was equal in station. As the carriage rumbled along the rough road down from the Black Castle, Amalina twisted this way and that, kicking her legs out like an acrobat, stabilizing herself by pushing her head against the carriage ceiling, sweating all up and down her limbs and back, to struggle into the dress of an Ardeelian princess.

"Any decent princess would expect two or three maids to help her with this," grumbled Amalina. "So she can eat treats and read a book while the dress simply makes its way on, not a drop of sweat."

"What's that?" cried Genadie from above.

"I need your help."

"There's no time, Ms. Dalca. Make due."

She seethed on silently. And from the Count's chest—the Count being a murderer, a troubling thought—and Lady Flauna's make-up box—Lady Flauna having been murdered, a more troubling thought—Amalina took the canisters and bottles (the possessions of a killer and his victim), and fumbled before a polished brass mirror to apply the make-ups in an attempt to age her appearance, and somehow leaven herself into something more than a baker's daughter, which is all she saw in her reflection.

"Help me, Genadie."

"No time!"

"This isn't going to work!"

"Never worry, all will be as Zeus demands."

"But I need your help! I won't be able to keep it up. I can't keep it up."

"Are you crying, Ms. Dalca?"

"What a charade! I mean, think about it: it was impossible enough when we were over there in the west!"

"Stop crying."

"It was like an alien world. I only had to disguise *myself*. But here, Lisbet's the outsider, and this is supposed to be *my* homeland. Princess Katarina Tepsji's homeland. And so now I'm going to have to spread a ... a curtain of lies over everything she sees and asks me about—everyone she meets, every place she visits—so that it looks like Princess Tepsji is real and belongs in it!"

"Oh, well ..."

"I'm going to have to improvise lies and sustain my falsehoods on a continuing, unending ... Oh, I can't do it! I just can't!"

"I *will* help you, Ms. Dalca."

"Will you?"

"I promise."

"I'm going to need it! All the help I can get! I feel so alone."

"Master and I will always be there for you."

And even while she continued to worry over the seeming impossible demands of her job, all the while she was agitated, too, by the thought of Piotr locked inside the high castle—trapped there—waiting for the Count to enter and discover him; and kill him. No, these were not the experiences and concerns of a countess or lady or princess. Not at all. And the princess was quick enough to notice something of a change in her friend.

"Did I say something wrong?" asked Lisbet after all the hugging and kissing, and the first flurry of compliments and the requisite recounting of friends and family came to an end; when Amalina plummeted from the reverie of being a princess, and remembered again who she really was, underneath all the imposter clothes and makeup, and recalled her darker circumstances. Lisbet traced her lithe finger along Amalina's cheek, then twirled the lock of hair hanging by her ear. Amalina recognized the sweet, almost subliminal scent of the princess' perfume—the perfume Amalina had mentioned liking so much before. Lisbet had thoughtfully worn it for their reunion.

Amalina shook her head, trying to stuff her unhappiness behind an upward slanted veil of teeth. It looked as artificial as it felt.

"But you look so sad, my dear. I thought I could never stop smiling and laughing when I saw you again. And I never questioned it would be the same for you. Oh, I was elated for the invitation. And though it was your uncle who extended the offer, I was sure it was your doing."

Amalina admitted it was her doing, "of course," still sounding artificially sunny.

"I hope I haven't come at the wrong time."

"Your timing is perfect."

"Are you well?"

"Quite so. I've never been better … until I got your letter and I felt I might faint from happiness."

"Then what is the shadow that's passed over you?" she said, with concern. "And so soon after our meeting, precious Kat?"

"No shadow, Lees," assured Amalina, returning to their pet names. "Oh, it's been a long travel here. Maybe my body isn't recovered."

"That must be it," she agreed, cheerily. "It took weeks for us to get here, but it wasn't until we entered your country I thought I'd never seen such hard roads. Have some of these cakes and tea, Kat. They will refresh you. Believe me, I can't have you leaving me just yet or I might die. I'm all alone here."

Amalina looked around the room. Lisbet wasn't alone, literally speaking. She had her entourage of three maids, and outside were the footman and drivers for her coach. She meant she wanted the companionship of someone her own rank and familiarity. *Her own rank and familiarity*, Amalina swallowed guiltily. Before another 'shadow' passed over her face, she grabbed a small plate with cake on it and put the piece into her mouth, making a pleased noise and closed her eyes until the shame of her deceit passed.

How am I going to keep this up? she wondered.

"Oh, I can see that doesn't quite please you either," she pouted. "Let's make plans, Katty, and look forward to our happy time together. Can we? The thought of getting to know you better, and to see the magnificent land you are from—so different from my own—and the castles, it makes me tingle. Can you feel it in my fingers? I'm so excited, let me rub it off on you." She caressed Amalina again.

And what can be said about a conversation between two young Lady Princesses reunited? They genuinely liked each other and enjoyed each other's company, and so anything they had to say was gentle and kind. The only item of note was after Lisbet mentioned, with some regret, that the governor and almost everyone of title in Tsobl had snubbed her. Even the purported kin of Tepsji had not responded to her inquiries, much less opened their homes to her. And so she felt very alone—for three whole days—as she waited for the Count or Katty to arrive or reply, and rescue her from this unfortunate solitude. And for all that shunning she was left feeling as if she had come down with leprosy. Amalina had to do damage control and thus create another set of lies to account for the shameful actions of people she did not know, much less know they even existed before Lisbet mentioned them. Amalina, thinking quickly to push them onto fresher ground, brought up their itinerary and the fact that they would be staying in the Count's nearest castle—after she'd seen to its preparation—before they then moved on to Netz.

"His nearest castle?"

"He calls it his Black Castle."

"If you are going there tonight, could I go with you? I'd beg you. The thought of another lonely night in this city is so dreary."

"Go with me?" Amalina took a sip of tea. Her mouth had gone very dry. The idea was to get away from the nice princess, get some space to breath and think. *Think, Amalina.* "But as I said, I came down from Netz. That's where I stay normally, and I haven't visited the Black Castle in so long, I couldn't even say if it is ready to receive ... Genadie?"

Genadie started as if from sleep, then bowed and stepped forward, "My lady?"

"Nice of you to help me, Genadie," said Amalina, sweetly. "Has uncle prepared the castle to receive? Lees would like to accompany me there."

He tilted his head this way and that. "You can return to it anytime you wish, my lady. For the Lady Spaarvierlet ... I expect perhaps in a couple days."

Lisbet made a sorry sound. Her fine, straw-yellow eyebrows came together in a pretty show of worry above her delicate nose. "Will you be leaving me here, then, Katty?"

"I'll stay with you as long as you want," Amalina assured her, feeling sorry for the older girl. Sorry that she was already exhausted by the interaction and couldn't hold off expressing it. "Who would I rather stay with, uncle or my dearest friend?"

Lisbet had Amalina's hands caught in hers and she squeezed them, staring into her eyes with a warmth she couldn't help being charmed by.

"Well then, tell me about your Black Castle," she said. "It sounds romantic!"

"Tell you about the Black Castle?"

Amalina glanced to Genadie, who'd withdrawn into the wall again and looked to have fallen asleep. Some help.

Amalina mumbled how boring the castle really was, hoping the disinterest would catch on. "It's large and amazing to look at from the outside, but I actually don't know much about it. I haven't been in it in a very long time. I don't like cities, and prefer the countryside. And we'll be visiting the high castle before long, which I can tell you in detail. If anything, that is my home."

"But before that," Lisbet said, nodding at what Amalina had just said, sensing the subject was not to Amalina's liking and very considerately not pressing for more details, "maybe tell be more about your uncle, whose generosity and kindness has not only provided me with a vacation and the promise of an exotic education, but gifted me your friendship. Please, even if you repeat yourself from what you told me in the spring, tell me again. We have hours, and just hearing you talk pleases me greatly."

Amalina cleared her throat. "My uncle?"

… You mean, that ancient blood eating monster? Whose true purpose for inviting you has nothing to do with providing opportunities to entertain yourself, or to allow you to strengthen a new friendship with his niece. Who is not, in fact, his niece at all, but a tradesman's daughter he kidnapped and made his servant? What he hopes to gain from you, I don't understand. What he will do with you once he has gotten what he wants (like so many of his victims' bodies from centuries past, from whom he fed), I don't know.

But if you timed your visit right, you could have arrived just in time to see him die at the hands of revolutionaries, or witness the expression of his unbelievable power as he rips them all, and me, to pieces.

The pain Amalina thought she could stow away reignited. As she lied to Lisbet of her uncle's exploits (adventures she borrowed from story books that she hoped her friend hadn't read), she realized how unbearable this mission was going to be.

I can't possibly keep this up!

Even actors get to leave the stage.

But she wasn't an actor anymore. She was a professional imposter. And for the time being—for her own life, and the sake of her father's—she would have to excel at it. Keep the smile on the face, keep telling the made-up stories to an innocent girl of the western kingdoms, until she herself believed what was coming out of her mouth. So that she could solidify the stories into stone, and not have to even think in order to spout them, but simply remember them as if they really happened.

Princess Lisbet Spaarvierlet listened attentively with a gentle smile, her eyes studying her and following along as if there were nobody else in the world more important than her dear friend Kat and what she was saying. It made Amalina feel terrible. When finished, Amalina was convinced to tell Lisbet Spaarvierlet another lie would be impossible. That she would keel over and die first.

Genadie cleared his throat.

"Genadie?" Amalina wondered what would cause him to interrupt. Had he found some way to help her?

He held out the tin.

"Oh, yes," Amalina said, wanting to roll her eyes. "You have to try these treats from Uncle Tepsji. They're delicious. They taste just like honey and I can't tell you how much I love them. Here take one."

•••

Two days later, as the Black Castle loomed over them like a thrown up shard of the mountain, Amalina, still in the grip of a black mood, thought it very strange that she, the supposed Ardeelian princess, would be seeing its insides for the first time right alongside a stranger who'd traveled nearly a thousand miles to visit this foreign land. The stranger, Princess Spaarvierlet, would be free to express her awe. Amalina must feign familiarity, no matter the surprises. She hoped Genadie would be able to cover her mistakes.

And Genadie's help *was* needed: through the small, blackened oak doors, they walked into what was the largest, highest enclosed space Amalina had ever seen. Stairs descended from the doorway to the deep pit of the hall, and in the distance the walls rose like solid, massive obsidian slabs to the height of the sky. It was difficult to see the vaulted ceiling, it could only be assumed to be there. Light sliced the darkness through narrow slits, placed at seeming random places and heights, creating bright, shifting shafts of dust motes in the air, and white rectangles on the black floor. Wide staircases snaked into tall, thin, rectangular openings along the wall. Their steps echoed in the cavern. Echoes which barely covered the combined, impressed gasps of Lisbet and Amalina.

"*Black Castle*," shouted Genadie (though too late to cover Amalina's audible surprise), "was built by Count Tepsji's great-grandfather, in the anticipation of invasion by the sultan. It can defend against a siege. But if penetrated, the forces can be withdrawn several more times, each hall a new battlefield to be taken."

"I've never seen anything like it," Lisbet said, squeezing Amalina's hand for reassurance. She had been so happy on the trip from Tsobl, and clapped excitedly when she'd caught sight of the castle. The smoky outer black walls hadn't given enough warning that a feeling of being immediately swallowed into the depths of a dark otherworld waited inside the main castle. Now her eyes blinked and she looked like a child who was suddenly menaced to death by a wild dog she'd at first taken to be sweet and friendly.

"You'll get used to it," Amalina said, tamping down a shiver of her own.

"No, no. I shouldn't want to get used to it. How amazing it is. And how long it must have taken to build. If it were closer to home, this castle would be very popular." It was nice of her to say, but her apprehension was written in her large, round eyes twitching in the direction of every clamoring echo, as if the sounds presaged an unholy attack. "Where is everyone?"

"Outside aren't they?" said Amalina. They'd passed nearly sixty hunched and toiling bodies, still chopping and pulling away the overgrowth along the road and inside the outer walls.

"I thought those were laborers."

"Gypsies," Genadie said. "They're hard workers, yes."

"But I mean," Lisbet looked all around again, "there's nobody *here?* Inside?"

"Yes," Amalina agreed. "Where is everyone?"

"Uh, they are down in the city gathering supplies, my lady. They should be here by nightfall—I hope. You know how your Uncle's main force of servants stays with him at all times in the high castle."

Amalina nodded understandingly, trying to help the lie along.

"Stingy," Lisbet laughed. "Sounds just like my father, if my mother would let him get away with it."

"We really aren't used to guests, I'm afraid," Amalina said. "And we didn't expect … I mean, though I'd hoped so very much that it would be so, but … we didn't expect you'd come at his invitation. And visiting us so soon—so very soon—was the greatest surprise. I thought it would be letters back and forth, and dates in the calendar set months before you arrived—"

"I'm sorry. I didn't mean to be so forward."

"I'm glad you were! We're both so very happy for it! Just forgive us if we're a little shorthanded."

The serviceable explanation was enough. The castle's darkness and echoes kept the princess' mind occupied.

"Before it gets too late," she said hopefully, "show me where you found those tulips. We should bring them into the castle to add some color."

Amalina suspected the poor girl just wanted an excuse to get back outside.

Outside, the princess sighed. "The land is very beautiful, the way the meadowlands roll out from the valleys, the valleys from the mountains, it's like looking down off the back of a bird when you're in the right spot. The air is fresh. The people so strong and happy. And the tulips you brought are incredible. I've never seen ones of those colors, and so late in the season. I'd think they'd fetch a fortune if they were brought to market back home. Thank you again, they are so pretty."

"My uncle will be pleased to hear how much you enjoy them. Your pleasure is his priority."

"Well, I can't wait to meet him," Lisbet said. "It was so kind of him to offer his home, and the opportunity to study this country. I have more gifts for him, of course, in return for his kindness. I hope he'll like them. And my father also sent some interesting and valuable pieces along." She looked embarrassed. "I feel like an explorer bearing gifts to the natives … oh, well, it seems ungraceful, but our hearts are in the right place, I assure you. There's nothing more important than solidifying bonds of family and friendship, and we don't want to spoil it or make the wrong move to frighten you off."

"You couldn't."

"To come here as precipitously as I did, and without much in the way of warning." She shrugged, falling into a deeper embarrassment.

"Please, Lees, we are so happy you did." Amalina took the opportunity to squeeze her friend's arm for a change, to finally be the reassurer. "My only surprise is I never thought my uncle could entice anyone into the Ardeel."

"My father hopes for me to stay here forever, I'm sure," Lisbet's embarrassed smile shrank, faded. Her yellow eyebrows moved ambiguously on her forehead, her thoughts fighting themselves, darkening. "The longer I'm out of his hair the better, really ... But that's the way it is. My mother didn't want me to go. She'd prefer I was back tomorrow. Somewhere in between those two is where my plan lies. Or rather, I suppose it will be as long as I please your uncle. I hope you live nearby to him?"

"But as I said, I live with him."

"You mentioned that you stayed with him often. But *always*?"

"It's a good arrangement," Amalina said, trying not to smirk.

"Your parents don't miss you?" asked Lisbet.

"My father more than my mother. But to tell you the truth, I miss my mother much more. I see her less, because she lives far, far away."

For the first time, Lisbet was silent. Amalina wasn't sure she'd heard her answer. Her remarkable blue eyes had dropped to the ground. Even her smile was completely lost. Her brightness withered.

What did this mean?

But the princess soon recovered from her strange upset and pressed Amalina's hands, and asked if Amalina really enjoyed the cakes she'd brought and really enjoyed her company. Amalina smiled genuinely. She vowed not to allow the shadow of her own deceit and misery to continue, as it had now somehow found its way into poor Lisbet.

But no ... Amalina saw this wasn't her shadow at work, infecting the princess. This was a darkness Lisbet owned herself.

So her friend wasn't as perfect as she had feared. Something troubled the older girl. Which meant there was something of trouble inside them both. Something different, but equally hidden. Just below the surface.

It would be easier for Amalina to proceed in this relationship knowing they had *something* in common—something real—even if it couldn't be spoken; even if it was bleak, sad or sinister. They could bond silently, she thought. Commiserate in spirit.

This was a happy thought.

But what in the world, wondered Amalina, could trouble a beautiful princess?

25

Destiny is Waiting

For Attila, night had lost its power of fear.

The ancient Ardeelian rule to bar shut all doors and windows, from dusk to dawn, in fear of darkness, was easier to ignore in a cosmopolitan city like Tsobl: so many people, mostly foreigners, had questioned the need for the prohibition, especially in the summer when an open window would relieve the closeness; and the locals, having learned of the foreigners' rule-flouting, figured it's a survivable breach; and habits—even ones known to keep you alive—have a tendency to die away. Besides, as the theory went, if so many people disobey the rule, falling victim to Ardeel's most famous creature of the night was less likely. There would be too many more targets to choose from, especially if you were not a young woman, who seemed to be the primary victims. Most everyone, it turns out in the end, is a gambler. And as soon as one person succeeds in violating a rule, no matter how serious it is, the next follows suit. The ancient Ardeelian rule became, in Ardeel's capitol, a quaint superstition.

But while Attila was raised from childhold in Tsobl, the rule was a strong reflex in his gut, because he'd been nannied by a true Ardeel native. She passed on the night's sense of danger, the consequences of disobeying superstition. And then he'd read the Secret History of the Tsobl Constabulary, and had her warnings confirmed. And he came face-to-face with them in his investigation of the St. Grigori graveyard. And had them backed up by the governor's admission. And so his anxiety grew during his flight into the rural lands. It took many days before he was comfortable starting or keeping a fire at his small camp. Only after nearly a month without being molested or hunted, and realizing there were many who lived outside that ancient rule, and slept comfortably under the stars—the hunters and trappers and woodsman, all lone men; and didn't Zsolt Marosh sleep without a tent on his famous hunts?—did Attila really begin to relax. After all, he reasoned, Ardeel was a massive land, with countless mountains and forests. What was the chance the creature would find one single person— and without a good reason to do so? Finally, after three months of silent agonizing, he could fall asleep in the wild with a fire still burning.

He poured river water onto the smoldering fire until it was a mush of grey ashes. Then he went to try his luck.

He took his position and saw that the day was starting well. Gug, Hak's wife, was stomping up the path, a determined look on her face—always cautious about leaving the farm alone in the hands of her husband, and in a hurry to return. She only broke concentration for birds, which she liked to stop and admire. Though she never fed them. Even when the feathered pretties came to her and begged for crumbs, she held onto her food like any handout was a robbery. Attila idly wondered if it was his fault for her strange unkindness, because she had been so generous to him, which spoke of a generous nature, and then he'd betrayed her.

At the right moment he whistled. Gug heard the morning bird and her expression softened. Her stride slowed and became less emphatic, and she looked into the forest canopy seeking the bird. When she took her next step there was the crunch-snap of weak sticks, and Gug dropped out of sight.

Attila rushed to the trap. His throat closed and he couldn't breathe. She hadn't yelled or made a sound after she fell. The thought of her having broke her neck because of him would stop his heart, he was sure of it.

Gug was laid out in the gloom of the pit, atop the pieces of underbrush he'd used to disguise the hole. She did not move and her eyes were closed. His heart didn't stop as he'd thought, but he was getting ready to vomit. The pit was very deep, but the multiple levels of sticks he'd used to slow her descent should have made it less than lethal, and should have just deposited her on the bottom. His real worry when fashioning it was that she would either see the trap for what it was and avoid it—thus his distracting birdcall to draw her attention—or that the aggregate of levels would slow her too much, and she wouldn't even reach the bottom, but stop at a point so shallow she could climb right out. Her dying was not only unintended and unsought for, it was unthinkable.

Gug moved. Her hands slowly crept around and patted her chest, her waist. She groaned. Then she looked up.

"Who's that?" she asked.

"I'm sorry," Attila said, his voice even, his eyelids at their steady half-mast. "I'm really very sorry, Mrs. Vogoneyevic. You aren't hurt are you? You weren't meant to be."

"By god, you're still here?" she laughed crossly. "You've done this to me, you criminal?"

"Not a criminal," in a calm voice. "Please, I only wish you to hear me out."

"I saved you and now I shall never be rid of you, is that it?"

"Please, Mrs. Vogoneyevic. I seek to reason with you."

"By throwing me down a pit?"

"You fell in."

"And who made it?"

"Let's not argue but reason here. Your husband has a duty he must perform for his people."

"His people?" she howled. She rolled onto her knees and brushed the dirt away.

"And his land. And his ancestors. There is a blot on his family line which he must erase. And he must free this country of its eternal tyrant."

"You expect Hak to do this for you?"

"Not for me," pronounced Attila. "For us all. For you and your children. Imagine if they could live—your son and your beautiful daughter, Lija—if they could live without fear."

She told him they needed Hak. Needed him with them. On the farm.

"I shall only borrow him for a while. I promise. He shall be returned to you a man come into his own. A hero across the land. His fortunes and dignity restored."

"He suits me as he is."

"Think of your children and their posterity."

"Let's discuss this hole you've thrown me into."

"Hear me out and you will be freed."

"Hear you out and agree with you, you mean," she said. "And if I disagree, I stay here and rot?"

"No."

"Then I agree. Let me up."

"You must be sincere."

"I am."

"I will let you know, Mrs. Vogoneyevic, that if you agree, I will not release you from the pit immediately. To ensure your honesty, I will go to your husband and take him away. Only after we leave I will send your children to bring you out."

"What nonsense!"

"I can't have you taking back your word once you're up and Hak listen to you and be guided by you."

"As soon as he finds out what you've done to me, he will tear you apart."

"That's why you won't tell him what happened. If you agree."

"Here's what's going to happen, Mr. Bronk: You are going to get me out of this pit. If you have the dearest shred of courage in you and you wish for my permission to let Hak leave this farm, you will let me out of this hole without my word. I will only give it to you once I am out."

Attila's dull eyes regarded her as he considered it.

"I agree to nothing unless you let me up this instant."

Attila gripped his shaking left hand. Then he nodded.

He took the nearby branch ladder and sent it down into the hole. As she climbed it with the same determined stomping motion with which she walked, his hopes sank a little. He'd trusted her, but she was about to attack him again. At least this time she didn't have a knife in her hand. He considered running. Instead, he held out his hand as she came to the top. Red faced, eyes bulging with the effort, she laughed scornfully and took it.

"You're a dismal man," she said as she patted herself off. "But you've at least shown bravery. You're no coward."

"Never," he said. "So I have your permission?"

She shoved a finger in his face. "Do you know what you are taking from me? From the children? Do you understand what you are taking from us, sir? Do you know the value of it? How much will you pay me if you lose him, Mr. Bronk? Eh? How much are you prepared to pay?"

"I understand," he said, nodding slightly. "I have your permission?"

"See what Hak says," she scowled like she was cursing at him. "Go see. I have a hole to fill so the children don't get hurt.

• • •

Hak set down his ax and gawked in disbelief as Attila wandered into the farm. Belatedly he chuckled and shook his head.

"You believe in *something*," chortled Hak. "You have your mind set, don't you, Mr. Bronk?"

Attila nodded. "I'm not playing games."

"Waited until Gug was gone to hook me, eh? You're lucky she didn't slice you into twenty pieces."

"I have you to thank that she did not." Attila bowed slightly. "But I've spoken to her."

"You have?"

"Just now. On the road. She was more favorable to me this time."

"She is a kind-hearted woman."

"I agree. And she has seen reason, Sir Vogoneyevic."

"Sir?"

"You are of the Vogoneyevic dynasty. You are a true lord of this land."

"Huh," was all he said to that. He wiped the back of his sweaty, sun-browned neck.

"Mrs. Vogoneyevic, your wife, she agrees with my assessment. She believes it, too."

"She does? She said that?"

"Sir, there is very little time. Too much of it has been wasted as evil reaches out into the world to regain its hold. While she is off to market, and will return to see to the needs of the children, you will come with me and we will do what should have been done long ago, and rescue this land from its tyrant."

"Sounds like a good thing to do," he said. "But she really said all that?"

"She's not a woman of so many words. She has agreed for you to go, and that is what matters. And we shouldn't waste any more time, sir. Destiny is waiting."

"We might waste a little more time, I think," Hak said, pulling up the ax. "Seems like I remember you were going to tell me something last time we spoke."

"Yes, sir."

"Don't see what's changed, Mr. Bronk. Aside from Gug being kind and giving you room, and all. It's a tough thing you say I should do. A tough thing."

"Striking down evil is always difficult. But it is necessary."

"Leaving Gug, Man, and Lija," Hak elaborated. He hefted his ax again. Attila nodded to let him know he understood. "So what you're going to do, Mr. Bronk, is you're going to tell me what you had to say before. Let's have it out. What is it you really want me to do, and what's the good reason I should. If I like what I hear, I will go with you."

"You will like what you hear," assured Attila, watching the sharp blade of the ax bounce up and down.

"I hope so, Mr. Bronk."

26

The Test

After nearly a week, Amalina began to feel claustrophobic. Lisbet naturally wanted to cling to her only friend in Ardeel. And so they spent every waking hour together, with Amalina desperately trying to invent new stories about her life, or retell old ones (recalling as many details as she could from their first telling), or more often redirecting their conversation to Lisbet's family and Lisbet's experiences; encouraging the *real* princess to expand at length. There were many quiet walks in the forest, picking pretty flowers, with Genadie and several gypsies close by, armed with rifles, to ward off the wolves. There was riding practice on the backs of the princess' indifferent carriage horses, while they spoke of the prettiest horses they knew. And they clucked merrily about the taste of the honey balls while conducting races to see who could finish one first, or who could make one last the longest. Amalina and Genadie began tutoring Lisbet in the eastern languages (which she picked up quickly). Twice a day Lisbet would insist on brushing Amalina's hair (one hundred and fifty strokes required), cooing over its luxuriousness and rich color, and Amalina would attack Lisbet's blond bramble of a head with the brush, amazed by how thick and cotton-like her hair was, and hoping not to pull out a chunk of her head if she pulled too hard. They tested and rated Lisbet's perfumes. They turned many different figures of many different dances, with music supplied by more gypsies lured from the nearby camp, the players restraining their fiddles and cymbaloms to imitate the staid court musicians. And Amalina outsmarted Lisbet at chess matches, while Lisbet taught Amalina a game with cards that (she assured) the church would not frown upon. Amalina was even able to leverage Lisbet's visit to reestablish regular prayer and bible reading on the holy days. And with their inclination to worship, the Count's hostility to religious practice—a fact which didn't seem to bother the spiritual Lisbet—was exploited to get out of the Count's castle and back down to Tsobl, in order to attend proper church services. And to try some finer food and buy some clothes.

But all the while, Amalina was crushed by fear of Piotr's fate. She wondered when he'd be discovered, every new day convincing her that it must have happened already. And before he died, what would he tell the

Count? When was her punishment coming? What was the Count waiting for?

What *was* he waiting for? For his medicine to take its effect on Lisbet? Even Genadie couldn't say when the Count would appear. And so, just as in the Count's previous extended absence, when he was testing his Ardeelian cage, and Amalina wanted to explore the study's hidden room but was being thwarted by circumstance, she felt her valuable time was being wasted. She had the secret message and the secret codes in her luggage. And she had the strange metal link, and Kralov's vial, too. Any one of these items might forward her cause against the Count. But nothing could be done because Lisbet, pleasing as her companionship was, was locked to her arm with the tenacity of a tick.

Amalina didn't realize how much Lisbet was affixed to her until they were riding to Tsobl, and the further they got from the Black Castle, the more the princess released her grip. Amalina's arm felt weightless when finally freed. Looking to her companion, Lisbet was gazing out the window, her light smile growing at the corners. The princess sighed (loudly) when they crossed the bridge into the city, as did the princesses' maids, who sat across the compartment. The Black Castle, now far behind them, was not to Lisbet's liking.

The carriage stopped short, sending Lisbet and Amalina up from their cushions.

Outside was a train of large men wearing peasant clothes, fur hats and sober looks.

"Oh my!" Lisbet said, her cheek pressed close to Amalina's in the window. "Who are they?"

"They look like farmers, or hunters. But they must be miners or loggers."

"Why do you think so?"

"Only miners and loggers walk around in big groups like that."

"And gypsies," Lisbet said, showing off her new-found rustic knowledge: she'd noticed how the laborers outside the Black Castle kept bunched, and never traveled in less than five. But she hadn't yet learned it was out of native Ardeelian superstition and precaution—the itinerant mountain people living lives exposed to the wild's most hostile elements. Elements the princess didn't fully comprehend, just as Amalina hadn't understood them until a little more than a year ago.

Amalina showed off what she had gleaned of city life during her travels by adding to their list: "And pilgrims travel in groups, and religious orders."

"And armies," Lisbet concluded.

Armies!

"What *is* it?" the princess asked, making room. Amalina had sat up straight.

She was now no longer looking at a line of miners or loggers or pilgrims or an odd sect of monks. She was witnessing Kralov's men on the move. She counted thirty of them. All with the same brushed fur cap, the same build, the same stern expression. They marched with an irregular step but a common purpose through the intersection, headed towards the end of town which led out to the highway to Netz.

"Oh, it's nothing," Amalina said, withdrawing and shaking her head. "It gets lonely up in the castle sometimes ..."

• • •

Amalina was unsettled to see Kralov's fur-hatted irregulars file into the Tsobl Cathedral at the very back, humbly crossing themselves and removing their hats, their heads bowed.

Their entrance didn't attact much attention, even with their intimidating size, moody looks and the massive knives on their belts. The bishop was already in full swing, his sermon bent on reminding everyone, rich and poor, outsiders, everyone, that their position within the church, according to heaven and the ultimate order of the universe, fit together as one single lowly mass; prone beneath the foot of the Pope. Be that as it may, Amalina and Lisbet, being royalty but strangers in town, had had to make room for themselves near the back rows, set far from the cordon of the wealthy and some political elite, who crowded the pulpit and made sure the mass had been arranged inside the church to a proper stratification. Amalina and Lisbet were within the commoners's ranks (which the nice Princess Spaarvierlet had no qualms condescending to do). This made it easier for Amalina to notice who was pressing in at the rear doors.

Throughout the sermon, Amalina kept turning in place, checking the men were still standing there. They did not look at her but stared with sober looks over the tops of the congregation at the distant gesticulating bishop. She peeked often enough so it caught Lisbet's eye and she poked Amalina, and gave her a playful look, then redirected her attention.

The bishop wrapped things up with something about healing divisions. Divisions that had caused a fracture in the world. That the bonds at the seams were still weak and should not be played with lightly. The threat to order was great, and the upset of order would gain little for anyone.

For some reason Lisbet was moved to tears. Her chin went to her chest, and she patted her eyes. Her little pink lips pulsed with red and pointed down at the ends. Amalina took her hand and petted it. The princess nodded her appreciation. Then she took out a handkerchief and dabbed at the tip of her delicate nose.

Hours later, when the day's service came to an end, Amalina excused herself. She realized only after she'd gotten out the door, by herself, that she'd broken a week of constant presence. A someone always looking at her, or over her, or to her, so that she could not be free. She let out a breath, and met her freedom gladly. And then she followed after the men in the fur hats.

They said nothing between themselves but, as if of one mind, they formed the ranks they'd had previously and resumed their march up the street. Tsobl was large enough, and cosmopolitan enough, that though they were obviously not native to Ardeel, they as a group did not draw attention. Only a couple people turned their heads curiously.

"They look marvelous, don't they?"

One arm steadied her on the right. Another arm, belonging to a second man, held on the left. Something with a sharp point touched her back.

"On their way to do some important work it looks like," the first man said from under a hood. She recognized the voice, and the large purple lips surrounded by the grey beard. "Now, tell me why I shouldn't kill you right now, Amalina Dalca, baker's daughter?"

"Kralo—"

Her voice was cut off by a short, warning thrust of the knife into her back.

"Commander," Amalina amended after a gasp.

"Just keep smiling and you don't die. For the moment. Now answer my question."

With a prod, the knife encouraged her.

"I'm helping you."

"How?"

"I'm carrying out my orders."

"You've used the vial on him?"

"No." She added quickly: "But I haven't had a chance."

"Keep smiling. We're just watching a parade. See, they are joined by a second division of good soldiers, should you wish to inform your master."

About ten more men wearing the same kind of hard peasant costume passed slowly by on the street, and turned to follow after the first group.

"I won't say anything," Amalina promised. "I just need more time."

"Isn't it obvious that time is running out? You understand that, don't you? Now, what have you done for me?"

"I haven't been able to—"

"No, of course you haven't. After months upon months at your disposal. Still nothing."

"You got my map, didn't you?"

"At the cost of good men. And tell me, where is Piotr?"

Amalina almost began to cry. The knife reminded her not to.

"He might be dead," she said calmly.

"Is he?"

"I'm afraid he's dead, sir."

"You think he's dead? Or he *is* dead. What are you telling me, little girl?"

"He's trapped inside the castle. That's the last thing I knew—"

"How was he trapped?"

"We went into a secret area of the castle and then the Count arrived, and he sent me away—"

"*Who* sent you away?"

"The Count. He sent me here to Tsobl."

"Is that what happened?" But he wasn't really asking. He said it with a doubt so heavy he was accusing her instead. He only wanted to weigh her response.

"You can blame me, sir," she said. "If that's what you want to do. I feel like it's all my fault. But I swear to you: I tried to help. But there was nothing I could—"

"Here's what it looks like to me. You thought you were a very clever little girl, and you trapped Piotr for your master to torture and to kill, and you ran to Tsobl before I found out and caught you. How dare you, little girl, think you can do such a thing and get away with it. Don't you remember that if you betray me and yet find a way to avoid your punishment, I will make your father pay for your crime? Or are you so corrupted by that beast of yours that you wouldn't even drop a tear at the loss of your own blood?"

"I swear to you, Commander. I swear to you, I am on your side. He is *not* my master."

"But you do everything for him, and do nothing for me."

She swore that wasn't true.

"What are you doing here?"

"I'm—I'm meeting a visitor. A princess from the western kingdoms."

"A visitor for *him*."

"For him and me. In order to be your spy, I have to obey him, and I already told you his plan where I play his niece to invite the princesses—" But as soon as she said this, Amalina wished she could take it back. Both men on either side of her shifted in a meaningful way. They were thinking, calculating. If they'd seen Amalina, they had also seen her companion inside the church. The two giant men could go in and take Lisbet right then and there. Or kill her. She thought to beg for Lisbet's life, but she couldn't work her mouth.

"His plans are at an end," said Kralov coldly. "We will be at his gate soon enough. Anyone inside who is not clearly on our side will die. But I've told you this before, Mouse. For some reason you did not believe me."

"I believe you, sir."

"Believe me now. And obey me. Because I don't believe you and I don't believe your stories at all. And you definitely want to make sure the one I end up killing is the *right* one and not, on account of your cowardice, a good man, whose death you will most regret. Or even worse for you, I kill a lying little mouse," He pushed back and bowed deeply. He said, loudly for anyone around them to hear, "Princess *Tepsji.*"

He and his man left her standing against whatever building they'd been next to. She couldn't tell what it was. Her mind was whirling. She gasped her breaths, but tried to control herself. To keep it in. Princesses didn't gasp in the streets.

Genadie wasn't there. She didn't recognize anyone ... except Lisbet and her train of maids, who were coming straight for her. With a glance around, she saw the caped Kralov and his fur-hatted soldier make their way after the rest of his men. She reached for the spot where the knife had been against her. She quickly felt for a hole in the fabric, and for blood.

"Are you all right?" Lisbet asked.

"Oh, yes. Yes. I just ... lost my breath. I needed some air and ... "

"Castle life again?" Lisbet smiled, with a teasing tinge to her voice.

"What?"

"You said it gets lonely up in the castle—and you like to look at men." Lisbet made a meaningful side glance after Kralov and his man.

"That's not exactly what I said."

"It's what you said, *exactly*." She looked to her maids for confirmation, which was a little unfair, Amalina thought.

"I said it gets lonely, nothing more. And that certainly wasn't what I meant." Amalina felt an odd blush flushing her cheeks. It reminded her of her cousin Jenna, and the look she'd get when Amalina and her friends mocked her interest in a certain boy or another. Amalina was sure she now wore the same embarrassed expression. But why? Kralov's men were no Erik Kosche, or ... Well, there was Piotr—or used to be.

"Don't look so sad like that. Please. You can admit it to me, Katarina. I won't tell. I saw how you couldn't stop staring, and how you tore right after them after services. I know they aren't princes. But lonely minds can make anyone curious about anyone else. Oh, I'd never thought it about you, dear girl. And those men ... well, they are a little rough looking."

At least she hadn't said they were 'too low'. It would have made her hurt.

"I just like seeing something new and unusual," said Amalina.

"Of course," Lisbet allowed kindly, not pursuing the matter to obnoxiousness.

• • •

"How do I look?" the Count's voice rumbled like thunder.

"What else?" Amalina sneered. "You have blood on your face."

He wiped at it.

"Can you help me?"

She leaned forward and wiped the blood away, feeling slightly nauseous.

"I can't believe you. Why have you come here? And now? Right after killing—?"

"Stocking up," he said. His face was huge, his skin full of blood and his eyes bulging with veins.

"I asked you before, sir: Can't you stop this, sir? Why can't you? How do you expect to hide this awful curse from your guests? I warned you about the wailing in the castle, didn't I? And wasn't I right?"

"And I took care of it, didn't I?"

"*I* took care of it."

"Well, it's taken care of. Now, I must see her before she gets bored and flies away. How do I look?"

Amalina shook her head.

"You look like strigoi."

His lips parted from his enormous teeth, the fangs of a wolf. He was trying to appear annoyed but he came off as a snarling beast. But the frown had its desired effect, anyway. She was warned off the subject.

"Well, you don't look right," Amalina said. "She'll know something's wrong and you will scare her away."

He looked out the window.

"It's raining."

"So?"

"Bring her onto the upper parapet to watch the storm. Dress well and don't get drenched."

"Bring the Princess out onto the roof, at night, in a thunderstorm?"

"When the lightning is far enough away it is a beautiful sight. Show her. She will like it."

"I was on my way to the privy when you stopped me, sir," Amalina reminded him. "So give me a few minutes. And it will take us some time to prepare ourselves. And that's if I can convince her at all."

"You will. Yesss. You will."

To Amalina's surprise, Lisbet liked the idea of going out to watch the storm. So much that she had to be convinced to stop and put on the appropriate clothing. They layered up with outercoats, and her maids carried above them an oiled tarp which Genadie lent. Genadie was a mass of knowing winks and nods toward Amalina, excited that his Master was around, but scaring the maids with his unaccountable leering behavior.

A strip of level roof extended out below the central tower. Since the stone of this landing was black, in the rain-filled night it was difficult to distinguish even in torchlight. The flashes of lightning caught where the rain splashed and pooled, letting them know there was something of a solid ground beneath them. They stopped at the short wall at the prominence's end by running straight into it.

The Count was right, of course. The storm was beautiful to watch. The Black Castle stood near the top of a mountain that soared over the valley. The clouds were revealed as great churning bundles by the arrows of lightning darting across the sky. And if you peered down, the treetops shook in the wind, in a staggered motion by the intermittent bolts of light, looking like an undulating sea whose waves were anchored into place, and could only sway as they strained to break free, bending low at once and then in the next moment throwing their caps into the air. One end of Tsobl could be seen from their vantage. A few vague lights shone. But the faces and then the silhouettes of the larger buildings were thrown into relief and then shadow as the lightning danced around them. The rain wasn't too strong, so they could stand. Even as the wind pushed at their backs, threatening to topple them over the edge.

"Whoa! Whee!" Lisbet cheered. "Did you see that one, Katarina? It looked like a hand with all five fingers shooting out of that cloud."

"Magnificent, isn't it?" a voice rumbled along with the thunder.

Everyone turned. Amalina's hairs stood on end, and she imagined the effect was the same for everyone else. One of the maids made a noise, and one of them dropped a corner of the tarp.

The Count was dressed in a long black cloak, with its deep hood covering his head and face. All that could be seen in the brightest flashes was his chin. He must have been holding his head at a downward angle. Maybe he couldn't even see them.

They stood in silence while the storm raged through the valley.

"You don't recognize me, Katarina?" the basso voice called out, speaking in heavily accented Deutsch, and raised a gloved hand.

"Count! Uncle!" Amalina went to him. "Of course! But, you've come here? I'm so happy to see you."

Amalina bent deeply in a curtsy and pretended to kiss his offered hand. He removed the glove and offered it again. She pretended to kiss it again. The Count let out a soft snort.

"And this must be our guest, Princess Lisbet of the Spaarvierlet family," he said taking Amalina's hand and pretending that she was walking him to the Princess. "Here, let me look at you."

"My lord," Lisbet said, getting down on her knee. Her maids were caught with stunned looks on their faces, unsure of needing to fall on their knees like their mistress, or to stay holding the cover. One of them bent to keep the tarp at a proper angle, two of the others bobbed foolishly, trying to read the signals.

"Here, let me see your face, my lady, or my coming won't have been worth it," he said.

Lisbet raised her face, and then ended up blowing the water out of her mouth and nose in a silly but graceful way. She looked at him apologetically, but then laughed. He joined her laugh and motioned her up.

"Can't see too much of this poor face with all the rain I'm afraid, my lord."

"Like the sun on a cloudless day," he intoned after a crash of thunder. "And just as delightful. Yes. But I've interrupted your fun. Here, let us observe this wonderful storm."

"Oh, we don't have to," Lisbet said. "We can go back inside. Katarina and I have been watching—"

"No, please," he interrupted, guiding her toward the edge. He was too tall for the maids so they gave up and let the tarp drop to the side. "I wished to join you. It isn't often we get to enjoy this view. Let us do it both together, our hands joined."

He took her by the hand and patted it. Nodding, she blinked awkwardly and tried to smile while fending off the rain. With her free hand she adjusted the hood forward, so now they were both obscured from view. The Count didn't object.

"I'm afraid my busy schedule has kept me away for too long." His voice was so strong no matter how low, it overrode the sound of the storm and seemed to exist in Amalina's chest. She felt it through her limbs. Lisbet's naked hand gripped the Count's at each of his sentences, responding to their impact. "And it will take me away again tonight. But we will meet again in several days at the high castle. My home."

"I look forward to getting to know you, my lord. You and your niece have been very generous. I know I didn't give you too much warning before my arrival, and I shouldn't like to think I've been putting you out."

"There are no expenses too great when it comes to friends and family, my dear. And I wish to count you as both."

Amalina looked at the two hands clasped together in the flickering light. His on top of hers. Hunter above prey. But that wasn't true, she thought. The princess wouldn't be one of his victims. It was innocent. Only, his hand could stay there for centuries, never changing, while Lisbet's grew old and withered into a skeleton. That was what was unnatural about it, as they held hands in the rain.

Hands.

Rain.

Something flashed inside Amalina's mind.

"Uncle, I didn't hear the carriage."

The large, confident hand didn't stir.

"You didn't walk here, did you?"

The hand kept still. His head tilted a little.

"Not the carriage. I borrowed a horse in town. I didn't know if there'd be any downed trees, dear niece, and I didn't want any delays getting here, when I learned you were at Black Castle."

"You won't be staying for breakfast or supper?"

"No. You know my schedule. Always on the run. I will have to leave well before dawn."

"Well, I'm glad that you have no problem staying up into the night," Lisbet said. Her voice was much lighter and hard to hear when the thunder split.

"What do you mean?" the Count asked, intrigued.

"I suppose I'm used to life in the city. But even here in Tsobl, it seems most people get to bed very early. Not much happens after sundown. Life in the countryside. I can get used to it, my lord. But at least someone else can enjoy a talk and a stroll at midnight. It seems only Katja and yourself—"

"Many things here are different than in your country," the Count murmured. "But I will see to your contentment, and make sure to my dying breath that you are never dissatisfied."

"If you have to leave tonight, uncle, you'd better make it soon. The heart of the storm is shifting and it might turn this way. I'll see that Genadie has your horse ready."

"Thank you very much," said the Count. If he could have winked at her he would have. Instead, while his one hand kept Lisbet's trapped, with his other hand he discreetly waved her goodbye.

Amalina trotted off the roof.

As large as the Black Castle was its layout was less confusing. She just had to take one set of stairs that fed into another which then fed into the final one, and then back up and out into the courtyard.

"Genadie, we need a horse."

"Why?"

"The Count plans to leave before dawn."

"And so why would we need a horse if *he*'s leaving?"

"We don't need it. He needs it. He can't just walk out of here."

"He doesn't need to walk."

"Genadie," Amalina said in exasperation. "He told the princess he rode in on a horse. He said he will be riding out on one. Now, since he didn't actually ride in on one, you'd better get one so it looks like he did. And that he then does. For the princess, you know? *He* might want to say a farewell to her at the gate."

Genadie nodded. And without a second thought, except to pull his hat down tight, he ambled out into the downpour to ready a horse.

Amalina ran to her room. Now was the time to act. Hands. Rain. It couldn't be a better opportunity, could it?

She threw open her trunk and fished through the clothes. Kralov's ampule was wrapped in several layers of cloth. She opened the stopper and swished it around. Still a bit left. Good enough. She only needed a little.

Before she left the room, she went to a basin and poured a dash of water into it from a pitcher. The water was slightly yellow. She didn't want to think about it. After dipping a finger into it, trying to draw just a drop, she then held up her hand and flicked the finger out from her palm. There was a small sound at the move, but the pellets of water sprayed into the area on the wall she was aiming. Easier than she'd thought.

She tucked the vial into the arm of her coat and ran for the roof. All that mattered now was that they hadn't moved and she could find a way to get close and unobserved.

Strange how the day was playing out, she thought. Worried about her circumstances. Confronted by Kralov. Being met almost at random by the Count in the middle of the night, and given the opportunity to finally act against him. It seemed as random and chaotic as the raging storm. But a higher force seemed to guide storms into being, pushed them on their path, and then emptied out their energy until they are wisps of white in a sunny sky. So maybe something was guiding this moment. Had intended it. Why else hadn't she been struck dumb when the Count appeared in the hallway, dropped to the floor in fear that he'd come to have his vengeance against her for letting Piotr into his treasury, for spying on him, for acting on behalf of his enemy? She didn't even wonder about Piotr until the Count had already dragged her to a side room and started peppering her with eager questions about Lisbet, and getting prepared to meet her. She had to assume Piotr was still safe; or he'd been caught and killed and the Count didn't let little things like that bother him.

The maids were in the hallway, just inside the door leading to the roof. They were huddled together and looked hopefully to Amalina when they saw her.

"My lady told us to wait inside for her if we wanted, milady," one of them said to Amalina, Astrell was her name, sounding apologetic. "My lady said she didn't see any sense in us standing around getting wet when we couldn't provide them shelter and they are in their coats."

"We're waiting to dry her highness when she comes in," added an older one tartly, as if resenting having to explain anything to the foreign princess who'd dragged them into this ugly place, and set their beloved mistress atop a tower in a thunderstorm.

Amalina was perfectly satisfied where the maids were, as long as they stayed put. They wouldn't see anything.

"Stay warm," Amalina told them. Then she went onto the roof.

Lisbet and the Count were still in their spots. The storm had increased but they were like statues on the tower. She couldn't hear what they were saying but was very curious to know. What could keep them there like that? He was still holding her hand. His atop hers. Unmoving. Drenched by rain. Perfect.

Amalina had to time this right. Within her sleeve, she opened the vial and turned it once, to allow a drop on her finger. It didn't burn or tickle. It felt innocent.

"I told Genadie, sir," Amalina said, coming up behind them. Then she suddenly wished she hadn't. It might break the spell. He could turn. She shouldn't have said anything. Except she didn't want to seem like she was sneaking up to do something nefarious. She added fast: "He said the horse will be ready in a quarter hour. Drying the saddle."

"Should you go, my lord?" Lisbet's hand squeezed his at the next flash of light. After a beat, the thunder blasted, making her shake. The Count was as unmoved as stone.

Amalina turned the bottle one more time, to make sure the drop was on her finger. The bottle would remain open, should it seem like tossing the whole thing at him would kill him. She swallowed, her heart beating. All she had to do was wait for a—

A flash.

Within the second for the thunderclap to reach them, Amalina raised her arm. From behind, in the doorway, Amalina was sure the maids, if they were watching, couldn't see the motion. As soon as the thunder hit, Amalina leaned forward and flicked her finger at the back of the Count's hand. Even in the darkness, and the rain, she was sure the flecks of Kralov's liquid hit its mark. Amalina righted herself, and held the vial at the ready, waiting, inside her sleeve.

The Count's hand twitched.

"Oh!" said Lisbet, as if it was hurt by the clench.

The Count turned, released her hand, and brought his own up to his hood, studying it. He rubbed it. He looked to the sky.

"Is everything all right, my lord?"

"Hm," he said. "It's time to go."

"But the storm is getting worse, my lord," worried Lisbet.

"It could never be as frightening as my schedule. I have hours that must be kept."

"Yes, my lord. Thank you for your company. It was very brave of you to come on such a night. And I had such a good time. Such a pleasant conversation. I look forward to meeting you again."

"You have a tender heart." He touched her arm, and then led her back toward the tower and into the castle. "No need to see me away. Get yourself dried and warm and have a good sleep." To Amalina, "Mouse, see that that horse is ready. I'm coming down."

"Mouse?" Lisbet asked.

"A term of endearment," the Count explained. "Isn't that so?"

"I haven't thought of a good one for uncle yet," Amalina played in, acting just as happy as she should. There was a struggle inside her sleeve to recap the vial and not let it spill or drop. "Maybe you can help me with a name, my dear."

The pleasantries of a night send-off were quickly concluded, with the Count not removing his hood and turning his back on Lisbet as soon as he could. Amalina followed him down the stairs. She watched for any reactions, any noises. Any signs that the liquid had done anything other than make him flinch. There was no reason for it to have caused any reaction, even so little as a slight tremor, considering the drops would have blended seamlessly—without surprise—within the deluge of the storm. It must have had some effect.

The Count didn't stop until he was outside and snapped the reins officiously from Genadie's hands. He peered upward at the near invisible building to check if he was under surveillance.

"Master, Master," burbled Genadie from the pool his face was buried in. "So happy you've come. I've missed you so much, Master. My lord!"

The Count then considered the back of his hand. He shook it at the wrist. He rubbed it carefully with his sleeve. He shook it again. Now he raised his head toward the clouds, shielding his eyes from the drops coming down. An uncertain growl escaped him, something like curiosity.

"So, little mouse," he said, shrugging off the mystery, "She is fearless: this is good. She has an open and adventurous spirit: this also tides well. But while my delighted seems content, I sense she is withholding something from me. Has she mentioned any complaints to you?"

"Not so much a complaint, but I think she was expecting more servants. For our meals we had to hire a cook from Tsobl. And he didn't really want to be here. It was obvious he and his assistants were scared to be here."

"More servants," the Count nodded. "I see. Anything else?"

"I don't think she cares for this castle much. But the high castle will be more to her liking. She loves to read and can't wait to see the library."

He nodded again. "Anything else?"

"She likes church service, and observes both holy days."

He made a face when he nodded this time. Then he shrugged. "Servants. I'll see to that. What does she enjoy the most?"

"Here?"

"Or in general."

"Above books? Flowers."

"Flowers," he nodded, again. "You should be in high castle by the end of the week, little mouse." He smiled at a thought: "And I noticed she has one or two young maids in her employ, do see that you share the medicine treats with them as well as the princess. Oh, but you did give our darling Princess Lisbet Spaarvierlet the medicine?"

"She liked them very much," Amalina nodded as he did. "She ate almost half of them."

His head shook so violently the hood fell backwards. His eyes were wide with surprise, his mouth a gaping hole. "She needed only one, or maybe three," he said. "I hope she's all right. I hope you haven't poisoned my princess, little mouse ..."

"You didn't tell me—"

There was a flash of lightning, with its crash of thunder immediately upon it. The storm had centered on the castle. But the Count was still aghast and only slightly distracted by the whinnies of the horse. As he brought the frightened animal under control, he shook his head, annoyed at having found out the prize goose he wanted might have been bought out from under him—the princess poisoned and lost. Then he was on the horse's back, and with the expertise of a cavalry veteran, turned it in a leap toward the gate.

The last she saw of him, just as he passed beyond the walls and into the mouth of the storm, he was absently flicking his free hand.

27

The Beginning of the Storm

When the Governor quit his desk and told his housemaid—over the retreating crashes of thunder—that he was turning in for the night and that he should not be disturbed until morning, his face resembled a cooked ham more than ever: pink and glistening. With a neat white handkerchief he dabbed the dew from his forehead, while somehow neglecting the rest of his spongy, trickling face. In his preoccupation he also forgot his desk and office key, leaving them on the sideboard next to the empty wine bottle.

Altering his route to enter the empty kitchen, and swiping a small wedge of cheese and another bottle of wine, he made his way up to his bedroom with his booty; and the latest report crumpled in his fingers. He knew he needed to read it again, to give it due consideration. There must be some other explanation than what it implied, what the rest of the council would agree it meant when the news circulated generally the next day. He knew that his post as governor didn't guarantee an easy ride, but he did not expect he would see a full scale rebellion—and so soon after they had utterly crushed the Ardeelian armies. He'd always assumed if he didn't apply judicious pressure to the native population that a half-hearted revolt could be expected within the next generation: when the boys who had not witnessed the brutality of their grandfathers' loss, yet still feeling a kind of handed-down embarrassment and dishonor and shame, envisioned themselves as a new counterforce to throw off the power that had defeated their honorable ancestors.

General Marosh, the coarse, hot-blooded rustic, along with his small battalion-or-so of soldiery, was marching north. He hadn't yet veered onto a course to run them through Tsobl. But he still had time to make that turn. And what other reason could there be to abandon his own lands? Yes, what other reason could there be?

"Poor Mush Mush," he told the cat threading between his ankles. "I didn't bring you milk. I'm sorry, I have generals to worry about."

"What generals?" rumbled a voice heavily.

The cheese dropped from the Governor's hands and split apart on the floor. Mush-Mush fled.

The Count, his face large and oddly pink, with a trickle of blood at the corner of his mouth—*had he left it there on purpose?*—stood beside the bed, as solid and seemingly part of the furnishings as a tall, grotesque candlestand.

"If I'd known you were here, Viscount," the Governor said coolly, his face pulsing red and gaining a new layer of sweat, "I would have brought up a snack for us both."

"You know that I do not partake of such things. But tell me, what generals are troubling you? And how?"

"All of them, Viscount," the ham smiled. "And they are troubling me by acting like—by *being*, that is—the native sons of Ardeel. They are like a broken horse that doesn't stay broken and begs for a lashing when you remove the saddle."

The Count's laugh was a staccato beat against the Governor's chest. But it was the Governor who should have been laughing, as he no longer needed to answer questions about his generals. Not specifically. Because of his quick and clever choice of evasion: lamenting the proud spirit of Ardeel. The monster nodded and grinned and enjoyed the idea that the people of his blood were unruly to the last. It was enough to turn his thoughts elsewhere.

"Have you heard what's happened in Netz?" asked the Count.

"I know a princess from the Netherlands has plans to visit that general area, if that is what you mean, Viscount. Supposedly she is destined for the high castle."

"What do you keep calling me?"

"What did you say?"

"That word, what do you keep calling me?" asked the Count.

"That would be 'Viscount.'"

"What does that mean?"

"It is a title. From the French. I believe it is: *Vicomte.*"

"No one has called me that before. What does it mean?"

"Much the same as a Count. Only it is a title that is … how would I put it?" the Governor see-sawed his head as if weighing his thoughts. "It is an honorific."

"And what does that mean?" the Count seemed tireless with his questions, his eyes full of fascination.

"From the records you declared yourself as Knight. And then later as Count. But you never declared your lineage, or how you came to this title of Count. Which, you understand, is a hereditary title with royally ascribed lands and duties. Since you didn't specify—you have never clearly stated— who you are within the Ardeelian histories, what family you belong to, and how they achieved this mark of rank, it stands that you have claimed this title. That it was not given. The people have chosen to honor you with it.

Bringing with it no powers or duties, it is an honorary title. An honorific. Thus, *Viscount*."

"I don't like this."

"Do you wish to declare your ancestry, Viscount?"

"I need not. And I don't like it."

"I don't see how it really matters, Viscount. The only reason to be concerned is if you were to die and you wished your title to pass on to someone of your blood. I don't think that is quite possible, is it? So you shall always possess this title. Unless, of course, you know something else— which I shall not pry into—and you wish to disclose to me a specific lineage, an *inheritor?*"

"Are you insulting me with this word?"

"Far from it. I am only being specific."

"You will call me Count. Because I am the Count of Ardeel, and I like the sound of that. And that is good enough for you."

The Governor nodded. "But you were saying something about Netz, Lord Tepsji?"

"They've hung out the body of a young Muscovite," the Count told him. Then he described the cage with the dead body in it, and the sign warning off foreigners. And how off-putting that might be to any foreign dignitary to witness such a grotesque and threatening display.

"But this is Netz you're speaking of. Not Tsobl. You can't handle the problem yourself?"

The Count's tongue snuck to the blood trailing to his chin.

"I can handle many situations," said the Count. "Do you think that is what I ought to do in this matter, to enforce *your* laws for you?"

"So let me understand: You want the body taken down and the sign removed, under my authority, because it violates our common laws against incivility toward non-native peoples? Or is it because *you* don't want *your* visitors offended?"

"You accomplish the latter by doing the former, it is true," the Count allowed. "But it falls on you to enforce the laws in this land, and ensure its tranquility."

The Governor raised his eyebrow, thinking: this is a strangely indirect approach. This one has always dealt brutally straight forward. And now he has come to request a subtle action, a roundabout action? What has changed?

"A funny thing to come from you, to demand proper services when you have never paid one cent in taxes," the ham smirked. But when he saw the Count's reaction, seeing his death in the ghastly face, he nearly fell to his knees. "Of course that was a joke and I never would have meant to say such a thing in any seriousness. You tell me of this violation of laws as a favor, so to draw my attention to what is happening off in Netz, and so I may properly remind the mayor of Netz of this country's proper order?"

"Yes," mumbled the Count agreeably, his bloodshot eyes not quitting the Governor yet.

"If I don't enforce my own laws," the Governor continued, recovering himself, reaching down to pick up the pieces of broken cheese, "I will look weak. Which I cannot afford."

The Count nodded.

"Perhaps I should go there myself."

"I think a letter would be all it would take. Nothing to arouse the spite of the people, but to remind those who control them just who controls the controllers."

"A neat way to put it."

"I want the mayor to understand that all the powers of the land are united on this, that it is not just my will."

But it is about your will, isn't it? the Governor thought to himself.

"I agree, of course, law and decorum should be restored." The Governor felt his heart slowing to its regular rhythm, and he cooled again. As long as I don't look directly at the Count, he reminded himself. It had been a while since their last face-to-face encounter—secondary as he was to it. He just needed to remember the old governor's strategies for dealing with the creature, and how to stay alive. The old governor's advice for how to deal with the human element of Ardeel, to survive in this land of savages, which he boiled down to 'be fearless and do something bold', did not apply to this one. Not exactly. Did it? "Have you spoken with your friend the bishop lately? I can't imagine he has forgotten his role, too."

"Forgotten his role," the Count repeated emptily, as if needing to be reminded.

"His duty to maintain the order and peace of the souls under his direction. The mayor would be one of those people."

"Bishop? Who are we speaking of? Which bishop?"

"*Your* bishop. The very Bishop of Netz, leader of the cult of St. Grigori."

"He is the *Cardinal* of Netz."

The Governor scowled, testily. "Just the fact that he goes around calling himself a cardinal—and the people believe him so—is bad enough. It shows his pretensions to a greater power than is within his grasp. He might even justify the title to himself because he has bullied the other churches to expand his influence and accept his rule. But until he produces a writ from the Mother Church herself, a writ confirming his elevation to that noble heading, he is, and will always be, a simple bishop."

"You have a sudden and curious particularity for titles," the Count's eyebrow arched, "which I don't remember you possessed the first time we met."

The Governor tossed his hands to acknowledge the fact. "However, we've never met *formally*. You are probably recalling the previous man to hold my position, Governor Groenhalt. At the time I was only his secretary. I'm sure I do resemble him these days, as I not only wear his age and his title now, but also his wig."

The Count smiled, his eyes fascinated again. "Yes, a more transitory thing your government is. Here, I wonder if your need to reduce—or further define—everyone else's title is out of jealousy, because yours is an appointment position, only temporary, while ours is not?"

"As I said, I am just being specific. I belong to a race who cherishes exactitude."

"Your fetish has twice now side-tracked my purpose in coming here. But I find I must pursue your reasoning: What's in a name?" asked the Count. "Honorific or not, what is in a name or a title if he has the *actual* power?"

"The power, yes." The Governor shrugged to concede and end the argument. "Well, we both know who we're talking about, whatever label—bishop or cardinal—with which we favor the man in Netz. So let's carry on. As I was saying, my secular powers can only penetrate so far into the bodies of these backward people, all the way out there. When they get their blood worked up, playing with their spiritual innerworkings can be more effective in correcting their waywardness than the threat of external force. Therefore: use the Bishop; or *Cardinal*, as you say. But then, I think again, perhaps I should go there myself. To speak with *all* parties."

"I say a letter from you to the mayor will suffice," the Count reminded him. "Unless you're telling me something else? Do you believe it was the Cardinal who put the people up to this barbarity and not the mayor?"

"The bishop, yes," he lowered his eyes as if trying to seduce the window on the other side of the room. "You believe it was the mayor's action alone, Lord Tepsji? You're convinced?"

"It was the loss of his daughter that caused this outburst."

"And just *what* caused the loss of his daughter?" the Governor put in snidely.

Again the Count stirred in a disagreeable way, and this time his body seemed to expand to fill the corner of the room. The Governor kept his eyes on the bolted window.

"Well, that's convenient then, isn't it?" the Governor told his evening's intruder. "The mayor would naturally be upset at the death of someone so precious. And this display of animosity towards the foreigners looks like a natural reaction on his part, even if it was contrary to the laws of Tsobl. But tell me: who could really feel comfortable—I mean feel that he has the righteous authority and power to work *contrary* to the *higher will* of Ardeel?"

The Governor's meaning was taken by the Count, whose shadow settled an inch. The higher will of Ardeel certainly wasn't what it was supposed to be, and understood by the outer world to be: the King, the Governor, and the assembly in Tsobl. *No, none of those were,* agreed the Governor and the Count at the same time. The land was controlled by currents which were stirred by its stronger, native forces.

"Yes, I understand my duties and responsibilities, Count," said the Governor. "I will post the letter with my seal tonight. But the mayor, as you already know, is just a figurehead post. And the man himself is even weaker than what I said implies. A weak, weak, weak man. My orders will be followed immediately, but only as far as that goes. I don't think any letter of mine can speak to the force of the *other* mind, which I mentioned. And that might be more *your* problem, than our distraught mayor's ..."

The Governor raised his eyebrow toward the Count, to try to drive home the meaning, in case the creature was as thick as he was acting tonight: the Bishop of Netz was the real power in that town, and was outside of the Governor's control.

But the Count was not there to receive the added point. He was no longer in the room.

The Governor smirked.

Be fearless, he heard his old governor's words trickle weakly in the silence. And do something bold.

28

Carila, the Defender

Kralov's liquid was capable of something. If the drops hadn't been diluted and washed off by the rain maybe there would have been more of a reaction. It would not have been lethal. If she'd emptied the whole vial on him, perhaps … But it was difficult to decide anything other than that the Count had reacted to it, and so she would have to experiment further. And the vial, wrapped in a leather cloth, would be kept on her person, secreted somewhere, at all times. If not lethal, it could be used as a distraction. She gripped it tight, protectively, as she headed back up to the living quarters.

The storm sounded as if it wanted to break the building in two. At any other time, Amalina would have been frightened and thrown her arms around her father for protection. Now she was energized by the maelstrom, the claps of thunder pushing her forward. She had dared to do something. She'd taken a first real step as Kralov's agent, and made her first real move against the Count on her own. And what she'd done had affected him. No matter how small, she'd flung her finger out like the barrel of a pistol, and a creature of the most tremendous power, one that had single-handedly tore through armies of knights in armor, had twitched. Recoiled. Had been moved physically. In this moment, Amalina felt if she jumped she would bust through all the floors of rock and fly to the stars.

More realistically, she determined to get as much accomplished as she could while empowered, knowing the Count was gone and she would have more hours alone. Who knows what had happened to Piotr, or where he was? He may be found later tonight and her mission brought to a bloody close. But it was important to at least take another step. That would feel good, no matter what came tomorrow. If Lisbet asked for company she would deny her friend in order to get one more piece of satisfaction.

Fortunately, by the time Amalina got back upstairs, Lisbet had already retired for the night.

"Begging your pardon, your ladyship," said Astrell, bowing low. "Our ladyship prays you will forgive her."

"No, that's all right, Astrell," said Amalina, as she walked past. "Better to get some sleep than try a conversation in all this racket. We wouldn't be good company."

"Begging your pardon, your ladyship," said the older one, in a voice less civil. "What was your uncle, his eminence—god grant him long life—thinking, eh? Keeping her out there to be drowned by the rain, frozen stiff by the wind, and torched by the fires of heaven?"

"Please, Carila," she heard Lisbet call from inside her room, "I've said nothing so unkind. You come here and get me to bed, and leave Katty alone. Katty, I haven't authorized her to say such slanders against him. I think he's wonderful."

But Carila's old eyes squinted all the harder now, and barely lowered her voice, as she sped onward: "Taking advantage of a young woman who doesn't know any better than to come out of the weather. Holding her hostage as he thinks she's made of marble and can't catch her death if she's not careful."

"Carila, mind me."

"Her life is entrusted to my hands," Carila concluded, now in a harsh whisper only Amalina could hear. "They aren't too old that they can't strangle the life out of an uncle and his niece, all in one go, should I be driven to such an act out of despair. You'll wish it wasn't true if you make it my cause—but it'll be true, and be so, all the same!"

Amalina nodded with an embarrassed blush to Carila, who Astrell was trying to lead away by grabbing the back of her blouse. Then she wished Lisbet good sleep through the rest of the storm and hurried on. This new drama would have to wait. There was a mission at hand.

Reaching under the mattress, Amalina took out the curl of paper and the several sheets of transferred code from the sticks in the Count's treasury. She set the sheets to the side on her desk and unfurled the curl into a small rectangle. Flattened between two fingers, she studied the strange characters on it, then compared them with the various stick codes. There were three possible keys. They had the same odd characters, but ran in different orders of sequence. From there, she need only find which one fit the message, by seeing which produced a real word from the first set of glyphs on the paper.

"Your recent activity has stirred the passions of the people, for which, great lord, they seek an outlet. This is dangerous. And it complicates my role here. I've uncovered a movement against you, one arising from the outside. The time of their arrival is uncertain. Their unknown confederates within the city secure their protection, and provide for their safe conduct during the burning hours. Turning a common people against them, people who sympathize with their goals, will be difficult. But you know that. Stay wise and cautious."

This message was far from the semi-literate and inarticulate hand which crafted the first 'Troubl wit yor servints' blurt. Whether the two knew each other or not, in the city of Netz there were two separate minions operating for the Count. It must be.

She tore the strip of paper into pieces and threw them into the fireplace. There was no regret as she did it. Saving the message could only get her caught. The shreds burnt green with flames and with a quick burst, as if they'd been treated in some chemical for easy disposal. They were gone instantly.

Amalina wondered why she'd taken so long to decipher the message. Now it seemed silly that she hadn't. If she were Kralov, she'd suspect her motives just as much as he did. The cold heart of a disciplined warrior now met with the heat of a newly minted revolutionary. A storm raged inside her. One to match the real storm now crawling off into the mountains outside her window. Why had she waited? What was the reason for hesitation? There would be no more of that. Only action. And more action, until the enemy was defeated!

While the note didn't reveal much, and Kralov's strange liquid hadn't destroyed the Count outright, she had tasted blood twice that night—so to speak—and had become ravenous. Her mind tore at her circumstances and sought for her next move. The vial would stay on her. The keys to the Count's secret codes were folded face down into the wider drawers of Katrina Flauna's make-up box, pretending to be the natural lining below all the little bottles and jars (which nobody would ever bother pulling out), and be close at hand if she needed them.

Only after she'd done this, and the hint of luminosity in the clouds suggested sunrise, did she grow sleepy and lay down.

• • •

Announced by Astrell, Lisbet came into the room wearing one of her finer dresses, her head bent forward slightly, with the wisp of a smile on her puffy lips, and was apologetic.

"I will send Carila home," she said. "I can't imagine what came over her. Please accept my apologies."

"Oh, no, you don't have to send her home. She was just protecting you. It's her job, isn't it?"

"Well, it's also her job to respect her station, and never to speak in such a rude and unacceptable way to anyone, much less someone of a higher rank." Lisbet bowed her head again. "It's really my fault. I don't mind it. And I've permitted her too many liberties. Father says so. But I've come to her rescue once too often, and kept her in our house, even when Mother and Father wished to dismiss her. For speaking her mind, of course."

"Maybe we're a little different here, she can speak her mind all she wants," said Amalina. "Well, of course we're very different here, aren't we?"

Lisbet turned her head and nodded shyly. Like she had to admit something she did not want to.

"I know we've made you put up with unusual living conditions already," guessed Amalina. "It will get better, Lees. But I know, though you didn't know what to expect, that you didn't expect our eccentricities."

"Yes, it's been a little ..."

"And if it makes your ladies nervous and they say a few things for it, believe me, I'm more than happy to accept the abuse."

"That's very nice of you. Can I hope to hear it is the same thought as your uncle? If not, I must insist that Carila return home."

"The Count and I are one mind on this, I can guarantee it. Let's hear no more about it. I want someone who will stand up for you, has the heart of a lioness, standing guard over you at all times. Uncle wishes the same."

Lisbet nodded, her smile grew by half an inch. She still couldn't bring herself to look directly at Amalina.

"Is that all, Lees? You seem to want to say something else."

She shook her head. Then gave a timid shrug.

"Believe me, you can tell me anything. Even if you think it would hurt me, I will listen, and take your side. Because you are a very good friend, and much better than I am." Amalina patted Lisbet's forearm, and then she held it.

"The count, Lord Tepsji ... your uncle ... he is ... different ..."

Amalina's stomach fluttered. What had she noticed? Did she *know* ...? or suspect ...?

"He's a man of supreme foundation," she said at length. "A stronger and hearty specimen of the male species I've never met. He could put shame to our boldest generals. I don't blame him at all for not noticing my fear. Why would he? He is a man who does not recognize the weaker attributes and frailties of the soul, because he does not possess them. I dare say, he cured me of some of my own childish anxieties last night."

"You don't have to say that," Amalina told her with a laugh. "I will apologize for him, because he would apologize if he was here. Carila was right. That was a bad storm to be out in."

"You are pretty courageous yourself, my darling. You didn't look scared at all. Just like him. Maybe I've spent too much time in the city, something my father has accused me of, and the natural has become frightening when it shouldn't be." She shrugged and smiled and laughed. "I wish I could be like you, Katja. And I will keep an eye on you, and do my best to imitate."

"Don't get as fat as me or you won't catch a prince's eye."

At this, Lisbet looked down and lost her smile. By her expression, it seemed she was worried.

What did I say? Amalina wondered

"I don't care for *princes*," Lisbet said softly. "What's in a title? I'm taking after you, my darling. I saw how you looked after those rough boys. So, prince or count, what do I care?"

Count?

Lisbet blushed.

Oh, thought Amalina.

• • •

The decision was made: They left the Black Castle and returned to the rented apartments in Tsobl, where they could take advantage of the restaurants and the several theatres, and be closer to the church and civilization, while waiting for the summons to Tepsji's high castle.

It was difficult for Amalina to liberate herself from Lisbet, who was now full of questions about the Count, many of which she had asked ten times before but wanted to hear the answers again, because now she had met him and had held his hand (though hadn't really *seen* him), and so the answers would seem fresh in this new light. As always, Amalina struggled to keep the stories quite straight enough to not appear a light-minded idiot; or worse, a liar.

The peasant revolutionaries were no longer to be found in the streets. They were either in hiding or they had naturally moved on to Netz, or the high castle itself. And when Amalina did manage to slip from Lisbet's side (and Genadie's watch) to search for Kralov, there was nobody safe to inquire after the Commander. This was a setback and major flaw in the revolutionary planning. She could not get her information to her leader or his forces. Not that anything she could tell him was vital—the liquid was probably not a solution to the Count, no matter that it had caused a reaction. But it would let Kralov know she was committed.

Amalina spent extravagantly, ordered the best meals, hired musicians and actors to play for the princess, and engaged a tailor to design dresses in the current mode of high fashion in Ardeel, hoping to attract the Commander's attention, to cause him to find her and make contact—if only for him to threaten her again. At which point she would inform him of her progress. But the Count bade them to the high castle first. The princess' carriage, loaded with her luggage and maids, and Amalina's less-sizable, more ancient, carriage riding before it, carrying Amalina's trunks as well as Amalina, Lisbet and Astrell, took immediately to the highway.

With no word of Piotr—of his capture and his death, and the revelation of Amalina as a traitor—by the time they were coming to Netz, and Amalina almost forgetting about this potential trouble, remembering it only in the odd, quiet minute, it came to her now, as Lisbet read from the bible, and Astrell woke from a deep, snoring nap and opened the blind covering the window and asked when they would see the high castle.

Piotr! Amalina thought, a small twist in her gut sending a wave of sweat over her. What do I do? Do I try to get to the secret door as soon as we arrive, try to open the Count's treasury and rescue him? Such an adventure would not only save both she and Piotr from his eventual discovery, it would be enough to convince Kralov of her loyalty. But what if he was already caught and confessed? What if when they arrived at the high castle's doors, the Count would spring a trap against her? Execute her for willful collaboration with his enemy? He had to have discovered Piotr by now. Or Piotr had died of his own accord. He couldn't have lived inside the treasury for weeks without food and water. So he was either dead or captured. If he'd died, the Count would have found him from the smell alone. She had to be driving into a trap, she worried, pulling nervously at her dress, or at least a thicket of the Count's questions.

But she couldn't let on. The cooler she appeared, the better to convince the Count any suspicions he had against her—egged on by the *prickly pair*, no doubt—were baseless. She had to be calm and unflinching, even in the face of death.

This reminded Amalina that she had better close the window as they came off the highway and headed into Netz, before Astrell screamed and Lisbet witnessed the corpse of Roti in the deadman's cage. Better not to have the princess aware of the Ardeelian brand of savage justice, or the village's low opinion of outsiders.

As Amalina sat forward to see where they were, and prepared to close the drapes, Astrell gasped and said: "Oh, look, my lady. Look!"

But her words were more in delight than fear. Amalina's eyes found the cage. She stared thoughtfully and without comment. Roti's body was gone, and so was the old sign warning away strangers. Now the iron structure was stuffed with flowers from head to foot, looking like a blazing, colorful trellis, with a sign reading simply—in both the native language and Deutsch— Welcome All.

Nobody was throwing stones at it.

29

Checkmate!

They arrived at the high castle in the early afternoon. The sun was still well above the horizon, and the two princesses were told by Georg, who met the carriages in the courtyard, that the lord of the castle was quite busy. He wouldn't be able to join them until the evening. Behind Georg, Amalina spotted two young men standing outside the main building's doors. The two looked like young farmers who'd been stuffed into old, outdated footmen's clothes. Drastically outdated clothes the more Amalina looked at them. The clothes of squires from centuries past.

Georg, who'd greeted Amalina and Lisbet with a cold smirk and had told them of the Count's regrettably unforgiving schedule, now pointed to the carriages and the footmen made their way with resigned steps to retrieve the luggage. Genadie, stepping down from the rider's bench, eyed the footmen suspiciously but kept quiet. Though he did exchange a curious look with Amalina. Georg then ordered Genadie to have the carriages brought around, the horses put into the barn and fed and watered, and to show Lisbet's drivers to their quarters.

Amalina, who was paying attention to this exchange, was reminded that it was unusual for a princess to be so preoccupied by her servants by Lisbet's gentle tug on her arm. Abraxa was ushering them inside the main building. "This way, my ladies. Please warm yourselves while your rooms are prepared. Come, Lady Tepsji, you should know the way better than anyone."

Amalina supposed Abraxa's remark was insolent and merited punishment. Ignoring it, and ignoring Abraxa, she led Lisbet by the hand into *l'entrée grande*. As they passed the threshold, Amalina remarked to herself that with the arrival of Princess Lisbet Spaarvierlet, this moment was the culmination of years of the Count's planning and even more so of his desire. Well, Amalina thought, here she is.

As could be expected the castle was immaculate and without a spot of dust—which would be uncommon even in Antwerp. It felt unnatural but most likely only Amalina noticed. Everyone else would be distracted by the size of the entrance hall and the colorful bunches of flowers rather artlessly thrown over everything, like a flower parade had detonated in the chamber. Oddly assembled bouquets were even tucked under the armpits and into the open visor of the armor standing by the stairs. Only the dull lead cup on the pedestal had been left out of the festivities.

"How very pretty," Lisbet said.

Refreshment of bread and fruit and drink was laid out on the long central table amid the pots of tulips, dogberry, etc., at which Abraxa pointed helpfully. Amalina stared past all this to the door that eventually led to the Count's private study. It was closed. And beyond that door the door to the study would be locked, too. And even if she could get through them both, the Count could be sitting there in the study, relaxing, plotting, or whatever he did while waiting for the sun to drop out of sight.

"Excuse me," Amalina said to Lisbet, "After the long ride, I think I'll lie down and wait for evening. I hope you don't mind."

"Good idea," the princess agreed. "I think we could all use a rest." She turned to Abraxa, "It looks lovely. Thank you for welcoming us. When we rise I'm sure I'll have some of that cheese and those pears. But can I have some water brought to my room now, please?"

"Milady," Abraxa bowed in acknowledgement.

"Abraxa," said Amalina, "you can show the princess and her ladies to her suite, I'll see my own way."

"Of course, Lady Tepsji. But, uh, where are you going?" she asked with a short, unpleasant laugh. Amalina was caught short as she walked toward the stairway to her own tower. "My, have you been gone so long that you've forgotten your way? Oh, no, I think I know what you're up to. You can't fool me, milady. But since you're headed up to the *servant's quarters*, I should warn you that—well, you may find this as sad news ... *she* is no longer with us."

Amalina turned, tilting her head curiously.

Abraxa smiled a mysterious smile, and then explained for Lisbet's benefit: "Well, Lady Katarina Tepsji is a very kind woman and makes friends with everyone, even developing personal relationships with us, the Count's staff. And she was quite fond of a young servant named Amalina, who was talented and could do just about any job in this castle. But while you were away, Lady Tepsji, I'm afraid there have been some changes. We've lost Amalina, who was known best for her bread making skills. We've retained another cook, and done our best to replace the girl. And you'll find that Georg has done a good job. No need to shed a tear, Lady Tepsji. Amalina was promoted, from what I understand, into a position higher than what she retained here in this castle. We should only worry that she doesn't get carried away with her new status. But you will not find her in her old room. She has been replaced. So you might as well have a rest in your room, a fire is already prepared. I'll see you and Lady Spaarvierlet are comfortable."

Now Abraxa pointed helpfully toward the other staircase, leading to the other side of the building. Amalina could already tell that her room would be the one she'd occupied when she first arrived at the castle. The one given to Lady Katrina Flauna when she came later. The room where Erik had tied Amalina to a chair, hung her out the window and made his last stand against the Count. The room was filled with unpleasant memories, and now she was being loaded into it again. At least Amalina could be confident that it had been cleaned thoroughly, and turned into a whole new, spotless room. Maybe Abraxa was so thorough with her obsessive cleaning that she had swept out any bad memories and reminders of that tragic event.

"Yes, you've been gone so long, Lady Tepsji," Abraxa said on their way up, "we also found a replacement for Genadie, so that we aren't crippled when he is away. As a matter of fact, he pleases the Count so much, I'm confident he'll be holding the position—if a second driver is no longer needed. It may be farewell to Amalina *and* Genadie before long."

Amalina made a face in the shadows nobody could see.

"Your ladyship will come to appreciate the new faces," Abraxa finished up with her sadistic grin. "Here you are now, your highness, Princess Spaarvierlet, a complement of rooms at your disposal, the outer chambers as you will, the inner chamber your own, the fire already lit."

"Thank you … Abraxa, was it?"

"Milady," Abraxa bowed formally. It was warm, but nothing like her splashing to the stones when the Count entered a room.

"Show her in," Amalina ordered. "No need to fuss over me, you know. Open the bed for her and see that everything is satisfactory. I can see to myself in my own home."

"Very well," smirked Abraxa, bowing again, and watched suspiciously as Amalina excused herself to Lisbet and headed further up the stairs.

Amalina paused before the turn in the hall leading to her room. To look down that passage would recall memories she would rather avoid. No sense bothering herself when she only wanted to duck out of sight until Abraxa was fully engaged with Lisbet. Something welled up in Amalina, and on impulse she stuck her head around the corner—to the scene of her poisoning, and the confrontation with the Count. It was cleared of any furniture. No small table and chair outside the door. Just blank, bare stones. And the entrance to her bedroom. Seeing it clean and ghost-free dispelled one of the knots in her stomach.

Now she ran back downstairs, listening as best she could for sounds of a footman or Georg on his way up. But the Castle appeared to be empty. Georg was probably instructing the new servants to haul the trunks through the service entrance in the back of the castle. In *l'entrée grande*, Amalina pocketed a piece of bread and a pear from the large table, took a candlestick, and could not stop herself but went straight for the Count's private study. If he was inside, she would find a reason she wanted to speak with him. If nothing else came to mind, she would announce the princess' arrival.

Tension welled as she approached the door. She needed to be quick about this, but she couldn't afford to be seen as rushing around—it would beg the question why. She had to knock on the door, even though it would be better to sneak in unnoticed. The Count might be on the other side. He might even be waiting for her, to catch her in an attempt to rescue the spy in his treasury (the dead spy; *Piotr couldn't have lasted this long*). And of course the question came: how would she get his body out without being noticed, even if she managed to get inside without being noticed? First things first, Amalina told herself. Then she knocked lightly on the door.

There was no deep-grumbled answer.

She didn't have time to waste. She could hear Georg now. Low, but he was shouting instructions in *l'entrée grande*, or some rooms away. From his tone Genadie wasn't his target this time but someone he wished to do as told, yet not sound too harsh in doing so. Ear to the study door, there was no sound from inside. But the Count had surprised her before. He was unnaturally quiet when he wanted to be, as in everything else about him.

She gave another knock. With no reply, Amalina breathed out and tried the handle. The door opened.

The count wasn't there.

"Sir?" she asked in a low voice. "Sir?"

She went to the cabinet and put her ear to it. She could only hear Georg's voice disappearing into a deeper area of the castle. Nothing stirred beyond the secret door. Amalina put her lips to the crack.

"Hello?" she said. Then louder: "Hello? Hello? Is anyone in there? It's Amalina! The little mouse! Answer me if you hear me. I seem to be all alone here. Hello? Hello? Let me know if you can hear me!"

No reply. No sounds within. She looked at the nearby chair and considered using it to help her reach the lock. It was just a passing thought, and she knew it would be more dangerous to try opening the door than not. Piotr was probably beyond rescuing. She could always explain away his body, if it were discovered, as a spy or a curious interloper who had nothing to do with her. But if she were found working the locking mechanism on the door, it would identify her to a certainty as an accomplice. The pressure built up quickly, and she went for the chair anyway. Why not?

But her eye caught a slight movement on the desk when she set the candle down. Shifted by the vibration: a small curl of paper.

A new message.

Opened, it revealed a long string of words written in mysterious glyphs. Some, it seemed, she didn't recognize. She took it up, but then set it back down on the desk. This wouldn't be like stealing it from a pigeon's leg.

Someone knew the message had arrived, and had set it on the desk. Most likely it was the Count himself. But he would have pasted it into the book in the hidden room, wouldn't he? Well, it was a known message to someone, and she couldn't just steal it.

Before she knew what she was doing, the extravagant feather on the Count's pen was tickling her cheek as she copied out the characters from the message onto a piece of parchment. Did the Count inventory the paper on his desk? If he did, it would be a problem she'd have to sort out later. She debated the sanity of what she was doing as her body dutifully copied out each glyph as quickly and accurately as she could. If she splattered ink anywhere, it could mark her own doom. So she held her breath to keep her limbs steady, breathing freely only when refilling the nib. Her hand and fingers began to cramp, and she blinked to keep the two copies in focus.

• • •

"I thought you were resting," Abraxa said when she found Amalina in *l'entrée grande*. Her thin lips disappeared in a tight line, her eyes narrowed. "What are you doing down here?"

"Turns out I was hungry," she said, removing the pear from her coat pocket and taking a bite.

"This meal was for the princess."

"I am a princess, aren't I?"

Abraxa snorted.

"Well, aren't I?" Amalina pushed, enjoying the flavor of the fruit. She wondered what market it had come from, and why they hadn't brought any to the castle before.

"You are a little mouse who is in danger of forgetting her place."

"That's strange. I thought you said my 'little mouse' had gone away. How could I be her? Can you not see well, Abraxa? It is me, Katarina Tepsji."

"This act will be tolerated in front of our guest and her people," she muttered. "When we are alone we will observe our proper ranks, Mouse."

Abraxa's face was screwing ever more into a frown. An expression of superiority tinted with resentment and malice.

"I'm hungry and I wanted to eat," Amalina explained softly. "I didn't know I wasn't allowed *any* of it. Why are you acting like this to me?"

"Come here," Abraxa said, and walked away without looking to see if Amalina was following.

When they entered the Great Library, Abraxa pointed to the closest wall of books. The one with the missing volumes.

"You blamed Georg for losing our lordship's books when he transferred them into the library. Isn't that right, Mouse?"

"I wasn't blaming him," Amalina said, wondering where this was headed. "I only told *you*. And that was to warn you that he might have made a mistake. I was trying to help you and him. We've been over this, Abraxa."

"Right," she said flatly. "And you stirred me up, didn't you? You used this fact to push me around, and get me to do things, secretly, under the nose of the Head of Staff, my own husband. Didn't you?"

"I was only trying to help. Please!"

"I'm not sure what game you're playing, little mouse. But it now comes to an end."

"Okay?" Amalina felt a tug in her stomach. "There is no game, but what—?"

Abraxa picked up a book—no, it was the catalogue of the library. She held it in the air for Amalina to see. Then she opened it, and walked the bank of books nearer the fireplace. Running her finger down the entries, her eyes flicked between them and the books on the shelves. Then, advancing, she put her finger where two books pressed together on a shelf. She looked to the inventory list, then back up to the shelf.

"Georg wasn't the only one to make a mistake, little mouse. You're the one who put up this section, not him. And here," she indicated the seam between two books, "is where a book *you* were responsible for has gone missing."

Amalina went to the shelf. Looking at the two books, she couldn't think of what would go between them. Looking down at the inventory in Abraxa's hand, she verified the titles, and, in fact, there was a title between the two on the list, which meant one was missing from the shelf. At first she couldn't figure out how this could have happened, and she didn't immediately recognize the title, as it was in a language she didn't know well. But then she remembered: Well before the inventory was completed, she'd had Genadie deliver this book to Dragomir Dalca, her father (the book containing a hidden message, assuring her father she was alive and well), with the intention of retrieving it before the first guest arrived at the castle.

Amalina's anger at being confronted this way, turned almost to a laugh, as she began to explain "It was lent out." But then the explanation hit a turn inside her, and switched back to a bemused anger.

"You mean to tell me," Amalina began, her breath panting, "that while I was away, you *searched* this whole library to find out if *I* missed a book?"

"Didn't you do the same?" Abraxa accused.

"*I* did the inventory. This is my work, so I had a reason to look it over. But you—you don't even know how to read! You went through each one of these books and matched its title, letter for letter, on that list!" After a thought: "Or did you have Georg do it? Is he in on this now?"

"I did it, you little witch. I went through it, just as you said. And I found it out, didn't I? I found your own mistake, your nasty little secret. Just as bad as Georg's, isn't it? And so what do I care if you act offended and start crying or shouting, you'll be bringing the same wrath down on yourself as you will my poor Georg if the Count should learn of it. So I'd say he will *never* find out. Checkmate."

"Checkmate?" Amalina fell back. It was such a strange word to come out of Abraxa. Even the contemptuous anger in her eyes couldn't stop Amalina from laughing at the oddity of it all. "We aren't fighting a battle here, Abraxa. I've told you time and time again, we're on the same side! Haven't I? What's the matter with you? And now you've brought in these new servants, and you plan to have Genadie and I replaced? As if the Count would side with you against us? As if we don't mean anything to him?"

Amalina wanted to get away. It was difficult to look at the angry, birdlike woman, with her lipless frown and beady, malevolent eyes. What could make her so mean? It's like she couldn't allow a friendship to form to save her life.

Admittedly, she thought, I did try to manipulate her. Maybe she sensed that.

"Checkmate," Abraxa said again. "Checkmate, little mouse."

Amalina went for the door, not knowing what to say. Before she left, something came to mind: "If that's the way you want it, then, it's a stalemate, Abraxa. Not a checkmate, a stalemate. And only for the moment."

She felt bad having said it by the time she was halfway up to her room. She'd never wanted to get on her bad side. She'd never wanted to get on *anyone's* bad side. It felt awful, and carried a palpable unease that would never let up, and could only get worse until one side or the other lost. It wasn't her kind of pleasure, playing games with people. It was bad enough she'd been swept up into one against the Count. And with Kralov. And now she had to deal with a servant's feud. She felt exhausted.

There was no sound from Lisbet's suite. She didn't bother knocking but went up to her own room. Now she could use a nap.

Her trunks had been delivered, set helpfully in the middle of the room. She was glad, when leaving for the Black Castle, she'd thought to take along her secret items. If she hadn't, it would have been that much harder to retrieve them from her old room in the other wing. That is, if Abraxa didn't shake them out first; she rummaging for incriminating evidence. Now Amalina only had the inconvenience of having to, for the umpteenth time, unpack her clothes into the newest bedroom, the secret items along with. She sighed and wondered what it would be like to actually have a maid. Or a whole regiment of maids. It would make life so much easier.

But keeping a secret would be so much harder.

Amalina decided she couldn't rest with this bad energy circulating through her body, and she could work it out by unpacking and getting everything settled in the bedroom. But when she went to open the first trunk, she saw the latch was loose. And when she opened the lid, the trunk was empty except for a couple skirts at the bottom.

Had the footmen unpacked her clothes already?

Opening the dresser, the drawers were empty, too. So were the cabinets.

She went back to the trunk, confusion and dread constricting her chest. Just two skirts, nothing more. Everything else was gone.

30

Uncle Georg

There was a boy standing at the end of the hall, the upper half of his face hidden by the large brim of a hat. He was slouched, his leg bounced uneasily. He wasn't wearing one of those ancient servant uniforms as the new footmen wore, but had on some raggy peasant clothes, which probably made him one of the new servants' sons. Who were they who Georg had hired? Where had they come from? A nearby farm? They all seemed a little slow and unpolished.

"Hey, there," Amalina called to him, "did you see them bring my baggage up to the room?"

The boy sprinted down the stairs.

"Hey!"

Nothing to worry yourself about, she thought. *Just find the make-up box. As long as it turns up, and it hasn't been ransacked, you're safe.*

All her trunks of clothes and accessories had made it up to the room, even if one of them had been emptied. The make-up box, which wasn't there, and which Amalina had insisted remain inside the carriage compartment for the ride to the castle, had probably been overlooked by the footmen. She just had to go down and get it.

Lisbet was still in her suite. But now she heard talking from inside. They would be out soon, so Amalina hurried away.

"Hello, I am Katarina," said Amalina, introducing herself to the footman in the entrance hall. His eyes lingered on her face in different areas. First the mouth, then the nose, then the eyes, then the ears, then her hair and cap, then they fell to her chest and arms. "The count's niece. Princess Katarina Tepsji. We should know each other before Princess Spaarvierlet comes down."

The footman stared and said nothing.

"What's *your* name then?"

"Ham."

"I'm glad to meet you, Ham. Were you the one who brought my clothes to my room?"

"Not just me," he said.

"Did you take anything out of them?"

"No."

"Did you see anyone take something out, besides me?"

"No."

She paused to see if he would ask why. He blinked slowly and unconcerned. Like a cow.

"Did you get everything off of the carriages—and out of them?"

He nodded.

She didn't want to mention what was missing. Not yet.

Before she left him she asked: "Have you met Count Tepsji? Do you know who he is?"

His shoulders went up and down.

Then she whispered: "You're supposed to give a small bow to ladies and lords, you know." She demonstrated. "And say, milady and milord at the end of every sentence, when you talk to them."

"Yes, Abraxa let us know all about it," the footman said. "We won't forget."

"You didn't bow to me just now."

"She said we didn't have to do anything for you if the foreign princess or her people aren't around," said Ham matter-of-factly. "Don't want to mess that up and get on my uncle's bad side."

"Your uncle? Uncle Tepsji?"

"Uncle Georg. You know ... he's the Head of Staff around here now."

• • •

The carriages had been put up in the large house near the barn and animal pen. The Princess' carriage was on the inside, trapped by the Count's carriage, the slow wagon, and the ice sledge; the sledge being the outermost. It must have taken a bit of work to bury the carriages so far back, and so that meant it had been done on purpose. Which, looking at it, and understanding this fact, that if Princess Lisbet and her attendants wanted to make a quick escape (as Erik, Lady Flauna, Odetta and Kralov had) it would take some time to get her carriage out, gave Amalina an ominous feeling. Even before she climbed up into the cabin of the first carriage to fetch her make-up box. The box wasn't inside. Now a chill crept up her back.

She searched the compartment three times, and pulled up boards and cushions, knowing that it would be impossible to stow the box below, above, or behind anything. But she had to try. Because if it wasn't in there, where could it be? Who might have it? And with it: her bottle and cryptograph sheets.

She felt a moan in the back of her throat, but checked it. Now wasn't a time to worry. There were already too many things going wrong. Why panic now? Just keep moving. Pretend everything is all right until one weak piece holding up her façade broke.

Georg was in the entry hall supervising the shifting of the bread and the pitchers on the table. The two footmen took their orders with constant looks to see if their uncle approved.

Amalina should talk to one of them. But she didn't want to alert Georg to her concerns. The last thing she needed was perking up his curiosity, which then, she was sure, would be transmitted to, and amplified by, Abraxa.

Wouldn't it be natural to ask after the box? she thought. If they were responsible for the disappearance of her clothes, and the box, they would be waiting for her to complain. This might actually be another move in Abraxa's imagined game against her. To irritate her, make her feel uncomfortable. And to have no recourse when she came to protest, with the threat to report the loss of the book in the library hanging over her (as meaningless as that loss really was).

This constant scheming and counter-scheming was so exhausting, she thought.

She had to get that make-up box. Even if who had taken it hadn't searched it and found the codes, she needed to have the codes. There was little chance to get back into the Count's treasury, so those pages with the solution to the code were her only chance to decipher the latest message. She had to have the box.

Eventually the dining table was sorted to Georg's satisfaction. The candles were lit and the footmen dismissed. Georg left in the direction of the kitchens.

Amalina ran after the footmen.

"Ham," she said. "I'm looking for my make-up box. It wasn't delivered to my room. Is it possible that you brought it to Princess Spaarvierlet's room?"

"There were many boxes," he answered simply. "They were pretty heavy."

"Well, this one wouldn't have been too heavy. It wasn't very large, either." Amalina demonstrated its dimensions with her hands. "About this big. It was in my carriage. That is, er, the Count's carriage. On the bench. It's made of walnut, I think. With little brass handles on it, on the front and the top. It opens in the front." It didn't look like he was following. "Do you remember it?"

Ham ran his tongue around inside his cheek as he considered it. Then he shook his head.

"Can't say I remember it at all. Did you check the carriage?"

"Yes. That's why I'm asking you, Ham. I've looked just about everywhere I can think of, and it seems to have disappeared. But that couldn't be possible, could it? Things don't just disappear."

He couldn't say, he said. It was impossible to tell if he was lying or just vacant-eyed. His expression was honest sympathy and concern.

"Well, my make-up seems to have disappeared."

"Maybe. If you can't find it."

"Can you help me find it, Ham?"

"I'd have to ask uncle."

"Are you doing something important right now?"

"Waiting for the princesses to come down so that we can serve them."

"I'm the princess here, remember?"

"Only when the *foreign* princess, or her people, are in the room. That's what uncle says."

"Yes. You told me that."

"Say, that reminds me," said Ham, suddenly animated. He dug out something from a bag at his hip. "Also have to make sure all the maids eat one of these when they arrive in the castle."

Ham handed her a round red candy ball.

"You're supposed to eat it."

"I've already had one."

"Uncle says I have to see to make certain. All the maids in the castle have to eat them. Uncle's orders."

"I'm not a maid."

"You are when the foreign princess isn't around."

"I've already had one, though. I've had many."

Ham stared at her.

"Will you help me if I eat it?"

Ham stared expectantly.

Amalina put the ball in her mouth. It was the bitter anise flavor. Even more bitter than before.

"Yuck," Amalina gasped. "Why this flavor? It's awful."

"There's no other flavor, Uncle says."

"There is, too. And much better than this."

"If they tasted any better everyone would want one," said Ham. "The children would be stealing them before the maids can get at them. This is the only flavor."

"Well, I'm eating it. Are you going to help me?"

He shook his head. Amalina spit out the ball. "Why not?"

"Uncle says you're to be treated as a maid unless the foreign princess is around. She's not here, so—"

"So, if the foreign princess asked you to look for my box, would you do it?"

"I'd have to."

"Well, then I'll go upstairs and ask the princess to ask you. How about that, Ham?"

"Okay."

"Or you could save me the time and energy of running up and down the stairs, and bothering the Count's guest, and just start helping me right now."

He didn't reply, but his head bounced at the impact of what she'd said. It appeared to have struck him in the ear more than penetrated. He was unsure.

"Uncle—"

"You do understand that the Count, who is lord of this castle, is more important than your uncle, yes?"

Ham nodded. "That's what uncle said."

"Did he tell you how powerful Count Tepsji is?"

Ham nodded again.

"Did he tell you exactly *who* and *what* the Count is?"

"Very powerful," said Ham, but didn't elaborate. There was no note of fear. It was just a basic statement.

"The Count wouldn't want his guest bothered. It is his purpose that the princess' comfort is seen to and met, and never have to deal with petty issues, especially ones that have nothing to do with her. So how upset would he be if she were troubled by this minor problem ... and who would he blame?"

"You, girl," Ham said. "'Cause you're the one who troubled her. Wasn't me." After a beat: "You going to do it?"

"Yes," she said, backing slowly. "Yes, I am."

"You aren't afraid of his eminence?"

"Of course I am. And so should you. I'm bringing you into it."

"Is the box *that* important to you, girl?"

"How important do you think a make-up box is to a princess?"

"To a pretty one?"

For some reason that comment hurt.

"I'm just going to bet that if the Count is upset by this, I am more important to be kept alive than you are. What do you think?"

It was the worst thing she'd ever said to someone. She was sure of it as she slowly climbed the stairs, wishing to go back to Ham and apologize. Even her fights with Jenna, her cousin, as insulting as they could get, had never had the threat of death attached to them. She couldn't afford to forget that, now that she was in the employ of the Count. Such threats were more than cruel, they were real.

• • •

It was like she brought the bad energy from the entrance hall with her. As she neared the princess' suite, with the argument between her and Ham still echoing in her ears, the voices inside the suite held the same stressed tones. Several voices volleyed back and forth behind the door. Astrell and Carila, passionately arguing. Lisbet was crying as she spoke. Amalina couldn't hear the words clearly. What could have upset them?

Amalina went to knock. What was the protocol here? Would sticking her nose into their business violate aristocratic etiquette by opening the princess to embarrassment? *Lucky for me*, she thought, *as much as I care for Lisbet as a friend, I have a more urgent (and higher) purpose at the castle*. And, in any case, she had the impropriety and rudeness associated with a foreign culture built in as an excuse.

Amalina rapped on the door. The heated voices stopped suddenly. There was a low hiss of whispering. Amalina knocked again. Four sets of feet scurried in many directions, most away from the door.

The door opened quickly and wide. Carila stood there with puffy red eyes, but her feet planted and chest thrust out boldly.

"Princess Tepsji, you call on our mistress personally? It is a pleasure." Her words didn't match her hard look.

"How is my darling Lisbet? Still resting?"

"I'm afraid it is so, Lady Katarina."

"I've no wish to bother her," Amalina said, lowering her voice. "But you might help me, Carila. I think the servants possibly made a mistake and sent some of my items to this room. If you could check for me, I'd appreciate it."

Carila looked stunned.

"Is everything all right?"

"Why are you asking here?" Carila said slowly.

"As I said, I think they brought it here."

"My apologies. I'd expect one of your maids. I'm unused to a princess conducting house business. You *are* very kind to them." She didn't make it sound like the idea pleased her.

"It's about this big," Amalina pressed on, and described the make-up box in detail—made of walnut, so many drawers, etc.—so that it could not be mistaken for anything else.

"We received nothing but what we brought, princess," Carila said.

"Are you sure?"

"Did they tell you they brought it to the princess' room?"

"They weren't sure."

"I am sure," said Carila. "I am very certain."

"Could you look again for me? Just one more time? I can't think of where else it might have gone."

"I will look," Carila bowed. Then, as she closed the door, "I will tell your maids the answer when the princess is awake again and releases us. Unless you prefer my lady report the information directly to you, when you next see her."

With the door closed it took a minute for the argument to resume. Amalina lingered by the door, ear cocked.

"What's the matter with you?" Lisbet cried out.

"You think I did something wrong, mistress?" Carila said. "Send me home then."

"I should. I can't believe how much you're willing to embarrass me. Did mother send you along to sabotage everything?"

"If you don't appreciate my help, send me home."

"Stop saying that!" cried Lisbet, then descended into sobs. "How can I possibly live this down, Carila? And I trusted you the most."

"Better to trust in me, milady. I am just looking out for you. Protecting you. Which is more than can be said about these common thieves you're trying to suck up to."

"Thieves! Thieves! You throw that accusation around pretty well. The only thief I see around here is *you!*"

"Unkind, milady," said Carila, sobbing herself. "I've taken nothing that won't be returned ... when your valuables find their way back into your possession! You accuse me of being a thief, but that is how you deal with thieves, milady. It's our only defense."

"You will ruin me."

"Only if you weaken. Now quiet yourself and play their game. We will win it, if you listen to me."

Lisbet said she wanted nothing of games.

"You know what I should have said to that Tepsji girl?" snarled Carila. "I should have told her: 'We received nothing but what we brought ... and even less than that.' That's what I should have said, and seen what she had to say to *that!*"

"I'm begging you to stop with this, before you force me to dismiss you."

"Do it, milady. I never asked to come. But while I am here, you won't be taken advantage of."

Amalina ran when she heard footsteps heading for the door. Up in her room, she thought of how much she sympathized with Lisbet. She was ready to break down and cry. So Carila had her own game she was playing. Just one more to add to the many. It seemed like it was the adults that had the endless energy for schemes. And they seemed to enjoy it.

But what was it she'd learned from the exchange? Carila was calling Amalina—no, calling the Count and his niece—a pair of thieves. Some of Lisbet's belongings had gone missing, it seemed. And it sounded like Lisbet's old maid might have taken something from Amalina in retaliation. The make-up box? It was possible. Or her clothes from the trunk? Maybe something she hadn't even noticed yet? Something belonging to the Count, maybe?

The important information was this: there was a thief in the Count's circle. Carila blamed Amalina and the Count. But had the thief made off with a little of everyone's stuff? including Amalina's personals? Including the make-up box? What thief would dare to steal from the Count and his guests? Only a fool, or someone who didn't know any better.

Amalina had been sitting there in silence, thinking over these new ideas, when she heard the door open. It was slow and tentative. She saw the fingers of a small hand curl around its edge, as the small person behind it pushed it further open. The brim of the hat came first, then the boy's face. He crept forward carefully, looking around the room for danger as he snuck toward the trunks.

"You!" Amalina said, jumping off her bed. "What do you think you're doing!"

But the boy had already spun and ran away, slamming the door behind him.

Amalina got the door open and followed after the small figure as it plunged down the stairs and dodged left and right through the hallways. The way his head spun every which way, he was still unfamiliar with the castle, desperately trying to find a good escape route.

"You come here," Amalina shouted after him. "What will your Uncle Georg do when he finds out what you've been up to, eh? You'll be lucky if he doesn't kill you! Come to me and I won't hurt you! If you keep running, he'll have the Count cut off a hand for everything you've stolen! Come here!"

He plowed through a door, throwing it closed behind him. But Amalina was faster than he was agile. She came through it, shouting: "Stop now and the princess will forgive you! I'm nicer than Uncle Georg—"

She knew she had him cornered when she hit the door. It was the privy, and there was nowhere for the little boy to run. Unless he took the only route out of the chamber. The door slammed open.

His hands, with his hat caught in them, were the last of she saw of the boy as he disappeared down the bench seat's black hole.

. . .

"I don't know how to tell you this," Amalina said to Georg, wiping the tears from her eyes. "I think you might have lost one of your ... uh, family."

Georg turned to regard the footmen, who were again rearranging the platters and bouquets on the entrance hall's table. Then he gave Amalina a curious look. "What do you mean?"

"I understand you've hired more of your family on here," she said. "To help in the castle."

"And which one told you that?" he said, bristling at the accusation, but his boiled-potato cheeks blushed guiltily.

"Your nephew, Ham."

"Ham, you're dismissed," he called to the footman, who dropped the jug of water, spilling it all over the table and on the floor.

"Uncle Georg!"

"I told you how to address me!" Georg snapped. "I taught you the proper words!"

"Yes, sir. Yes. But you just dismissed me, uncle! Do I still have to call you—?"

"Stop blubbering and dry that mess."

"But you dismissed me, uncle."

"You haven't been dismissed. You will clean that mess. And you won't refer to me as your uncle again, upon the pain of death. Do you understand me, Ham?"

"Yessir. Yes, sir!" Ham busied himself with drying the table, knocking items off as he did so.

"But something happened," Amalina said. "One of them is lost."

"What nonsense are you talking about?"

"I mean," Amalina was starting to anger, "One of your family who you brought into the castle has been stealing. He stole from Princess Lisbet, he's stolen from me. And when I caught him in the act, he ran away and—"

"Which one? Who do you mean?" He was looking ferociously at the footmen. "They would never."

"The little boy."

"Who?" Georg turned on her.

"The boy."

"The only people I've hired are Ham and Gull. And Drus, who is no little boy and I know for a fact has been in the kitchen all day long. So I have no idea who you are referring to. These are the Count's servants, and no more: The Head of Staff, Abraxa, Ham, Gull, and Drus." He added with downturned lips, "Except the dog Genadie, and you."

"Oh."

Georg straightened up and closed his eyes, finished with the nonsensical conversation. Curiously, he didn't seem interested in the subject of the boy or a thief, or that anyone might have died.

Then again, she hadn't gotten to the point that he'd fallen down the privy hole.

She didn't want to ask anybody where the hole let out. There was still some light left in the sky and the gate was still open. Amalina ran around the outside of the castle, climbing onto the rocky area near the back of it, assuming that is where the castle's refuse would fall. She anticipated the bloody and pulped body of the child and found it difficult to look too far ahead. Instead, she searched high up on the wall for where the privy vented.

The boy's legs hung out a square hole amid the grey stones. The hole was very high up, and had a small lip of deteriorated wood. Amalina felt a rush of relief that he had stopped there. He might have survived the drop if he'd fallen, but if he didn't snap his neck he would have come away with broken limbs that might never be repaired.

"Hello?" Amalina called to the legs. "I see you! Can you hear me?"

The legs kicked.

"Don't move! I'll be back!"

She found a ladder by the barn that was long enough to reach the top of the walls. It was too heavy to lift. Should I get Genadie? she wondered. She looked at the sky. Its blue was darkening, a reddish tinge on the clouds' western edges. If the Count was in the castle, he could've been awake and moving around at any point, so anything she did might be detected. But if he was away, he wouldn't be able to arrive for another hour. Maybe less.

Amalina went to the barn and collected the reins from the horses. She looped them into a heavy roll and took them up to the parapet atop the walls. The height, looking down, was dizzying. But not as bad as it would have been from one of the towers. She did feel nauseous when she saw the small legs again, kicking outside the hole of the chute. It was much further down the wall than it'd looked from below.

Amazed that she was doing this once again, creating a castle-high rope to dangle over a ledge the way she'd done a year ago, she tied the reins' leather straps together, one after the next with practiced precision. She made a loop at one end, large enough to cinch around the boy's waist.

She lowered the rope as far as it would go, to see if she would be able to lower him to the ground outside, or be forced to pull him back up. It barely reached the hole. This was going to be tricky. Hopefully he wouldn't be too scared to try.

She swung the loop toward his legs and called, "Here, put it around you. I'll pull you up!"

His arms shot out and grabbed the loop. He hadn't even hesitated, but flung his body out and jumped on.

Amalina wasn't prepared for his weight. She hadn't even considered it. The boy taking hold of the reins almost pulled her right over. She cried out and held on, cursing for having not wrapped the rope around her. It's not like she hadn't been in similar situations. Now the thin leather was slipping through her fingers, her sweaty hands making it all the harder to hold.

To her shock, the boy hadn't put himself through the loop, but had used the loop as a foothold, and now stood up in it, holding onto the rope with his hands and looking to her. It was a precarious choice to have made. His foot could slip, he could lose his grip. Falling was easy.

But it was lucky he hadn't secured himself by the waist. No sooner had Amalina recovered and began pulling up than the loop's knot unraveled. With a shout, the boy lengthened uneasily, and looked down on the rocky doom below. He couldn't let go. So he began pulling himself up, hand over hand, towards the top. Amalina fought the added shaking of the rein-rope and heaved harder—really wishing she had wound it around her, where she could have just now turned in place like a wheel and winched him up. Instead, it was a struggle to haul with her arms, losing inches in the other direction as it slipped through her palms. She hauled back, bracing her body against the wall. She couldn't look down, but faced the top of the wall. Willing him to appear there. But there was always more rein, or a clump of knot that fought against coming over the edge. A clump she was sure would burst open before it turned the corner.

The latest knot was caught firmly. The angle was too severe, and she had to fight with her whole body to pull, her hands cramping, the rein biting into her skin, her arms aching. At first she thought it was just her imagining. But the knot began to unravel. She saw the small leather bud at the top of the knot pull through the hole it was sticking out of, and then there followed a small popping sound. And the knot broke.

Amalina shouted at the same time she heard a small cry.

A hand hit the top of the wall. The fingers flexed, and began to slip on the rough surface.

Amalina jumped forward. She grabbed at the hand, its wrist. Bracing with her knees, sure she was toppling over, she used her other hand to reach over and grasp the slender forearm. His free hand slapped at her, and she let go his wrist and took it. They were no longer crying, but breathing heavy and grasping, flailing at each other, pulling at their arms as gravity pulled much harder from below.

Drawing backward, feeling the muscles in her back strain, she hauled the boy over and threw him onto the narrow landing. She fell down with him. They gasped and grasped at each other, like they were falling and trying to catch themselves. Eventually they settled down.

Panting, she said, "You idiot. What do you think you were doing? You could have killed yourself."

"Thank you! Thank you!" Oblivious to her insults, his eyes blinded with an alternating fear and relief. "Oh, I might have killed myself. What was I thinking?"

It took her a second to realize he wasn't speaking the same language. And another to realize he was no relation to Uncle Georg.

31

The Palace of Pleasure

The boy moved around the room with a restless energy. He went to the bed, he peeked out the window, he circled the room, he shook his head, then he went to the bed again; completing this circuit seven times or more before he gave in and sprawled onto the mattress and cried himself out. Then he sat up and looked irritable.

"You aren't going to tell her," he said. "You can't tell her."

"I already promised not to," Amalina told him. She sat in her chair and observed him warmly. He was no more than 10 years old, with a thick head of blond hair that, freed of the large hat, broke away from his head in wild clumps. His skin was the kind of red very pale people got when they'd been in the sun too long; revealing clear white in seams, under the jawline and near the roots of the hair. He had a long thin nose punctuated beneath it by small but fat lips. Under his heavy blond eyebrows were two round blueberries for eyes, shot through with light blue ice crystals. His eyes gave him a magical quality, a liveliness. But his expression was of a small child who'd caught his foot in a wolf-trap. He was tough, but temporarily vulnerable.

"You're going to tell her," he said. "But you'd better not. What a fool mistake coming here."

"Why don't you want your sister to know?"

"She'll kill me. She'll send me home. Then I'll *really* pay for it." Then he repeated under his breath, "Fool coming here at all! Can't understand a word anyone's saying."

"How in the world did you even get here?"

The boy—his name was Aklan, Aklan Spaarvierlet—explained with enthusiasm how he'd got there, like he was recounting an adventure. But his conclusion was that it wasn't as much fun as he thought it would be, and littered with more complications than he'd bargained for. First, he'd smuggled himself in one of Lisbet's trunks. He'd overheated, and starved, and dehydrated, and nearly smothered. But, worst of all, as he kept lamenting, he couldn't understand the language and nobody in this backward place could understand *him*.

"Why did you do it? Why did you come?"

"That's easy!" Aklan smacked his fist in his palm. "The barbarians!"

"Barbarians?"

"Everyone knows the barbarians are in the eastern kingdoms. I've heard all about 'em, and I wanted to come see one in person. Figured I'd kill ten or a hundred if I got the chance. Drive 'em all the way back to the Steppes and the desert, or to wherever they pour out."

She asked how he figured he'd kill even one, considering his age and size.

"They're a bunch of scared buzzards," he cawed. "I'd scare off ten of them just at the sight of me. What'll make it a challenge is catching one, as them cowards will be running so fast! I brought my daddy's sword but I had to trade it—or else I'd send twice as many to glory. You believe that! My hands will serve them good enough. I'll make a name!"

"You'll be caught quick if you don't shut up."

Aklan swallowed his lips.

"You stay here and keep quiet. I'll bring you food and we'll figure a way to get you out of here."

"Can you show me where the barbarians are?" he asked in a quieter voice.

"There haven't been barbarians here in ages."

"Must be some."

"You understand what I told you? You'll keep quiet and out of sight?"

"Yeah, sure. Could you get me a sword, Princess?"

"I'll try," she said. "But it's important nobody know you're here—"

"My sister, especially."

"*Everyone.*" Amalina went to him and kneeled low to meet his eyes, the way Erik Kosche had done when trying to reassure her. But she wasn't trying to reassure the little boy, she needed to make something very clear to him without saying it. "You aren't at home anymore."

"Don't I know it!"

"Keep quiet." She put a finger on his lips to shush him. He recoiled from her finger playfully and giggled. "You need to understand you aren't just in a different land. You're in a very dangerous place. Never mind barbarians. There are things much stronger and more dangerous than them."

Aklan nodded, his eyes wide, awaiting for some new, interesting information.

"The Count ... my uncle ... Lord Tepsji. He is a very powerful man. I can't tell you too much more than that, but he can be very strict. More than anything you've ever heard of at home or in stories."

"He pulls peoples guts out? and burns them at the stake?"

"It's not that he doesn't like children," she continued. "But I have no idea how he would react if he were to find out you're here. As I say, he's very particular, and sensitive to many things—loud noises being one. And when he's bothered, he can be a beast."

The boy's eyes narrowed crossly. Prepared for a fight.

"Well … you don't have to hate him. He might even be nice to you. But since we don't know, though, we'll need to get you out of here safe and sound as fast as we can."

"Forgive me, Princess, if you think it's rude," he said, pumping his chest up, "but I'm here to protect my sister. No barbarians, or a mean Count, are going to lay a hand on her. You understand?"

"You're protecting Lees from the barbarians? Is that it?"

"For fun … *and* that," he said. "Anybody who'd do her wrong gets me as his dread enemy. Even your uncle if he's the mean sort. Pardon again, Princess. I don't care if they're supposed to marry or not. I'll plump his eyes if he makes Lisbet cry."

Amalina's eyebrows went up: "Marry?"

"Yeah. But I don't care. And I don't care how scary you think he is. I can get pretty scary myself. See?" Aklan crossed his eyes, gritted his teeth and growled, trying to look like a lion. Amalina wanted to laugh, but it wasn't funny under the circumstances.

"I'm sure she'll be safe with him," reassured Amalina. "But I can't say the same for you. You weren't supposed to be here. And if you think you look scary, you haven't seen him. No, you haven't seen the Count's kind of scary."

"What's with all the flowers everywhere in this castle? Looks like a florist's basket. He couldn't be *that* scary."

"You listen to me, and don't fool yourself, little Aklan."

· · ·

The first thing Lisbet Spaarvierlet did, when after a considerable time she emerged from her room to visit Amalina, she bypassed the meal being rotated on the table in the entrance hall and asked to be introduced to Amalina's horse, which had been the subject of discussion for hours (when last-resort topics usually plunged to favorite pets), and who they had neglected to visit on the way in. She just *had* to see the great White Snow, beloved creature of Amalina's pride and worship. Perhaps they could enjoy a late afternoon ride in the fresh air, and see the local sights before it was too dark.

Praying she wouldn't be asked to ride Snowy, fearing it might buck her right off, with an obliging smile she brought Lisbet to the stable. Lisbet's driver was playing groomsman and brushing down the carriage horses. They were beautiful horses, of course. All velvety brown with serene, sinewy postures, noble bearings, and a sensuous flip to their thick, near-black manes. Amalina had Genadie, who'd been feeding the nearby pig, and who Amalina assumed would have better command over the mercurial moods of the horse, extricate White Snow from its stall and bring it around front. He did so and stood it beside Lisbet's carriage horses.

With the acute perception of a child whose toys have been placed next to another child's much better toys, Amalina saw clearly how her horse—now directly comparable to specimens of Antwerp's royal stables—was not the horse she'd long claimed it to be. Not lithe nor handsome, White Snow was, more than anything, a blocky, pleasantly-bleached burden-beast. Something a fully armored knight would trust in battle than a fair damsel would be caught riding. Lisbet must have noticed the poor showing just as everyone else. But since the princess was free to talk, she just said, "Oh, what a beautiful, beautiful, courser, Katty, dear. I'd almost guess it a draft horse. So powerful looking. I'd be afraid to ride it, I think, with all that power. It could probably pull my carriage right up the mountain all by itself if it were harnessed to it. I suppose the horses here have to be very strong because of the mountains and all the climbing. You can keep him under control?"

"It's too bad the sun has gone down so quickly," said Amalina, sounding confident, "or I would show you how much easier it is than it looks."

Lisbet agreed and turned quickly from the stables with one last lingering look at White Snow, an ambiguous smile on her face. "Can I have a tour? Or should we wait for your uncle to join us?"

It was getting into evening, and the Count hadn't shown. Georg, who met them at the door, couldn't, and wouldn't, explain his lord's absence, and left Amalina to act as the castle's host and guide. When she scratched her head, not knowing where to start, or how the castle might have been altered while they were away, Lisbet said: "The Great Library, Katty? That is, after all, one of the wonders I came to see."

For Amalina, one of Lady Katrina Flauna's more annoying traits was how she'd roam the castle with an appraising eye, like she was taking an inventory and running a thorough tally of the worth of the tapestries, paintings, armor, candlesticks, rugs, decorative goblets, plates, etc., right down to the rivets. Lisbet Spaarvierlet's eyes had that same furtive flicker over all the décor, and all the people, too. With her upper lip massaging her lower lip in active consideration of something she did not give voice to. But her eyes were mild and lacked Flauna's ravenous greed. Still, it made Amalina wonder what she was searching for.

"This is wonderful," Lisbet said of the library once they were in it. "Very wonderful. It might be as large as the King's." She clarified: "In Antwerp."

She'd settled down. Whatever had been bothering her and preoccupying her mind was gone. She spun in place trying to take it all in, then went to a wall at random to begin her perusing.

"I so love books," said Lisbet. "Anything I can get my hands on. My father thinks it's improper, but I think he's wrong."

"Books are improper?"

"Women with books are improper. Women with any curiosity is tantamount to sin. Funny how it is that my brother is really more of a problem than I could ever be."

Aklan's admonishment not to let his sister know he was in the castle ran through her head, and she sensed this was dangerous territory. "I'm glad you came," was the only thing Amalina could think to say.

"So am I." Lisbet spun in a circle, holding out her arms at the shelves, then fell into a chair with a satisfied smile, as if in a happy swoon. "The palace of pleasure! I could stay here forever."

"Is this why you came? For the pleasures? Not to see me?"

"*You* didn't invite me, did you?" She wore a wry smile when she said it. But then it was like that peculiar shadow flitted across her face, suddenly sad. After the inner thought passed, she became calm, if stoically resolved. Her voice got lower and more serious. "It was your uncle. I came for him. My father encouraged it. Yes, he encouraged me most avidly. Forcefully. So I came for *him*. And his *palace of pleasure*." She opened her blue eyes at Amalina. "But you were its charm and lure. For me."

"Can I get you anything, milady?" Astrell asked, and it felt like she was trying to interrupt something her mistress might say next. She stood beside the door, eager or anxious. Or both. She was a young maid looking to make good.

"No, thank you, Astrell," said Lisbet. Then to Amalina, closing her eyes once more. "Strange, but now that I'm here, with unlimited books at my disposal, I feel too tired to open one. I couldn't think of reading."

"Do you want me to read to you?" Amalina went to the shelves with a bounce, and searched for a title that might amuse her friend. "Unfortunately, as you know of Lord Tepsji's thoughts on religion, there is no bible."

"Find me a good romance," Lisbet said. "Something spirited, and with a fair, loyal, brave knight. One who will sacrifice everything for the woman he loves, though all her enemies have spoken falsely against her, and made her a villain to all eyes in the kingdom. Only he knows the truth, and believes it, and would die, if needed, to rescue her."

"Sounds like you've recited one already," Amalina laughed, now devoted to finding a romance.

"Just the outline. I haven't given its body poetry. Only the mind of an expert lover can do that. I lack the skill. But I can be trained, I think. Or at least be motivated, if I could hear some sweet words that convince me the world is made of love. Of beating hearts of passion, and lives in the arms of others. And dreams always yet to come."

"And now you're reciting poetry."

"Find me a story or a poem, before I embarrass myself any more with pathetic imitation."

"You are very pleasing, what you say, milady," Astrell burst from beside the door. Then sheepishly, when both Amalina and Lisbet looked to her in surprise: "If you don't mind my saying. Apologies, milady."

"That was kind of you, Astrell."

"It's strange," said Amalina, pacing the shelves again. "Now that I think about it, I don't believe I ever came across a romance. No. No poetry, no love stories."

"Really?"

"I catalogued these books here. Every last one of them." Amalina brought her the inventory book. "See? But I can't remember now ... No, I can't think of a one." She ran her finger down the list. "There are histories and works on science and industry and vocations. On math and law and treaties. On royal families, and explorations, and natural discoveries. I'm sure there must be. Shouldn't there?"

Shouldn't there?

Amalina had read more than a dozen romances, most of them supplied by her closest friend, Cristine, when she was still living in the village of Korr. She'd read adventures and dramas on top of all the romances. She couldn't remember if she'd actually seen any of these titles as she worked her way through the Count's stash, or if she just imagined she had. She shook her head and pursed her lips.

"It would be a pity." Lisbet sat up and followed Amalina's finger down the list. She sighed. "A great pity to have such a large collection ... but with nothing *living* in it."

"Are you missing something?" Amalina asked.

Lisbet's head spun towards her, looking wary. "Missing? What do you mean? But ... no."

"Home, I mean," she said calmly. "Missing something or someone? So that you feel sad and lonely?"

"Oh," Lisbet said as she straightened herself and searched the catalogue. "No. I just really enjoy romances. More than anything else. A history will do. But nothing beats the sighs and tears of a romance."

The door opened, startling Astrell. Georg entered stiffly, lifted nose first.

"His eminence, and lord of the high castle, Count Tepsji." After making the announcement, he bowed deep at the waist.

The Count nodded slightly to his head of staff and entered. He was dressed in his finest, the garments he wore to receive Erik Kosche and Lady Flauna. He'd added several chunky necklaces with massive rubies embedded in them. One centerstone, on a large disk, was blood red, with veins of pink running over it like an eyeball where the colors exchanged. He was enormous, of course, dwarfing Georg, who dwarfed Astrell (who was trying not to cower too obviously in the corner). His hair was pulled back on his head, and under his thick eyebrows his massive, brooding eyes fell onto Lisbet, and Lisbet alone. He pulled at his long black mustache like he was massaging the tail of a cat.

His mustache had returned in full glory.

Lisbet sucked in a sudden breath. Amalina was careful not to glance over at her, to check her expression. She didn't want to make her feel as if she were being studied. The Count's eyes were enough to withstand.

"Princess Lisbet Spaarvierlet," he said in a voice so low and deep it rattled the chair. "You were gracious enough to travel far from your native land, with nothing promised but to experience the hospitality of relative strangers. I welcome you again, into my favorite home: the high castle … my palace of pleasure."

He bowed, but kept his eyes steadily on Lisbet.

"Yesss, perfect," he said. "You are lovelier in the candlelight than what the storm was generous enough to reveal to me. Oh, so much more lovelier so. Yesss."

"Are you speaking to the princess or me, uncle?" Amalina snorted. "Let's not be overly familiar with our guest, hm?"

"You don't mind me commenting on your obvious and superlative beauty, do you, Princess Spaarvierlet?"

"I will not dissuade you," said Lisbet with a coy smile. "But you'll call me Lisbet, won't you?"

. . .

Amalina excused herself as soon as she could. Astrell and Georg were left behind to keep Lisbet comfortable, and propriety observed. Amalina nabbed some food from the waiting feast to bring up to Aklan. As well, deliver him a warning to keep still and not talk if he could help it—the Count was in the castle. She'd wanted to take some cheese and a small half of a chicken. But she took what would be less obvious: a hunk of bread and a pear. If the bread had gotten too hard (by waiting all evening for someone to eat it), he could dunk it in water to freshen it up.

But in the hallway, Carila seized Amalina's arm.

"He's in there with her?" the old maid demanded, angrily sucking at her teeth.

Amalina nodded.

"Well, now she'll die!" she blared.

"What?" Amalina glanced up the hall toward the library doors. "Why do you say that?"

"Embarrassment! Shame! Humiliation! Any one of the three, or all of them together. She isn't the strongest girl in the world, and she's weak right now. And vulnerable. And it doesn't matter what I tell her, she's dying of one of those sinful things right now, even though I told her ... I told her she's got nothing to be ashamed of. It wasn't her fault. If there's anyone to be shamed, it is these devils of Ardeel!"

Amalina was amazed by Carila's insult but not offended. Even with the old lady eyeing her with venom, and squeezing painfully on her arm; her fingers wriggling through the muscle to scrape painfully at the bone.

"I don't see why anyone should be shamed or humiliated," countered Amalina. "Everyone seems to be getting along well. Ouch!"

"This visit was very important to the princess and her family. I can't tell you how important. And my grace is careful of her appearance. Call her vain, but she must be dressed in the finest of clothes. What she had planned to greet your uncle with was the most expensive garments the best tailors of the city could provide. Thirty men and fifty women worked their fingers to the bones to create her wardrobe. A wardrobe to impress kings!" Carila wiped her lips. "The princess would never tell you this. She would forbid me to open my mouth about it. But seeing she's putting me out when her drivers leave, I've no problem telling you to your face: We've come halfway around the world to make an impression, and what do we find but thieves and imposters!"

Carila looked Amalina up and down when she made the accusation, spraying the epithets onto her. Amalina shrank. The bread and pear in her hands felt heavy and she wished she could hide them.

"You keep saying thieves, but I don't understand. We've taken nothing from you, and—Ouch!"

"The wardrobe, held in the special trunk, to be opened once we arrived at this so called 'palace', so that her highness might match her surroundings ... was emptied!"—"*Ouch!*"—"Relieved of almost every dress and gown and sash and what-have-you. Have you. Have! You!"

"Ouch! Stop that! What are you saying? Me? I didn't."

"Who else would take the dresses? Who would they fit? I've seen all your clothes. What do you have? Two or three of them? So old and reworked. You think you are fooling anyone? No, you might fool nice people who have reason to want to be fooled, like milady, but not me. And you fill their heads with all this fancy talk of dream castles. *Palace of Pleasure?* I've been to palaces! No palaces here. The first wreck we see is ugly and empty and surrounded by gypsies. The second is just a small thing, and decorated by a handful of bumpkins trying to pass for proper servants, run by another bumpkin who doesn't know how to set a proper meal, and stuffed full of dandelions to throw us off the scent. I've not been tricked, even if my mistress has. You've brought her here and stolen her things. I should dare expect at the next meetings of society back in the civilized world—after we've been stripped and sent home naked—you will step into our company a shameless thief, and flaunt to our princess the princess' dresses and jewelry as if they were always your own."

"Her trunk was empty?"

"You're quick. Should I repeat the rest for you?" Carila shook Amalina again. "And her jewelry box plundered … as if you didn't know it."

Amalina swore her innocence.

"You asked me to look for your make-up box, Princess Tepsji. I've no fear of you now, so let me just say this: I took it. I have it, and I know right where it is. Took it out of your carriage when I saw it wasn't attended. And you'll get it back as soon as you return the princess' belongings. All of them."

"What if I were to tell you," Amalina said in a low voice, hoping to calm the woman, "that my own trunk was emptied?"

Carila stared, not knowing how to take this new bit of information. After a moment of grace, her eyebrows came together and she looked skeptical.

"I'm telling you I didn't take your mistress' clothes or her valuables. I'd never do such a thing. I don't know how to convince you if you won't believe me, but I need my make-up case."

"If you didn't do it, I trust you to recall the minion you sent to do your dirty work. You don't get the case until milady's wardrobe and jewels are restored. Send your uncle after me and I'll destroy it. See if I don't."

Amalina paused, unable to resolve the dilemma in her mind. It might have been fatigue, or how long since she'd last eaten. She eased herself, relaxing her whole body, and took a bite of the pear, and tried to settle the old woman with her casualness.

"You've got it wrong," she said with a sly smile. "All wrong. But I do have something that belongs to Lisbet. I'll show it to you, but you have to swear on her life you will not tell her about it."

"What kind of thief's trick is this?"

"When you see it you will understand that I'm not a thief at all. You'll trust me all the more, but I need your word. I can't show you unless you swear to me."

"You have something that belongs to my mistress, the princess, but it will prove your innocence? And further, I must swear on her life I should tell no one about it even if you show it to me? I won't stand for this nonsense."

"If you don't, you won't see it. And I will deny ever having said it. And you will never ever know what it was. And even more, you won't be able to calm dear Lisbet with the comfort that her belongings weren't stolen at all."

"You can do all that?"

Amalina nodded.

"I already warned you I'm strong enough to strangle you and your uncle with my bare hands, and that goes for your imposter servants thrown in. If you try anything tricky, you will pay with your life."

"You talk like that to other princesses?"

"I've never met a princess who I thought wasn't a princess at all. And since I am no longer in the employment of the Spaarvierlet house, though I will protect them with my life, I have no reservations telling you just how things stand. So, that being said, lead on."

"You swear you will tell nobody what I am about to show you?"

"I swear I will tell nobody what you reveal to me, but I will tear the limbs out of anyone who tries to do me harm. Or the princess harm. Do you understand?"

"Come to my room."

Amalina started to move, but she was still caught in Carila's incredible grip. And Carila was struck by what Amalina said. "Ouch!"

"I'll tear the limbs out of *anyone* who tries to do me harm," she muttered again. Then she followed.

. . .

"Traitor!" cried Aklan. "I told you not to tell my sister!"

"I didn't," said Amalina in a low voice, waving her arms to tell him to stay quiet. Carila was standing just inside the door, staring in disbelief. Amalina shut the door and ushered her in. "And I swore her to secrecy. She won't be telling anyone."

"But why'd you tell *her?*"

"Master Aklan," breathed Carila, still astonished. "Is that you?"

"You can't tell Lees," he demanded of the maid. "Swear to me."

"What happened to your clothes?"

"Traded 'em. Now swear."

"What's happened here?" Carila asked Amalina, her head shaking in bewilderment. "How have you brought the young master all the way here? You've conjured him, have you?"

"It's all very simple." Then Amalina told the maid what Aklan had told her. Of how he'd wanted to fight barbarians at the frontier so he emptied out one of his sister's trunks and stowed away on the voyage. He'd avoided their detection for the trip. And by luck he'd left the trunk in Tsobl or he would have starved to death. He'd traded with those peasants he could, to keep himself fed while he looked for adventure. When, at the last minute, he found that his sister and the foreign princess had returned to town, but were leaving to Netz and the palace of pleasure, he'd then hollowed out one of Amalina's trunks and got inside.

"Amazing, even for you, Master Aklan," Carila goggled at him. "I wouldn't believe it if I didn't see it with my own eyes. Your parents must be worried to death. Why would you do such a thing?"

"Who wouldn't want to see a Palace of Pleasure? … And fight barbarians, too?"

"So you threw away all your sister's new dresses?" Carila's face was growing red, her cheek twitched. "You knew how much your parents paid for them. And how much she looked forward to wearing them."

"I threw out *hers*, too," said Aklan, and pointed to Amalina.

"As if that makes it all right?"

"She's not mad." Aklan took a step back, recognizing a mounting danger in the old maid. "You swore you won't tell her."

"Her jewelry. All that fine jewelry. Without it she will look like a plain beggar in the street. That wasn't in the trunk. You threw them away, too?"

"No," he said matter-of-factly, "I traded them for food."

"Boy!" Carila took after him. He avoided her painful grasp only by knowing from experience she was about to pounce.

"I'll tear you apart," said Carila. "I'll tear you to pieces for such a thing! Oh, to think! You are the most!"

Aklan tried to dodge around Amalina. But Amalina didn't want to get between the two. Carila would bowl her right over. Amalina shushed them as she flew to the door, and with her body barred anyone from trying to open it.

Carila took Aklan by the sleeve, and then reeled him into her arms. Amalina had experienced the agony those fingers could inflict, and felt a sympathetic pain as the maid went to work on him. Carila tossed his flailing body around, and plucked at him like a hawk tearing the wings from a kill.

"Ouch! Oh! Ow! Get my sister, princess!" he cried. "Get my sister!"

Putting her hand over the boy's mouth, his tears gushing over her fingers, Amalina said to Carila calmly, "I am not a thief. Now, can you *please* return my make-up box?"

32

What Do I Do?

"Now what do I do?" Carila fretted to herself. "I can't tell her highness he's here. I've sworn to the little master I won't. And so I won't. So, what?"

"You both keep quiet," said Amalina testily. "I have important things to do, and I don't have time to deal with any nonsense."

"How long do I have to stay in here?" came a small, muffled voice from inside the trunk in the middle of the room.

"Until it's safe to come out," she answered. Then, seated at her desk, she compared the secret message to her cryptographs, and muttered, "You'll get your food and water, don't worry."

"Is your uncle really that beastly?" Carila asked. "He'd harm the young master?"

"I'm sure he wouldn't be pleased at the surprise, if he caught the little prince. So let's not find out."

"But he couldn't bring harm to an innocent little child. It'd be unthinkable."

"The harm would come to the relationship between the princess and my uncle. Her visit would be at a quick end. Would that please Lisbet? Or her parents?"

The old maid made a face. "You spoke nothing but sweet poetry of your uncle. Now that we're here, he's a brute? Tell me you haven't laid a trap for my fair woman."

"What I said of the count, on his behalf to the princess, was the truth. Had I spoken with the little prince, I would have told him not to come. But he did, so ..."

"What are you doing there?"

"Just stay over there and keep him in the trunk. I'm almost finished."

But the lettering didn't match up with any of her solutions. She hadn't recorded all the coded sticks, which meant she'd have to get back down to the desk in the treasury if she wanted to read this one. Amalina groaned in frustration.

It was only because Carila was a servant and unused to challenging those of a higher status that she didn't further pester Amalina. Amalina was aware of this, and for the first time was thankful of the convenience of social class and order. Even if Carila, while idling by the trunk, was wondering and guessing what Amalina was up to at the desk, she couldn't demand to know or interfere. In fact, now put in her place, the old woman was more probably acting like any other servant in the circumstance, and barely taking notice of the activities of the princess. Instead preoccupied with her private dramas—her relationship with Princess Spaarvierlet, the other maids, and what was to become of her now that she was dismissed—and only monitoring for signs in the outerworld that someone needed her help.

"I need your help," said Amalina.

. . .

Keeping the boy a secret from the Count was going to be difficult, especially when the Count could appear anywhere within the castle on a gust of wind. Knowing he would try to hide his supernatural nature from his guests from Antwerp, Amalina concluded that if one of those guests was permanently lodged in her quarters, it would at least prevent him from entering without knocking on the door first. And secondarily would keep the prying Abraxa (and family) from scouring her bedroom while she was absent. If anyone entered the room, especially the Count, someone needed to stand near the trunk, so that Aklan's breathing or other sounds could be attributed to that person instead. It was the best strategy she could think of. And she did her best to explain to Carila and Aklan how important it was that this be done *"in order to not upset Princess Lisbet's visit."*

But this would work only if Amalina succeeded in the first step of her plan.

The Count kept Princess Spaarvierlet talking until well after dawn. She did not rise until the afternoon, and was surprised to be met by Carila in her chambers.

"I know we've had our disagreements, milady," the old maid said with her head bowed penitently, "and that you've dismissed me. But I have thought on the matter, and I want to please you, dear lady. I want to honor your will to have me discharged, and yet still continue to serve you in some capacity. And show you I have reformed my prejudices against this Ardeelian family. All of these things, I believe can be accomplished."

"Well, tell me how that can be," asked Lisbet, with amusement. "Keep in mind, you were the one who demanded I let you go, and you were the one who was so hardened about matters. But continue, and reveal how you can accomplish all three of these at once. I wonder how it can be done."

"Not knowing when your highness was planning to send the coachmen home, and me with them, I have volunteered my services to the Princess Tepsji."

Lisbet's eyebrows flew halfway to her hairline. But then she smiled so wide that some of her teeth showed. "And she accepted you?"

"She is short of maids. As she was when she visited us—uh—that is, when she called on your parents back home. Well, the Lady Princess has kindly accepted."

"If you want to serve me you will not do anything against her. Even if you think you are serving me by doing so, or feel it would please my parents."

"I can serve her and be loyal to you, milady."

"You will act as her faithful maid, and not my spy, or family saboteur. This I insist. If you are to be my gift to her, you must not be an unpleasant one."

"The agreement is to serve her until you order your parent's carriage to leave these gates, at which time I will return to your parents and they can deal with me as they see fit. And while I will never reveal the deeper secrets of your family to Princess Katarina—you couldn't possibly wish for that—I will be entirely faithful to the Tepsji house. Only until you wish it otherwise."

"My dear Carila, you are always full of surprises," Lisbet said. She observed the old maid with kind and delighted eyes, but when she dismissed her she regained a sad, reflective air. This, the sad, reflective air, Carila reported to her new mistress.

"I think your uncle isn't as pleasing to my princess as she'd hoped," Carila supposed.

"Well," replied Amalina, with a frank tone, "I don't know what he hoped to gain by asking her here. And, while I love Lees very much, I don't know what *she* hoped to gain by coming."

33

A Problem, Mr. Bronk?

Attila Bronk petted the air at his hip. When Hak Vogoneyevic didn't stop walking or slow down, having not noticed the motion, Attila turned to block his path. And then he caught sight of the little figures in the distance, just before Hak's massive body eclipsed them.

"A problem, Mr. Bronk?"

"Now that we are here, sir, we must make one last attempt," said Attila through dramatically gritted teeth, though his eyes held their same characteristically heavy-lidded boredom. "You will have to go alone. But I am certain you, of Ardeelian high blood, will be able to stir General Zsolt Marosh where I, an outsider and perceived traitor to my own people, failed. He once had the fire in him to do this work, the work that needs doing. The messenger (myself) was flawed."

"Thought you wanted me to raise my family's people, Mr. Bronk."

"I do. But we're outside Zsolt's home. While I trust that a Vogoneyevic army can be victorious—undoubtedly—two armies would be all that much better, it would represent to that criminal creature a larger portion of the country is against him. And, besides, more force is better than less, and General Marosh has commanded forces in the field and his mind for military strategy and tactics could be advantageous."

Hak shrugged.

"What's the matter with you, sir? I sense something."

Hak chopped at the air with his palm, waving away the question. But Attila wouldn't let it rest: "Tell me, sir."

Hak looked over his shoulder. "Gug yelled at me last night."

Attila looked past Hak to the figures who'd halted two hundred yards away. One tall, two small. Gug and the children. They'd been at that distance, never closer, for the journey so far.

"Your wife came to you?" asked Attila, surprised. She must have slipped close to Hak while he and Attila were sleeping by the campfire. It must have been. And Attila hadn't woke. This bothered him.

"Quarreled something awful," Hak told him. He lowered his great blond head and his lower lip thrust out.

"I didn't hear any of it," murmured Attila, even more surprised, though his expression kept neutral. This *really* bothered him. How had they managed to have an argument without waking him? His nerves squirmed at the thought of the many deadly creatures inhabiting the forests which could have, apparently, feasted on his body while he was prone; believing he had one eye open, ready to spring into action at the least movement, and yet actually in that most vulnerable of conditions: deep sleep.

"It was in my dreams," Hak explained. When Attila didn't say anything, but stared at him for a long time, Hak elaborated. "She was furious about how I'd gone and picked the cabbages too soon. And it made no sense either, because it wasn't our farm—we don't have cabbage—and it was the lady Okye who'd asked me to, 'cause her husband wasn't feeling well. She said I misheard the lady, and I was supposed to come at harvest time. But now I went and pulled all their cabbages too early and they weren't going to survive on them for sale or eating, and we'd have to take care of the woman and her husband and we'd have to kill our only two pigs to fit them in. And it didn't make any sense, because Okye doesn't even live here, she used to be a serf on my father's neighbor's property."

"No, it doesn't make sense," Attila agreed. "You're acting like this—like a scared and hesitant child—because Gug was angry at you *in your dream?*"

"You didn't see her. She was pretty mad. Never seen her so mad."

Attila looked again at the distant figures. He could feel the press of Gug's stare even if he couldn't see it.

"What's she doing there?" Attila asked. "Can't you tell her to go away?"

"I can't tell Gug to do what she doesn't want. And I reckon she's there to keep an eye on me."

"You won't try?"

"They aren't hurting anyone."

"It's all the more difficult to move anonymously with the protracted shadow of a wife and two children behind you."

Hak chopped his hand in the air again, studiously not looking back. "They're all right, Mr. Bronk. Least I know where they are and they aren't starving. Not sure how, seeing *we* haven't had much to eat. But having them in sight eases my mind."

"Not when she's giving you nightmares," Attila said. "You would be better focused if we were by ourselves. I promised her that you will return to them when our good work has been done."

Hak wiped the back of his neck with his large hand, and with an expression so anguished by conflict Attila had to look away.

"Let's go see Zsolt," said Attila.

. . .

Walking along the approach road to Zsolt Marosh's mansion it became clear the property had been abandoned. The mansion and outer buildings were as eerily silent as skeletons. After a brief search of the grounds its only tenants were three stray mongrel dogs, seven tom cats, a skeletal cow, and a shabby game warden who stared at them curiously.

"Excuse me," Attila said, approaching the warden. The warden leaned his large cudgel forward as they neared, his concern drawn more toward the massive Hak at Attila's side. "Do you know what's happened here?"

"Gone," said the warden, eyeing Attila up and down now. Then his eyes narrowed shrewdly as if he was about to say something. But then he didn't.

"It seems everyone's gone," Attila prompted.

"Took his home out by the root," the warden agreed, eyeing Attila up and down for a second time, only taking a longer time to do so. "Who're you?"

"This is Sir Hak Vogoneyevic," Attila introduced with a side-step and a gesture. Hak bowed unsurely.

"Now that's an old name," said the warden almost enthusiastically. He set down his cudgel against his thigh. "*Vogoneyevic*. My cousin served under 'Antlers' Vogoneyevic. A great man."

"His relation." Attila now encouraged Hak, pointing to him.

"My grandfather, of course," said Hak, adding another superfluous bow.

"No, allow me," the warden bowed. The two traded several more bows. "'Antlers' was a brute like no other. Saw him once take on three men, and they weren't in no shape to laugh about it when he was done."

"Can you tell me what's happened to Sir Marosh?" asked Attila, politely, and suffered the wrath of the warden's glare for the interruption.

"I told you. He left."

"With everyone?"

"I told you. By the roots."

"Where?"

"Hunting party. It's his way, you know. The greatest hunter on this continent."

"What is he hunting presently?"

"Anything he wants," declared the warden with a snort. "The mountains themselves someday, and I'd bet he'd bag at least one, that old Marosh."

"But did he *say* what he was hunting? Did he put it about what he was after?"

"To me? Why should he?" the warden put his hand on his cudgel again. His eyes shifted between Hak and Attila, as if wondering how the two of them could be together. He looked Attila up and down again for a third time and his mouth curved down.

"You're right, there was no need," said Attila, patiently. "But by observation, my curiosity is piqued. You say he is hunting. But not only has he taken everything expected in a hunt, he has also taken with him his guns of artillery, and by the condition of the grass, a sizeable shod cavalry, and at least a battalion of infantry. It makes one wonder what exactly he is hunting."

"Doesn't me," said the warden as he hefted the cudgel into his hand again. "Now, tell me just who you are."

"I am aid to Sir Vogoneyevic."

"And just why are you wearing my cloak?"

Attila did not react. But the pause wasn't a good argument on his end. Even Hak seemed to want to know.

"That's my cloak," the warden said. "I recognize it sure as anything, now. Look at that patch. Sewn it on myself. And that cloak was stolen some time ago when it was hanging out to dry from washing. Stolen the day a traitorous rogue, destined for rightful execution, escaped from General Marosh's custody. That is you! *That is you!*"

The warden's cudgel flew up and started swirling in circles toward Attila. Attila backed away, but couldn't prevent the warden from drawing a line between him and Hak.

"Please, mister," Hak said, waving his big hands in a placating way, with a soft smile on his face.

"Is the grandson of 'Antlers' going to stand partnered with a traitor and a thief?"

"He's mistaken," Attila said drowsily, his voice more bored than ever. "This is not his cloak. I am not a thief."

"Tell me, are you with him?" The warden now backed up and rotated the heavy end of his metal-studded club towards the mountainous Hak. From a distance he would look like a dwarven hedgehog spinning a branch at a blond bear. But the warden was full of fury and undaunted. "Declare yourself, sir. Are you with this thief?"

"I'm afraid so, mister."

"Then by the love of my cousin, down with all Vogoneyevics! Confederates to degenerate swine! No matter how big they think they are, they shall fall to the righteous!"

The warden charged Hak, who dodged and weaved with wide eyes. Panic stricken he yelled at the top of his voice: "Run!"

The warden required the cudgel to walk any distance further than his own gate, so Hak and Attila were out of his range immediately. Hak kept running. Off the road and over the gradually undulating hills of this valley, with Attila right behind him.

"I will report you, thief!" the warden shouted after them. "You will be hung for your crimes!"

In the distance, the three figures shifted position.

. . .

"Will you tell me what happened back there?" Attila scolded indifferently, though he was still clutching his shaking left hand. "Can you explain?"

"What?" asked Hak, scratching his head. He glanced to make sure Gug and the children were still in sight.

"That warden came at you with a weapon and you ran."

Hak nodded with a small laugh. "Yeah, that was pretty scary, wasn't it?"

"You did not seek to defend yourself. Never mind that you didn't defend me, but your own person. You showed no motion to match him or to make a counterstrike. You simply cowered and ran."

"He had that big club."

"Yes, I saw it. And do you think someone as small as a chipmunk is going to hurt you with it? It would have been like tickling you with a feather."

"*You* didn't stick around to get tickled," observed Hak drily, but sounded hurt.

"I am not a man of violence."

"Neither am I," Hak said.

"How can that be when you are going to meet with the creature of death and kill it?"

Hak shrugged.

"You understood what I told you, didn't you? You must defeat this monster in combat. There will be violence involved."

"I heard what you said," Hak said. "And it made sense. But tell me why you can't do it."

"Because you are a native son of this land—"

"You don't have to tell me all that again, Mr. Bronk. I'm asking *why* you can't do it yourself. It doesn't make any sense why I have to do it, if you have no problem killing someone."

Attila's expression remained dull, but his entire body shook.

"That isn't true," said Attila. "I cannot kill someone."

"What's that?"

"I am a man of law. A man of Heaven's law. I cannot kill another man." Attila slowed as they walked. It was getting dark, they would have to make a fire. They might be able to push further, but he had Gug and the children to take into account. They'd need to make camp, too. They were probably thirsty.

Attila saw the face of the soldier in the water: the one he'd met before the falls, the one who'd tried to skewer him with a lance but ended up in the water. And that's how he saw the soldier now: bubbles climbing out of his mouth, terror in his eyes, his strength growing slack.

"Even now I tremble that I might have accidentally killed someone. It wasn't my fault, but it doesn't matter. He came for me and I … Well, it doesn't matter the circumstances, I am haunted by his face, and the knowledge that I might be damned for what I have done."

"Mr. Bronk?" Hak began timidly.

"Yes?"

"I can't kill someone either. Just like you."

Though Attila was stunned, he didn't show it, and unconcernedly swished the edges of his cloak.

"Why do you say that?"

"I just can't. Just like you, Mr. Bronk. I am a man of law."

"But I was sworn to it. With a book. I was an officer sworn to uphold that law. I was the low constable."

"Oh." Hak frowned. "But I am a man of Heaven's law, too. Why can't I say the same thing as you? I don't see how that's fair."

"Because," Attila began with a patient nod, "You are not me. And you have violence in your blood. Didn't you hear the warden back there? Your grandfather 'Antlers' killed three men with his bare hands, without blinking. It was a joke to him. This is the line you are descended from."

"Sometimes it doesn't feel like it."

"I could go on about what I said before. About how you have a duty out of shame and guilt—"

"No, I wish you wouldn't."

"Do you mean to tell me that you have never killed anyone, Sir Vogoneyevic?"

"No one's even called me 'Sir'. But … no."

"Looked like you were capable of killing me a couple times."

"Naw. I can look pretty mean, though. Truth is, I don't think killing is in me."

"You've killed animals. Chickens and pigs."

"Those are things without souls. And, anyway, I never liked it. Gug does it mostly. I think the kids have taken to it better than me. No, I don't like it. I don't like the pain and the hurt and the blood. I don't like killing, Mr. Bronk."

"For the creature," Attila said, "you can think of him as something without a soul. Because he has none. And you can think of him as a threat to you and your family, if that helps get you mean enough to do it. Because he *is* a threat to Gug and Man and Lija."

"I suppose that might help," conceded Hak. "Maybe."

"I can only remind you that it is in your blood, and it is in your destiny."

"I sure wish it was in yours, too, Mr. Bronk. I wish I'd have been sworn into law, like you."

"It takes a bit more education," said Attila, feeling guilty but not showing it. "Besides, someone has to do it, and that person is you."

"You sure about that?"

Attila regarded the mountain lumbering at his side, his skin so dark from the sun that he was beginning to match the evening gloom, and hair so sun-bleached it stood out against that gloom like a torch. The massive man felt elemental in his strength. How could he be so timid and weak? Attila marveled, as they stopped to make camp.

"I hope Gug doesn't yell at me tonight," Hak mumbled to himself.

34

The Cue

It took two nights and days of keeping Aklan muffled. Two nights and days of fretting over Piotr's fate, and over how much time had passed that he was certainly dead, or being kept prisoner—being kept alive only to be tortured for information. Two nights and days of fearing the Count would come to her at any second, accusing her of spying, and all the while Amalina formulating excuses that might be credible enough to save her. Two nights and days of wondering what the meaning of the new message was, how important it might be to the cause, but couldn't translate it. Two nights and days of wearying vigil, and entertaining her guest, Lisbet, that she almost missed her cue when the opportunity she was so anxiously waiting for finally presented itself: Early on the third evening, a cry of wolves announced the Count's leaving the castle.

"You will help me," Amalina told Carila and Aklan. "This is very important, and it needs to be done quickly and without anyone noticing."

Carila was suspicious but Aklan was just as happy to be freed of his prison. He looked goggle-eyed at his surroundings when he emerged from the trunk and bounced with restless energy, though groaning at his rusty joints.

"Carila, you will keep Abraxa distracted. Complain there wasn't enough variety in the evening meal."

"There wasn't," Carila agreed.

"I know, I heard you."

"I can't believe you put up with it," she said. "Master Spaarvierlet never would."

"No, I wouldn't," said Aklan.

"I meant your father," Carila corrected.

"Oh."

Amalina continued her instructions: "You'll tell Abraxa what you think they should be serving. Take her to the kitchen and show her what you know."

"I don't know how to cook anything."

"Well, pretend. I'll come get you when we're done."

"What exactly are we doing?" Carila asked.

"There's not much time to explain," she said, feeling the minutes being lost for every second. "The politics in the mountains are less comfortable than in Antwerp. And the frontiers even less so. The young master Aklan told me he wants to fight barbarians, and he can help do so if he helps me now. You'd like to help me fight against the barbarians, wouldn't you?"

"Yes!"

"So then you come and help me. Both of you. I need to get into a part of the building only my uncle can reach, and he's left the castle. But it'll all become clearer when we—"

"What *exactly* are we doing?" she asked again, even more suspicious because of Amalina's quick talking.

"Opening a secret door in this castle. Which leads to a secret chamber."

"Let's go!" cried Aklan eagerly, his eyes shining bright. Amalina assumed, to him most of all, it would sound like an adventure: what he'd been looking for all along!

As they moved along the hallways, Aklan kept himself just behind the corners. The plan was simple enough, if only it would work and they didn't get stopped along the way.

Astrell bustled up to them, "Oh! There you are!"

She bowed to Amalina, and glanced nervously at Carila, looking unsure how she should behave towards her former coworker.

"What is it, girl?" Carila grumbled. "The princess doesn't have all night."

"The princess ... um, the princess ... um, *my* princess ..." Astrell turned to Amalina, panting nervously. "I mean to say, your ladyship, that Lady Spaarvierlet is in the ... the library. She knows you wanted to rest after dinner, but wished to extend an invitation to sit in the library with her. Count Tepsji will not be able to keep her company this evening ... due to business."

"Yes," said Amalina. "I'm aware of his business. And important it is. I am also a part of this. But my role tonight is here inside the castle. So tell Lisbet I will go to her when I can. But I will be occupied for at least another hour. Maybe two. Afterwards, I am hers."

Astrell bowed and ran off.

Ham and Gull had disappeared to wherever they went after the evening meal. Georg would be in the kitchen with Drus. Abraxa was stoking the fire in the grand entrance hall, looking worn from the day's activities and trying to keep awake in case she was needed in the night. Carila went to her and started grumbling. It took a couple minutes before they headed off to the kitchen.

Inside the Count's private study, and after scouting the Count's desk to make sure there weren't any new strips of paper, Amalina went through all the motions of getting the secret door open, with the boy watching her interestedly. He looked around the room like he saw concealed doorways and tunnels behind everything pushed against the wall or was large enough to hide a staircase. After she'd triggered the lock on the cabinet, she jumped off the chair and called him over.

They fought with the bulky cabinet. The boy's strength wasn't enough. Somehow it seemed heavier with him helping.

She hadn't heard the alarm of the wolves, so she still had time. But it was wasting away.

Carila was conducting a cooking assignment with Drus. Abraxa and Georg were observing with unveiled outrage.

"If you could come for just a moment," Amalina begged Carila's assistance. "You can return to this afterwards. You three," she ordered Drus, Abraxa and Georg, "wait here and get to work on applying whatever suggestions she has already given you."

With Carila putting her back into it, the three of them got the cabinet inched far enough open. Carila and Aklan stared with open mouths into the darkness beyond. Taking her candlestick, Amalina ordered Carila to return to the kitchens. Aklan would remain at the entrance to the treasury, *"to keep the door open,"* Amalina explained to him.

She wanted to run into the hidden rooms, but part of her held back. She dreaded entering. Piotr would be in there. She pictured him—his body—slumped and rotting. Hung up in a black cage. *Intruders' Fate!* the sign would read.

But the treasury proved innocent, and so did the cavernous room attached to it.

No Piotr!

She called his name softly. When no reply came she could only move onward with the rest of her mission.

She went to the desk in the message vault. Before she opened it, she noticed on its flat surface a book and two flat bits of paper. They weren't curled the way the pigeon messages were, but were the exact same size and shape. The paper was the same. And, looking at the writing on them, both papers had the same message written on them. It didn't take her long to figure it out, and she opened the book to confirm her suspicions.

The messages were the same, of course, because one of them would be tied around the leg of a pigeon and sent away. The second one would be pasted inside this book she hadn't seen before. It was a place to put copies of the Count's own correspondence.

She didn't have time to get distracted, but this discovery was enough to check the code with her cryptographs. They didn't match.

She opened the drawer and pulled out all the code sticks. First she'd have to match the ones she'd already copied, to clear them out of the way. This done, there were seven more. Amalina blew out a sigh. Then she took the quill and ink and transferred the glyphs to whatever empty space she had on her papers.

"What are you doing?" Aklan said next to her.

Amalina screamed and splattered ink. Then she cursed as she mopped up the black before it could stain the desk.

"What are you doing? Why did you come in here?"

"You were taking too long. I thought a barbarian might have cut your head off."

"You would have heard me scream."

"Not without your head," the boy said.

"You've never seen someone get their head cut off, have you?"

He shook his head.

"You need to get back up to the door, to make sure it doesn't close on us."

"There's no way it's closing by itself. We couldn't push it open, remember?"

"You also have to make sure nobody comes in and finds out I'm in here."

"Why not?"

"Because they aren't supposed to know about this place. Only uncle and I. He's the one who opens the door for me."

"Whah. He must be as strong as a river. What are you writing there?"

Amalina stopped what she was doing and leaned back. Her wrist was hurting.

"What language is that?" he asked. "It that how barbarians talk?"

"I can't say."

"'Cause it's secret?"

"Yes."

"I'm helping you. Why don't you tell me what it says?"

"Because you're too young. This is serious business."

"You aren't that much older than me. Why do you get to do it?"

"Just get back up there!"

"What are these keys for?" Aklan asked, after pulling one of the iron keys out of the desk. "Are they to treasure chests?"

"Some of them, probably. Some of them have deadly traps, too. I don't know which."

"Whah! And what does he have in the bags in that first room? His money?"

"Yes," she said distractedly. When she heard his noise of excitement, she said, "It *will* be anyway. Right now it is lead. He's studying alchemy and plans to turn it into gold. Can you imagine? All of it gold."

"But it's just lead now?" said Aklan with a deflated tone.

"Mm-hm."

She got done transferring the codes. She compared them to the message on the two strips. The first looked like it matched maybe two of the code sticks. She'd have to figure out which one. But for the message she found two days ago, no cryptograph matched its first few characters. She blew out a breath of frustration.

"What's the matter?"

"You need to get back up there before someone comes into the room," she told him.

"You don't have the right alphabet?" His eyes were darting over the sticks and the sheet of paper she'd laid on the desk.

"Doesn't look like it."

"What about this one?"

He was shorter than Amalina and from his vantage he could peer farther in to the back of the drawer. He darted a hand in and pulled out another stick. This one was grey. It was made of some sort of dull, dark metal. The letters, which looked even more unusual than the others, matched some of the letters on the old message. She now transcribed this new code key. Her heart beat hard. She was taking too long.

When she was finished, she looked at the book of messages. These were signals the Count himself had sent out. It must be valuable. But if she took it, he'd notice. Should she rip a few of the strips out? Or copy them?

There wasn't time.

So the Count had books of these messages. Many, many books on many, many shelves. She marveled anew at all the correspondence in the room, just as she had the first time she'd seen it. With how much he had stored here, it could span at least a century.

She closed the book and stared at two small paper rectangles on the desk. She had no time, but she couldn't help herself. She had to know what it said, what the count wanted to tell someone. It was just too alluring to know what went on inside his head, what really mattered to him. And what if whatever the message said told her she needed to do something else, immediately, in these hidden rooms? Or that she had to put a candle to it all, to prevent some outrage from happening. Or that she should escape the castle before he returned that night, for fear of her life?

She nodded and tried out the codesheets on the message. The second one was a match. Before Amalina retrieved Carila, and they shut the secret door and locked it, she watched as her hand worked the translation, spelling out the words in the spare space left on her sheets. Very fast, she had the Count's message translated.

The wolves tell of a scouting party in my forest. They killed many, but couldn't prevent their bodies being recovered or I could tell you who and where to make inquiries. But it seems they are still in the village. I have less time to devote to this annoyance. You will take care of it.

Scouting party? Wolves? Was it about the men who'd come with Piotr and his comrade? The ones screaming in the forest against the snarl of the wolves as he entered the castle? That happened weeks ago. Strange that the Count was getting to it only now. But then, how exactly did the wolves *'tell'* him anything? Just like the pigeons and the bats, he can speak to them? So it seemed.

No matter how late these messages may be, there was something important and urgent here. Someone was about to be instructed to deal with Kralov and his rebels. She had to get warning to them. If only she had pigeons of her own. But she didn't. Even if she hijacked one of the Count's birds, it would only arrive into the hands of his agents. Or if they knew where to deliver her message, Kralov would *definitely* be in trouble.

She would have to go to Netz herself.

35

Lisbet's Complaint

"His lordship has gone away," Lisbet said, nestled in her chair beside the fireplace in the Great Library. "His business keeps him away during the majority of the day. Now it has robbed us of his company this night. He's busier than my father, who runs five companies, as well as all our estates; and holds three ministerial titles, not to forget his crown. What precisely does your uncle do?"

Amalina cleared her throat to buy herself time. Lisbet sensed her hesitation was due to embarrassment. Because her question was, in fact, more than indelicate. It was a violent breach of etiquette.

"Forgive me for asking such a thing, my darling Katja," cried Lisbet. "Please, forget I ever asked. I don't know why I … I meant nothing by it. It's just his occupation, or *occupations*, seem all consuming. You never mentioned …"

"It seems normal to me, you know," Amalina said. "I grew up with it. Don't worry about asking. Let's just find something to keep our minds fresh and happy while he is away."

"Is Carila working out for you?"

"Too early to tell. But yes."

"Another forward thing to say," Lisbet chided herself. "What's the matter with me tonight?"

She slapped the covers of the library's catalog closed.

"I have checked through the whole thing three times," she said with a quick sigh. "There are no romances. Can you believe it? All these books, and nothing to do with stories of love. Does he have another library somewhere in this castle?"

"No."

"In another castle?"

"Not that I know of. He's most proud of this one."

"But what does it say about someone who doesn't have one single scrap of paper, in a collection of thousands, on the contemplation of the sweetest, the most pleasing, the most pleasant, the most pleasurable, the most pleasure-giving subject?"

"Is love pleasure-giving?" asked Amalina, as she sat on the arm of the chair and petted Lisbet's head. "I've read many romances. And while I love them, if they end happily, for most of the story they were unhappy before. Or if they start happily, they end tragically. There's a lot of sorrow mixed in, anyway, so it feels pretty equal in the end: pleasure and unhappiness. Why even begin?"

"You're joking with me."

Amalina nodded. "Just trying to console you and cheer you up."

"So where are the romances you read? They're not in here."

"Borrowed them from an old friend. Years ago. I might be able to get one. Nothing in the castle right now, though. I think I could recite some if you'd like to hear it."

Lisbet pouted.

"Are you like your uncle, my dearest?"

"How is that?"

"You care for business over love? But that can't be true. You are one of the warmest, most genuine people I've ever met. And I can feel your heart. I can sense it. You love love, don't you?"

"I think so."

"You desire it, don't you?"

"As you said, it is sweet. Who doesn't want that?"

"Are you in love with someone? Or have you ever been? I don't mean those big, strong ruffians marching around. But within your soul, have you a love for somebody?"

"No," Amalina said too quickly.

"Maybe you're still too young."

"Do you? Have you?"

"I fall in love every day. But I am perhaps more passionate than most people. When I was born, my mother's servants drove away two nesting lovebirds who were keeping me awake with their songs. Mother thinks my temperament is their revenge." Lisbet laughed. She made a face to acknowledge she was being silly. "Why am I so sour this evening, Katja? Do you mind if I complain? I don't do it often. And only in front of those I trust and care for. Once the storm is done, it is over. And like a depleted storm calm and peace reign."

"I've never seen you like this." Amalina held Lisbet's hand and felt a deep sympathy for her. "Complain as much as you like. I can take it."

"Bah, I think I'm done," Lisbet said. Then after a pause, "But …"

"Is everything all right?"

"Your Uncle … Everything is so different than I expected, I have to admit. You promised me nothing, and he promised me nothing. But my parents had expectations … And I suppose I did as well. Why else did I come this far? And this quickly? So rashly."

"We've disappointed you." Amalina felt a stirring in her stomach that was not exactly a pain, but it didn't feel good. It felt like she could feel her friend withdrawing from her, even with her arms around the princess. "What's the matter?"

"You spoke of the *Palace of Pleasure*," Lisbet said, her pout wiggling awkwardly, unsure of becoming a frown or a smile.

"Well, that's what uncle calls it," Amalina shot in.

"It conjured some ideas, this name. Some images in my head. When we think of the east, we see sultan's palaces, and exotic, sumptuous, overflowing ..."

"That's *south* east. Very south. My uncle ... our families loathe the sultans."

"And you despise the invaders from the west, too, I'm sure," Lisbet added apologetically. "Though I hope you don't associate *us* with *them*."

"I wouldn't have visited you if we despised you," assured Amalina. "We're well over that."

Lisbet nodded, though her look held a cautious doubt. "Anyway, my parents had visions, perhaps unrealistic. And coming here ... I am pleased by everything. I promise you, Katty, I love the company you've given me, and all the comforts. But I must confess a surprise at how different life is here. Here in this castle. In both castles I've seen. I mean, when we think of castles, and palaces ... well ... It's actually very amazing how you two get along here. It's very amazing, indeed. Very," and her next word probably didn't fall out with the grace she intended, "*impressive*."

"Meaning?"

"Well, I don't know how you manage. In Antwerp, on any estate, for any family, we have armies at our disposal. Maids, valets, butlers, stewards, cooks, groomsmen, coachmen, peasants. I mean, for a Count ... there are potters, messengers, hunters, masters of the kitchens, wine stewards, bakers, heralds, racers, tailors, fisherman, trumpeters, barbers, stable wardens, masters of the dogs, falconers, archers, smiths, maidens, physicians, chaplains, comptrollers, marshals, artists and performers—"

"That's quite a list."

"Like a little city tacked onto the walls surrounding the castle." She sighed again. "Maybe that's why your uncle is driven day and night, as he must make up for the difference."

"It feels too lonely for you," said Amalina, guessing at what she was getting at. She kept mentioning the Count and his absence. Could she really be feeling emotions for him? *Would I?* she wondered, *if I didn't know what he really was?* Aklan had said something about marriage. Had the romantic Flemish princess built a fantasy of escaping her parents, and becoming a Countess in the mountains?

"I was just surprised," she said with a small shrug. "There's nothing wrong with it. The castle looks beautiful. Look at all the flowers. It is a natural beauty, without all the bedlam of horses and staff under foot. It is probably frugal and wise ... Or ... But ... Or ..."

"Are you trying to ask me something else?"

"Is it because ... Can he not *afford* it?" Before the sentence had fully come to a stop, Lisbet trembled, then smashed her hands to her face, then let out a cry that would have turned Kralov's head all the way in Netz. Tears burst through her fingers, and her tiny mouth became a gourd shaped opening of teeth and lolling tongue. She threw Amalina off as she ran for the door. "I'm sorry! I'm sorry! Please forgive me! How could I ask it? Forget! Forget me!"

And then she was out of the room. Her howling carried up the stairs and ceased when she slammed closed her door.

• • •

Amalina didn't hear the warning alarms, she was asleep. Large, firm fingers shook her shoulder, taking her out of her dreams in an awkward way, so that she was still half in them when she saw the Count pulling at his mustache beside her. She jumped with a start and landed at the other side of her bed.

She immediately looked for Carila and the trunk. The two were by her desk. Carila was snoring. She thanked their prudence at having kept the trunk, with the little boy inside it, closed.

Amalina put a finger to her lips and took the Count out of the room. The Count was visibly annoyed by this petty inconvenience, but also amused by the novelty of it. Amused enough to permit it. At least, to Amalina's relief, he wasn't looking like a winesack gorged with blood. No blood striping his face or dripping from his clothes. But then, where had he been all night?

"What are you doing here?" she whispered. "What's going on?"

"The servants tell me of an outburst in the castle." Amalina heard a strange echo: *The wolves tell me of a scouting party in the forest.* She shook her head to wake up. The Count interpreted her movement: "There wasn't an outburst?"

"You mean Lisbet?" Amalina asked. "She had a good cry, that's for sure."

"What happened?"

"She's a bit lonely and bored. But that might not be all of it. I think she might want to marry you."

He didn't say anything, but stroked his mustache twice.

"When did you have time to grow that mustache back?" Amalina asked.

"Hm?" He stopped groping it. "Marriage you say? So soon? I've only just begun to talk with her. And there might be others coming to visit me."

"Can I ask you something?"

"This is what made her cry, little mouse? Tell me, what did she say to you exactly?"

"She said a lot of things. I'm telling you, she's lonely. We don't have half as many people as she expected to be here." Amalina repeated as many of the servant titles as she could remember.

"She expected an entire royal court?" the Count blurted in surprise. "I haven't had anything like that in centuries."

"I wouldn't tell her that," Amalina suggested. "And about the library ..."

"What about it?"

"Why aren't there any books on poetry, or romances?"

He made an odd face.

"What is it?" she asked.

"Romances? Romances? That is what she asked for? There is a whole world of knowledge packed like a powderkeg in that room, and she finds the one thing missing?"

"You don't like romances?"

"They are loathsome, little mouse. Meaningless trifles with the power to conjure whole cities from anthills, and warp the mind into wild beliefs of the impossible. I have eternity at my disposal, and I wouldn't waste another second on them."

"But you invited her here. All of those princesses. Your mission ..."

"What about it?"

"You don't ... You don't believe in love and romance?"

"Have you ever been in love, Ms. Dalca?" The way he said it, it sounded like a challenge, as if the likelihood were as realistic as her having swam the length of an ocean.

"No," she answered the question of love for the second time that evening.

· · ·

But she was lying. She'd once been in love.

Something similar to the stirrings she'd felt for Erik Kosche. And in a different way, now, towards Piotr.

But it was also a love entirely more.

Ivanti Ion Vokent.

A much older boy.

And a much smarter boy. Because he'd seen in Amalina's eyes the fury of love in them—an immature love, of course—before she knew such a thing existed.

The boy, Ivanti, was easy to fall in love with. He was smart (as stated), and kind and warm, and of an optimistic and jovial nature which shone like a rose in Ardeel's perpetual field of mud and ice. And he was tall and handsome in a way that did not happen often in the village. It was said the deputy sheriff and the mayor had once been handsome, and you could see that they might have been once—there were telltale signs—before time had run off with the better parts of their attractiveness. Her father had been good looking, too. He still retained much of it in the natural, happy expression on his face. But this boy—*Ivanti Ion Vokent!*—with his strong arms, legs, and chest; with his head of thick, luxurious dark brown hair which flew aside in great locks to reveal his gentle, bright face; with his face's apple cheeks, large, soft, understanding hazel eyes, straight nose, and smile surrounded by ... well, why not? ... let's say, his exquisitely shaped, red lips; and let us never forget his clean, fresh-smelling skin—he was *now-and-present* in his beauty. And though older than she was, he was so within her reach (age-wise) that he'd sometimes recognize her, and say things to her like: "Hello", and "How's your father doin'?", and "Can I get inside for some bread, or are you blocking your doorway on purpose?" To which she'd smile.

Like Amalina, every girl fell in love with him. He was the cause of an unhealthy bitterness and spite among the entire female populace, which arises from silent rivalry. And it wasn't that he'd understood it—something which in his good nature, had he noticed, he might have laughed at. And perhaps in his kindness labored to solve to all their satisfaction. No, what he perceived was only the front of that dark forest: The unrelenting fire of love in all the girls' eyes. Even Amalina's.

Anyone on this earth who is approached by another person possessing that deep, questing, unquenchable gaze—but without also, prior to that moment, seeking that look for oneself, hoping to find it in their eyes as a return for one's own desire; or at least with an understandable provocation for it to happen; or a good reason to expect for that look to be there—it is only natural for one to reject it. The passion unsought is not understandable, and therefore unreasonable. And the bearer of those amorous eyes considered mad. Full of madness. And is, therefore, again, undesirable. It is a too sharp noise, a cloying smell, a direwolf with fangs exposed by a hideous snarl, readied to snap into one's flesh. One recoils at it.

If one wishes to fall in love with someone, or be in love with someone, best to do it behind the target's back, and never look at them, and never attempt to speak to them. Or, by ignoring this course, one engages in a frontal assault and ruins the whole thing.

Better still: withhold one's emotions at all cost. Engage in society with a stiff spine, without any eye toward passion or in kindling kind interests with anyone else, no matter how attractive; besides one's own family, who are essentially a captive and cannot fly away. Then, by remaining stoic, if love for a someone else appears, it will most likely come in regular, off-hand moments, nipping at both victims equally and in small proportions, so that it grows proportionately, and the star-aligned two won't know what has truly happened to them until they realize together—and most likely at the same moment, trapped in a wet-eyed, mirror-like gaze—that they most happily (and equitably) have been boiled in the cauldron of love.

But this was not what happened with her and Ivanti, *the boy*. He'd been at the sharp point of love, and surrounded in lethal gauntlet by all the girls of the village so that his handsome face grew to have a bewildered, suspicious cast when he walked the streets. He stopped talking.

Then he escaped. A recruitment gang had come into town shouting out the need for brave and strong men to fight for the king against his enemies. And before a day of worry could expire (for his many admirers) of his being made off in irons by these hard kings' men—to be placed into the king's army as an unwilling conscript—he joined them silently in the night, gone the next morning. According to his father, with whoops of martial and national zeal that made them all proud; if a little concerned who would now help when serious heavy lifting was needed.

For Ivanti, it had been preferable to be in a cold and far off place, to face the sword and cannon of a faceless horde of cruel strangers, than to brave the ranks of the throbbing hearts at home.

Those hearts broke, and the miserable little village's misery became only more obvious, even when the sun was out. But it was always worse at night when one was alone with one's private thoughts. Thoughts which were always crueler and more adventurous in their cruelty with the backdrop of darkness and silence (as darkness and silence speak with the breath of eternity).

Eventually the girls recovered themselves, and either turned quietly inward or found interest in the boys they hadn't considered before. Amalina was perhaps the quickest of all of them, since she was younger, well learned, and could find ways of chopping at the lost boy's character while he wasn't around to defend himself; or otherwise prove she was wrong about his perfections. She'd disposed of him so quickly that other girls who had known she was also in love with him observed her and wondered how she'd done it, and tried to learn her method. Even the older girls, like her cousin Jenna, who were *really* after the boys now. Only Amalina hadn't been as successful in ridding herself of the ill-emotion as she had thought.

Ivanti returned one year later. His powerful form had only grown larger and stronger in the meantime, and now he was outfitted in the most handsome of uniforms. With the fine cut and upturned fur lapels and grand hat with a colorful plume, the costume caused even the deputy sheriff to grow pale with jealousy. The boy strutted into town, eyes glinting, smile beaming, cheeks glowing bright red. He was such a sight that most the villages in the surrounding counties emptied—animals abandoned in their fields, projects left off, one careless crafter neglecting to douse his fire so that he returned to see his workshop and attached house burned to the ground— just to see him.

And when she saw the boy, she knew she had never fallen out of love in the first place. And all the horrible things she'd thought to break him down into dissolvable pieces had been falsely crafted lies—crafted by a cheap and inexperienced mind in order to prevent its owner's collapse: Hers. He was that wonderful boy she'd loved since the very beginning, utterly unstained.

She was old enough to get in close at his return. She elbowed out another girl to serve drinks to the men, as they surrounded him at the hearth and encouraged him to tell tales of what he'd seen in the outside world. She listened. He was vague, and spoke only of the sport in the camps, and the great victories the king's army had had over their enemies. Because they had so decimated the invaders, and pushed them back, extending the country's borders back into the land of their enemy, and harassed them into peace treaties that should never expire, the army was given leave to return home. The village men—top to bottom, young to old—were very happy at the news and with him, growling approval and grasping his shoulders and thighs and thumping him on the back. The women were very happy, too, of course.

There were only two people that were unhappy. One was she. The other was the boy.

She saw the unhappiness in his eyes and his actions as the days passed after his return. It took half a week for him to leave his house. He bumbled around, paying visits as he should to those who mattered in the village. Sought occupation, if not for money—because he had somehow impossibly come by some money in the army—but to give himself something to do and fit himself again into society. But he was strangely quiet at odd moments where he should have rather been singing a song or telling a joke. And his manners were more reserved than before. He held his head back when a friendly sort leaned close to him, as if he were trying to shift his head onto his far shoulder by scooting it back with his chin. And his eyes narrowed at them all. Not in an unpleasant or angry way, but in a manner that disclosed a distance between him and them. He saw them as strangers now. He'd been to the outside world and had become one of it. And now he could not be common with them—as he was now most *uncommon*. That was the worst of it: She saw the look and understood it to mean that he regarded them as something lower from which he'd ascended. And he, though springing from them, and caring for them still, pitied them. Pitied them for their backwards natures and ignorance.

Perhaps that was another encouragement for her to dive into her books. To find everything that she could know, and show him that she could contain all this knowledge, to know more than anyone else in the village or in the world, but then remain one of them—remain unchanged, happy, and still the same girl that she'd always been. To avoid—or otherwise overthrow—Ivanti's arrogant pity which had left her feeling so ashamed.

Anyway, the point was that she'd lied to Lisbet and the Count, because she had loved someone once. A boy that had gone away and then returned, and then—inevitably—left once more. He left on the second and final occasion to show bravery and gain rank in the king's next war. And so he escaped twice the small village and his many admirers, never to be seen again.

And now she remembered love, romantic love. The feelings that it brought. Like the throb of a small beast that was caged in her chest, the electrical impulses across her skin; surpassing her childish curiosity of Erik, and her tempting fear of Piotr. She remembered it, and after playing with its physical ailments for twenty minutes with a clever smile, she shut it hard away. She'd learned that important trick years ago, thanks to the boy, Ivanti Ion Vokent.

And apparently, she now understood with a brief shudder, the man in the castle with her, the one who scorned love with a sneer, had learned the same neat trick.

36

The Activities of a Tricky Girl

When they arrived in Netz, the same lurid transformation to the high castle had been worked on the village: it had turned into a gloriously colored flowerpot. To Amalina it didn't look like the same village of her previous visit, which housed a hostile, lynch-inclined populace; a gathering place for a revolutionary army and its commander, and the eternally drab and relentless toilers of the Ardeel. All those elements were still there, of course, but undetectable to foreign eyes. For Amalina, it was like someone had set a painted helmet on top of an unhappy head. Its frown and glare visible through the slits, if you knew to look. But for those who didn't, it was a glorious, showy thing.

The purpose of the visit was for the two princesses to attend the holy services in the renowned St. Grigori Cathedral, conducted by the equally renowned Cardinal of Netz. It was not Amalina's true purpose, however, only her excellent cover story. Her real plans she kept to herself, not even shared with her unwitting co-conspirators. For Carila and Aklan, who rode in the Count's carriage—behind the Spaarvierlet carriage containing the pleasantly chatting princesses—it was a way to remove themselves from the castle, and allow the boy to spring from the trunk and breathe fresh air for a few days. For the Count, who remained in the castle, it was a chance to rest, to mind his many ventures he was neglecting, and repair some of the castle's faults before Lisbet's return. For Genadie, who was told the Count was going to be away surveying his lands again, it was a way to slip out of the depressing circumstances of watching his prime place before his master be usurped by Georg and his wife, the perfidious pair. It was on this last detail that Amalina would work her cunning to enact her actual plans.

As they settled into their apartments overlooking the cathedral, Amalina took Genadie aside and said: "We have only a few days. Can you get me to Korr?"

He was surprised to hear this. "What, Ms. Dalca?"

"We need to go there. It is very important. I can't tell you how important it is that we do this while there is still time." Then she told him of Abraxa's plot to humiliate Amalina by revealing the missing book from the library. "If I don't get that book back from father, the terrible two will turn the Count against me."

"But the book was borrowed from the library. Master agreed to it. Don't you remember?"

"But it was supposed to be returned before the library opened. And even so, who knows if the Count will remember, he's very distracted—"

"Zeus knows and remembers all!"

"So he knows you brought me to Korr on our way to the western kingdoms, to drop off the book? I seem to remember we snuck there to do it. You disobeyed his orders."

"I stretched them, is all." Genadie didn't look as concerned as she'd hoped he'd be. "He must know about it, girl. He's the king of all Gods. He permitted us, and from his kindness and manners, he doesn't bring it up."

"All the more reason to go then. We have the time, and he won't care if we do it. We'll be getting back a book the library is missing, which the visiting princesses might wish to read. And I can pretend to Abraxa that the Master had been reading it in his study after all. Which would embarrass her, knowing if she'd brought it up with him it would have just made her a nuisance to him."

"You called him 'Master', Ms. Dalca," Genadie said, pleased.

"But what do you say? Does it sound like a good plan?"

"If you want to handle it that way, I won't object. I'd like to see that rotten apple's face when you tell her." After a panting giggle he changed course: "Is there something else going on, Ms. Dalca?"

"What do you mean?"

"You seem very distracted lately. You hardly come around to meet with me. Our language lessons have *rallentato a nulla*. Rather trailed off."

"The princess," Amalina excused herself.

"No. You've become quiet and ... I'd say, secretive. I see no reason for it. I fear you are troubled by something but won't tell me. You can always confide in your *istruttore*."

"I've just told you everything."

"Perhaps something more dangerous to you than a blackmail attempt by Abraxa. Really, what could Master really care about such a small thing?"

"Nothing more. Now let's go."

. . .

Amalina apologized to Lisbet for abandoning her in Netz at the last minute. Important family business called her away to another village, and she must see to it alone. And so she left her with the promise of returning in a day or so, and left Carila and Aklan with the warning not to stray from her apartment while she was away.

The ride to Korr was slow. Genadie didn't push the horses. Amalina wondered if there was something more to his foot-dragging than reluctance to wear out their horses in his usual fashion (sometimes unto death) while Lisbet and her servants were around to be offended or frightened by it. With his odd question to Amalina about there being *'something else going on'*, *'something more dangerous'*, it sat on her mind that he might know more than he was letting on. That he might know about the rebels. Somehow knew that Kralov had survived the attack and was leading them. And knew that Amalina was somehow recruited into the movement. And he was testing and probing her loyalty, a loyalty both to him and his master.

"Can't you move any faster?" Amalina called to him on his driver's seat. "Lisbet isn't with us, and we're well out of Netz."

"Do you know the town of Olex?" he asked in return, actually *slowing* the horses. "You've heard of it?"

"The name sounds familiar."

"People don't speak of it anymore. It is a forgotten place. " He shouted in Italian: "Except in the *secret histories of Ardeel* … Well, it is forgotten there, too, now isn't it? Olex and Vijku, both. Two towns that once existed, thriving for hundreds of years, and then were removed from all of time and memory."

Olex and Vijku were the cities that had somehow violated the secret compact with the Count—or so the Count claimed—and he had not only razed them to the ground, exterminating all inhabitants in the process, but caused their names to be removed (literally burnt) out of the compact, and the histories, and the maps of the region—or so the Count also claimed. A process which had taken another couple centuries. So that the two names were entirely forgotten by even the oldest Ardeelian.

The only people who knew of them, knew their exact names, quite possibly, were the Count, Amalina, and Genadie.

"Yes, Genadie," Amalina said. "The Count told me all about them."

He pointed, in an off-hand way, to a wide piece of overgrown land, covered in weeds and patches of wild straw, with fangs of forest sinking into it.

"This was Olex," he told her.

There were no signs of buildings or even stripped foundations. It was all given over to nature and looked like nobody had even considered settling there. Virginal land.

"How do you know?"

"Master has shown me."

She didn't bother to ask how he could trust the Count's word on such a thing.

"Why did he show you it? There's nothing here."

"That was the point of it, Ms. Dalca. Think of his awesome power."

"Did he do it by himself, or with others?"

"By himself. He needs nobody else."

"Sometimes he uses birds, or wolves. Or other things, too, I imagine. So he could have called up some elephants to smash everything to pieces."

"You're being deliberately ridiculous, aren't you?"

"I've seen him talk to the birds. And the bats. Can he talk to any animal?"

"He is Zeus, he can talk to anything he has created. Which is everything."

"You know this for a fact?"

"I've seen him hold conversations with flies. I've seen him! Told them not to infest the castle or the privies, dungheap and outer midden. See if it didn't happen."

"Talks to flies," she said with a sense of unease. What would be the point of having human spies when all of nature could supply him with all the knowledge he needed? He could cut out the pigeon middle-men. There must be a reason.

"Anyway, the point is: here is Olex."

"And why are *you* telling me this?"

"No reason," he murmured in his scratchy voice.

The best reason Amalina could think of was that he was subtly warning her of the dangers of disobeying the Count. As if, once more, he knew what she was up to, who she was associating with, what she was plotting; and was revealing the folly of all three activities.

It only seemed more plausible when, many hours later, Genadie called out to her, and threw his hand lazily out toward another strip of wild countryside, announcing: "Vijku."

And it became more disturbing when, much later but with the same off-hand delivery, Genadie announced to her: "Korr."

• • •

It was impossible she hadn't seen her village in over a year. And yet it was true. In that time Amalina had escaped death on several occasions, witnessed the inhuman crimes of a monster, became a princess, travelled to the western kingdoms and been accepted into the ranks of their nobility. From one perspective, it felt like she had just stepped away from Korr on a long walk that had taken half a day. From another, more challenging one, she felt as if she had never lived there for one second. Her memory of it was quite distant. How had that little span of time caused such an alteration of her memory and feelings?

Seeing the familiar road into the village, and spotting the telltale landmarks, her heart began to beat a little faster. The reality of its closeness pushed her over to the side of the wall that contained the part of her personality that belonged, had belonged, would always belong in the village of Korr. She could feel the people—and the buildings and streets containing them—within her soul. Literally feel them. And if she closed her eyes, she could picture it all as clearly as if her eyes were still open. Even the air matched the air within her lungs, having never fully let go the breaths she'd taken there.

This brought with it the flood of feelings she'd locked away inside her and forgotten. She'd been so close, just a half a year before, when Genadie had driven her to Korr's outskirts. She'd been chained to the floor of the carriage, and only gotten a surprise glimpse of the minister and his wife, Sadra, who were taking a stroll along the road. She had cried then, the emotions crashing around her insides, but she hadn't found a full release. Now she was sobbing as she thought of her father, poor Dragomir, who hadn't seen his daughter since she'd been taken to the high castle. He must be a complete wreck: hair white with grief, his hands wrinkled and shaking, addled by the pain of a missing daughter and the crushing duty of having to bake his bread and run the shop alone. A sad, solitary figure he cut. Tears pouring down his cheeks, just as hers were now.

Her cries were so violent, it was hard to get the false nose to stay in place.

"I'm going by myself," Genadie said after he'd parked the carriage in a hidden turnoff, and come down to see what the commotion was. "You're staying here, Ms. Dalca."

"No, no. I promise I won't say anything. But I have to see him, Genadie. Please. Even if it's just through the window, I need to know how my father, my flesh and blood … how he is holding up. That he hasn't worn away to nothing since I've been gone. You see I'm putting on this make-up. He wouldn't recognize me even if we ran into each other. But we won't, I swear. Look, I'll change into your clothes, and wear your hat, so everyone will think I'm a man. How about that? There's no chance anyone will know it's me."

"Are you saying I should put on your dress?" he asked with a disdainful laugh. "You convinced me to come here for a specific purpose. Now it seems you have something else you want to do. What are we doing here?"

"I'll tell you, if you swear not to tell the Count."

His whole body quivered at the suggestion. "I'll *report* you to him," he declared proudly. "What is it, Ms. Dalca?"

"But he must already know, Genadie. Mustn't he? If he knows everything? So I am not asking you not to tell him for his sake. He already knows. I'm asking you not to tell him, to prove yourself to me."

"One is as bad as the other. I'm true to you, but never more than to Master."

"That I know. And if he asks you, you are free to tell him the truth. But only if he asks you. If not, you don't tell him. Because then he doesn't want to know ... or at least he doesn't want to know it from you. Do you understand?"

Genadie looked puzzled by the girl in the false nose, as if he just realized he'd mistaken her for a young, innocent, naïve girl—and she might actually be more than equal to him, in some confusing way.

"I'll promise to keep your secrets, Ms. Dalca, but only if Master does not ask for them."

Amalina swore him to it. Then she sighed heavily, as she prepared to tell him the full truth or something like it.

"Do you know where Georg and Abraxa are from?" she asked.

"No."

"Neither do I. I've never seen or heard of their family before. But Abraxa said she knows me. And she implied that she has family nearby. She suggested—but didn't say it directly—that she has people around my father. Watching him. And that if I get her or Georg in trouble with the Count, they will do something awful to him. So, you see, I need to see him. I need to know that he is okay, and to see if what they say is true: there are men watching him."

Genadie looked grim.

"Why does Master allow *them* into his home?" howled Genadie full of contempt. "Why does he allow them to plague us, his closest and dearest servants?"

"Here is what we'll do," Amalina told him. "I'll wear your clothes. You'll wear my old dress, which I brought along, right here. Just keep your head down and the bonnet as low as you can. You go in first. Then I will brush by the store at some point and see how my father is. I promise I won't do anything more than that. You'll see. I'll keep my promise. Then, before you get the book from him, you will position yourself nearby the store, and watch for anyone who is watching him. We'll give it the day, until an hour before sundown. If anyone from Abraxa's clan is shadowing him, we should know by then. I'll have gone back to the carriage in the meantime. I'll drive in and pick you up, just after the evening bell. Sound like a good plan?"

"No!" he howled. "I can't fit into your dress!"

But he could. And, as it turned out, *his* clothes were a little too tight for Amalina.

37

A Return to Korr

It was difficult to breath in the false nose. It hissed and reverberated behind the painted leather flap like she was breathing into a small cup. And the hat and wig, pulled down low, barely held it in place. She thought of taking it off, but didn't know if the make-up she'd applied—from the Count's actor's make-up supply box—would be enough to disguise her from the people who'd known her all her life. She kept it on, and tried to breathe through her mouth as much as she could remember to.

Of course she'd lied to Genadie about what she was up to. If he—or she—spotted one of Kralov's men, that was all fine and good. But verifying the Commander's threats against Dragomir was still only a side benefit of this trip. She had still other purposes.

Amalina put off going to the bakery. It was a difficult choice, but she had to stay on mission. She knew it was too much of a temptation to see her home that she circled around Korr and entered from a different route. One that would keep her away from the store and her father. Only when it was time would she head to that side of town.

Keeping her head down, avoiding people she must surely know, and they know her, she took the streets that would have the most people in order to hide herself in their numbers. All the more chance that those around her would be talking among themselves. Caught alone, a stranger in Korr could easily be accosted by a friendly villager wanting to know if the stranger needed directions, or if the stranger would like something to eat, or purchase, or would like to talk about the weather or the politics in Tsobl. She weaved and moved like someone who wanted to be left alone, all the while her heart beating heavily, imagining she would be stopped and recognized, or that she really would run straight into Dragomir.

She ran into Cristine.

Amalina froze, wide-eyed, after slamming into her old friend at the shoulders, and each spinning in a tangential direction. They looked at each other with what must have been the oddest expressions. Cristine was confused, and tried to identify this odd, small man who'd rudely barreled into her. Being a girl, she would normally apologize to the man for the accident, whether it was her fault or not. But Cristine was a different sort, and her cold eyes narrowed sharply, while the equally sharp mind behind them manufactured twenty different insults for this stranger.

Amalina wanted to burst out with tears and throw her arms around her best friend—the year away having changed nothing about her but her size and had honed her razorlike gaze. Then, knowing she was blowing her disguise, she thought to apologize—but that wasn't something a man should do to a girl. And worse, if she tried, she would use a voice that would not sound like a man at all. She could say nothing. Almost as a joke—which she would laugh about later—she shook her soiled-gloved finger at Cristine. Then she turned and went her way. Glancing back when she felt it was safe.

The reason why they'd collided so spectacularly was because they were both walking with their heads down low, and moving with quick strides. Amalina didn't know where Cristine was off to early in the morning, but her friend was hunched and trodding with the air of a loner who wanted to get out of the street before the bullies descended. Cristine, her old friend, was by herself. No doubt under siege by the older girls—the jealous girls— without Amalina at her side to give her shelter, Amalina, the baker's daughter, who was much more friendly and popular (because she was so nice, and dutiful, and hardworking, and *plain*). There was another impulse to follow Cristine, to rip off the disguise and comfort her best friend. She had worried this would be the case—that Cristine was all alone. And it was true. And was that the shadow of a black eye the poor girl sported?

She was near Cristine's house, which meant she wasn't too far from her first destination. The chemist who worked for Cristine's father's company had an outbuilding he used for an office which was attached to his employer's row of buildings. When Amalina recalled how Cristine's father used to amaze them with the effects of acids and combinations of chemicals (to create colorful smoke and small explosions), she then remembered the place where he got those items: the chemist's warehouse.

The chemist's office, which some people in the town entered for helpful aids in cleaning, or to see if they'd found some rare metal in the mountainside, looked like a bookkeeper's office. Now that Amalina had seen the Count's scientific lab, she was surprised by the lack of ostentation about the place. It was pure Ardeelian not to be too boastful, but the chemist had truly masked his occupation. Only when called upon would he open a cabinet and reveal the bottles and jars of the profession. Or pull out a scale from his desk. Somewhere in the back rooms must have been his beakers and burners and the metal structures to hold it all together.

"Hello?" Bistl the Chemist said from his chair beside the window. He had been reading something in the sunlight. "Now, who are you?"

Amalina gulped. She forgot that she'd have to speak. She made her voice low and scratchy. It came out lower than Genadie's voice, to her surprise, but still sounded too feminine; girlish.

"I would like to know what this is that I have found."

"And what have you found? Can you show me?"

Amalina nodded, keeping her head down, looking at Bistl's hands and shoes. Not daring to look directly into his face. The false nose waggled precariously under the brim of the hat.

Amalina took a piece of cloth out of her pocket and opened it. The chink of the chain's metal glowed magically in the palm of her hand.

"Oh!" Bistl exclaimed. "Oh! And where did you find this?"

His fingers trembled just inches away from the broken link, afraid to touch it.

"It was given to me to test. My friend knew I was coming to see you and asked me to inquire about it. Can you tell me what it is?"

"I'm fairly certain I can," chirped Bistl confidently. Now he touched it. Stroked the oblong loop of metal with his finger. "But I will need to test it. Is it okay for me take a sample?"

Amalina agreed and he pulled a blocky set of clippers out of his desk and removed a generous piece out of it. She didn't look at his face, but wished she could. Had he taken that much because he needed that much? Or because he knew what it was and wanted to keep some for himself? Or wanted to test Amalina to see if she knew its value? or how far he could take advantage of her?

"There was something else?" he said.

She hesitated, wondering how he knew.

"You said your friend knew you were coming to see me," he explained. "Was it to test something, or another matter?"

Amalina took out a leather cloth now and opened it. Kralov's vial.

"A bottle of perfume?" he said with an upward lilt to his voice, as if he were amused.

"Not perfume. There isn't much of it left. I can only afford a few drops. Five at most. But I want to know what kind of liquid it is."

She opened the bottle and held it out to him.

"No color, no smell," she said. "Looks like water, but it isn't."

"What is it?"

"That's what I'm paying you to find out." Amalina took out one of the gold coins. Bistl made a small noise. "I don't think it's an acid. Some kind of poison? I need to know its components. It's important to me."

The chemist probably had a lot of questions: Where did you get it? Did someone try to use it on you? What do you plan to do with it? But he was used to keeping people's secrets. So many villagers, he'd told her and

Cristine years ago, trusted him to keep private their finds in the mountain, their finds' locations, and never to pry too far. The gold coin would also envelope his curiosity.

He cupped his hand and waved it across the vial's opening, wafting any scent it might have toward his nose.

"Can you test it now?" she asked.

"When do you need your answer?"

"Now."

"This afternoon."

"You aren't busy. You were reading when I came in."

"Yes," he made a small derisive laugh. "And I've set my book down. You have hired me for the day. Assuming you want an accurate assessment of the items you've given me, you will allow me until four to run all the tests I need to."

Amalina wanted to apologize for being rude, but also didn't want to talk too much. She nodded, and pocketed the gold coin.

• • •

Her heart was beating hard again. This was it. She was rounding the corner that would take her to the bakery. After so long she would finally see her father again. The last time she'd seen his face, he'd told her to fetch some water—had lied to her and sent her on a mission from which she would not return. According to the note he'd given Genadie to give to her, he'd come to some private arrangement with the Count, and she was to be taken immediately away to his castle, no return date given. In the message, he'd confessed he'd sent her out of the house without her knowing what was to happen because he knew he couldn't handle saying goodbye. But a return was promised. Someday. For good.

The Count had forbidden any communication between the two while she was serving him. This small bit of cruelty hadn't been explained, but it was worked around. She had sent him one message, to assure him she was safe and healthy, in a secret message hidden inside a book lent to him from the castle. Now Genadie was going to retrieve the book. She would find out if he'd written a reply. But even before she read it, she would also see for herself how tragic his life had become without her. How often had he, in a melancholy mood, confided that, since she was all he had in his life, he could not live without her? His bread would suffer. His business would suffer. He would suffer in loneliness.

She'd pictured him many times, with grey hair and as wrinkled as an old apple, withered away by the shock of her absence, and stooped by the guilt at having sent her away, tending to a store given over to dust and rodents.

Coming to the bakery, she could barely bring herself to look. She thought if she saw him as she'd imagined him over the years she would throw off her disguise and run to him, as she blubbered and declared her forgiveness.

Just for a second she thought she would hold back. She'd pick out Genadie in the street and also look for any of Kralov's agents. And then wait in a garden somewhere for four o'clock to return to Bistl and the results of his testing of her magic items.

That wasn't possible. She had to see for herself.

She swung past the lamppost where she'd seen Lucinda Skeldar savaged by the Count, and then walked straight toward the shop's open doorway. Genadie was nowhere to be seen. He was either hidden well or he was too embarrassed to stay in the street wearing a woman's dress.

It was around the time of day when a small rush of wives picking up loaves for the midday meal crowded into the store. This would be perfect to give Amalina cover. She slipped into the small crowd entering, and felt a wave of fondness, familiarity, and nostalgia break. A light and enthusiastic energy was bursting through the customers. They were chatting merrily and laughing at something that was happening around the sideboards. Her heart leapt when she caught sight of her father.

Dragomir was smiling and laughing and calling out between Miss Urtugoyic and someone in the back. A loaf of bread flew through the air. He caught it one handed, plopped it onto a sheet of paper, wrapped it expertly with a grinning flourish, and then set it into her wide-mouthed basket. This happened a couple times, the juggling act entertaining everyone to the utmost hilarity. His hair was thick and dark, his skin plump and fresh, and his thick beard seemed to be trimmed. Far from a wreck, the man had never looked better. Amalina smiled happily at this, forgetting how deep inside she wished he might have suffered, at least a little bit, for having exiled her into the care of a known monster and hadn't seen her for over a year.

He was now singing a song, accompanied by a female voice: the hurler of the loaves. The voice wasn't familiar. And she never would have guessed who it was until the two danced and traded places, and Dragomir became the one pitching the loaves, while Jenna, her cousin, smiling and singing and shimmying with delight, caught the bread and packaged it for Miss Wojtjak's entertainment. Jenna's hair was up, hidden underneath her white cap. Amalina had never seen her cousin so happy.

This displeased Amalina utterly. She felt a weight drop in her body that made her feel like she would fall down to the floor. Instead, she caught herself and reeled backward out of the store.

Amalina didn't know what was happening inside her. It felt like she would be sick. Her vision blurred, but without tears. There was a red pulsing in them.

Anger. She was mad. Violently mad. She wanted to run back and knock the bread out of everyone's baskets, throw the loaves off the shelves and stamp on them. She wanted to gouge at Jenna's face with her fingernails and pull out her father's beard.

Why? she wondered. Why were they so happy? She wasn't there. She'd been gone for a year. With no word of return. And how she'd worried and suffered over them for it! How could they be enjoying themselves when working the store was such a boring grind day-in and day-out? How was that store, and her father, and her cousin, and all the customers she knew, so much happier—so much better off—without her?

"What?! Watch where you are going! Who do you think you are? Who are you!"

Amalina picked herself up off the ground, wondering how she'd gotten there and who was speaking so crossly to her. Then she felt the pain in her arms and gut and knew she'd run hard into someone else. Only this time she'd fallen straight to the ground. The wall she'd run into was standing over her, running a string of angry reprimand.

Amalina looked up. Sadra. The minister's wife.

Sadra shut up. She stared at Amalina. She bent at the waist and examined Amalina's face.

Hands going to her head protectively, Amalina found the nose had flown off. The critical component to her disguise was lying on the bricks next to her knee. She rolled and scooped up the nose, pulled the hat down low, and waved her gloved hand apologetically. She made it to the corner of the building before whatever shock was holding Sadra in place wore off. Amalina tore off as fast as she could, and took whatever alleys would get her to the other end of Korr unobserved.

She heard Sadra's last word echoing in her ears: "Amalina?"

• • •

The desperate sprint through the alleys, and the surge of adrenaline at the surprise encounter with Sadra, was good enough to cure Amalina's outrage. Exhausted, panting, she cooled off physically and emotionally. She shook herself and became Kralov's spy once more, putting to the side any of the confusion that had overwhelmed her. Overwhelmed her beyond anything she'd ever experienced before. Greater even than when she'd seen Lucinda Skeldar murdered. She focused on what needed to be done. That created a healthy wall between her soul and the strange anguish she'd just suffered.

Save it for later.

The bad feelings rose again, from her gut and into her throat. She swallowed it down, shook her arms and body and then straightened her spine. After a deep breath of hometown air, she was balanced again.

She would revisit what had happened later. Now she would occupy herself.

With the hours at her disposal, Amalina toured the village as an outsider, and made her way through the streets she seldom traveled, looking for things she'd never noticed before, studying the store fronts and the people she only recognized from religious services or town meetings.

When the fourth bell struck in the church tower, Amalina was at the chemist's office.

The way Bistl sat up from whatever was laid out on his desk, he was interrupted in his work. He took a lens away from his eye and nodded at Amalina in greeting. He gave her a strange look.

Lowering her head, she made sure the false nose was properly placed.

"What did you find out?"

Bistl pointed to the piece of chain laid out on a red sheet on his desk. This was what he was working on.

"Let's start with this. It is what I expected it to be. Knew it as soon as I saw it."

"Which is?"

"An unusual alloy compound, but mostly made up of silver."

"What's that?" said Amalina.

"Silver," Bistl repeated. "It's silver. You've heard of it?"

"No," she admitted.

"So you're from Ardeel and haven't gone abroad," Bistl assessed with a smirk. "Anyone else would know. And they would have had it confiscated at the border if they tried to bring it in."

"Why?"

"It's a rare metal. A precious commodity. We export it from these mountains, if ever we find it. That's what makes us so rich."

"By getting rid of it?"

"Trading," Bistl said flatly. "We settle for the tremendous amount of gold it brings in."

Amalina nodded. Silver. Okay. Why hadn't she ever heard of it before? She'd been to the outside world, to the western kingdoms. She'd seen metals similar to this, for rings and jewelry, and decorating boxes and inlaid in furniture. At the time she thought it was a polished steel. Or white gold. Maybe it was silver. But none that she could recall were as bright as this specimen.

"So, you are from Ardeel, and you found this piece *inside* of Ardeel." Bistl winked. "You are paying me enough not to say anything about it. But I wouldn't show this piece around if I were you. Could get you into a bit of trouble with the powers that be. Arrested for dealing in contraband. You *are* paying me, aren't you?"

Amalina nodded. After an uncomfortable silence she pulled out the gold coin. But she held onto it.

"Of course," said Bistl, "you said someone else gave it to you, didn't you? Well, tell your friend they took a chance having you look into it." He paused, then scratched his patchy eyebrow. "Or maybe your friend knew this and wanted to avoid getting himself in trouble. Or maybe wanted to get you into some."

"You aren't going to tell anyone."

"Not as long as that coin winds up in my pocket by the end of our conversation."

"It will."

"Then we're fine."

"If you knew what it was as soon as you saw it, what were you doing with it when I came in? Looked like you were studying it pretty close."

"Yes." He pointed to the piece. "I noticed the manufacture stamp, but I couldn't quite make it out. Had to use a solvent to clean it a little."

Amalina bent over. All it looked like was a solid bit of metal.

"Where?"

"You don't see it? Right there."

She looked where he was pointing. He put his finger right on it to help guide her eyes. There was a blurry smudge.

He offered his lens.

It took a few seconds for her to make the adjustments with her eye, but then the piece became clearer than anything she had seen before. There was a small oval depression in the shiny surface, and in the middle of that: AXP.

"What do the letters stand for?"

"It's the mark of the smith who made it. Must be pretty old. I don't recognize it. And nobody in their right mind would put their name to contraband now. May I ask where it came from? I'm very curious."

"I can't tell you."

"By its shape, it looks like a link of chain. Which would mean there would be more like it, as it likely being from a chain."

"My friend didn't say." Amalina started to feel uncomfortable. She wanted to leave.

"I have friends as well," he said, after clearing his throat. "Friends who would be willing to pay you more than that coin you are about to pay me to know where you attained this metal. I can't stress how much they'd be interested. They would be at your mercy. However much you ask, probably. Within reason."

"I'll let my friend know. It's none of my business."

Bistl cleared his throat again.

"May I have my payment?"

"The liquid."

"Oh, yes. The greater mystery." He had returned Kralov's vial to the leather square and stored it in his drawer. Now he fished it out and gave it to her with a brief shrug. "Didn't use much. Several drops, like you said."

"And?"

"There's a reason it resembles water the way it does, in all of its qualities."

"Why? What is it?"

"Water."

There followed a great silence. She sensed he was staring at her, waiting for an explanation.

She paid him and left.

• • •

The new information was a convenient distraction. Her upset earlier in the day was an inconsequential haze behind its wall. The chain was silver. She'd have to research just what kind of metal that was, and how much of it there is. By how it kept the woman underneath the castle weighed down and bound, and how the Count refused to touch it, it was—wait, hadn't Lady Flauna mentioned that word? 'Silver'? When she was talking about her jewelry? And the Count insisted she wear gold instead. Yes, he avoided the metal … maybe like he avoided the sunlight. The way it weighed the woman underneath the castle down, and effectively bound her, it wasn't lethal outright. But it affected them both negatively in some way. And by how solid it was, Amalina was sure a weapon could be forged from it. A silver spear? Who was it who'd made the chain? Had he done it at the Count's request? If she could find the silversmith, maybe he could create the blade.

Kralov's water remained a mystery. It had had an effect on the Count. There was no doubt about it. However, like the silver, it didn't seem it was outright lethal. But it couldn't just be plain water. He stood in the rain plenty of times. And she'd seen him drink water on occasion, and wash the blood crusted on his skin with it. So how was this water different? Bistl might have been lying, of course. Maybe he'd found what it was during the testing— some unique poison or irritant—and kept it for himself. And replaced the vial's contents with water, and gave Amalina a simple answer. It would have been easy enough for him to do. But his indifference to it was genuine enough, as was his slight contempt for Amalina having brought it to him.

Maybe he suspected the water was a ruse. A ridiculous, shoddy, cheap excuse for her to introduce, under its cover, the real prize for examination: the silver link, which was only along for the ride "at the asking of a friend."

Amalina shook her head at the way her mind was snaking around. Seeing plots and lies and subtlety in everything, because it existed within her now. Every time she realized this, that she was a plotter and a professional liar, it felt like a weight on her. It made her feel older. Sometimes this artificial aging made her feel empowered: to be so quickly elevated to adulthood! But other times, like now, it made her feel too old. As if she looked in a mirror, she would be stooped and wrinkled.

She wondered if something had happened like that to Ivanti, the boy she'd loved, when he'd left town; to cripple him; to separate him from the people he once loved by changing him. Only he chose to return to whatever it was. She doubted she'd return, if given the choice, to her current confusion of deceitful living. But, even if she would, she'd never want to be like him. He seemed all the more miserable.

When the church bell sounded the end of the day, Amalina brought the carriage into town. She kept the brim of the hat low, but she still saw, as dusk fell, her old neighbors and acquaintances seal their doors and windows against the coming night. She slowed the carriage as she neared the bakery, but tilted her head so that the bakery itself was blocked from her view.

Genadie, instead of getting into the carriage, climbed up onto the riding board next to her. He tried to take the reins, but she elbowed him and hurried the horses on.

"You went into the store," he reprimanded under his breath. He was speaking French. "You broke your promise."

"I couldn't see him from the street. If you saw me, you saw I didn't stay long. I didn't even make it past the entrance, really. Just enough to see him."

"And run away. Like a little girl with a guilty conscience."

"Hopefully I looked like a little man. That was the point of the disguise. Did you spot any of Abraxa's people?"

"Everyone looks suspicious to me here. Especially the men. I couldn't differentiate, except for the silly little man who was you." Then he asked, "Where are you going?"

"I have to turn this around, don't I? I can't do it here."

"We need to get out of here. People are looking."

"They're probably wondering who's in the carriage. We don't get many fancy types coming through at sunset." She looked at the bag he brought with him. She had a sour thought, but she had to ask. "Did you get the book?"

"Of course, *mademoiselle*. I do as I promise."

Amalina snorted. Just then, as she turned to face the street, she saw what she couldn't believe. She had to blink, looking again and again. Her face flushed, her body became electric. To cover her cry of shock and disbelief, she shouted at the horses, and launched them down the brick street at a precarious speed. The carriage wheels cried at the cracks they faltered on or fell into, and they barely avoided sideswiping the front of buildings as they hit the curves. Genadie howled as the carriage almost took down a lamppost. Then they were free of Korr.

As they rode away, slower now on the highway, and the two on the riding bench felt the first cold breeze of autumn whisper across their skin and cruelly through their clothes; and back in the village, some spoke of what they would gossip about the next day, of the mysterious out of control carriage, with the woman who looked like a bearded man and the man who looked somewhat like a girl, shouting like maniacs behind the reins; and the children told their parents of the frightening old man with paint on his face they saw running and crying through the alleys; and Sadra swore to her husband, the minister, that, for the second time in half a year, she had seen Amalina, (*it just had to be her!*) who was supposed to be away in Germania visiting a relative; and Bistl chewed on the edge of a gold coin, weighing the temptation of breaking his word and telling someone about the day's visit by a curious little boy, wearing make-up and a ridiculous false nose, who not only had gold coins, but friends with silver relics; Amalina seethed and swore under her breath, and replayed again and again the vision in her mind, the last thing she'd seen in Korr before she sent the horses flying: Dragomir, on the street at dusk (when everyone should be indoors), with a great smile on his face—a beaming smile she rarely saw, and one of pride and tenderness—walking shoulder to shoulder, hand in hand, *scandal upon scandal*, with the equally love-struck Widow Lidsz!

38

The Battle of Vogoneyevic Fields

In the peace treaty which cemented the control of Ardeel to a foreign power—a character-testing trial unheard of in the nation's history, and one unthinkable in the hearts of the county's staunchest natives (rivaled in its unthinkability only by their abominable contract of obeisance to the Knight of Ardeel)—there was a provision which allowed Zsolt Marosh to hold onto his cannons. It needn't have been included, and the problem really should have been remedied in the terms of surrender. But the provision was included and it was a problem. A nagging worry in the background of the Tsobl government's endless worries. He couldn't use them in all practicality for hunts, and their only other possible purpose would be for the purpose of war. And when would there be a war in Ardeel's central provinces? Whispered inside the councilrooms (and then in the bars and restaurants where the members of the assembly habited), like the telling of a ghost story, was the dread imagining of Zsolt's artillery utilized as weapons of insurrection. But they were only stories, and the cannon had remained in place for decades, even when the bread revolts occurred.

Those cannons were now out of chains and being hauled through the mountains. Where they were going, Attila could not know for sure. But since there were no rumors of insurrection, and since Zsolt Marosh was so beholden to the government in Tsobl, there was really only one logical destination: the Count's castle.

Attila cursed at himself for having been so stupid as to tell Marosh the Count's exact position (or what he assumed it was). He'd idiotically given Marosh the directions and the motive.

But really, at the moment he'd done so, standing soggy-clothed and worn out before General Marosh, he'd had no hope for a better outcome. Even if Attila was discarded from the campaign, this was the best he could have hoped for.

It was that last bit that tasted so bitter to Attila, and tormented his waking moments. Long gone for him was concern for Hak's surprising pacifism. Or, rather, it became an issue to be put off. It was being worked on. But the larger, persistent thorn in Attila's thoughts was that an avenging force against the Count was now out ahead of him, led by a competent general, without him being part of it.

Why had Marosh thought to punish Attila? Why execute the man who had given his marooned life renewed purpose?

Attila considered the puzzle logically: it could only be for the reason the old mad general had said it was: Attila had been disloyal. It didn't matter that Tsobl was odious to him, or that Tsobl was in cahoots with the Count, and both Attila and Marosh shared the same dislike of the foreigners and shared the same interest to take advantage of the Count's momentary weakness. Attila was also foreign. And Attila was, or had been, a piece of the Tsobl government, and had turned against that government. This disloyalty offended a man of military heritage. Anyone who turned against their superiors, even if they were right to do so, deserved execution.

And maybe the general thought by doing so it would buy him good favor with Tsobl, as he then set out to conduct a private war that they would never condone.

But for the general to enact Attila's plan felt like a different kind of betrayal. An insult. A work of spite.

It was no consolation to Attila that his ideas were in motion in the body of Zsolt Marosh and his army, they ready to swing a deadly blow against a creature that long deserved its comeuppance. The fact that Attila wasn't attached to it, wasn't a part of it, wasn't riding at the head of the assault, throbbed in his chest like a wound.

His only hope was to have his own army meet with Marosh's before the fight began—or, that is, Hak's army, under Attila's indirect control, to meet with Marosh's. Zsolt Marosh could squash Attila when Attila was alone, friendless and pursued. Sitting side-by-side with the Vogoneyevic heir, and at the head of a consequential army with its own pieces of artillery, the old general could only nod in respect and true friendship.

. . .

The reintroduction of Hak to the Vogoneyevic homeland and its peoples— or most importantly, the men who would make up his revived army, and the mothers and wives who would support them in their decision—was a process faster than Attila had anticipated. Which was worrisome for Attila Bronk, because he was hoping, in the extra time to gain a following, as Hak made himself known with his handsome and magnetically simple personality, he could train the boy up to be a true leader. And, more to the point, build him into a convincing bloodthirsty warrior. His people would need to see him as something larger, something commanding. Something of a legitimate shoot of the ancient and savage Vogoneyevic roots.

"Please, Mr. Bronk," Hak said wearily, "Why are you down today? I promise I'll be able to do my duty. I have always done so."

"That's reassuring." But even if Hak was too simple to ferret out the sarcasm in Attila's deadpan delivery, he didn't think the words fit too well.

"I wish you'd be more than just reassured, sir. Really I don't understand why you're fidgeting like it's some race to get to that knight of yours. We can wait to see how General Marosh fares, can't we? Maybe he'll cut that monster down without us."

"We have to be there," said Attila. "Or is that how you want history to be written: General Zsolt Marosh destroyed the infamous Knight of Ardeel, while Hak sat around picking his ass to see what would happen?"

"I suppose that doesn't sound too good."

"No, it does not."

"Why do people have to write history anyway, Mr. Bronk?"

"That isn't the question you should be asking."

"Well, I'll tell you Mr. Bronk, you don't have to worry."

"Unfortunately, worrying is my job."

"With all that worry, too bad you can't get a raise in your salary."

If Attila was capable of rolling his eyes now would have been the time. He didn't even sigh.

"Gug's still there with Man and Lija," Hak observed. "Looks like they picked up a dog somewhere. Looks friendly and nice."

"They're counting on you," Attila reminded him. "Now is the moment I've … or, rather, this land has anticipated for ages. You'll remember to speak to your people as we've discussed?"

"I heard what you've said, Mr. Bronk. Look, I know you have your hands full with me, but don't worry, I got it. I got it."

• • •

The men of the territory were assembled first, as this would have more to do with them than their wives. Hak arranged the place and the day and one-by-one they came, looking shy or cautious or resentful. But they were an assembly of nearly one hundred and fifty when the time came. A sizeable force for a first-time man of the people.

"Something's wrong," said Attila, his half-closed eyes focusing across the wide dirt of the field and into the distance.

"What is it?" Hak said, squinting his eyes and trying to follow his gaze. Then he looked back to make sure Gug and the children were still in their place along the horizon. Then his eyes roamed over the crowd and back to the road at the far end of the field, where a four horse carriage sat.

"That's the governor's carriage," whispered Attila. "The governor of Tsobl. It might not be him inside, but there is someone official there."

"What do they want?"

Attila's heart thudded hopefully for a moment. He remembered the letter he'd sent to the governor. Had it reached its target? Had the governor actually read his letter and come to parley? Or was it something else? The game warden had also threatened to report him to the authorities. But a dispatched carriage from the governor would seem a strong reaction.

"It could be a coincidence. Unfortunately I don't believe in such things. Word must have reached Tsobl, somehow."

Some in the crowd were turning to see what had their attention.

"They're just sitting there."

"Perhaps we should try this another day," Attila suggested with a sleepy smirk.

"I thought there's no time, Mr. Bronk."

Attila shook his head.

"Then on with it," Hak said. And he waved his large hands to announce his intention to speak. Attila pushed down an acidic belch.

"You've got us here, Hak Vogoneyevic," said one man in the front of the crowd, a man with a pot-belly and mangy patches of hair along his jaw. "You go and tell us what's in your heart."

With a rumble of voices and stamps on the dirt, the men agreed.

"Well, I haven't much to say," said Hak. "I'm not a man of words. Not like Mr. Bronk here."

Attila side-stepped to put himself behind Hak. On the road, four men came out of the carriage. They were too far away to identify. Four tall, thin shadows.

"But as the man I am, I don't much understand difficult subjects. Don't get me on politics and national economies or I am lost."

Laughter from the crowd.

"This subject is not difficult. It is very easy. And Mr. Bronk lays it out well."

"You tell us, Hak!"

"I will," nodded Hak. He righted his posture so that he looked like a heroic city-center statue, double the size of an ordinary man—and just as dark brown, but with a yellow wig thrown on it. "You've had some sense of it already. But here we go: There are animals who we naturally fear. When they cause us harm, we hunt them. Now tell me why, when there are monsters who we fear, we don't hunt them?"

Silence for a moment. Then, one voice: "We haven't the power."

The four men came off the road and entered the field.

"You know who I speak of. You men. If you haven't signed your name, you've heard of this wretched deal that was struck with the worst creature of all. You know what I'm talking about."

A guilty murmuring.

"That fellow, he laid waste to armies. And he humiliated us. Oh, much the same way them foreigners come through here and took away our government. We've been beaten down, and then beaten down again."

An unhappy murmuring. The four men crossing the field drew close enough to make out detail. They were soldiers wearing light armor. Scouts. The kind that had hounded Attila for weeks, driving him through the snow and rivers. His bored expression did not change, but he fluttered the edge of his cloak and fought the urge to take a step back.

"There's not much to be done about our government. They're here for good, and that's that. But there's one thing we can do to get our pride back, fellows. And listen to me: we can do it, too. That creature, while we let him, he's run off with enough of our people to make us weep for the rest of our lives. And hate ourselves for the shame of it, because it was no deal we should have struck. And we didn't strike it, fellows. Understand that. It was our grandfather's grandfather's grandfathers. And they were afraid because they'd been beaten down, and they were beaten down hard. So they did what they felt they had to, and no shame in that. But you think they wouldn't be proud if we were to rip that piece of paper right up, and throw it in the monster's face?"

"And get killed for it, Hak?"

"I'm not going to say one or two of us might not make it. Or one or two of us will be the only ones to make it. But we have more numbers now than that creature had to face at once in the old times. And we have weapons now that he never even seen or thought of at the time. We have weapons that can outfire him, outrace him, and outdamage that sorry, fermented apple who hides in our hills. Imagine, as Mr. Bronk tells it, living free. Our nights not spent in fear, but with our windows open, breathing fresh air. And telling our children how we've cut down this monster like we did this field here, and cleared away the evil. Drive it out, we will. And be heroes to our families again. And live lives with our chins held high. And let me tell you, those boys in Tsobl, they like that creature, and they think he's a good thing. And what more else do you need to know than that?"

"You," said one of the soldiers from the edge of the crowd. They had their swords out and forced a path—the Ardeelians parting easily—to the giant Hak. Then they spotted Attila behind him and their teeth shown.

One of the soldiers—Attila would swear to it—was the man from the river. The one he was close to drowning. Many of these soldiers looked alike, from one to the other, but it was too uncanny a resemblance for it not to be. Attila would swear to it. His face had scars.

"And there they are," said the soldier, pointing out Attila and Hak for the benefit of the crowd. "The men we've come for. Infamous across our counties. A pair of thieves the likes of which you've never seen."

Attila stepped out front. "I am the low constable of Tsobl."

"Yes, that's easy enough to spot," mocked the lead soldier. "How well acquainted we are with the signals of the Tsobl government: Stolen boots, stolen pants, stolen shirt, stolen cloak. Now that cloak belongs to Zsolt Marosh's warden, and put those patches on himself. It was those by which we could identify the culprit. And here he is: our culprit."

Their swords came up.

"We aren't as lame as the warden," said the soldier. "There won't be any running away from a poor, old, hobbled man."

"He was mistaken," said Attila. "This is a mended cloak, it is true. But not his. I am no thief. I have broken no laws. I am a man sworn to the law to uphold it. And Sir Vogoneyevic should not be included in any accusation against me. He is a noble of this territory."

"Another pretender," laughed the soldier. "Get a look at this giant yokel. King, did you say he was?"

The crowd made a disagreeable murmur and stepped forward. The soldier, a bit of a showman, felt the shift in mood.

"That's Hak Vogoneyevic," said one of the men. "He's a proud son of Ardeel."

"Can't be too proud if he's running with a known thief and heretic."

"Now I'm a heretic?" said Attila. "These slanders will be disproved in a court of law. And then we will see who laughs."

The lead soldier shook his blocky head. "Going to make it to a court, are you? See that carriage back there? Your judge sits inside. And sentence has been passed. Step forward, Attila Bronk."

Attila did not move. "Who's there?" he said, pointing at the carriage. "It looks like the governor's carriage is it?"

"Judgment has been made, sentence has been passed." Now they stepped forward, swords at the ready, their free hands clenching and unclenching. Their backs were hunched and knees bent, bracing for a fight. They fanned out at each other's shoulders.

"This man is innocent," Hak shouted. "I rescued him, shot by a killer's bullet. He is a man of honor. He is a Godly man, and not known to lie. He's never killed anyone and I've never seen him steal. He may be of foreign blood, but he speaks of our heritage proudly, and against the voices of his own people, our old enemies. Our oppressors."

"Well, that's treason for you," said the soldier, coming at him. "Enough of that."

Attila withdrew and Hak jumped in front. The first sword slashed down into air. Hak brought his giant brown hand across the soldier's arm and hit the breastplate, shoving him off his feet and into the soldier to the left. The first toppled the second like a pin. This opened the way for the next two soldiers, who approached Hak more warily.

The crowd was silent, their faces drawn and grim. The only action they took was to glance back at the carriage to see if any more were coming to join the fight, and widen around to circle the action, to get themselves a good look at what was happening.

As the tip of the heavy sword punched and waved at Hak, he knocked it aside with a swift punch. Then he stepped forward and sent his elbow into the soldier's nose with a loud crunch. The soldier's helmet flew off at the impact and he went straight down.

By now the first two had regained their feet and the fourth was already on Hak. Hak swung his massive leg and kicked the sword out of the fallen soldier's hand, sending it hilt first at the two on the left.

The soldier on the right swung his sword into Hak's side.

Attila drew back, looking bored but inwardly feeling a stabbing pain where the shot had gone into himself so many months ago. He hadn't really felt the pain at the time in the moment, had he? He wanted to close his eyes and turn away, but his dull eyes stayed fixed on the action, even as the blood fell from Hak's side.

Hak grunted with an effort and took the man's sword hand, wresting control of the blade. He pulled him and then swung him around. It was a sight to see a full grown man in armor be swung around like a sack of onions. Only the toe on his left foot touched the ground. Then he was barreling face first into his friends.

The soldier with the broken nose stabbed his knife into Hak's calf. Hak screamed and squatted down, shocked with pain. The soldier, blood pouring from his flattened nostrils, tried to grab hold of Hak's hair. His fingers slid through it. Hak punched the man. Then he punched him even harder a second time, with a sickening splintering sound breaking over the soldier's coughing gasps. His eyes rolled to the back of his head and he collapsed completely.

Hak stared at the dagger stuck through his calf. He was frozen as if trying to comprehend what he was seeing.

The three soldiers came forward, Attila entirely forgotten. In a sense, everyone, even Attila, had forgotten he was there. Everyone was looking to Hak, and the three soldiers charging him with their swords out.

Attila dove forward and pulled the knife out of Hak's leg. It didn't come like a knife from a sheath, the way he thought it would. There was resistance. A rubbery grab to it that made the motion sickening. Attila thought of the bubbling face of the drowning soldier. The same feeling of unreality and nausea overtook him.

Hak grabbed the helmet off the unconscious soldier and threw it into the approaching soldier's face. The soldier tried to bring up his hand to block, but it smashed him square in the nose. They were too slow. Whether it was their armor and Hak's light farmer's clothing that made the difference, he had a speed that reduced them almost to statues.

Taking the sword from the stunned soldier's hand, Hak lifted it up, bobbled it, juggled it, and then seized the grip, anger set unusually in his gentle features. He brought the sword up and down in a wild chop and the soldier's forearm broke apart in a spray of blood. He screamed. The two soldiers behind him fell back.

The crowd gasped and stepped closer, their eyes growing wide or cautiously narrowing. And something hopeful growing on their lips.

The soldiers were in a fury. They separated and came at Hak from front and flank. One swung at Hak's head, the other his knees. Both blows landed and he flopped over onto the ground.

The men surrounding the fight grumbled and wailed. A few stepped a foot forward as if they would come to Hak's aid. But those toes quickly withdrew.

The soldiers pulled back. The lead one lifted his sword over Hak's sprawled body and prepared to cut him in two. A shout from a distance, a female cry, made him pause, sword in the air. It was Gug. She'd shouted but stayed where she was. She couldn't have seen too much, but must have seen Hak's blond head drop from sight and known something was happening she'd like stopped.

The lead soldier wound up his sword, and this time struck downward. Hak rolled toward the soldier and the blade caught in the ground before it could hit him. Hak made a strange shove with his lower half, and then he was on his feet, and he rocketed his shoulders upward into the soldier's face. The upwards blow sent the soldier's arms into the air and the sword flying end over end. The crowd gasped and parted, cowering and covering their heads.

Hak punched the soldier and grabbed his head, turning him to put his body between himself and the other soldier. He sent a knee into the man's breastplate, which pushed him back against his fellow soldier. And though that soldier was ready for it, he wasn't ready for Hak to leap forward over his comrade's body. There was a terrible red gash in Hak's skull, running a yellow-pink swath in his sweat-and-blood matted hair. Hak punched that gory noggin right into the soldier's face.

Now the crowd made a hopeful noise. All the soldiers were on the ground. One wasn't moving, likely dead. The other was without a forearm and was unconscious or in shock. The other two were scrambling in confusion, dazed at Hak's assault. What had started as an execution of two unarmed men had turned into a routing of this mob's old enemies: the Tsobl establishment.

Hak took a sword from the ground and stomped on the back of the lead soldier's head. The helmet deflected the blow and the giant almost tripped. He then kicked off the helmet and tried again. The soldier's head turned at the blow as his skull was driven flat into the ground. There was another cracking sound, and he said "Uh!" but then his body began to flap in the unconscious throes of a newly made dead man.

The crowd cheered.

Hak went after the last conscious soldier, who was stumbling his way backward, the crowd kindly parting for him. The soldier's eyes roamed from face to face as he saw them jeer and he knew he was in trouble. Some of the men looked to the carriage, which sat without comment, the rider atop it holding a hand above his eyes to help him see what was happening. Even Attila came forward, chasing after the action with methodical steps, coming to join Hak's side.

Hak tread forward, his shoulders twitching and flexing, his large muscles obvious under his sweat-soaked shirt. The soldier tripped and fell, only catching himself at the last second. But it was the pause Hak needed to overtake him. He lifted the sword high, and with the motion it took to split a piece of wood and the stump underneath it, he cleaved the soldier's helmet and head in two.

The crowd roared with lusty delight.

Hak paused to survey what he'd done. Then he turned suddenly and rushed toward Attila.

"Run away!"

Attila caught him by the hand. It took his whole body and his heels creating furrows in the earth to get him to slow down.

"There's no need to run, Hak. You've done it. Look, and there's four of them. Even better than your grandfather 'Antlers'. I've never seen anything like it."

Hak recognized the cheers going up around him. And the men surrounded him, clapping him on the back.

"Well," Hak said, looking downcast and ashamed. "It was a tough thing. A very tough thing to do, Mr. Bronk. But I did as I promised, didn't I? I hope you're proud."

"You're a hero, Sir Vogoneyevic."

Hak shook his head. He pointed. Gug was walking away with Lija. Only Man stood in place, watching, patting the head of a dog, and he would probably follow his mother when she got far enough.

"Here, Hak!" said one from the crowd, full of mirth. "Let's go see what that Tsobl judge has to say to you now!"

The crowd, like a sentient wave from the sea, pulled Hak to the front and rolled towards the carriage. Attila dodged through the arms and tried to keep pace, wondering just who was inside. Could it really be the governor? The driver was turned on his seat, as if relaying some message to someone inside the carriage.

"Come out, come out!" went up a cheer. "See what Vogoneyevic has done! Come speak with our hero, Hak Vogoneyevic. Son of great 'Antlers'!"

"I'm his grandson," Hak tried to correct.

The wave paused at the edge of the road. The driver was winding up his whip in the air, looking nervously at the hard peasant faces. The interior of the carriage looked dark and as if no one was inside.

"Are you in there, judge? Come and speak to Hak Vogoneyevic, the lord of our land."

"Lord of the land is he?" a reedy voice shouted from the window. "I think not. Treason is what I just witnessed. High treason. Are you all subjects of the Ardeelian government or are you traitors as well?"

There was a dumbfounded silence. The voice was confident and contemptuous.

"Come forward," said the voice. "Let me tell you something. Come forward and hear out this voice of law."

Hak was left behind as they moved around him, creating two protective ranks in front of him and Attila. The way they shifted and screwed up their faces, they were figuring how to turn the carriage over before the horses could tear away.

"There is a reward for the capture of traitors," the voice said. "A handsome reward."

A hand came out of the window and dropped coins onto the road. Then it dove back inside and threw out two more handfuls.

"Traitors die! *Capturers* shall enjoy these fruits!"

Some of the men had already leapt to the side of the carriage to snatch the coins. Almost all turned to regard Hak and Attila, a new, ugly aspect showing on their faces.

The driver cried and cracked his whip, and the horses yanked the carriage.

"Capturers shall enjoy these fruits—these golden fruits, *and more!*"

As the carriage left, the mob shifted on the road.

Attila grabbed at Hak, and said: "Run away!"

39

That Was Very Nice of You

Genadie drove the horses overnight, stopping to rest and water them occasionally. Amalina kept silent company on the rider's bench and would have stayed there, lost in thoughts as she was, but he reminded her how she must be found inside the carriage and wearing her "princess" disguise when they reached Netz. So down she went, and with the remaining hours at her disposal she inched closer and closer to the book Genadie had recovered from Dragomir. The pressure built within her to look inside. To check if her father had made some mark to let her know he'd seen her message. Maybe he hadn't. Maybe, not knowing its purpose or what to do with it, or thinking it had been a gift from the Count and not Amalina, he had set it aside unread. And then, in his despair, after so much time passed without a word from the castle, unable to cope with the loss of his wife and daughter, he had succumbed to a madness and idiocy that allowed him to accept Jenna as his own—to actually enjoy her company, and allow her to work in the store—and allow the Widow Lidsz, with her long, wrinkled face, and her horse-like laugh, to seduce him.

Convinced of this fact, it was easier for Amalina to finally open the book, with the understanding that she was doing so to review her original message; to see if she'd made some mistake in crafting it, or see if it was impossible for anyone (her father, that is) to notice it. And secondarily to review it from her present perspective, to see if it wasn't the writing of a pathetic, still-naïve little girl. Something to be embarrassed by its openness, its vulnerability, and its eagerness. Then, at last, to check if Dragomir had made some alteration, to let her know that he *had* found the message.

Right beside each of her letters (which she had spaced cautiously throughout the book, placed inside illustrations of machinery and touched by little flowers), Dragomir had added a letter of his own creating a second hidden message she could not miss.

> "i love you too we miss you very much stay safe and come home
> when you can"

Well, what was she to say?

Amalina huffed. *Come home "when" I can? Not: Come home "as soon" as I can?* No hurry there, she told herself bitterly. Dragomir was having a grand old time without her. He'd never been happier running the store, now that Jenna had replaced her and the Widow had swept in to replace her mother. It was like Jenna and the Widow had been waiting to pounce the moment Amalina was out of the way and her surprisingly weak-willed father was free to be wowed and wooed. And: *"We" miss you?* Not just *I*, but he'd chosen to include Jenna, and maybe even the Widow Lidsz, as if his daughter could not help but, due to her absence and helpless position, accept them as her family.

After a quarter hour of steaming anger she quieted and tried to assess the value of her upset: What was she feeling, really? Betrayal? Woe at the unfairness of her home's happiness just because she wasn't there to share it? Hostility at the unjustness of Jenna's sudden promotion in life? Wasn't her cousin the perpetual unhappy one? Wasn't *she* the one destined to die by wolf attack (really a victim of the Count's)? Wasn't *she* the dispensable one? And now, she'd fit herself into the hole Amalina had left and had become something she wasn't ever supposed to be. She'd found a purpose. She'd exceeded the position. She had taken Amalina's place, and not just credibly filled the gap, she'd done a better job of it.

All while Amalina dealt with the lonely, private, unhappy struggle of living with, and trying to rid the world of, the monster.

• • •

Carila was red-faced with anger, but tried to control her voice when speaking with her new mistress: "You left us as prisoners. There was no way to return to the castle without your carriage."

"Why would you want to go to the castle?" Amalina asked, relieved to find Aklan loafing on the feather mattress, uncaring about their imprisonment.

"You didn't notice? Her ladyship—that is, the Princess Lisbet—has gone. The day after services she left. I couldn't convince her to wait for you to return. I wouldn't be surprised if she's married by the time we reach them."

As doubtful as an elopement was, and as much as Amalina had hoped to keep Aklan in Netz until she could find a way to send the boy back to his family, she decided to have Genadie load the carriage, destined for the high castle.

"Do I have to go in the box?" Aklan asked from the bed, looking like he'd prefer to roll over and go to sleep.

"You'll be out of there when we get you up to my room," she said, as she grabbed at him to move him along.

"Be careful then." He winced and moved with stiff limbs, and tried to avoid her. "She broke my legs."

"Who broke your legs?"

"I didn't break anything," barked Carila, and seized him effectively at the arms and pushed him into the trunk. He looked like a cat trying to be stuffed into a too small sack, complete with howls. "But I will if you give me the excuse."

"She did so! I heard my bones snap and I still can't walk straight."

"Taught him a lesson, is what I did," said Carila, trying to close the lid on his flailing limbs. "How else was I going to keep him in the room, instead of sneaking out the door, or climbing out the windows when I wasn't looking? He's as restless as a mouse.

"Keep it down," Carila advised the boy inside the trunk, once the lid was on. "If you make a peep, I'll break your mouth. Then how'll you cry for your supper?"

He knocked from inside the box in protest, but made no comment. Amalina had Genadie put the trunk into the carriage, just so she and Carila could keep a watch on it.

• • •

Before the road they were traveling dog-legged to the right, winding around the edge of the forest and led into the long approach to the castle, Amalina spotted a curious grouping of peasants at a cart. Not only was it unusual to see so many bodies together in the sloping Ardeelian landscape, even when it was the month of harvest, they did not have, individually, the regular shape of an Ardeelian field worker. Where long, lanky limbs should have been, with the occasional barrel chest thrown in, these specimens were tall, and bulky in every sense, like they were built under their skin by clusters of cannonballs. And while they had discarded their foreign uniforms, and adopted plain wool shirts, it was plain by their distinctive beards and darker-skinned faces—all glowering and watchful, with the heavy muscovite features—they were Kralov's men. Their commander didn't seem to be among them.

Decoupled from horses, and with no obvious riding board, it was difficult to tell which direction the cart was headed. It was on a trail that led from the highway to a small farmhouse. Amalina supposed the men were pushing the cart toward the farmhouse by the way they broke off at the sound of horses and the carriage. Most of them kept their backs to the road, trying to avoid being seen. Even though the field was flat but for the khaki stubble of post-harvest stalks, and besides the intermittent titanic domes of hay just beyond the farmhouse, they were the only thing of interest for miles. After a sudden movement from one of them, some hurriedly began reshuffling straw within the cart.

They were trying to cover what was in the cart's bed. From this distance, it was brown and long and cylindrical, resembling a tree trunk. The closest end seemed to be rounded. Amalina leaned up to the window, staring harder, trying to discern what it could be, even as the straw fell on top of it. There was something metallic about it. A cannon? But it looked ribbed, or corrugated all the way along its length, with no protrusions for wicks, legs, or stand placement. It more had the feeling that the closed, rounded end was the important one. Was it some kind of battering ram?

The men glared at her, or at the carriage, or Genadie atop the carriage. For them there could be no one else speeding along the road, en route to the Count's castle, than their enemy. Were they already en route for the assault? But it was too late in the day. They wouldn't arrive til night. Late at night. Having already been exposed to the Count's attack for hours along the way. No, they must be heading for the farmhouse, to place their cart inside the protection of the barn. Preparing pieces of equipment for a future assault. Whether it was a cannon or battering ram, large as it was, what she knew of the Count made it seem as useful as a chess piece. Bravely, Amalina shifted her body out the window, letting them see who was inside. If they reported back to Kralov, he would know she'd returned. Maybe that would affect his plans. Delay the attack. Contact her to see what she had to say. She had vital information now, which he might be able to use. She put her arm out, low to the side of the carriage, and discreetly signaled: *They should not attack. Not yet.*

Only after a sudden thought did she turn to see if Carila was watching. The maid's body was slumped, taking up most of the bench, her knee braced against the bottom end of the trunk with Aklan in it, and her head was turned. She was either sleeping or staring absently out the other window. She hadn't seen anything.

Amalina wondered if any of Kralov's men had noticed her signal. Or understood her meaning.

• • •

Where the Ardeelian countryside after harvest was sun-bedraggled and wasted, and could be broken down into three categories and color: yellowed straw, copper grasses, and chunky brown soil (either mud or dry earth), the high castle was in full bloom. There were new bouquets of flowers adorning the gates, bunched together artlessly, with different sizes and no mind to colors. Some of the flowers were broken at the stems. However gaudy and tasteless it was, Amalina came to the conclusion that someone had been industrious while the princesses were away.

Inside the gate, the courtyard was similarly irregular. It was as alive as a kicked anthill, with people scurrying in all directions looking busy and alert. The air was filled with the loud murmur of conversation, the shouts of children, the cries of animals, the clanks and clunks of physical labor, and the smell of fire pits and cooking meat.

"Oh!" said Carila, taking the surprise out of Amalina's mouth.

Who were these strangers?

Most were dressed in the wools of Ardeelian commoners. A handful wore the out-of-date uniforms of the castle's serving staff. The two men who approached the carriage, followed by Georg, whose head was tilted high enough for Amalina to see up his nose, were neither Ham nor Gull. They had the same clueless, barely-trained mien of the former footmen. They also had, around the ear, or a brow, or the bridge of a nose, the telltale signs of a blood relationship to Georg.

The perpetual banquet was still set in *l'entrée grande*, with Ham and Gull seeming not to have left off their shifting of dishes. The only change was more plates and serving trays now heaped to spill at all positions of the table (goose, wild boar, and venison added, among other treats), with two maids, an additional butler, and two or three little children following in their parent's footsteps. The nephews had deep lines growing on their faces, and they appeared bleary, as if they actually hadn't stopped in their rotations. The additional crew looked to them for instruction. The children did cartwheels. When Georg entered things slowed, as all of them gawped at their head of staff with a combination of fear of judgement and hope for reward.

"Is this meal for us?" Amalina asked Georg as the two new footmen wrestled the trunk to the stairs under Carila's direction.

"For anyone that will have it. How long has it been ready, and nobody has partaken of it." Georg didn't sound as insulted as his words implied. His look was one of haplessness as he surveyed the grand untouched meal.

"I don't understand, why don't you wait until there is a desire to eat? Or until the Count calls for a meal and the guests are summoned for it?"

"That isn't the way in the *Palace of Pleasure*. This is a banquet! We are to have the food ready at all times, in case the princess should have the urge."

"That's the way of the Palace of Pleasure?" asked Amalina, incredulous. "It seems wasteful."

"Our high liege said to set the table. He has given no other instructions other than to fill out the staff immediately."

And so this is the way it was to be. The Count whispers an idea, Georg fulfills with a shout.

Princess Lisbet was in the Great Library, not reading but staring pleasantly at Abraxa, who stood by the door. Abraxa was looking expectantly to Lisbet, even after Amalina entered, as if they were in a duel of companionability.

"Ah, you've returned to me, Katty," Lisbet embraced her and then directed her into a wide chair where they could sit close together. "How was your trip? Your father is well?"

Amalina kept from looking at Abraxa, who had withdrawn far into the corner. She couldn't appear to have anything but a natural reaction. "By the time I arrived, he was already away on business. He is worse than the Count. But the others were well." She apologized for having left her alone in the village. "But why did you leave before I returned?"

"It wasn't the same without you. The St. Grigori Cathedral was nice enough. But the cardinal is nothing like your uncle. And the castle has the library."

Their conversation picked up where it left off and went along with pleasantries, with Lisbet expressing wonder at all the amazing things the *Palace of Pleasure* offered. Such as so many flowers in the fullness of their season, though it was autumn now; a peculiarity of the Ardeelian atmosphere, or the resilience of its plant life, or novel techniques in their preservation, no doubt? Amalina evaded the harder questions until they were both without subjects to talk about and sat in each other's arms. Amalina felt she could go to sleep, for how comfortable and already exhausted she felt.

Lisbet sighed and turned to Abraxa.

"Abraxa?"

"Your grace?"

"Where are you from?"

"Where am I …?" Abraxa looked nervously at Amalina. "There's no need to ask me … unless there is something you wish for, and then I am at your command."

"I don't see why I can't learn a little about you. You are a living soul, just as I. Our value is not any different, even if the roles we've been given are." After a pause she saw this wasn't enough for the old maid. "In fact, you might even have more of a value, being so close to toil. The Great Cardinal was sermonizing on how the first of us will be the last, and the last of us will be the first, and how it will be much harder for the rich and powerful to enter the grace of Heaven than those who serve them. But please, you seem very nice, and are so attentive, I wish to know about you. Come, if you are Katarina's friend, come be my friend, too."

"But I'm not—"

"But I've told you what I wish," she said maintaining her sweet voice, making the words sound like something between a gentle tease and an earnest plea, with her head still casually set on Amalina's shoulder. "And isn't my wish a command? Should I make it a command, Abraxa? Don't delay anymore, but come to us and sit down and tell me your story."

Shy, embarrassed, fearful, Abraxa lowered her head, and came to them with hesitant steps.

"Well, nobody around here's ever asked," she said softly. "I wouldn't know what to say. I am a simple person. *We* are. My husband and I. That is, Georg."

"The head of staff?"

"Yes, princess. That is so."

"That's unusual," observed Lisbet. "Doesn't happen often. Most stewards try to keep the personal attachments to a minimum. Less complications. But that's interesting, you two. I never would have known you were attached in any way besides a devotion to service. But tell me more. You've always served the Count?"

"No. Uh." She seemed to reconsider. Then: "No. No, no, no. No we have not served our lord and master long at all … within *this* castle. But in a sense, we've served him all our lives, haven't we? Growing up in Ardeel. He is a very powerful man. He and his family have served as the law and protectors since time began. It is an honor that he brought us close to him, to serve him directly, to provide for his delightful guests."

"Well, that's enough of that," Lisbet said with a short laugh. "But tell me about *yourself*, personally, Abraxa. What was it like growing up in the mountains? What food do you like to eat? What dances do you most enjoy?"

"Does milady wish me to pick from among those questions or to answer them all?"

"Them all."

Abraxa looked horrified, as if she'd been ordered to endure a torture in the village square. Her eyes darted up, and raced between the two princesses (or rather, the princess and the Mouse), and then returned to the floor. But then a smile crept onto her face, and she told them a story of picking flowers when she was a child, while her parents worked in the fields.

"That was very nice of you," Amalina said to Lisbet, when Abraxa was done with her confession and had fled the room in embarrassment and horror at this uncomfortable exchange, with never-before-seen blush on her grey cheeks. "I've never seen that side of her."

But Lisbet's small lips were slanted in an unsure way. "May I tell you something, Katty?"

"Of course. Tell me now, if it'll cure you of this sudden unhappiness."

"It's not sudden, my darling. I've carried it since I arrived. But you know that, and it has been gaining size and weight all along."

"Tell me, Lees," Amalina said, squeezing her hand the way she would Cristine's. "Tell me now and release it."

"This palace of pleasure ..." Lisbet's smile didn't look like true contentment, and she tilted her head as if weighing a thought. "It is quite amazing, isn't it?"

"Is it?"

"I said I enjoy flowers, and it is packed full with them. Walls covered in them. When at the black castle, I remarked how few servants there were. And when we came here, there were just a few, as well. When I suggested I expected more, now it is like a city full of them. Whatever I ask for, it appears. Like you are the Count's spy, and all my complaints and worries are answered to my satisfaction."

Amalina gulped. "Don't think of me as a spy. The Count only wishes to see you happy."

"Yes. And he and his palace meet my every wish. Once it was empty, and now it fills with my tastes and wishes and dreams. Only not as perfectly. Not that I am complaining. It is just ... These aren't natural things here. These are decorations put here, without having existed here before my arrival. At my anticipation and not preexisting. Somewhat artificial. Please do forgive me for saying this," and now tears formed on her blueberry eyes. "But it is a little strange. And here is this library. This great library. And I can't help but think that it was never here before, until you returned from your visit to Antwerp and told him I enjoyed books. And so he, in a rush, created this room to please me. This palace is like a looking glass—"

"But that isn't true, exactly."

Clear droplets pattered down from the princess' eyes to her silken lap. Her lips twisted and flexed in a way that made her angelic face ugly. "I don't know how to say this, but I must, Katarina. I must."

"Just say it," Amalina insisted. "You aren't going to hurt me, if that's what you're afraid of. Say anything."

"The flowers, despite their amazing longevity, can be gotten anywhere in these forests. This city of servants ... well, how long have you known Abraxa? It couldn't have been too long. These aren't trained or skilled people. Not in the least. They were probably gotten from anywhere in your countryside, bought off by the promise of a meal and lodging. Not that feeding this many is cheap ... but ... This really does hurt me to tell you any of this Katarina. I don't wish to insult you, or hurt your feelings ... And worse, I ... I feel like I can only bring shame on myself, and my family ..."

For some reason Amalina wanted to laugh, even as her stomach knotted in sympathy with Lisbet's obvious struggle and suffering. She squeezed her hand. "Get on with it, Lees! Get it out!"

"It seems the Count hasn't any money. Has he? Has he, really, my dearest? But I can't call you that, can I? If I'm asking you such a thing. Because it reveals me for who I really am."

Amalina no longer wanted to laugh. Leaning forward, she waited now for the confession.

"It was my father, you see," Lisbet said, flopping her free hand in show of irritation. "I mean … I liked you, Katty. You were very nice. But just a little girl, weren't you? And a strange little girl … who spoke so well, coming from the exotic east in a beat-up old carriage, a ratty driver and one dress. No maids or attendants. It should have been obvious. But my father … my father. He thought that was the shrewd frugality of the old world mindset. And that your uncle, who had funded your explorations to our side of the world, was like a dragon sitting on a hoard of gold. And my father … my father … well, Katty, despite everything you saw on your visit, and all his excellent qualities, he was never good at managing our estate. He thought, upon receiving Count Tepsji's invitation, that a rich old goat was looking for a pretty young wife, and my father could supply him one, and provide him access to our country's court, provided he could accept a cheap dowry … and be willing to finance his wife's family."

Lisbet shook her head and dabbed at her face with a handkerchief.

"That is what I am," she said after awhile. "A cheap gift. Or rather, an expensive one. As long as the Count could afford me. That was the first part of my mission: to assess Lord Tepsji's holdings. Then, if he lived up to my father's fantasies … to seduce him." Lisbet's mouth opened fully, and she let out a loud cry. But only two sobs after that. Then she shook her head again and buried her face fully into the kerchief. "That is what I am, little Katty. That is all I really am."

Lisbet's tone had changed, and her body had seemed to harden, to withdraw. She was taking her true shape, which was something other than a tender friend. And even though Amalina knew it was nothing personal, and that her weeping and alteration was more brought on by self-disgust than a coldness toward her, Amalina felt a dramatic altering of their circumstances.

Now Amalina knew that her visit into the western kingdoms, the fraud of it, had been all too obvious. She'd only been led to believe it was a smacking success by the politeness, curiosity and self-interest of those who'd let her in their door. And she had convinced herself of her accomplishments, more than a little, by hopeful self-delusion (abetted by the indifferent Genadie). Now she saw how it had been, and how things really stood for them at present: Lisbet was an older girl, fully into her young womanhood. Older even than Amalina's cousin, Jenna. She was someone with more worldly interests, looking after handsome princes with genuine affection and true hopes for romance. She had emerged from the coddling of childhood long ago and was seeking for an acceptable place within adult society. And to the princess' eyes, Amalina was as Amalina appeared to be: a silly little girl. Not her equal. Not a true friend. A kind enough thing that she could use to get her to her true destination: Count Tepsji.

"You think the Count doesn't have money?" asked Amalina, suddenly curious. "Or are you afraid that he *is* rich, and you will be forced to carry out your mission?"

"How can I be afraid of the answer," she burbled, "when the answer is so obvious?"

"Listen to me, princess," Amalina said, now trying to sound older for her companion. "I am asking you a question, because I have many answers that I can give you to warn you away, to have you fly back home this very instant. But that's only if you want *those* answers. Because I can also give you answers that would please your father, if *that* is what you wish. Tell me, princess, what do *you* want to hear?"

Lisbet looked up out of the kerchief in surprise, and observed Amalina as if for the first time. Seeing Amalina as perhaps wiser, or cannier, than she ever expected. But her tone was still sweet, and her answer still hopeless: "What can you *possibly* say, little Katja?"

40

The Pleasurable Girl

"What do you want from Princess Lisbet Spaarvierlet?" Amalina asked plainly and directly, then quickly added: "Sir."

"I ask you if she's satisfied with the increase in staff," said the Count, pulling on his mustache and giving her a curious look, "and in reply you ask *me* what I want from her. Haven't we been over this?"

"The princess is satisfied, sir," said Amalina. "But only to a point: It's obvious to anyone who isn't blind Georg's people aren't qualified. They're just uneducated peasants here to fill up space in the castle."

"I see."

"Stop pulling on your mustache, sir, and tell me what you want from her. Because that is what she would like to know: What is your concern in her being here? She feels like she's being handled more than treated as a guest. It's so distressing, she even called me your spy. I know it's difficult to meet in the daytime, but your absence is more notable to the person you invited personally to be your guest. She can only be entertained so long with your flowers and servants and books. And since we're on that subject, the palace of pleasure's pleasures don't impress her all that much. Not that she's looking down at you but she is used to luxury. Princesses are pampered, and to her it looks like you are at pains to reach the level she is accustomed. Not that she wants such a thing. That is not why she came. But since you've made that your primary occupation it seems, the awkwardness is strange and … and awkward for her."

"I thought I'd made it clear," said the Count. "I want her here for my entertainment. To be able to experience a fresh mind. Enjoy a fresh thought. Touch fresh blood and flesh."

"You'd better hurry then. I think she'll be leaving. Soon."

"Leaving you?"

"Leaving *you*."

"But aren't you her cherished friend?" he said with a snide look and mocking tone.

"You're the one who invited her, sir, so you're the one she came for. And she isn't going to stay if the person she wished to meet is a blatant seducer; with his inadequacy in providing delights, a deceiver."

He said nothing for a minute, but twisted his mustache and lowered a brow in thought.

"Deceived?" he said, finally.

"She doesn't believe you are a true count." This caused him to smirk. "Or, more exactly, she believes the castle and everything in it is a show. She doesn't believe you have any real title or any real wealth." He snorted. "That the rumors in the western kingdoms about Ardeelian nobility is true."

"And what are these rumors?"

"We're poor. *Their* pauper nobles have more money than twelve of our counts and barons and kings put together."

"Yes, we're all *Viscounts* to them now. You said she was nice."

"*She* didn't say what I just told you. It's the common belief there. She came to us thinking otherwise, but now is entertaining the rumors might be true."

"I don't have anything to prove to a spoiled Flemish tart of a princess," sneered the Count. His angular sneer showing teeth—so that it was almost a smile—and the glimmer in his eye betrayed his amusement. As if he were playing with himself a clever game of some kind inside his head. Typically circular and self-involved of him, which irritated Amalina.

"No you don't have to prove anything," she agreed, trying to keep the sarcasm out of her voice. "But just so you know, sir, if she leaves, and she tells everyone back home her impressions, I wouldn't expect to get too many more answers to your invitations. Which is fine if that is what you want."

Nodding slowly, eyes slitted, he said, "There's a fine point. *You* don't believe her, do you? That I am poor."

"You're rich to me, sir. Very rich. But what do I know?"

"In ten minutes I want you to come to my private study."

"With Lisbet?"

"Not yet."

And ten minutes later, Amalina presented herself in the private study. The Count was at his desk. He opened a bag of gold coins similar to the one Genadie carried to town. He sifted his pale finger through the spilling pile of flashing metal.

"How does the princess think I pay my expenses? Or yours?"

"That's a lot of money," Amalina said, forcing excitement into her eyes, restraining the urge to glance toward the hidden vault. "I've never seen so much."

"Her father has more," the Count supposed.

"I couldn't say ... But ..."

"He does. They all do. I'd expect this is a year's income for a duke. Perhaps a little more. These are gold coins, you understand, little mouse."

"I know what coins are what," Amalina said. "A gold one would have kept our store in business for a year. Maybe five."

"Yes, I know," the Count murmured. "Keep that in mind." Then he stood.

Amalina almost staggered backwards as he went to the cabinet. In her mind, she saw him opening it. And his every step forward made her heart beat louder. Then, after the clack, he opened the cabinet wide and motioned her inside.

There were torches burning in the first room, the counting house. It was obvious he'd planned this moment, to reveal it to her. It was as theatrical a presentation as anything Lady Flauna and Erik Kosche would have come up with. And Lisbet would suffer over its strained delivery. Standing in the middle of it all, the Count brought up his arms to proudly indicate that the lot of it was his.

Still, in the back of her mind, and contending with the underlying—if distant—fear that he planned to show off Piotr's lifeless body, Amalina had to remember to look confused.

"What *is* all this?" she asked innocently.

"My treasury, Ms. Dalca. Every bag contains a square block of many bullion. A bullion produces five coins." His hands still in the air, he rotated at the hips, including the entire room of shelves with his sweep. "And so you understand, this is the merest tip of it all."

Amalina stood there, mouth appropriately agog.

"Is it true?" she asked, walking further in.

With a brief flick, he tore the side of a bag open. The bars glowed in the torchlight.

Amalina went right up to the shredded bag and then touched its heavy, solid contents.

"The merest tip," the Count repeated.

She looked around, then she walked further in. Her intent was to use her amazement to get herself as far into the vault that she could. How far would he let her go?

The Count backed up several paces, but then lowered his arms, like he would catch her in them if she went any further. He was deliberately blocking the entrance to—the very sight of—his message center. No lights were in the lower room. It was never meant for his grand revelation. It was still off limits.

But he'd let her in this far.

"You would admit then that I have adequate wealth for a count," he said with mock understatement. "Even one from lowly Ardeel."

Amalina nodded. "You want me to tell the princess about this?"

"Nothing of the sort," he said. "It would ruin the surprise I have planned for her."

. . .

Amalina prepared Lisbet to meet the Count, perhaps for the last time. It was forbidden to tell her of the surprise waiting inside the private study. Amalina had to resort to vague reassurances that tonight's encounter would break to Lisbet's liking. That the Count was indeed financially stable; more so than Lisbet thought anyway. And that the gold necklace and earrings *did* look nice with her pale pink dress. Then it was on to the hair brush, and one-hundred fifty strokes through her fantastic, voluminous hair.

Georg knocked at the door. He announced *his excellency*, the Count. Lisbet sat up. Though she put the proper curve on her small lips, still she held the same doubtful and despairing air she'd dampened the past hours with since her confession. Amalina patted her pale shoulder one last time to reassure the princess. But the princess, distracted as she was, pointed Amalina to the opposite chair, like she would have directed Astrell or Carila. Amalina obeyed without offense, interested to see what was to happen. And also to get them both on their way. It promised to be a big night. Either the Count would convince Lisbet to stay, or she would make her decision to return home (and without an engagement for marriage). And while they were embroiled with each other, Amalina would finally have time for herself and her mission.

Lisbet bade the Count to enter. He swung in through the door with the same verve he had once greeted Lady Flauna when she had first entered the castle. With the same smiling, mustache-twisting, twinkle-eyed gaze of hunger; a lazy but predatory hunger. He appeared relaxed. Instead of his customary set of outdated velvet coat and leggings, he wore his regular bumming around outfit. His right hand casually petting his white silk shirt.

By the time they left, Amalina couldn't remember their conversation. It seemed that there hadn't been one. The intercourse had been conducted by their faces (mostly in the eyes), and the sway and posturing of their bodies. He did the swaying, and the princess' figure picked it up, and when he left, her body was so in synchronicity she was forced to follow right after.

"I expect we'll see you in the morning, little mouse," he said. "I'd imagine it would be best for you to go to your own room and get some good sleep rather than wait for our return. There's no telling how long we'll be."

She didn't have to be told twice. Once they were down the hall Amalina went straight to her own chamber. If Lisbet decided to leave, it would be right away. By morning, most likely. And so there was no danger to the princess if Kralov attacked. She and her people would be out of the castle as the men were on their way in. The Commander wouldn't be stupid to attack at night when the Count was at his fullest strength. But if Lisbet was convinced to stay, then Amalina needed to get to Kralov before the attack to alert him who should be spared—to plead Lisbet's case.

Anyway, she needed to get the information to Kralov about the Count's weakness to a certain metal and susceptibility to the water he'd provided, just in case it could help them. Remembering the piddling ram in the back of his men's cart, she knew she'd better let them know as soon as possible.

Only there wasn't a good reason to sneak away. None she could think of.

In the morning, Lisbet's leaving would give Amalina good cover. Or if she was staying, Amalina still might be able to convince the princess to make another run down into Netz for a church service. Or find some other excuse Amalina could sell. So, since Amalina had until morning, and she felt a charge of energy at having been given full-blown entrance into the treasury, and there was the pervading feeling that matters of all kinds were coming to a head, she decided to forgo sleep.

Amalina arranged her cryptograph sheets on the desk, then she pulled out the curl of paper. She'd already gone through the codes before, with no result. There weren't any more in the desk and these glyphs definitely fit the unique characters to be found on numerous ciphers, beginning with the cast metal one. She tried it again. But not all the characters belonged to that one cryptograph. And full words—seeming they were full words as there were spaces between blocks of letters—made no sense. Rearranging the letters in the words to see if they were some kind of anagram structure didn't result in anything other than a wasted hour.

She sighed and restarted from the beginning. The first character was an odd one, and found only on the metal cryptograph. So that *had* to be the master key. Why didn't it work?

She tapped her lower lip and stared at the letters, then at the cryptographs, then at the letters.

It begins with …

Wait.

It *begins* with the metal coding. But who said it had to stay that way throughout? Maybe the spy was such a nervous sort, or devious, that he took deeper lengths to obscure the message. Maybe each letter, in their turn, belonged to an individual code.

Now that she thought of it, Amalina remembered there was a letter printed on the side of the code sticks. Even the metal one had a letter stamped on its side … And its letter was 'A'. The first letter in the alphabet. So which one was B? Closing her eyes, she thought she could picture them and their order.

Only she didn't recall them precisely. It became a grueling trial by error working through the proper side designations. Another fifteen minutes to get excited she was definitely on the right track. Real words were forming. Only after an hour did she have it.

She had the secret message:

> Your services are always appreciated. In compensation for the unforeseen complications, due entirely to my own miscalculations, I propose a one-time doubling of exchange, at my expense. I will be more careful in the future. AXP.

Amalina frowned. Okay, so it wasn't of imminent importance. Despite the length the writer took to hide its meaning it was just a 'thank you' note. Whoever it was had made some mistake, and would compensate the Count for his troubles. Nothing exciting. At least, it wasn't exciting without context.

Amalina blew out a sigh.

"Is everything all right, milady?"

Amalina yelled and flew out of her chair. Carila shouted in return and fell back, staggering to recover from the fright.

"Oh, Carila! You startled me. I completely forgot."

"I didn't want to disturb you, milady," Carila said, bowing apologetically. "You were very busy, and deep in concentration. But you made that noise."

Amalina looked around the room for Aklan, surprised he had sat quiet for so long once she'd returned to the room. He could only be asleep in the bed.

But he wasn't.

And then she noted the open trunk.

He wasn't in the room at all.

"Where's the little prince?" asked Amalina, becoming nervous.

"The little master? He's taken off."

"Where?"

"I don't know. He promised he'd stay in the castle, though, until his sister gives up the castle and leaves."

"He's loose?" She felt a fury grow inside her. "What were you thinking?"

"It wasn't my choice, milady. But it was the best we could do under the circumstances. When the footmen brought the trunk into the room, the binding gave and the little master fell out. Well, the footmen had a start at that. I pretended it was a surprise to me as well. Aklan started howling a bunch of nonsense and running around the room, and the footmen, for some reason, thought he was one of their own and had gotten into the trunk."

"But why did you let him leave?"

"They were after him, milady," she said. "It was all he could do not to get caught by them. Before he ran out the door he told me he'd hide in the castle, but out of the princess' way. He'd join up with her again when he saw her leaving. And then he was gone."

Amalina pictured the boy hanging out the privy chute. He wouldn't have gone back there, would he?

"You wait here for him to come back," Amalina told Carila, as she quickly stuffed her ciphers beneath her mattress. She ignored Carila's curious look. "I'll see if I can find him."

After calling down the privy and receiving no response, Amalina decided he hadn't tried that route again. Or if he had, he'd fallen out completely and might already be dead outside the castle walls. Downstairs she went. He wasn't among the children in the grand entrance, or the main hall, or in the kitchens, or outside in the courtyard. If he was truly hiding, he was doing a fantastic job of it.

Abraxa had been in the kitchen with Georg discussing the next day's preparations. Amalina decided this gave her time to wander more freely, though who knew for how long.

Following the same meandering route she'd used once before, when Lady Flauna was in the castle, Amalina made her way to the Count's private study. The doors were shut, possibly locked. But the keyhole was of a generous size, and she and Erik had once used it to spy on Flauna and the Count. Now she would do the same and see if Lisbet was being shown the treasury as the Count had revealed it to Amalina. And whether the revelation was enough to convince the princess to follow her father's plan: to wed her family into money.

Amalina kneeled down and put her eye to the hole.

At first she didn't understand what she saw. The room was lit by one torch, so the room was lit at the edges, with long black shadows being cast sideways toward the wall. The movement within the room helped make things clear.

What she saw in that room, if it were described here in full, would shock a sensitive reader. For Amalina, it came as a surprise only in that she had not expected to see such a thing, and that she had never thought to see Lisbet in such a delicate position. But she understood, by the slow and sensual movements of the two bodies, and the heated looks of passion upon their faces, that this was an embrace of a consensual nature, and a tender one at that. And it had the shock of education to it, as what she now perceived very clearly near the center reminded her of the longest arm of the clock as it rattled up towards midnight. She'd never seen anything like it in that condition, her only glimpses of those parts being moments during swimming or bathing, or being used to evacuate a body's water. Never this way. *And look where it went to!*

What she saw informed—and confirmed, too—what she encountered in her lucid dreams. And that it was Lisbet there in the room, experiencing the endless grasping, and her making guttural noises, moans of protest but not protest, in the deep, earthly enjoyment of it, sent Amalina's own body panting.

She pushed away from the keyhole.

This was not what she'd expected to see.

Her mind was in a whirl.

She couldn't think. Couldn't think of anything. She wanted to return her eye to the hole. She wanted to knock on the door to disturb what was happening. She wanted to do something.

Do something.

How long would this take? A minute? An hour? For dogs it took less than a minute. For birds less than a second. But them …

Amalina's thoughts, and the murmurs from the study, drove her from the outer room before she fell back to the keyhole, back to being their uninvited witness. She still couldn't think, but she knew she needed to get rid of this out-of-control feeling within her.

Trying to wrest control of her thoughts, she decided that this entanglement in the study could only mean Lisbet was going to stay. And the Count would not be leaving the castle that evening. Lovers did not leave each other in the night, according to all the romantic poems and stories. They never quit each other's embrace, night or day, except by force.

So Amalina went to the stable, and in ten minutes was riding for the gate.

41

The Cardinal of Netz

With hurried steps, Rosczy entered. "Do you know who's come? Come *here?* to the *church?*"

The Cardinal lifted his head slowly from reading the roll of accounts, his face deformed into a punishing expression: eyes slitted to points, mouth cinched to that of a small trout's anus.

"I-I'm sorry, Cardinal. Most sorry. I did not mean to intrude. I beg your forgiveness a thousand times over, Cardinal. But I didn't know if you were *expecting*—well, he's *here*. His carriage has just arrived and his man has announced his request. An audience with *you*, Cardinal."

By the shock on Rosczy's face his unexpected guest could only be the Count. The Cardinal felt a stone plunge from his throat into his stomach. But when did the Count travel by carriage, or enter the church by announcement? "Tell me," he said calmly, "*who* requests an audience with me?"

Rosczy told him. And for who it really was, the Cardinal didn't even know how to begin hiding his surprise.

. . .

The Governor was kept waiting for three hours. Well into the night. By the fourth time the scurrying assistant Rosczy begged his forgiveness, and told of the bishop's—*never cardinal!*—need to attend to some bit of important work, and was offered plates and pitchers of refreshments while he waited, he supposed this was the expected punishment for having arrived without warning. He would wait. That was all he could do.

That and avoid eating or drinking anything within the vicinity of Netz. He'd been warned of the suspicious deaths that surrounded the Bishop of Netz like a graveyard. His enemies and rivals tended to wander to eternity after a meal or a drink shortly after departing the cathedral. Hadn't the bishop slowly replaced the priests and bishops in other parts of the country this way, until Tsobl was surrounded by the bishop's sympathizers and collaborators?

But the Governor had to wait—and wait patiently—because he had to know the answer to these two questions: Was Zsolt Marosh and his makeshift army under the bishop's orders? And then: What were they up to? The reports had continued to roll in of Marosh's movements within the wilds and mountains of Ardeel. And long ago the army had passed any logical turning point toward Tsobl. The threat of a direct attack on the government was over. His only logical destination at this point was Netz. Unless his intention was to attack neighboring Moldavia. Unlikely. And so, what would so interest Marosh in Netz that he would not respond to direct orders from his government; orders for answers as to what he was doing; and direct orders to about-face and return at once to his county bounds? The messengers had returned empty-handed, and with tales of a General who would not meet with them, or they could not find within the caravan. And once came a tart scribbled note: "You wish I had left the cannons unattended at my home? They are with me because I am with my men and I wished them all to remain in my control. Whatever you fear I am about to do with the central defense's artillery pieces, I will have already done it by the time you come to take them from me—a feat I'd like to see you try."

A minister had opined that the hunt-mad Marosh was just being himself, stalking a great caribou or bear. For the Governor there were only two realistic explanations. Either Marosh had been in communication with the bishop, had developed an alliance, and now they had decided to make public a new military force in Ardeel, one controlled by a true-blooded Ardeelian. Which would be, of course: the bishop. The second possibility was more curious and less likely, but still possible. The old low constable Attila Bronk had been in Marosh's territory shortly before the general's army girded and set itself in motion. The low constable had been working his fanatical way through the old Ardeelian aristocracy, imploring them to join him in an attack on the Count. Had the old general taken to the idea? It was a mad one. But was Marosh now on the move to strike at the Count?

If Marosh did so he would probably die. This wasn't unacceptable to the Governor. One less Ardeelian hero to deal with. But if he were to succeed against the Count, then what? It was the old nightmare scenario: should the native Ardeelians remove the threat which had haunted them for centuries, what would then stop them from also throwing off their secondary oppressors?

"The Cardinal is ready for you," said Rosczy.

The Governor's face reddened and he held back a curse at the bishop's bogus title upgrade. Anyway, he thought, do something fearless, do something bold.

"Governor," the Bishop said, sitting stiffly in a high-backed chair as the Governor entered his office. "I am pleased, if not completely surprised, to see you in St. Grigori."

"Your eminence," the Governor bowed—swearing now he'd never say the word *Cardinal* within earshot of the man, unless the Pope actually hired him. And put it in writing. To ease the situation he kissed the Bishop's offered hand. Or more precisely, he kissed the large ring on that hand. The Governor would not allow his rival to feel the direct press of his lips. Gloved or not.

After a tense exchange of meaningless protocol, the two settled into the night's business. The Bishop/Cardinal remained in his chair, drinking from a chalice at his side with gleaming, challenging eyes. The Governor sat in a smaller, plain wood chair, ignoring the cup of wine Rosczy kept pushing at him. It was the Bishop who finally broke the spell and asked why the Governor had come.

"How well do you know Zsolt Marosh?" asked the Governor.

"I know everyone in Ardeel," bragged the Bishop. "What about him?"

"But how *well* do you know him? He's from further south, after all, and has his own church to see to his soul. When have you last communicated with him?"

"I don't know," said the Bishop with tightened lips. "I am rather busy. If you would get to the point."

The Governor could actually sense his face become redder, and feel the flush of sweat that covered his face and body. His expression could always be as flat and neutral as he wanted it. His body betrayed his inner state.

"Why are you here, Governor?" the Bishop/Cardinal said again.

"I thought you might tell me why Zsolt Marosh is on his way here, along with most of his men."

The Bishop's head quaked, then he regained control. The fingers on his right hand did a little dance and Rosczy offered the wine. It was a motion to buy time.

"Is he really?" said the Bishop. "His men?"

"His army. Most of it, anyway."

"And you think he's on his way *here*?"

"I predict he will arrive in Netz at any hour. He is in the woods."

"So why don't you go ask him yourself?"

"He is in the woods *somewhere*. I don't know where. And he's rebuffed any communications, and won't reply to summons." The Governor flicked an accusatory look at the Bishop. "It amounts to insubordination. I don't want to have to act against him. Better we avoid the chaos and confusion of the bad times, if you remember them well enough." The Bishop nodded.

"And so if I can derive his purpose by other means ... and certainly there is the possibility he is coming to meet you."

The Bishop's mouth pursed. Then a light trace of a smile. At first the Governor thought it was a sign of acknowledgement, an admission of guilt. But then the Governor read it another way: the Bishop saw how it was bugging the Governor, his evasions, and he was enjoying it. And he didn't have to say a damned thing and it would make the Governor's life even more miserable. The bastard intended to let him dangle and twist.

It was a mistake in coming. Unless he could find a way to get the Bishop—*the Cardinal; whatever*—to talk. To give in to him and respect his authority. Maybe he needed to rattle the man back.

"Zsolt could always be on one of his legendary quests to bring down an outlaw bear," began the Governor. "But not with cannon and a supply train."

The Bishop nodded and said nothing.

"So he is either on his way here to perform some maneuvers. Perhaps in violation of our country's desire for peace within its borders ..."

Silence persisted as the ham glistened before the Bishop.

"Or?" the Bishop added as patiently as he could.

"Or he has fallen prey to a man you have met. Attila Bronk. The low constable of Tsobl." The Governor drew his fingers alongside his mouth, feeling sweatier than usual but knowing he had to look in control. "He returned from Netz with wild tales of the Creature, who has been gathering his strength. According to the story, the Creature reached inside your very own grounds to kill your intendant, Neku Jonker—"

Rosczy's platter clattered to the floor. He was forced to set it on a nearby table. The Bishop flicked an annoyed glare at the servant, and motioned for him to leave.

"The creature killed Neku Jonker?" asked the Bishop with a straight face.

"That was his conclusion."

"He didn't conclude that to me."

"He preferred to bring the information to us," smiled the Governor. "So that we might bring the *legitimate force* of our government against the monster's growing threat. You see: the creature had violated your grounds. Something he was not supposed to be able to do. According to some of the histories."

"So it has been said. It *is* true, he has never bothered this cathedral."

"Well," said the Governor, his smile becoming playful. "Until last year."

The Bishop/Cardinal wondered aloud what all this had to do with General Marosh and his army.

"When we refused to move against the creature, the low constable decided to lobby some of the old guard directly."

"You couldn't prevent him?"

"We tried. He isn't an easy man to catch. He met with Zsolt. Shortly after that, he was on the move."

"Is your constable with him?"

"The initial report was that our soldiers caught and killed him. But that's no matter. His idea that our modern armies can kill this creature lives on … in the force that is headed toward Netz. Or more to the point, aimed toward the castle outside Netz. If you have not summoned General Zsolt for your own purposes, there is only one other explanation: He is on a mission to attack that creature."

The Governor paused. His stomach fluttered. He didn't know why he was so nervous. But he was coming to the truth now, wasn't he? The Bishop *had* to react one way or another, and he would know if this robed power-monger was opening a revolution against him.

The Bishop steepled his fingers. Then he consciously took a moment to drink. "Are you sure you wouldn't like some wine?"

"I'm not thirsty. I've just come for answers."

The Bishop waggled his eyebrows, and a smile returned to his mouth. "I don't know," he said. "I supposed I've gotten all I can from you, haven't I? Zsolt Marosh has been turned by your constable into an avenging force—"

"So then it's true," the Governor gasped, almost out of his control. "You haven't sent for him."

"Please—"

"But do you understand the implications! The danger of it! If he should fail … well, just the attempt alone will violate the compact. I was no signatory to it, as are the thousands from the west who have made this region their home. But they will suffer all the same when *he* comes to punish!"

The Bishop nodded gravely.

"And he will suspect you!" the Governor said, almost slobbering, wondering why the Bishop could keep his cool so well, when he himself felt like he was falling apart.

"Some wine," the Bishop insisted. "It looks like you need something to drink."

"Are you listening to me?" the Governor said, his complexion looking mottled and frightful. "Do you not understand the ramifications for you and your church?"

"I understand you are agitated," the Bishop said, rising from his seat. "But you must calm yourself. Here, have some wine. Please, some wine. Rosczy, come! Bring water! You will at least drink some water, won't you?"

"Damn the wine and water. Is there some poison you need me to ingest? Get your hands off me. I'm telling you: He will destroy you and everyone in this town, in this country, if we don't stop Marosh in his act of suicide."

The Bishop rose coldly from the Governor's collapsing body. He let the man slip out of his hands and onto the floor.

"You think I'm attempting to poison you with my wine and my water?" His wrinkled cheeks grew red, the result of having been offended. "I am trying to *save* you with it. And if you had eaten anything Rosczy had offered you while you waited, you would not be collapsing on the floor before me."

The Governor began to gasp. On his knees he reached out for the cup of wine, guided by the Bishop's suggestion. It was the only thing he saw now. The cup. Something to drink. To drive out whatever was overtaking him. But the Bishop now pushed it away.

"No, too late for that. In fact in a matter of minutes you will be dead. And you'll know the answer to a question I have often wondered." His voice growled cruelly: "You spoke of Marosh committing suicide. But, I wonder: Will *you* suffer the punishment of those who have killed themselves? Because it was *you* who kissed my ring. I did not force it on you. I only put the poison on it. And with every offer of food and drink I sought to withhold its effects, to keep you alive for hours after you had already gone. So I wonder now, as I often do, might I still hope to avoid the punishment of murderers when my turn comes for judgment, because I never raised my hand directly to harm, but only to allay the effects of the poison others took through their own actions and their own lips? I don't pretend it is anything beyond an idle hope." He said with a dubious, almost contemptuous note, "But it could be true."

42

White Snow

It had taken some minutes to get White Snow out of the castle. With the gates full open, he faltered there, and fell back again and again as if the stone passage Amalina was trying to send him through was not an exit but the mouth of a beast ready to swallow him into its black depths. But she held on. She gripped the reins and hugged his body with her legs. She felt wild, and her wildness was going to conquer *his* wildness. She growled at him and berated him and told him as much. And once he'd plunged through the gate and was on the road, he was more than obliging to break into the fastest sprint she'd ever ridden, so that she was forced to rein him back before she fell.

"Good, Snowy, Good!" she'd whispered soothingly into his ear. "Just get me down to the Commander. That is all I ask. I'm no Genadie, I won't wear you out into bones. I promise. Just get me there and I'll be off you and you can rest!"

Even at top speed, the ride felt ever-long. The sky was clear, the moon was near full, and the details of the fields and the front of the forest was not much different than what they looked like in daylight, just with a particularly grey flatness to it all. And all the landmarks along the road that Amalina had grown used to over the years passed by, one after the other, at an interminably yawning distance, so that it felt by the time Amalina had hit the dog-leg and rounded the toe of the forest and arrived at the farmhouse she'd seen the Commander's men approaching, hours had passed. Her mind hadn't settled, though. And while she knew she would report all her findings to Kralov, and warn them of the dangers of a siege, she didn't know what she would exactly say, or where to begin.

The old stone farmhouse was sealed up as tight as any proper house in Ardeel. Also, it was unsettlingly quiet. White Snow's protesting snorts—he would've preferred to continue to Netz, or gallop on through to the other side of the continent—was the only noise she heard after she'd climbed down from the saddle. Then came her crunching steps on the hard dirt and dry grasses, and her own beating heart. *But the men must be inside*, she thought. She knocked on the door. She knocked a second time.

"Who's there?" came a tremulous voice. "Who could be outside this simple family's door so late at night? But I beg you to leave us alone. We've left out the signs. We've obeyed all the rules. So leave us in peace, I pray to you. I beg you, sir."

Amalina touched the round of garlic at the door and smirked. Did he think it was the Count knocking?

"I'm looking for the Commander. I need to speak with him."

Her voice was probably unexpected, there was a pause. Then: "Who?"

"Tell him it is Mouse. Here to report vital information. Please open the door. What I have to tell him is urgent and I know he is using this house."

The voice came again, "We are just a simple, law-abiding family—"

Amalina knocked loudly to interrupt. "Tell the men I am here with knowledge that will aid them. And prevent their deaths. Or are they in your barn? Or hiding in a haystack? Come out, Commander, if you are here! Listen to me! Or the Count may destroy you all!"

"Do not shout his name, little girl!" the voice wheezed behind the door. "You will summon him!"

"Or is that your intention?" a new voice asked from behind her.

"What?" Amalina gawked in surprise when she spun and recognized the figure holding the sword. "Piotr?"

Piotr didn't nod, but grinned darkly.

• • •

"The monster's cherub returns." Laughed Kralov. "What timing. Are you here to draw away my focus at the most crucial moment of our operation? Or are you telling the truth?"

The Commander sat on a stool in front of the cart, the one with the metal ram inside it, which was, in turn, housed in the small barn. Though he was sitting and Amalina standing before him, he appeared taller than her, and so much larger than she remembered. He was now in a commander's uniform, and wearing a new fur cap. Flanking him in an outward line on both sides were a handful of his men, with swords restless in their hands and pistols tucked into their waistlines. The uniformity of them and the symmetry of the scene was striking.

And still, Amalina could not keep her eyes from Piotr, who was as handsome—and alive—as she'd last seen him. He'd spoken no more words after his initial greeting, directing her instead with the sharp end of his sword to the barn.

"I saw them bringing the—the, uh, the cart—to the farm. I was afraid you were planning to attack before I got word to you."

"What did you want to tell me?" asked Kralov. "Is the Count coming for us?"

"No."

"Led to us by you?" Kralov's eyes were hard and distrustful even if his tone was light and humorous. "Or ... has he left the castle? What is it?"

"I did as you asked, sir," she said. "And I think I've uncovered other weaknesses that you can use."

He nodded, encouraging her to continue.

"The water in the bottle you gave me. I couldn't get him to drink it. And I couldn't get much on him. It was just a few drops. Or a little more, at most."

Kralov's eyebrows went up, and his lips pursed. He nodded again. "Well?"

Amalina described the Count's reaction as best she could. Emphasizing that no matter how minimal the result, in quantity it may have a stronger, or at least a distracting effect.

Kralov grunted, and smiled appreciably.

"But I don't understand," Amalina said. "All it is ... it's only water. Isn't it?"

"Do you know how I survived that night, little girl, when all the rest died at the Count's hands? Fought him off?" asked the Commander. "I'd have to be very strong, and as capable as him, hm? Not so much *that* then, than luck. When the storm kept us from reaching the village, and night fell, and we knew he was coming for us, we escaped in separate directions. With only three horses on the sleigh—because our unruly fourth wouldn't be put to the harness that morning without a fight—Katrina and Odetta took two of them, and the third pulled the lure-sleigh and Genadie. Katrina went straight for Netz. Odetta rode to the mountains. I, on foot, ran to the forest. We could only hope that the storm was too strong for him, or would throw him off enough that we—or at least one of us—could avoid him. He must have taken Katrina first. Then Odetta. By the time he came for me, without a horse and less easy to track, it was already on toward sunrise, and the storm was slackening. I had made it as far down as the tip of the lake.

"I didn't know where I was," he continued. "All I saw was deep drifts of snow before me, which I dragged my exhausted body through. I hadn't really even noticed that beneath the snow the ground was harder, and smoother, and cracked under my feet after every step. The Count, that creature, he should have known where he was. Maybe he did. But he was so intent on killing me, and in a hurry because of the coming dawn, that he discounted everything around him but me. He came directly, you see, like a charging bear, a roar in his throat filling the valley, and blood vomiting out of his mouth. And he would have killed me as he did Katrina and Odetta had the ice underneath his left foot not given way, and his entire leg fell down through the hole that opened.

"I couldn't understand what was happening. He was twisting and squirming helplessly, like a worm upon a hook, his eyes filled with a wild madness. It would have been rather easy for anyone to have removed their leg from the hole, got it out of the water. But something overcame his senses. At first I marveled he'd been grabbed by a great fish. But no matter, he was immobilized. I couldn't get close enough, with his arms and with those claws—and admittedly, to my shame, from my own cowardice—to take advantage of the moment and strike him. I ran as fast as I could, praying that he would be stuck there until the Spring thaw. He was trapped in a mindless rage, and I only stopped running when I saw the colors along the mountain ridge and knew sunrise was approaching quickly and might catch him. I turned in time to see him cry out, and in a stroke of luck for himself, get his leg out in time to flee from the coming light. Before he did so, he grasped at his leg, as it crumbled under his weight, as if he wished to get hold of the pain itself. Then he burst into a stream of black air that flew toward the forest and the castle.

"Afterward, it occurred to me that his agony might not have been caused by a second creature under the ice, or the deadly cold of the water which would have killed an ordinary man with its shock. But I suspected the Count was impervious to all those things. And so I began to wonder if it wasn't a particular quality to the lake that could drive him to such pain and distraction. And so, with your report, I know it is so—"

"But there's something else," said Amalina, stuffing away Kralov's tale for another time, to think its details through. "Maybe better than that. Have you heard of the metal 'silver'?"

Kralov laughed as if it was a ridiculous question.

"Well, you know sir that it's forbidden within the mountains?"

"I know it is heavily taxed," said Kralov. "It's an export-only material. It's how these bastards keep in business."

"I don't know about that," rushed Amalina eagerly. "But it doesn't do *him* much good, I can tell you."

She told him of the woman hidden below the castle, bound with the silver chain. And the Count's reluctance to touch the metal. His aversion to it.

"And why didn't you tell us about all this before?" Piotr said, matching the suspicion and heat in Kralov's eyes.

"Because I didn't know. I didn't figure out the metal had any importance until recently. Or what the metal was, until a few days ago. And I tried to get to you as soon I could, to tell you. I swear. That's why I came. How should I know you'd be attacking so soon? But now, maybe if you could put it off—"

"Put what off?" said Kralov.

"Delay your attack. For just a little. Make some weapons with this metal. Make nets out of it. Get it on him or over him. He will be at your mercy. I've seen its effects. He's afraid of it.

"That may be," Kralov admitted with a careless shrug. "Or it may not. But it's a little late now. We already have our plan. And we begin tomorrow. When the sun rises."

"But why not have the best weapon?"

"We have it, girl," said Piotr. The soldiers grunted their approval. "And he will never know what hit him."

Amalina glanced at the cart. What was so extraordinary about a ram? or a cannon? She could see the Count laughing at it, dodging it, shattering it into a thousand pieces.

"Are you sure?" she asked, with too much doubt for their taste. They all bridled, even Kralov.

"Oh, without a doubt," grumbled the Commander. "And don't you worry. If it wasn't for you, we never would have known. Well, even if you didn't realize it, and sought to hide it. And then tried to trap Piotr inside that vault so he could not get us the information." Amalina frowned at the accusation. "The lad was smart enough to get the book out, despite your little treachery."

"I didn't seal him in," Amalina protested. "And I tried to rescue him."

Kralov patted the air. "We haven't time, little mouse. What's happened happened."

"I swear it's true. I cried when I couldn't find a way to release Piotr. He knows how difficult it is to open that door. Tell him, Piotr. I tried everything I could. And when I *did* get in, he wasn't there."

"You supplied us with a map of the Castle," Kralov said, charitably. "Not much, but there's that. Piotr, using his wits and all the senses he could in that dark vault, found another route out. And has provided us with a second map, with the secret rooms, extensive as they are, that the monster would have hidden from us." Kralov pulled a folded square of paper from a purse at his hip. He flourished it for Amalina's benefit. "We even know where he sleeps. My, how I have questioned what I was doing—blamed myself for the deaths of my friends, and worried that I was betraying them by not running to a safe land so that at least one of us survived. And how often I've wrestled with my purpose for staying here and risking the lives of even more in pursuit of revenge." He waved the paper again, confidence and triumph in his eyes, even if his lips were set in a scowl. "Tomorrow, the sun rises on his final day of rest."

A secret weapon, a secret map. It was all planned out. So then this was it. The coming end to the monster.

Amalina felt a terrible tug in her stomach. Almost as if something inside her didn't want it to happen. They must have seen it. The men shifted. They eyed her with contempt.

"You've something to say?" asked Kralov.

"Are you sure you don't want to wait? For stronger weapons?"

Kralov shook his head.

"You know he now has—I don't even know how many—maybe close to a hundred new servants inside the castle."

"Twenty-five," said one of the men, a sorrowful look on his face. "Total."

"I wasn't sure," said Amalina. "I just found out today. When I returned. There seems so many more. Are you sure?"

"You returned … from Korr," Kralov added.

"That's where I had the silver identified," explained Amalina.

"Not trying to warn and save your father from us?"

"No," she countered. "And that's why I returned so fast. I was looking for you, to tell you about the silver. The silver!"

Kralov sat quietly, observing her coldly as she squirmed. Maybe the same way he had watched the Count with his leg stuck through the hole in the ice, suffering in the lake waters.

"Well, then if there's nothing to be done with *my* information," she began hopefully, "I'll go back and get things ready. I can keep the gates open for you. Or whatever I can do to help when you come."

"You aren't going anywhere," said Piotr.

"You'll be staying right here," added Kralov.

"But I can help—"

"Better you stay."

"But I might be missed," she said, beginning to feel desperate. "The Count might know something is wrong."

"Nothing was wrong when you left the castle in the middle of the night?"

"He was busy. With his guest. He doesn't know I left. But if I don't come back, he *will* notice."

"Good," said Piotr.

Kralov nodded. "When he sees us coming for him, and he discovers who is missing from the castle, he will know who among his people is responsible for the treachery. And you will be known for what you really are: Kralov's little spy. That is good, no?"

• • •

There were thirty-seven Muscovites including Kralov and Piotr. They moved like shifting hills, slowly and deliberately, and with a physical weight one could feel at a distance. They'd had little rest in the night, even after the

Commander's final pronouncement on Amalina. There was a lingering suspicion among the men, which carried until the early morning, that she'd been sent by the Count to identify their hiding place. So in place of sleep was an agitated wariness, and hands near weapons anticipating a sudden fight. Their fatigue at early-morning light did not show, unless it was an extra length of grimness in their expressions (hidden under voluminous beards) and the downward set of their collective eyebrows. Still, after the Commander observed the brightening sky, and with no cloud to be found, he nodded and sent their attack in motion. And they lumbered forward with undiminished strength and a force of will and determination that held a feeling of inevitability: The Count will fall.

It seemed true. And Amalina felt ashamed that she could not be there, or be a part of it. Her initial hesitation, or unhappiness at the thought of the Count's death had now come round—perhaps because of that air of inevitability—and she couldn't imagine not being present when it happened. Whatever he might think of her, of her betrayal, the vision of Lucinda Skeldar, and of Erik Kosche, and Odetta, and Lady Flauna, and the countless victims she did not know but knew their numbers were legion, made any suffering he might experience at her treachery seem appropriate and fitting. An added twist of the knife. An increased weight to his comeuppance, which justice and vengeance approved of.

But it wasn't going to happen. As the small force shook its arms, stretched, then hauled the cart out of the barn and pushed it to the road, Amalina was held back at the farmhouse door by Piotr, who kept her there with warning glances.

Kralov had recognized White Snow as Lady Flauna's old courser. He nodded and put his head against its muzzle, grabbing it firmly on either side. Then he kissed it once and said: "Lunnsvyet, Lunnsvyet ... if only you'd taken the harness, we might have made it. Well, no matter. You are free. Time to go home." He untied White Snow—or Lunnsvyet as he called the horse—and whipped him on the rump to send him away. "Go! Go!" The horse sped off gladly—toward Netz and beyond—not even sparing a moment to look back at the girl who had hoped, and tried, to love him.

"Are you sure this is going to work?" Amalina asked Piotr as he picked up his sword, knives and pistols.

"We are going to bury him," Piotr answered. Strangely, his voice and attitude had also altered. He spoke with the cheer of a comrade-in-arms. "These past few months we've been stocking the riverbed, just inside the forest, with sealed casks of powder. It'll be enough to send every stone in that castle to the moon. He'll have nowhere to hide."

"I think other people have tried that," Amalina said tentatively, not wanting to upend his positive outlook.

"Not like this," Piotr said. "The book I found in the chest: It's the solution. That's why the bastard had it hidden so deep. He feared anyone knowing its secrets, and they'd come use it on him."

The book from the locked trunks? Amalina could barely remember its title. A Latin text. Or Greek. Something about burning glass. Fires from the sun.

"Believe me," he was saying with a delighted grin, "he will have no refuge but the grave. Should have destroyed that book is what he should have done. And he'll rue the days he kept it whole. Now its knowledge will strike him down. We've been training, and training again. Those men are the sons of Kralov's old circus friends."

Amalina's growing confidence was sabotaged by this last fact. Circus friends? They were performers? Despite their appearance as hardened warriors, what could they really do in the way of combat? What an army!

As they shoved the cart at the road, the string of them looked mighty and deadly. Maybe Kralov knew what he was doing after all. Obviously Piotr knew something from the book that had convinced several dozen men they were about to win a fight no army for centuries had ever done.

"I can't come along?" asked Amalina in her plying, sweet voice. "I really want to. To help."

Piotr's smile slackened and became doubtful. He chewed on its corner.

"You know I didn't lock you in the vault," she said. "You know it wasn't my fault, and I tried to get you out. I've always been on the Commander's side, even before he was a commander."

"You heard his order," he replied indifferently.

"But I can help."

"Not likely."

"You don't know anything," she said. "Look at you. You *and* the Commander. You push off anything you don't like even if it will help you. You see, you sent away my horse, even when you could have put it on the cart and saved yourself the trouble of hauling it to the castle—"

"Shows what you know," Piotr interrupted.

"What do you mean?"

"No horses."

"Why no horses?"

"Because the Commander's men listen to him and obey him. And we're going to the castle to meet the creature. The Commander's seen that thing talk to animals and tell them to do things. Better to never trust some animal our Commander can't command personally, or have them turned against him by a monster who can. Understand now, *Mouse*?"

"Well, I'm no animal. At the very least, I can get the princess and her people out of the way."

"You weren't paying attention," Piotr's smile widened once more but it was hard and cruel. "Anyone inside that castle will die as his accomplice. Nobody will be spared."

"You can't kill the princess!" gasped Amalina. "She's not on his side. She doesn't know what he really is. None of them do."

"And this is why you stay behind, little girl."

The thought of Lisbet being shot, or run through with a sword, or stapled by knives, or being blown to bits by explosives, or burned without remorse, or hung from a rafter, or beaten and kicked to a pulp, hit Amalina like a force which sent her to the ground sobbing. Her friend, the sweet-faced and delicately natured innocent, Lisbet Spaarvierlet, who had been lured by an invitation, and fallen in love, and only hours ago enjoyed the embrace of her future husband ... whatever she had expected by coming to Ardeel, she didn't expect to be caught and executed in a rebellion. Amalina's body shook and she beat the ground with her fist, wishing she hadn't ever gone to Antwerp, hadn't participated in the fate of someone so fair and mild and undeserving.

When Amalina remembered Carila, and Astrell, and the other servants, and considered their demises, she felt like she would faint. She was falling to pieces. Then she remembered Aklan. Matters clarified.

She picked her face out of the stubbly dirt. A string of spit holding bits of mud hung between her lower lip and the ground.

Had she fainted?

The train of men were almost out of sight far up the road. By how slowly they were moving, she wondered if they would get to the castle before the sun fell.

She thought to run after them. It was possible to catch up.

But they would send her away. Or kill her, maybe.

The thought that she had to be there at the castle, to warn her friend and her people—and maybe even Genadie—to get them safely out of the way before the assault began, was as strong an impulse as she had ever known. Such impulses had sent Amalina into dangerous situations before—confronting elemental creatures, leaping out tower windows—and this impulse could not be disobeyed or she was sure to faint again. And she could never forgive herself. Even if it meant her own death at the hands of the invaders—who would see her presence as a confirmation of her alliance with the enemy, the Count—she knew she had to save her friends. Or at least try.

But how to get to the Castle with Kralov and his circus in the way?

They would need to take the road's dogleg around the forest and stretch of mountain. The straight shot would be to cut across the mountain's edge. That would put her in front of them by maybe an hour. But to do so, she'd need to be able to navigate a wild forest, and climb the mountainside at the speed of someone travelling along an open road.

It was an impossible thought. Unless she grew wings there was no way she could get through and over the obstacle—an upthrust of rock which had forced the surveyors of old to, reasonably, build the road *around* said rock— to reach the castle before they did.

At the thought of growing wings she wished she had a pigeon she could send directly to the princess. To tell her to flee the castle (but also to tell the Count nothing). Even if she could do so, Lisbet was probably still in the Count's arms, and her new husband would learn of the warning alongside her. Or even if she were by herself now, the Count being her husband, she would be compelled to tell him. Better to send a message to a servant, or Aklan. Have them take her away to safety.

But there was no pigeon! Stop thinking about it!

Amalina looked to the forest, and the hump of mountain which stood between her and the castle. She sighed, wiped her mouth, and stood up with a growing determination. It wouldn't work, but she had to try. She would get a drink and maybe take a piece of bread from the farm owners. And then she would be on her way.

As if hearing her thoughts, the door to the farmhouse slammed closed. The whunk of the crossbar falling into place behind the door sounded next. She wouldn't be taking any bread or getting any kind of assistance.

Before she began the journey, before she took her first step, she heard a noise.

Just around the side of one of those mountainous piles of hay, White Snow came into view, his head bent toward the ground. He was stupidly snuffling around for a bite to eat from the stubs of grass instead of chewing a hole into the haystack.

She'd seen him galloping off at high speed. When had he turned around? There was no doubting why, though. By design of fate and destiny, he'd been *delivered* to her.

It was still too chancy to barrel up the road past the Commander. They would not only see her and deem her an enemy, they might get off a lucky shot and take her or White Snow down. But with the horse, she thought, as she took his reins and climbed up onto the saddle, she might be able to give Kralov and his men a race by going the hard way.

Amalina set White Snow racing for the mountain.

43

The Wolf, pt. 2

The leaves were red and orange and yellow and brown. And with the bright sun rising overhead and shining through them, the color within the forest was altered and uneven. The sum hue was mostly orange-brown. Which made things murky, but in a pleasantly autumnal way. The heat of the sun was strong where it broke through the canopy. But within the protection of the trees, the season's cool air dominated. Which was a relief. Amalina's body was so coated with sweat by her exertions to stay in the saddle that her clothes were gummed to her skin. Moving the wrong way too quickly was painful as the less flexible material she wore resisted her movements. High summer heat would have been so much worse. She would have fainted by now. Or given up.

She assumed White Snow's opinion—if he had any—would be the same.

Amalina had expected to abandon Snowy not long after they entered the forest, confronted by impassible knots of vines and debris in the underbrush. The idea was to push him as far and as fast as he could realistically go, knowing whatever ground he gained would be faster achieved and farther than she could have gotten on her own. And it would save her the energy she'd need to finish the journey, after the inevitable happened and she was forced to abandon her mount.

But this morning her mind was sharp and her eyes found openings to direct White Snow's hooves. And the horse did not balk at the incline. And though there were no paths or animal trails, he didn't hesitate in the confusion of vegetation and uneven footing. He just seemed to nod his head when she pulled one way or the other, and cantered steadily through the bracken and spaces between fallen branches and rotting tree trunks, and up the side of the mountain until, surprisingly, they reached its crest.

There was no clear view into the valley. But she knew if she hugged the slight curve of the mountain, and kept to relatively the same elevation, she would reach the castle. No need to plunge down the other side unless she wanted to reconnect to the road itself. She could always do that if needed. It seemed the forest was less cluttered at this higher elevation, which argued further for keeping at it.

Her legs became sore. She stopped White Snow when they reached an outcropping that surveyed the valley. She'd never noticed the outcropping from the road. From its ledge, the road was a thin grey-brown line against the yellow-brown fields. It must have been the angle, but Kralov and his men weren't visible. She debated waiting until they came into view, to give the horse some time to rest. White Snow's flanks were dark with sweat, the hair clumped together in tiny wet licks across its sides. She petted him, and flicked away some foam. His breath was even, and he shifted lazily, which made it seem he wasn't too taxed.

It was at this point she sensed a presence behind her. She whirled around. Nothing.

Had it been a sound in the woods that alerted her?

She couldn't tell. One moment she was scouting for the Commander, the next it was like a monster was looming over her shoulders. She coughed once, and then scanned through the trees.

Somehow she had put out of her mind that she was traveling alone in a mountain forest, and in a mountain forest seldom traveled by humans. This made it the domain of the wild. Even if it wasn't a bear, or a wolf, or a wildcat, something as seemingly harmless as a deer or a moose could become dangerous if she wasn't careful. Anything that took her for a threat, and maybe hungry enough, could bolt from cover and stamp, or butt, or claw, or bite. She was weaponless and tired and scared. Not a recommendable condition here.

"Hello?" she said.

Some of Kralov's men might also be on the mountain. Piotr had said they hid their ammunition in the river. They'd been within the treeline when Piotr had come to visit, posing as the messenger. So there might be a set of eyes above a bushy beard staring at her, wondering who she was and what she was doing on the mountain with him.

"Hello? Is someone there? It's Amalina. The Mouse. You can come out." She drew the line at declaring she was with Commander Kralov. What if it was a lost relative of Georg's? "Say something if you're there."

Then she thought: Those men in the treeline—Piotr's men—had been attacked by wolves. A number of those men killed.

Wolves.

The memory of the wolf-pack, led by that massive, vicious black wolf settled over her like a blanket of ants. Her skin crawled at the thought of it watching her, and she felt where its eyes were touching her, drawing lines around her body until they settled on her throat.

"Go away!" she shouted.

Nothing answered.

She regretted thinking of that wolf. Returning her mind to that night— not so long ago—when a set of blood-red teeth snapped at her relentlessly, the death skull gleaming in its eyes, she felt herself weakening as its claws worked at her.

She shook off the memory as best she could. The last she'd seen of it, its hair was on fire and it was running off into the forest. It might not even have survived the burns she'd given it, or the bruises. It was known that wolves, when hungry, would turn on their own for food. And any member of his pack might have taken his weakened state as the perfect moment to depose him, and rule the rest. To have his share of food, ladies, and glory.

With a *nk-nk*, and a rearward kick to White Snow's haunch, Amalina resumed her journey, letting the presence—an ominous presence—provide the pressure at her back, like a stiff wind against a kite. It moved her along.

· · ·

In another hour, she noticed the pitter-patter of dry underbrush that followed in the wake of White Snow's hoof falls. It could have been random drops of rain, if the sky wasn't entirely blue and the sounds so regular. Sounds *keeping pace*.

For the first time in her journey, she came to an obstruction of fallen trees and choking clots of vines that White Snow couldn't find a route through. She would have to backtrack. Amalina had noted a lower clearing a quarter mile back, and without debate turned White Snow around. In the distance, a blur of grey and black shot between trees. She could almost make out the triangular head with shiny black beads for eyes.

She turned White Snow again, and sent him higher up the mountain. Eventually the forest would thin and become more passable, as long as it didn't transform into a thicket of evergreens and fallen trees.

White Snow didn't want to climb. His breaths were becoming labored. Foam was building on his shoulders. But Amalina had no interest in climbing off him. She spurred him with her heel, and encouraged him with her voice.

"Get on," she said.

There was an answering growl to her right.

"Get on … now."

The horse seemed to agree. He snorted but picked up his pace as he found solid footing.

In several minutes, there was an opening to the left and they took it. The oaks had changed to evergreens here, and the spaces in the floor eased into a soft litter of orange and brown needles. White Snow gingerly crunched along, still letting out low snorts. Anywhere else, he might have stopped or bucked her off, just to get some rest. His interest was to leave this forest, just as much as it was Amalina's. Return to the safety of those massive stone walls where there were no predators.

A small growl rose behind them. No lurking, furry shadows ahead. The horse started to trot, but was forced to slow with the branches closing in.

A small growl below them, to the left. Amalina pointed White Snow diagonally upward, to the right. He sounded agreement.

She caught a grey-black shadow out of the corner of her right eye. She couldn't tell if the panting she heard was imaginary.

Amalina didn't know what had convinced her to take to the mountains. Any native of Ardeel knew what lived in them, and few had the courage to enter alone (and never unarmed). And of those few who entered, just a small fraction returned to tell the tale.

"Get on. Get on. Nk-nk."

One growl came from behind and was immediately echoed by the one on the left. Then she thought she heard a wolf at a charge, until she realized it was scrambling through—or over—an obstacle. They seemed to be on all sides and behind, but still no one in front. She had to keep ahead of them. It couldn't be too much longer before they reached the naked strip of land that circled the castle.

But two alternating growls sounded to the left, much closer. The low leaves of a bush shook, and she saw a hairy back. They were pressing from the left. She had to go right, higher along this mountain, toward its summit instead of around to its other peak where it met with the high castle.

A heel to his flank and White Snow picked up speed, pressing forward instead of to the right. Amalina ducked anything that might hit her head and shoulders, but the remnants of lower branches, and reaching arms of shrubs, nicked and clawed at her legs, tearing and pulling at the skirt's fabric. If one clung too hard, it might pull her off. Or if one gouged too far in, it might take off her leg or set her blood flowing.

The wolves knew they'd been detected. One barked. And they came scurrying after White Snow. Their low, slender bodies were built for this terrain. They must have been holding back because they could have easily distanced the tired, dodging horse. Or, anyway, caught it. But they held their distance, only letting themselves be known when it was convenient to their purpose.

They were tiring their prey. It was going to come down to whether White Snow could stay up for the time it took to reach the castle. The wolves couldn't know where they were headed. They could only suppose they were playing their own game, one they had worked many times before. At this point, with the foam dripping off the horse, and its complaining grunts, and loud, huffing breaths, their tongues must be hanging out of their mouths, drool dripping in anticipation.

A decline opened in front of them, with the ground rising on either side. There were no trees in the depression, and it appeared like a naturally formed road, carpeted by debris from the over-arching trees on the opposing rises. White Snow's hooves crunched through this strange pass eagerly, and he broke into a fast trot. Amalina wanted to hold him back, just so she could make sure his leg wouldn't strike a hidden hole. Another voice told her to never mind all that, she should put him into a sprint while she had the chance.

The sides rose higher, and the rock broke through to become walls. She heard the growls above them. When she looked, heads with tunnel-like, violent eyes ducked in and out of sight. They were still tracking parallel. But a leap from that height wouldn't help. They'd missed their opportunity. Still, they followed along, their growls rumbling louder, as if in protest.

Amalina didn't know how far down this path was going to take them, but as long as they were headed in the right direction it had to let out at the castle. She bit her knuckle.

There came a low, rumbling growl, whose vibrations ran right up Amalina's spine. It ended with a bark. A bark of admonition, to draw their attention. It came from behind.

Amalina felt as if her neck and hands were locked into place, and only her lower body was free to follow the rhythm of the horse below her. She could not turn. But she knew if she did, just what she would see. She could hear its weight in its steps in the brush floor.

She forced her chin to the side, and with a wince sent her eye over her shoulder.

The black wolf. It was smaller only because she was atop the horse. But it was massive. And she could tell it was that horrible menace that'd almost killed her by the pink and black scars on the side of its face, where she had pummeled it with the torch, and the flame had sparked and marked it. Even without the scars, though, wouldn't she recognize it from the fiery hatred in its eyes? and its champing, snapping teeth?

Amalina knew what was about to happen.

This cut in the mountain was leading to a dead end. At some point it would stop, and they would be cornered by the black wolf.

The pack had been steering her—shepherding her—the whole time.

Now the black wolf's comrades chittered and yapped, telling their commander that they were there if he needed them. But he would be free to take this reward himself: a pretty white horse, and a delicious little human.

Amalina told White Snow to sprint. He did.

The monstrous black wolf howled and sped right after. He increased his speed, gaining ground on them.

There was no way to escape the alley, its walls were too high and steep. The only exit was back through the wolf. Unless, by some miracle, it did not stop but let out.

The walls curved to the left, and when they straightened, Amalina saw the end. The stone walls pinched inward, with loops of tree roots connecting the two sides. The roots were like fingers, or wooden bars of a cage. There were large holes below and above them, allowing a flow of water or air, should it wish to pass through. Anything larger than a small dog was trapped. To confirm this, after a second of analyzing their plight, Amalina noted the bones on the ground of animals that had been caught just so, and had been too big for the wolves to drag away or section off.

White Snow tried to pull up short, hauling itself onto its hind legs. She thought he was going to try to leap over. Instead, as his back legs skidded through the clattering remnants of previous kills, he brought his forelegs down on the roots, as if he could smash through them. All he accomplished was to break one of his hooves through, and then crash bodily into the rock; coming to a full stop.

With her momentum, Amalina flattened into his neck, the horn of the saddle punched her in the ribs. She gasped. But feeling White Snow's body falling backwards, and time seeming to slow, she grabbed hold of his mane, and hand over hand, now using the saddle horn as a ladder rung—and with the wolves in the upper margins howling at her, or chomping their teeth at her in the hope of snagging her—she carried on over White Snow's head and fell to the ground. On the other side of the barrier.

She stumbled, and tumbled, and rolled through the bits of branches and broken pinecones and carpet of brown-orange pine-needles. The sharp ends of everything tore and pierced her hands and she was carried along by momentum, down the slope, and tried to right herself.

White Snow let out a cry of terror she'd never heard from a horse.

She didn't want to look back, but when her head and eyes turned of their own accord, the black wolf's face appeared in the lower hole, with its forward paw digging into the ground as it tried to work its large shoulders through. It had its eyes fastened on her, their burning yellow black telling her how much it wanted to rip her to shreds.

How much farther to the castle?

What did it matter? She ran. There was nothing more to do.

She tried to keep at the same elevation and not slide down the decline. Wherever the forest let out, she wanted an even plane to the castle, or still have a downward slope as an option. If she had to run uphill, she was doomed.

The rock walls fanned out to the right and left. She didn't hear the wolves who'd taken the higher ground, but had to assume they were there, even if they were being led further away. It was still too high for them to jump down safely. Or so she thought.

She ran, wishing she'd worn something that didn't drag her. The skirt was billowing between her legs, checking her speed.

When the black wolf wove its body through the hole, it howled in ecstasy. The horse was stuck and could be taken at their leisure. The morsel of human flesh would not be allowed to escape.

The walls were coming down to meet with her current level. The trees thickened and grew before her, with large branches and fallen trees creating new walls, with thick foliage filling in the cracks.

The black wolf tagged Amalina's legs with a paw.

She fell to the ground and rolled, hoping it wouldn't be able to climb on top of her before she could turn to face it.

Just like the night so long ago, his shredding claws fell to her chest as his open mouth, white fangs inches long, descended toward her face. She felt the claws dig into the fabric of the cloak, and its weight knocked her breath out. But somewhere inside her terror-numbed brain, there was a part that was alive and racing to keep things that way. She accepted the claws and the weight, there was nothing that could be done with it. Her fists swung up on both sides to catch the wolf's head. Her left thumb accidentally hooking into the corner of its mouth, her right thumb catching the upper lip, and index and middle finger landing on either side of its eyes. Her fingers instinctively clenched inward, even while her arms fought the force of its neck, its body, as it champed toward her face. Her body curled, slipping between its hind legs, and her knee went upward into its groin.

She screamed as it howled.

Their momentum had them rolling end over end, like a fur and fabric wheel, sending up needles and leaves in their wake. The wolf's forelegs couldn't sink its claws in as deep as it wanted because of this unnatural movement. In the meantime, Amalina used her fingernails to dig into the soft flesh at the corner of its lips, and gouge and scratch its eyeballs.

But there was no way to avoid its fangs, it dove its snarling snout down toward her soft, vulnerable neck, its head turning in anticipation of clamping into a death clutch, with a power she could not overcome. Instead, she lowered herself, and curled even more, and met its nose with her forehead. She felt its sharp teeth cut into her skin there. When the mouth shut, she turned her own face up and bit into its chin.

With its mouth forced upwards, it couldn't howl as it wanted. Her fingers continued to gash and gouge as she bit chunks out of its chin and along the jawline. The wolf squirmed from side to side, trying to find an opening on her. She became aware of a fatigue within her own body, and felt the stings of its front claws, cutting finally through the fabric and into her body.

They threw each other away, its back claws digging into her stomach as it did so. She didn't care to see where it landed, but turned and plunged down the slope of the mountain, wishing she knew where she was, and where the castle was. And maybe Kralov had men in the forest after all, and they might hear the struggle and come to her rescue.

Instead, there was nothing but another fence of fallen trees and branches. The black wolf had fallen back to make sense of where it was, and what had happened to its face, trying to lap the blood with its tongue, but now it was ready to return for her. But here she was: boxed in. With another glance, as she saw the black wolf make its charge, the other shadows of its pack were coming down from the earlier slopes to meet with it. They would all be on her. And she saw in her mind Erik Kosche laid out in the snow, his body nothing but a bowl of finely chopped-and-stirred gore. This would be her.

She could climb the fence of interlaced logs, or try to go through the small space at the bottom. She knew she was too tired to climb, and she would be too slow, and they would bound right over her if they wanted. She dove like a rabbit through the lower opening, imagining and hoping she might be able to fly right through it. She didn't.

Her hips and the skirt caught on the numerous teeth of broken roots, twigs, and branches. Her legs were still back out on the other side. The black wolf bit into her ankle. She kicked hard, and spun around and figured the other wolves would leap over the wood and onto her upper half. She scurried and shimmied, and felt more paws and teeth tearing at her legs.

Amalina spun and kept spinning, hoping the movement would confuse them and deflect snaps and claws. When she spotted the large branch in front of her, she grabbed onto it and pulled as hard as she could. Instead of pulling herself through the hole, the branch pulled free of the ground cover. She cried as a tooth bit through her shoe and into the bottom of her foot.

She kept screaming as she worked her way through the hole, hoping there'd be something left by the time her leg came out. The wolf held onto her foot and it became a tug of war. She began to move in the wrong direction.

She took a handful of whatever was next to her and threw it over to the other side. Screaming all the while.

Whatever happened was distraction enough. She was able to pull her hips through and then her legs and then her foot. The shoe came off in the wolf's mouth. She saw its face through the hole, a portrait of hateful eyes and teeth. It came right after her, shoving itself through the hole.

But its upper body was much larger than Amalina's hips. And in its virulent, unthinking hate, it managed to wedge itself just as carelessly as she had.

She thought to run, but then she saw the heads of the rest of the pack come peeping over the branch-and-root lattice fence.

Amalina grabbed the branch that had come free. She brought it down on the black wolf's head. Its howl of protest only drove her mad. She ignored the red pool that was gathering below her feet, coming from her own body, and pummeled that big, furry head with a fury she hadn't known since their first encounter. Only this time, the wolf was caught, and she was going to bludgeon the thing until its brains were falling out of its open, white shell.

She yelled at its stunned pack: "You see that? You see that?"

• • •

Amalina's small figure emerged from the edge of the forest just feet away from where the black wolf had entered it so many months ago, howling, its head on fire. She stumbled and brushed her face, and tried to recall just what had happened, how had she gotten here. Then she remembered the plan, seemingly hatched months ago, of riding through the mountainside. Where had White Snow gone? Oh, yes. And where had the wolves gone? She saw herself battering the black wolf's head. Was it dead? She didn't know.

She found Aklan outside the open gates.

"Princess Katarina?" he gasped, taking her hand. "Are you all right?"

"Yes. Yes," she said, running a hand over the bloody trails on her face, taking away the leaves and needles from her head, and trying to compose herself. "Here, let's go inside and find your sister."

"What happened to you?" he looked appalled, and distraught at her obvious injuries, her slight limp. Then narrowed his eyes at the tree line for what might have hurt her.

"Never mind, just a little accident," she said. "Hurry. Let's gather everyone we can. We're leaving the castle this beautiful morning." She winced at the pain from her ankle. "To pick flowers."

44

The Subdued Siege

Carila finished wrapping Amalina's ankle and gave it a light kiss. Then she said: "Now you should get some rest, dear."

"It's too good of a day," Amalina groaned as she sat up. "Let's round up the princess and everyone, and we will find some beautiful flowers in the forest. Late bloomers. It's like spring in the fall. And there's a spot of irises I've never seen before, with purple and black and red dots. And there's so many! Let's go."

"You're a very silly little girl," she clucked. "You stay here until you're recovered."

"There's nothing to recover from," Amalina argued, feeling the ache from the claw rends on her chest, which the old maid still didn't know about. Not that it mattered if the rends had been tended to. Even with the bandages on her legs, and her head cleaned and tended to, the bite wounds all around felt like strips of fire. "Just some scratches."

"Did something hurt you in the forest?"

"I just fell, I'm telling you."

"Into a thorn bush?" Carila's old wrinkly cheek dimpled as she smirked at her mistress. "You won't tell me, milady, what you were up to all night?"

Kralov and his men, no matter how slow they were, must arrive soon. Whoever wasn't outside the gates—whoever she failed to get outside the gates and hid away from the siege—would be dead before nightfall. Amalina pictured the large, white-shirted men coming up the road. That sent her off the bed. She covered the limp well enough. She went to the window and removed the covering. As the cool air blew in she heard only the birds in the forest. The road wasn't visible from her side of the castle.

"Find Lisbet. Find the princess," Amalina said in a commanding tone.

"That's easy enough. She's been in the Grand Gallery all morning. Or, I should say, that's where they found her this morning."

"The Grand Gallery?" wondered Amalina.

"You know ..." Carila fumbled, unsure how to make it clearer. "The *Grand Gallery*."

"I'm not sure what you mean. You mean the rookery?"

"The what?"

"With the pigeons? The birds?"

"No, I mean Count Tepsji's Grand Gallery, with the paintings and the sculptures."

Amalina looked at her curiously.

"You don't know of it?"

"Maybe I just don't know what you're describing. Can you show me?"

Carila conducted Amalina down to one of the many doors that had always remained locked, one which the Count would often shoo her away from when she was poking around. This door, she noted, was on the exact opposite side of the castle as the one to the Great Library. So, a Great Library on one end, a Grand Gallery on the other? And where once the hallway used to be plain stone, new tapestries and decorations announced there was something here to be discovered.

Astrell stood outside the door looking glum, but when she noticed Carila and Amalina she fixed them with a cold look.

"Is the Lady still inside?"

"She doesn't want anyone bothering her." Astrell's eyes flashed at Amalina.

"The Lady Tepsji should be no bother," Carila admonished, sharply. "They're close friends. This is her home. And the Lady would see her guests are comfortable."

Astrell made a face, but bowed and opened the door.

"You remember now?' Carila whispered to Amalina.

"Of course, of course," returned Amalina. "Now go get all the princess' people to her suite to prepare for an outing. Do it right away. I'll send Lisbet up as fast as I can. We can't delay or the day will grow too hot for anybody's comfort."

Amalina went through the door.

The Grand Gallery was as immense as the Great Library, though without the massive wall of windows at one end. It had a roaring fire in a fireplace so large one could walk into it, and many torches in the wall, and a giant chandelier with all the candles lit. All this light made it possible to appreciate the hundred or so paintings, and its four collosal statues. Amalina decided fine art must have been another of the Count's various interests through the years which he'd found valuable enough to keep and warehouse.

"Good Morning, Katty." Lisbet was at the far end of the room. She wore the same dress she'd worn last night. Her hair was an unkempt bush. Even when Amalina reached her, her gaze fell upon the walls in an unfocused way, only her chin slightly turning in Amalina's direction. She was smiling, and both her eyes and mouth moved between expressions of thoughts of pleasure and recollections of pleasure. Amalina recognized this as a sickness of love, so often and so eloquently and passionately recounted in poems and romances. Only it came off terribly in the moment. It was nothing Amalina would want to mess with, especially knowing what was fast approaching the castle. "How is your uncle this morning?"

"I haven't seen him." Amalina threaded her arm through Lisbet's. That seemed to break the spell a little. The princess relaxed into her side. "But I'm glad I found you. We have to go."

"Where?"

"No time to discuss it, Lees." Amalina quickly related her amazing finds in the forest, while she pulled Lisbet, the thin girl, from her spot. It was like trying to put a boulder into motion.

"Flowers," Lisbet said politely. "I don't think I'm done here yet, Katty. Such a marvelous collection. I'm surprised you never told me of it. That you never showed me. All this time practically imprisoned in that library. Quite embarrassing to think I didn't know of the gallery until this morning, Katty. It was naughty of you to hide such a quality aspect about your uncle. If only you'd let me in, I should never have questioned your uncle's *standing*, which led to, well ... and then ..."

"And then?" asked Amalina.

"Do you think he cares for me?"

"Now's not the time for that sort of thing when the irises await, Leesy! They might be wilting already!"

"But let me see this one more time before we go, Katja dear. My beloved."

"Just a quick turn."

"Do you think he cares for me?"

"You spent some time with him," was all Amalina could think to say. "And he you."

Lisbet sighed and hugged Amalina's arm.

"What a beautiful collection it is," she said.

The Grand Gallery's paintings were mostly pastoral scenes, featuring vast shafts of light striking down on barely clothed people, who were either falling over onto grass or into bales of hay, or were dancing, or were swinging on swings, or were eating great meals off a blanket. There were a handful of portraits of sober looking monarchs with voluminous amounts of hair on their head, and eyes that told the viewer they were prepared to leave the painting to do more historic things.

One painting Amalina recognized immediately: It was the gift she'd been given by the Princess Derhovna. Amalina made a noise, something like a gasp of outrage.

"What's the matter?" Lisbet said, peering into the harmless portrait of Derhovna's favorite horse.

"I was going to put that one in my room," Amalina growled resentfully. "The Count apparently thought better of it. I'd wondered where it had gotten to."

"I'm sure he didn't mean any harm. We can ask him. Where is he, do you know?"

"I'm sure there's some business."

"Oh, no!" She was crestfallen. "He won't be joining us on this flower expedition?"

"He might," Amalina lied hopefully as they approached the door with Astrell watching them from it.

"But I'm still not done, Katty, let's just give it one more tour. I promise."

They circuited the room one more time, almost as if in a dance, turning around and this time looking inwards at the marble statues of beautiful women in Greek fashion lounging on uncomfortable rocks, with cascading hair and powerful faces and bodies. Amalina tried her hardest not to look at them too much, or seem as if it were her first time seeing them. She pretended to be casual, if not out-right bored of them by their familiarity.

All the while Lisbet carried on with her sighs.

"Do you really care for him, then?" asked Amalina, in wonder at the power of love.

"He isn't happy with me?" she gasped suddenly, almost in tears.

"I told you I haven't seen him, dear. And of course he is happy with you, or he wouldn't have you here."

Lisbet sighed.

"But I was talking about you, dear silly love. I was talking about you. Yesterday you were so upset, today you are something else. I can't wonder if it might change again so fast."

"Oh, no, I don't think so ... He is quite an interesting man."

Amalina nodded, thinking, *only how much do you really know?*

"I mean, you are a very religious girl, aren't you?" said Amalina. "If you were to stay on and to love him, you will spend half the time in town because, as you know, he doesn't go to church, and he spurns most things that are of a religious quality. He doesn't even possess a bible."

Lisbet shrugged, smile still firmly set. "He says he's lived a very long time, and seen many things, and that he has his own convictions, spiritual and otherwise."

"As devout as you are, this doesn't bother you?"

She shook her head. "Really, my father is *much* older than Lord Tepsji, and so he has seen *many* more things than your uncle. And my father has opined negatively as much as your uncle has opined negatively upon religion. Also, my own uncle, who was once ordained a priest, he renounced his religion after suffering some terrible blows he does not speak about. And, as well, my dear Katty, there are those holy men who go into the woods to speak to god, and never again set foot in a proper church. But they are still holy men. And even more so: Who's to say my Lord Tepsji isn't the same as these hermetic holy men, living up here in the mountain, speaking to nature and hearing heaven's voice speak back to him?"

"The Cardinal—who we both like, I remind you, Lees—would call such things heresy."

"Count Tepsji doesn't strike me as a heretic so much as a free thinker. And if he is one, well … I see myself as a tether to his soul, to pull him up if he should fall too far." Lisbet looked at Amalina now, but her eyes were still dazed. "You don't love your uncle?"

"Not like you," she evaded with a polite grin.

"He's so very intelligent," Lisbet went on. "Wise. Knowing. Insightful. You know, he speaks of top smells and bottom smells. He perceives and understands the world far deeper than anyone I've ever met. He can look at chaos and describe its order. Do you understand that, Amalina?"

"Not really. What is chaos?"

Lisbet smiled at her own thoughts, then regarded the Grand Gallery again. "Why, Katty, why didn't you tell me of the gallery?"

"Oh, I knew of the room, of course, and of all the pieces of art," she said. "The Count is quite a collector. It is well known. But he's certainly done it up better than I've ever seen it. Anyway, I'm sure he wanted to impress you without my getting involved."

At this, Lisbet gave a strange, almost swooning look and capped it with a light nod. "I'm impressed beyond expression. Looking into this room … It seems he's captured everything in the world."

Yes, it seems he has, thought Amalina, as she passed the love-struck princess into Astrell's embrace, the princess seemingly unaware of the change. Unaware of many changes. She was another person. The darkness that had haunted her since her arrival had definitely lifted.

"Please get your Lady ready to leave … Fast!"

• • •

How much time had they wasted talking? Amalina couldn't wait any longer. She had go to the wall to see if Kralov was nearing the castle or had already arrived.

As she climbed the stairs on the inside of the outer walls, she heard the creak of a wooden axle. She peeked out a narrow lookout. Coming up the approach road was the small force of men, their white shirts stained with sweat, their beards and hair matted down on their heads, but looking no less determined. Some pushed the cart along, some were before or after it. Kralov and Piotr marched at the head of the column.

My god, it was too late! They were here! There wouldn't be an escape for anyone. And when they found Amalina, besides suspecting her of witchcraft (by having transported herself ahead of them), there would no longer be a doubt in their mind to whose side she belonged.

She fell back from the opening, but then realized she probably couldn't be seen in the darkness as long as she kept to the right angle.

There's no telling how long it would take for them to enter. Georg's family had closed the gate when Amalina and Aklan came back inside. Did anyone know there was now an enemy force set to invade? It's not like there was a proper watch along the battlements.

Running down to the courtyard, chest and legs aflame, her scalp feeling like there were nails driven into it, Amalina caught the new footmen loafing outside the main building. They were watching two children playing with a dog. The day well progressed, the courtyard was a lively place, with smoke rising from several small huts, and the murmur of many people engaged in whatever craft Georg had assigned them. She was about to tell them to fetch their head of staff, but then she thought to look towards the gate doors.

Amalina's felt a lump grow in her throat.

"You two," she said quickly, "bar that gate! Bar it now!"

They started to move in the gate's direction, startled into action by the roughed-up little girl barking at them. But their heads kept turned in her direction. Staring. Wondering who she was that she felt confident enough to tell them what to do.

"Go!" she said, going for the castle door, driving them there, "There's no time! There's a bunch of marauders outside who will kill all of you! Hurry, save your skins!"

Now they went for the gate at a trot, still throwing back looks. Who knew if they'd get the locks up in time?

Charging back into the main building, Astrell and the other maid blocked Amalina at the entrance.

"Oh!" said Astrell. "Princess!" In the morning sunlight, Astrell now noticed how worn and bruised Amalina was. The bandages. "What's happened? Are you all right?"

Amalina assured her so. "But where's Lisbet?"

"Sh-she's thinking of resting, milady," Astrell stuttered, unsure, eyes surveying the damage on Amalina's exposed skin. "If Count Tepsji will not be coming, you see. That is what I'm to ask you, Princess."

"Go to her!" Amalina panted. "All of you! Find the footmen, your drivers, everyone. Get to Lady Spaarvierlet's chambers immediately! I'll meet you there."

Recognizing Amalina's urgency, and coupled with the fresh and disturbing wounds evident on her body, the maid's face contorted into a mask of panic. Amalina shook her head, spun Astrell around, and sent her bowling back through the other maid and into the castle. She shut the door on them.

There hadn't been any shouts from outside the walls. She had to see what they were up to, to gauge how much time she had on her hands. How much time to plot some solution to this new predicament.

Back at the top of the battlement, she leaned the top of her head out, holding her cloak over it to obscure who she was—and not present an inviting target for any marksmen among them.

Strangely, Kralov and his men were ignoring the castle entirely. Only two were faced toward the castle, the rest had their backs to it. Kralov was talking with Piotr and a couple others, his hands describing something slowly in the air. The rest had pushed the hay out of the cart and were retrieving their weapons from its bed. Somewhere along the way they'd decided to strip themselves of their swords and pistols. Perhaps to lighten themselves as they shouldered the cart up the steep approach to the castle. The blades flashed in the sun as they swung them and returned them through loops in their belts. Brown powder flasks went on their sides too. And pistols, loaded, were stuck in at the waist of their pants.

Piotr removed his fur cap and wiped his brow. From behind, his shoulders were wide, and the way the shirt hung damply from his body it caused her to think of Erik Kosche. Erik had been blond, blue-eyed, and sweet—sweet up until the end. Piotr was darker skinned, brown haired, brown-eyed, and with a hardened disposition. But, from Amalina's vantage point, looking down upon him from the high castle wall, they shared a vulnerability that made her fear for him.

"Who is that?" Aklan said at her side.

"Get down!" she cried, sweeping him off the stone lip. "What are you doing here?"

"What are *you* doing? Who are they?" then Aklan got a look in his eye. "Was it them? Were they the ones who beat you? And you escaped!"

"No."

"And they followed you! Are they barbarians? But I recognize them from the big city. That's them, isn't it? It is! Look at them!" he didn't look the least bit frightened. He repeated excitedly: "Are they barbarians?"

"No," Amalina insisted, trying to calm herself, remembering who she really was: their spy. *The spy that shouldn't be in the castle.* "They're good men. Unfortunately they have a dispute with my uncle. It's too long to explain, but we can't get in their way. They're riled up and they might just kill us if they catch us."

"They don't look riled up," Aklan said. "It looks like they're planning a picnic. They're cold-blooded barbarians is what they are."

"No, they're not."

"They are if they're gonna kill us. Why are you sticking up for them?"

"I told you it's too long a story. Now we have to get to your sister and remove everyone to a safe place until they leave."

Aklan cocked his head and narrowed his blueberry eyes at her.

"But Leesy doesn't know I'm here."

"That doesn't matter now. You want to protect her, don't you? Now, go! I'll meet you at her room, just give me a minute."

"What are you doing up here?" said Abraxa, coming along the narrow walkway just as Aklan ran in the opposite direction. "Who was that?"

"Isn't he one of yours?"

"Never seen him before," she said. "Now, tell me. Who are those men outside? My gracious, you have this whole house worked up."

"*I* have them worked up?" said Amalina in amazement.

"They think there's going to be a massacre. Why would you lie about such a thing?"

"You asked me about those men outside. Well, they're the ones who are going to do it! They plan to kill everyone in this castle."

"How do you know?"

"Can't you see them?"

"They're just standing around."

"Have you seen their weapons? They're preparing for a siege."

"They could just as well be here to defend the castle. If they want to attack, why haven't they done so already? Why haven't they declared their purpose? No, it doesn't make any sense."

"I'm telling you, I heard them. I know who their leader is. He was one of the people who tried to destroy the Count last spring."

Abraxa's non-existent lips retreated into her mouth in a strange pucker.

"Stupid little girl, riling everyone up like that."

"Listen to me, everyone has to get out of this castle. Get as far away from these men as we can or—"

"No, no, no, no," Abraxa cut her off, closing her eyes and shaking her head. "What disorder you bring! Leave the castle? While we are *inside* this castle, we are safe. While we are under the protection of our great liege lord, we are safe. You said it yourself, Mouse: They tried to kill him before. And they didn't, did they? Nobody can harm him. He is all powerful. He will turn their violence against them and send them to the fiery pits. How can you have any doubt about this?"

"Their commander? He's survived the Count's attack. He has come back with a way to destroy him. I'm telling you—"

"No, no, no, no. And again: No." Now a fear was in Abraxa's beady bird-like eyes. "You doubt. You doubt, you doubting, ill-bred mouse. You doubt our master, when he is everything. It will be noted and told. When we have stood by him … and trusted him. How else could"—and here she gulped on her words—"how else could Georg have devoted his entire family to his eminence's care and protection? How could Georg, with all good conscience, have assured the sum of his flesh and blood that they would be safe if they should come here and serve this—this man of *perfection* and *grace?* Would that beautiful man, Georg, now have them believe he lied to them? That he put them all in danger? Would he have them doubt—as you dare to—doubt the great Lord Tepsji in this trifling moment, knowing full well when it is over, that if our sudden doubt in his ultimate power is learned of, we would suffer the fate of all those who've stood against him, and felt his wrath?"

"You have to believe me. Prepare them. At least some of your people can escape. The women, the children."

"The men outside the *palace of pleasure* are nothing."

"The palace of—?"

Amalina's words of incredulity, in the face of Abraxa's blank-eyed terror, stopped when the whole wall shook, dropping them off their feet. And the report of a great explosion echoed through the courtyard and the castle.

45

Attack on the Palace

There were some shouts, the barking of dogs, the cries of children, but it all died down quickly as the smoke rose from the courtyard below, like an unusual dark mist. The smell of sulphur and burning wood brought tears to the eyes, and now came coughs and choking. Amalina got to her feet first and offered Abraxa her hand. The old maid ignored her. Propped up on an elbow, her head was bowed toward the stones and she croaked despondently: "Told them they would be safe ... Swore on his life they would be safe ... No one would come to harm ... Georg promised ..."

The battlement walls wrapped around the castle, and in the rear one sprit of it connected with an upper floor of the main building (it was below this bridge that Genadie's hovel stood). Amalina would use the route to reach Lisbet and her people. Where they would go from there, she didn't know yet. Better to have them in her sight, anyway. Then come up with a plan. She gave up on Abraxa and headed around.

Kralov cursed angrily down in the courtyard, Amalina paused, saw him waving his arms. His men joined with him trying to drive the cloud away.

"... Going to cost time!" he yelled. "Get those fires out! Get this smoke out of here. What the hell were you thinking, Piotr?"

Georg's extended family, standing in small groups, stared at Kralov and the handful of men who had entered. Some of the children and older folks joined in with the arm waving. The smoke lingered in a swirling form, though its lower skirt was already lifting. None of them engaged with the invaders, not so much as to begin a conversation. There seemed to be a general understanding that speaking to these strange mammoths who'd blown through the gate, and even looking at them for too long, would be unhealthy. Some of the giants' long, curved blades caught the sunlight through the smoke with random, blinding flashes.

Had the Commander's secret weapon done this damage? It would be something if the Count could survive such a burst if it were directed at him. But according to the histories: *he had survived cannon fire.* Or he had at least evaded their blow and went on to demolish the weapons, and with them, the men who'd brought them.

Looking over the other side, Amalina saw that the cart had been removed to a safe distance from the doors, off the road and onto the grass. Whatever the secret weapon was, it hadn't blown the doors apart. It was still resting half-buried in the hay.

"Huh," Genadie grunted ruefully, standing opposite Amalina and peering down into the courtyard. "The Muscovite. Come to have another taste. There are fools at every age."

Genadie was hunched over, he had his hand on the hilt of his knife, which protruded from his belt much the way Kralov's men's pistols did. He sniffed and rubbed his face. "Look at those pathetic mudsitters, the whole clan, parading around without a thought. Might as well strike up a dance with Kralov's brutes—and just where did he get them?—for all they're doing." Amalina realized he was complaining about Georg's family now. He seemed to become chatty when his nerves were worked up.

"What are we going to do?" she asked him.

"Nothing to do but wait for the Master to clear them out. It shouldn't be long. Nobody lasts long."

"But they've sworn to kill everyone in the castle."

"Have they?" Genadie asked with raised eyebrows. "Well."

"What can we do?"

"Stay out of their way until Master strikes. He can't come outside, you know. The sun is still up. I suppose Lady Flauna's toady thought it would give him some advantage."

"Won't it?"

"Only if Master decided to meet them outside. He isn't that stupid."

"Where is he? Do you know?"

"Ms. Dalca," he chided in his scratchy voice, his eyes still squinted down into the courtyard, with lips struggling awkwardly between a frown and a smile, "Master is everywhere."

• • •

It would be impossible for the castle's hallways to be any quieter than what Amalina experienced on a mid-winter's day when only the Count, Amalina and Genadie lived there. But the silence *felt* greater because of what was happening just outside the main building. A storm of violence was gathering, and yet the stone corridors were hushed in a way that suggested peace. A peace Amalina had grown accustomed to. And now, as she headed for Princess Lisbet's suite, she regarded the tapestries and bits of armor clinging to the wall and the bowls of crocuses, and felt an amazement to know that at any moment they might all be torn down or blown into the air.

She knocked on Lisbet's door. But then hearing the stir of voices behind it, pushed in.

The conversation stopped. Princess Spaarvierlet, at the center of her people, hair down and make-up half applied, was the most surprised by her entrance, but then the most relieved. There was a step in between the two expressions—surprise, then relief—a slight pause, almost like a hiccup, when a shadow passed across her blueberry eyes, corrupting them. Shame, or embarrassment, or circumspection. An inward realization of her own falling away from something. She had woken up fully from her love-spell in the gallery. But then she was coming forward with her arms flung wide, her face declaring her relief at seeing someone who, even if Amalina could not save her and her people, could at least explain what was happening. Surely this group of men who'd just blown through the gates weren't here to escort their flower picking expedition.

"There isn't much time," said Amalina. "Theirs is a private quarrel with the Count, but they will be hostile to anyone they find. It is in their nature."

"Where is your uncle?" Astrell shouted. The way Lisbet batted her eyes, and guiltily avoided Amalina's gaze, it was a question she had been asking her servants before Amalina arrived.

"But as I told your Lady, I haven't seen him since yesterday. When did you last see him, Lees? Last night, or this morning?"

Again, the guilty eye flutter and the glance to the floor. She evaded: "I don't see how he will be able to protect us. And I know he wants to protect us. Doesn't he? I'm afraid, Katty."

"How are you going to save the princess from this?" Astrell shouted again. "If she dies here, don't you think her parents will be here with an army to repay you?"

"If she dies here, we all die here," Amalina said calmly. "Those men plan to blow the castle to pieces, so there won't be any place for her family to look for us to give payment."

Lisbet's footman and driver, the two men of their party, smirked and traded glances. One ran his hand through his hair and fixed his eyes on the door. The other rubbed his fist in his palm, as if buttering it for a punch.

"Your uncle," Lisbet reminded her.

"Of course, Lisbet. He will see to our safety as best he can," she said. "And protect his beloved high castle."

"The Palace of Pleasure," brayed a voice, sarcastically.

"Yes, there's not much of that right now, is there?" Amalina answered the heckler. "I'm under the same threat, so I'm just as worried and frightened. But ... now where's Aklan?"

"My brother?" Lisbet asked, surprised. "He's at home. What are you—?"

"You mean he didn't ... ?" He hadn't revealed himself. That was obvious now.

"Are you all right?" said the nameless maid, concerned.

"Yes, I'm fine," nodded Amalina "Never mind. I meant to say … no, never mind. Carila hasn't been here?"

"She was," Lisbet said. "But she went to look for you again."

"Well, we have to see to our own protection, just to be on the safe side. Right now this is probably the best place to be. They are looking for the Count and they wouldn't expect him to be up here. Please, for your convenience and comfort, if we have to move, it would be best if you had whatever it is you'd like to carry with you. Nothing heavy, but do gather what you think best to bring … if we are forced to leave."

Lisbet nodded.

"I'll find where Carila's gone. And see where we can move safely should needs require."

Amalina started downstairs, thinking she'd see what kind of defenses were being mounted in *l'entrée grande*, the grand entrance. If the Count wasn't there she'd seek him out and learn what he intended to do.

She slapped her forehead (setting off the pain in her scars).

Wait. Whose side am I working for? Better to pin him down, somehow. Sabotage his chances against the Commander.

She thought of tearing down any covering on the windows. Letting the sun in where she could.

The thought of doing it was too much. She was already exhausted. The pain in her lower legs and chest were connecting and building a trail to join the pain in her head, making it pulse.

I'm working for myself, she thought. *And to return to papa in one piece. Let everyone else battle it out.*

It would be helpful to know where the Count was. But she knew Kralov could be battering down the front door any moment—or exploding it and the whole entryway to splinters. Better to not be there when it happened.

She returned to the wall. She would spy on Kralov. See what he was up to and then make a decision.

Genadie was no longer on the upper walkway. Neither was Abraxa. Thankfully Kralov hadn't sent any of his men up to scout the castle. Evidently he had his own strategy and was comfortable letting some strategic points alone. His manpower was limited, after all. She hoped no one would spot her from the courtyard when she peeped over.

Under Kralov's supervision, small kegs were being stacked near the main building's front door. It didn't appear they were going to be used to blast the door, but were being properly arranged for some other purpose.

He looked up into the sky and seemed to measure the position of the sun.

"Princess," said Aklan, pulling at her dress.

She whirled and snapped at him: "I told you to go to your sister!"

He put his hands out in a gesture of what-can-I-say? "She was already in her room. They all were, so …"

"But you weren't!" Amalina accused in a harsh whisper. "What if we'd all left?"

"Where are you going?"

"That isn't the point. You wouldn't be with us!"

"She can't know I'm here. Please, Princess Tepsji, she can't." Then he motioned. "But here, look what I did."

"What did you do?" Amalina growled impatiently. Then, seeing his wounded look, realized she was being unfair. "Well show me. What are you talking about?"

Without a second thought, Aklan grabbed her hand and pulled her around. They arrived at the point in the wall she had tried to save his life. He pointed over the side.

She looked down but didn't see what he wanted her to see. It looked like the plain stone wall, the castle's midden below.

"Look," he insisted, not elaborating.

Then her eyes found the darker area where the privy let out, where Aklan's legs had been dangling once. From the hole there was a barely visible line descending from it—it was an effort to focus her eyes, so that it was more than just a vague blur—a line with a bulge every so many intervals in it, until it ended in a delicate swirl on the ground below.

"What is it, boy?" But she already suspected. There was an upward lilting note of hope in her voice.

"A rope. A proper rope," he said, his face looking dead serious, but proud. "Wouldn't reach down there from here, but it's fastened tight where it is, and the hole's big enough even Carila can get down through it. As long as she's good to climb on a rope. We can leave by it, princess. They haven't any barbarians down there. They're all in the front, like the bunch of stupid savages they are."

"They aren't savages and they aren't barbarians," Amalina reminded him sternly. "I'm telling you, they have their reasons for doing what they're doing. But we can't get into it now. Let's just get everyone moving in the right direction."

"I'm not going," Aklan said.

"Yes you are."

"My sister must never know I came. My parents will kill me."

"Your parents already know you're gone, don't you think?"

"But they don't know where. I could be hiding at any of our homes. I've done it before. Fooled them for three months, once. I swear she can't know. Ever."

Amalina shook her head. It didn't make any sense, but she didn't have time to waste. If he didn't want to go, he didn't want to go. She'd find some way, probably at the last minute, to convince him to get to safety. Maybe when more of Kralov's bombs shook the castle apart.

"Go out first then, if you like," Amalina said after a thought. "Hide in the forest somewhere close. And watch out for animals. But get going. I'll have one last look and then we're coming, too. Though I can't imagine how I'll convince your sister the dignity of this exit."

Aklan beamed, nodded once and ran.

Amalina crept to her old vantage point. Each time she moved, she lowered at the waist, and crept like a hunted rabbit.

In the courtyard, the kegs formed three neat and tall pyramids. She assumed these were loaded with gunpowder.

Kralov shook Piotr's hands, while all of the men formed themselves into ranks. He nodded at them, too. Then he came around to give each one a hug, sometimes pushing his forehead to theirs, his fur hat knocking theirs back.

She thought to go but was entranced. There was something happening here. Something important, and solemn. It needed a witness other than Georg's family, who had given them a distance of yards, and who were being ignored like harmless farm animals.

Men broke away from the ranks.

The cart entered the courtyard.

Sixty some hands cleared aside the hay in the cart bed and clutched at the metal ram. Amazingly, the large metallic cylinder began to separate.

At every seam in the "ram" the metal split off, until Amalina understood these were individual pieces. They had been stacked, one after the next, until they appeared to be of a piece. Individually, Kralov's men held what looked to be wide and deep metal bowls with handles affixed to them. The men took to polishing their concave side with cloths, giving them some last minute touch-ups.

A few of the men pulled from the hay large crystal orbs, which, for their mass, the muscled men had to hold with two hands.

They found their places again, after adjusting pistols and cutlasses, and gave each other grim nods. At the Commander's direction, two of them— one with a bowl, another with an orb—parted from the group and trotted to the door beside the blown gate. Amalina supposed that meant they'd be heading up the stairs, and would be joining her on the parapet in a moment. She had to clear out. She checked around for Genadie, to warn him if he hadn't seen the men coming.

Down in the courtyard, Kralov kissed Piotr's cheeks one last time, hugged him. And then, with a theatrical flourish, he pointed towards the front door. His men began marching straight at it, like they could pass right through as if it was a beaded curtain.

• • •

In the hallway just outside the privy, the princess' two footmen and driver were slowly letting out lengths of rope. Their faces were red, a sheen of sweat on their brow. The driver had taken off his jacket. The knotted rope extended in a taught line from their hands and down through the large square hole where the privy seat had once been.

"The last one," one of the footmen told Amalina. "Then we can let you down. We'll come after. No need to worry, the enemy isn't below. It's no time to turn your nose up at an escape, whatever the route, milady."

Amalina was confused: "How did you know about this? I was just coming down to tell you."

"Carila."

"So everyone is outside the castle already?"

"The second driver and all the lady's maids."

"Except Carila," said the driver. "She's stayed behind."

"I'll be staying, too," announced the second footman, bravely. "To see to our lady's defense."

"Lisbet is still here?"

"The Spaarvierlet's are never ones to run," said the second footman. "Same goes with their daughter. She's a brave one."

"You all go," Amalina commanded, passing them to head downstairs. "This is my home, you know, and the Tepsji's never back down from a fight."

Lisbet's rooms were empty.

Heading down the stairs she could hear Lisbet's voice crying out, searchingly: "Count! Count Tepsji!"

"Lees," called Amalina, then she met Carila and Lisbet. "For your own good, come back upstairs. You have to leave here until this threat has passed."

Lisbet hugged Amalina. "You're alive. I thought they'd taken you."

"They won't take any of us, dear Lees, if we escape. Please let's go back upstairs and—"

"Where is your uncle?"

"I don't know," Amalina said. "I still haven't found him. He's probably laying a defense with what he can. But you're my responsibility."

"I am *his* responsibility," said Lisbet, her eyes growing harder than Amalina had ever seen. Her sweet, gentle face turned downward, the tiny petal-lips descending almost rudely at the corners. "I am most certainly *his* responsibility, if the eastern gentleman would claim it. Will he?"

The princess was clearly wounded at being abandoned after a night in his arms. Amalina recognized, in this moment of peril, Lisbet had assumed her lover would be at her side. But he'd forsaken her, coldly abandoned her. The wound was doubly sore by being so close to her early morning's reverie over him.

"Whatever he is doing, he is doing it for you," Amalina told her. "But he must do it in his own way. Let the men have their war, we'll clean up after them. As long as we survive, Lees. That is our job here. To get out alive."

Princess Lisbet petted Amalina, then turned back down the stairs: "Count Tepsji! Count Tepsji! Why are you not here? Please, good and honorable lord, come to my side. Come to me. Where are you?"

"She won't come with you," Carila apologized to Amalina as they trailed after her old charge.

"What about you?"

Carila shook her head. "Even if I wanted to I couldn't fit down that hole."

Amalina asked her how she knew about the escape route.

"Master Aklan showed me when he found me. He wouldn't tell his sister himself, but ran away and left me to it. As much good it is. Small as she is, she won't go. Big as I am, I can't. And I would have liked. But if the lady won't see sense, I'll at least see she gets out of the way when the battle begins. Save yourself now, Princess."

"I'm trying to save everyone!" countered Amalina hotly. "But nobody's interested!"

She didn't follow Lisbet and Carila, but listened as the princess' pleas faded and took on a longer echo when she reached the lower floors. Where was she going to go?

Where am I going to go?

She didn't know where the Count was. She didn't know where Genadie was. She didn't know where an agent playing on both sides fit into this scenario.

After a thought, she ran back upstairs, hoping the footmen hadn't already cut the rope.

46

Kralov's Circus

Kralov's plan was to enter the main building in full force through its front doors. The invaders couldn't afford any more unruly motes of smoke as what had filled the courtyard when they brought down the gate. Gunpowder was now withheld, even though the bolt barring the building's front doors was so thick that, without an explosion, a large battering ram, which they didn't have, would be needed to crack it off its hooks. Other measures were taken.

Minutes ago, one of the men was hoisted on three of his friends' shoulders, stacked like a ladder, to a high window. He carved through the skin covering it and found his way through the castle and to *l'entrée grande*, the castle's large entry hall. He had only to show his pistol to Georg's nephews, who were bracing against the door (and with slumped shoulders they broke off and found something better to do for the afternoon). He knocked the bolt out of the way and pulled the doors wide.

Three men charged into the hall. The way they made little hup-hup noises under their breath, and their whole form bounced at the knees with a shared rhythm, it had the look and feel of a trained performance. The first man stopped at the door and held his pistol threateningly to all that were inside gaping at him. The second man bolted across the room, over the table, and then landed with an extravagant roll next to the pedestal with the goblet along the furthest wall.

When this second man came up, in a defensive crouch position, he held between his two hands and at chest level the metal bowl. The concave part of the bowl pointed into the room.

It wasn't until the third man bounded in, on the opposite side of the door of the man with the pistol, and held up his own bowl at chest level, that it became obvious the second man had some definite purpose. The second man rotated at his hips, pointing the bowl at the third man. The third man shifted his bowl back and forth. And a strong beam of light lit up the room as its brilliant point traced along the wall, directed by the third man and his bowl.

The second man was reflecting sunlight from the courtyard. And that light was redirected in turn by the third man so that there was not one point within the room that could not be instantaneously hit with a powerful and concentrated shaft of sun; should they want it so.

Hup-hup-hup, and the sweaty, white-shirted musclemen flooded through the door, trying as best they could not to disturb the flow of the light. Some men placed down kegs of explosive, others brushed back Georg's people with the sharp length of their swords. It was a deliberate and well-paced performance, with the only odd element being the servants, who did not understand what was happening and couldn't decide where they should put themselves.

Piotr entered quickly and regarded the top sheet of paper in a small stack he was holding. He pointed at the closed door, the one which led to the antechamber feeding to the private study.

Some men stuck their heads into other rooms and doorways: the rooms leading to Genadie's old closet, the great hall, the hallway leading to the kitchens, the passage to the Great Library, the passage to the Grand Gallery, and the stairs of the towers. Each man shook his head negatively at whatever he'd seen.

Piotr nodded and waved back to the entrance.

Kralov entered. He was holding a cocked pistol in one hand and a set of pages in the other. He consulted the sheet and then pointed at the door that led toward the private study. Piotr agreed. He directed more men in.

The human sun machine's gears rotated as more connections were added. Five new men sprung in from the courtyard. Piotr opened the door to the next room, the private study's antechamber. One man rolled in and set up unseen at its far end. Two more men ducked in. The beam transmission was adjusted and the other room lit up, and a large bright dot could be seen flicking back and forth across the inner walls. Then the kegs of powder went in. The operation was so methodical and well trained it appeared as fluid, as mechanical, as regular, and as smoothly inevitable—and yet as delicate—as the inner workings of a clock.

Kralov pointed to the side hall which led to the kitchens. Piotr acknowledged. A new force was sent in that direction so that the beam could be directed there if so desired. Kralov prepared himself for that route, but gave his young captain a final signal. Piotr went into the antechamber, intent on entering the private study.

• • •

Coming through the shattered front gates, circling the rubble and fractured planks in the courtyard, Amalina saw how the men stationed along the parapet of the outer walls had arranged themselves at angles so they could turn their mirror bowls and direct the sunlight at each other. They were playing with it, creating a mirror-sun on the mammoth stone wall of the main building. With their great strength, the metal bowls appeared supple enough to bow inward or outward when they flexed their arms, so that the beam dispersed or concentrated as they preferred. They rehearsed their motions and their control of the ray until they were satisfied. Down inside the courtyard a man on his own was able to capture the sun directly from the sky and sent its reflection into the building.

Understanding what they were about, she avoided the beam as she passed through the wide open double-doors. Two men with pistols and swords positioned on either side of the door glared at her, warning her to stay out of the way. They didn't seem to recognize her. Or if they did, she'd become just one of the rest of the Count's meaningless crowd now.

Despite the light ray, Amalina's eyes had to adjust to the darkness inside so that she didn't trip over anything. She followed the trail of relay men to the inner rooms.

"You," said Kralov behind her. Piotr turned from his position at the open study door. His jaw fell open. Kralov pointed his pistol at Amalina, but his voice was gentle, even as his brow lifted and he eyed her with a suspicion so strong it looked like he expected her to rip her skin off and reveal herself as the creature he'd come for: "How are you here, Mouse? How?"

"Snowy ... The horse," she said, matter-of-factly. She traded glances between the two men. Kralov's boys looked unsure on what they should do. The hot light brushed over her, and she was forced to put a hand up to protect her eyes. She squinted painfully, and saw a trail of red over everything she looked at. She blinked to try to dispel the effect, while telling them: "I told you I wanted to be here."

"So the Mouse declares her loyalty to Kralov!" Kralov shouted. "Did you hear that, foul creature? Your Mouse is mine and always has been! She has been working these many months for your destruction! How do you like that?"

Amalina tried not to choke on the sudden lump in her throat. If the Count was around, he'd heard it. She could only shrug now and hope Kralov's plan worked. Apparently the idea was to bring the sun to the Count by way of a network of mirrors handled by seasoned acrobats. Another lump, one of fear and doubt, joined the first one in her throat.

"Stay next to me," Kralov told her under his breath, his pistol aimed at her chest. "He may still have a softness for you."

The operation continued. They entered the study. Two men opened the cabinet and then pried it away from its hinges with their swords. Next was the treasury, the counting room. Then down the stairs into the massive vault of letters, books and papers: the Count's message archive.

The act altered. The first man leapt expertly atop one of the low, central row of shelves and held aloft one of the heavy crystal globes. The shaft of light was sent from the treasury straight into the ball. The room glowed suddenly with the approximate light of ten blue-flamed torches. The shelves and especially the papers seemed to glow in that strange cyan light.

Piotr stood by the central shelves and studied his map. Then he surveyed the room and found the shelf he wanted. He indicated a place on the left wall for the benefit of the men and their commander. A new man, holding only a mirror, jumped up on the central shelf while others placed powder kegs all around the room. Then those men prepared their mirrors.

Amalina tried to get a look at the map in Kralov's hand as he lowered his head to study it. Even in the brighter light, it was difficult for her to make out anything more than a network of unevenly sized squares.

Piotr went to where he'd pointed. A secret switch caused the shelf to slide backward, creating a new passage. Kralov's men flooded into it without hesitation. The old commander prodded Amalina and she followed them in.

Except for some strangely shaped alcoves spread unevenly around the room, the room was a barren, stone cube. But after a second glance, Amalina saw that the alcoves were not alcoves at all, but spaces between stone brick protrusions. Each protrusion was a little taller than a man, and a little wider. Their shapes were mostly the same, but some had rounded tops and some flat and a couple were pointed. Above each one was a word in fading black paint. One said: Cellar. Another: Kitchen. Another: South Egress.

It occurred to her that these brick protrusions were the seals for doors and passages, which the Count used to plug up or cut off access to parts of the castle. How many times had she thought a door should be somewhere, but it no longer was? Or a door she'd never seen before had suddenly appeared. Here was the solution to the mystery: The Count's door-stone storeroom.

This revelation to Amalina meant nothing to the men. They registered no expression beyond their incredible determination to grind forward.

Two open passages, on opposing walls, led out of the room. Piotr looked to his map and then pointed to the passage on the right. The sun machine— not quite as bright as in the grand entrance but still bright enough to make one squint, or feel an uncomfortable heat if it passed over one's skin—went into action.

Any doubt that Kralov's plan had potential was put to rest in the next room.

The first man died in a spectacularly bloody fashion. As he sprinted for the far wall, a sudden blur hit him from the side and his body sprawled out across the floor, spraying blood from a headless stump. The next man charged in, but running backwards, with the crystal globe in his hands. The light piped in from the courtyard filled this new room with its eerie glow—except where the shadow his body and hands cast—and the count, as a blur, shot around the room until he fit into a shadow.

What Amalina hadn't noticed was the small powder keg attached to the man's waistband, with the short, lit fuse sparking near his belly. She only caught a glimpse of it as someone's arm pulled her backward hard. And she saw the man with the lit keg turn with a shout toward the Count behind him, who'd been lunging to tear his head off.

The explosion rocked the castle, and sent dirt and debris flying into the storeroom, falling from the ceiling, tearing through her clothes and skin, and clattering with a drizzle of muffled clicks and clacks against the walls and onto the floor. The sound and its concussive force had Amalina's ears ringing.

She heard a yell, which would have been loud if it didn't sound like it was under water, as she was pulled further back by the wrist. Back into the message center. Back to where the air was still relatively clear and the sun beam was visible through the haze—though perhaps not as potent. Piotr was holding her wrist, guiding her to safety. His hand was sweaty.

Kralov's invasion was delayed ten minutes for the air to become clear enough to return to the next room and continue on.

But as they pushed forward, the black blur blew past the front man and entered the message center. The blur was not as fast, and not as blurry as before. And it moved in a jerky, uneven way. There was a desperation to it. Like an insect that had been blindsided by a swat but not killed. And when the blur stopped, here and there, at a conservative and careful distance from one of Kralov's men, the Count was seen panting, his large eyes glancing around the edge of his shielding, uplifted cloak, regarding the abdomens of his enemies, searching for the smaller kegs. His face was pure white, and his expression neutral. But he was looking, and searching.

One man hit him directly with a beam of concentrated sunlight.

The Count went for the mirror that provided the light to the one attacking him, to take it (and its man) out, only to have the mirrors shift and that man now sweep the Count into his light path. The Count shot away toward the exit, only to be blocked by another man holding a mirror. The Count reeled backward, his eyes spinning and he looking confused. Everywhere he tried to move, one of the acrobats, almost with prescience, met him with a bolt of sunlight that forced him elsewhere, from the front or the back. Their faces were tight and angry, and they played with him—or so it seemed—for almost a full minute, as they targeted him and prevented him from moving—no matter how fast—to the safety of shadow.

When they got him into a corner, three men had already anticipated the move, and with lit kegs jumped at him.

At the same time, several loud pops sounded, as the men positioned atop the central shelves, and one near to the Count, fired their pistols. The blows pushed the Count back and stunned him.

There was enough time for Kralov to burst out a laugh of triumph.

The Count threw backwards the men with the lit kegs and rammed through the one blocking the door to the door-stone storeroom. This last man's mirror hit the ground along with his right arm.

The three men with the lit kegs knocked their burning fuses to the floor, where they hissed impotently like sparking, fiery worms, to a finish.

Kneeling, Piotr wrapped a cloth around the torso of the one who'd lost an arm. His skin had become as light as ash and his eyes fluttered, but his face was still set in that same grim determination as earlier.

"It's all right," Kralov said to Piotr and his men. "It's no matter that we only made it here. Here is good enough. Piotr, shut that door. Molko, set the petards."

The door was shut and then everyone went to work, with the bulk of the powder kegs transferred from the courtyard into the message center. It took a tense half-an-hour to convey it all, under the protection of the lights, and gunmen ready with their pistols.

Amalina was unobserved, and she brought water for the dying soldier, who'd been dragged to the side and was now crumpled up against one of the shelves. His eyes were closed, but his lips pressed weakly outward to meet with the cup. He drank. She petted him, and had to press hard at the thick hair before her palm reached his head.

He muttered something.

Amalina looked to Piotr.

"He wants wine," Piotr translated.

It sounded like things were coming to an end. Conversations grew louder, with their manly voices ever more confident since the Count hadn't returned.

When she looked about, light glinted off a piece of metal inside one of the shelves. It left a ghost trail in her eyes. Blinking, she walked toward the shelf opposite where she stood, from where the reflection came from, and saw that it was the section—the single shelf—devoted to Korr, her village. Amalina took a candle. The glinting metal had been so shiny, it reminded her of silver. But the Count wouldn't stock silver right on the shelf, would he? She lifted the candle and squinted into the deep but barely-occupied space.

Sitting on top of some scrolls and other pieces of paper and envelopes was a book of considerable size. On its spine were three large, raised letters made of polished steel. The letters spelled: AXP. Amalina sucked in a breath. *AXP*, the sign-off on the Count's most difficult coded message! And this book was AXP's correspondence. It originated from Korr. She reached for the book.

Raised voices made her turn around.

"I told you it's no matter, Piotr," Kralov was saying. "All he had to do was show his face. We know for a fact he is here and he is injured. Now, if he isn't dead already, we bring the castle down on top of him. There will be no escape."

"I want to see him die, Commander. I want to kill him. It was because of him my brother was murdered. I will have my vengeance, Commander. You understand that."

"If you go after him, my silly boy, and he isn't dead, he will kill you."

"I'll take some men with me. They'll be more than willing to take the chance. To kill him with their bare hands. If you want to stay behind, keep a torch and no fuse. If I die, let blow as you will. But with the chance we have, let me have my vengeance, Commander."

The Commander did not look at Piotr, but motioned to him and said almost tenderly, "So do it, Piotr."

"I'm telling you," said Piotr in a pleading voice, "there is nowhere for him to go! With the sun in the sky, he will be there. He has to be."

"And I said: Do it!" growled Kralov, irritably. "Who am I to deny any man his vengeance? It's why we're here. Only, take men who are willing and understand the risks."

But all of them were willing, it seemed. If they weren't, they wouldn't have come on this impossible mission.

Piotr opened the door. The men were ready with their mirrors and pistols and swords and kegs tied to their waists. He didn't even hesitate but pushed the first man through (the man holding a crystal orb), and then went straight for his position right after. The rest followed in, just as resolved as before, but their upbeat hup-hupping had disappeared in the tragedy and the loss of their comrades.

Amalina couldn't bring herself to touch the AXP book, to bring it out. There wasn't any time to be messing around. She couldn't take the book and leave the castle to study it. She should see the mission through and witness the end of the Count, if that is what was going to happen. Just like Piotr, she had to know for sure. Raining tons of stone onto him wouldn't satisfy her. There was always the chance that he'd somehow escaped.

So she left the book on the shelf, and the Commander and the remaining men inside the message room, and followed after the brave, handsome, vengeance-minded Piotr.

In the door-stone storeroom, Piotr was readying his men to push into the passage where the first of them was killed. The circle of light being sent in struck the wall above the man's crushed and minced body, illuminating a splash of blood. Amalina noticed the man's eye staring at them over his charred forearm. His head had toppled and come to rest between his elbow and his shoulder, as if he were holding it. She closed her eyes and turned.

When she opened her eyes, she noticed what she should have seen upon entering.

"Piotr," she whispered.

His head spun and he glared at her, his eyelids half-lowered and deadly. She pointed around the walls.

Along the walls, the gaps between some of the standing doorstones were wider. Six piles had been taken away. Centered above the now empty places were the words: Corridor; Cellar; Wheel; Wine; Egress; Chamber.

Piotr referred to his map, dabbing his finger on it in places.

"Swords, Commander," he called to the message room.

Five men came through, cutlasses and torches at the ready, kegs tied at their waist. There were no fuses on the kegs, only open holes. Amalina hoped no sparks came off the torches at the wrong angle.

There had been two passages the first time they'd entered. Piotr pointed to the seemingly solid wall where one used to be. The Count had sealed it up. Piotr consulted his map again. Then he looked between the open corridor and the now blocked and hidden passage, his face pained by his own indecision.

"Did he think we'd notice he'd blocked a route, to make us want to move in that direction?" said one of the men with a heavy accent. "Or is he trying to force us in the direction he wants, by leaving one open?"

Piotr smirked irritably, the man's words only echoed the questions he was trying to answer himself.

"If he put up a wall, he must have gone that way," Amalina said helpfully.

"Take her," Piotr told one of the swordsmen. The man dropped his sword, and with lightning speed had hold of her neck. "If she says another word, cut her throat."

Amalina wanted to gasp, or react in some way. She shut her lips tight, so that they mashed and wriggled. The hand gripping her neck tightened, making her feel the pulse in her veins, and caused strange patterns to shift in front of her eyes. She coughed and his fingers withdrew minimally.

"He doesn't know we have a map," whispered Piotr. "We go where he will most logically be, never mind his evasions and mis-directions. He's trapped in this castle and he will be found."

Piotr gave one last glance at his map, nodded confidently and pointed to the open passage. "That way."

The men poured in first, setting up the sequence of mirrors to light the way. Before he went through, he told one of the men with the kegs: "Stay at this wall. If one stone in that blocked door shifts, blow the room. The Commander will take care of the rest."

Piotr didn't wait for a reply. He moved forward.

The swordsman gripping Amalina's neck shoved her after him.

Beyond the scorched passage came a room with a tub and several large murals of food and figures frolicking in sundrenched landscapes. Then there was a room containing large jars sealed with dried skins. It had the air of the treasury, with a small standing desk in one corner. No one was interested in stopping to find out what the jars contained, and they kicked through the door leading to the next room.

They didn't even stop to look, but went through impatiently, and they found themselves in a chamber whose walls were stacks of skulls. Piotr grunted, as if remembering something when he'd come through the first time, presumably with nothing to light his way. And he'd come alone, and desperate, and expecting the Count to swoop down on him at any second.

Stones were locked into the opposite doorway; or what Amalina assumed was the doorway. It was as smooth as any of the other castle walls. Solid blocks of stone set immovably together. But that rectangular clearing in the skulls is what marked it.

"Out," he said. Three swordsmen attacked the stone joints with their weapons. They prized the stones, one by one, grinding and cracking with metallic ringing sounds, until they removed the first layer.

Piotr grunted again when it became obvious there was another wall behind it, but this time the sound was accompanied by a savage smile.

"He's inside."

The ghoulish chamber of skulls warmed until stifling with the heat of the light concentrated on the stone blockade and the churning of the swordsmen at work. When they were done with the next layer, they were breathing heavy and staring at a new wall.

"Has to be the last," said Piotr. "A round of water and catch your breath."

They shook their heads and heaved at the wall. They'd all been at work since early in the morning. It must be mid-afternoon by now, if not moving towards the evening. They hadn't paused, they must be exhausted. But they chose to continue on, knowing if they stopped they would feel their exhaustion even more and be tempted to stop altogether.

"Parley," said Genadie.

Everyone stopped. Amalina saw the opening before Piotr found it. One of the skulls had been removed, and a black void stood behind it.

"Parley," Genadie's scraping voice said from the hole.

"What is that? Is that you, Count?"

"The Master of all there is in the world waits for you behind this wall. Should you enter in peace, he will grant you it. Should you enter in malice, know this is your final act on earth, and he shall meet you on the other side to enumerate your eternal punishments for having dared try him."

Piotr scoffed.

The men carried on at the wall.

"Don't let Kralov have misled you," Genadie argued, or taunted, or both. "Why isn't he among your number now if he so believes in this mission?"

Piotr put his face up near the hole, but at a safe angle to avoid anything shot through it. "If the Count is in any condition to offer the parley, let him speak for himself. Otherwise, he's already halfway to his doom, and all I can say to you is: prepare to die alongside him."

Stones were coming out of the doorway at a fast clip. The sunlight was shone there to protect the hands working around it.

"Fair warning," chimed Genadie. "Enter on your knees, you will be preserved. Enter on your feet, you will be spread across the mountains, even your skulls will not find a resting place within the room you are laboring. You will die. Evaporated. Forgotten by the living. Forgotten even by those who once bore you and loved you."

"We have a hostage," Piotr told him. "Move against us, the baker's daughter dies first."

The skull was placed back into the opening.

The doorway was freed of enough stones so that entry was possible. The room beyond was pitch black. The men looked to Piotr for his command.

Piotr nodded.

One of the men holding the globes backed into the next room, while two men stood on either side, prepared to dive in after him, their torches ready to touch off their kegs—instant death for everyone. Piotr had tossed aside his map. He shook his sword's weight in his hand and cocked his pistol.

Amalina was shoved through next. Then came her escort and Piotr. Then two more men with mirrors, who caught the main beam and directed it at the figure lying in the large bed.

Genadie was huddled up next to the bed, his knees to his face, looking like a large dog who'd been shot in the groin. He peeked through this hands at them, unable to bear the light shining at him.

The Count was in the middle of the bed, atop the white silk sheets, but under his cloak. His whole body was pulled tight and cowering beneath the black cloak, and only his hand was seen at the upper edge of it, clutching it protectively. When the circle of light went to the hand there was a mild hiss, and the hand withdrew.

The grip on Amalina's neck relaxed.

"Master," Genadie whispered at the cloak. "They are here."

The white hand, in the shadow provided by the cloth, waved weakly and dismissively at him.

Piotr's teeth were gritted in an animal snarl. His eyes concentrated on the thick cloak. Amalina wanted Piotr to attack, as did the men around him. But he stood there as if mesmerized. He wanting to draw out the moment of revenge until it satisfied him.

Amalina worried that this is what the Count wanted, too. Everyone was looking at the black cloak on the field of white silk. Maybe he was going to fly down from the ceiling in a sneak attack from the shadows. But when she looked to the darker corners of the room, nothing was there but an old dresser, a tapestry and some paintings, and a couple black-lacquered standing cabinets.

Genadie hissed at the Count's enemies. And the lump under the cloak moved slowly, the sign of a wounded, dying creature. Maybe the explosion and the bullets had done enough damage to him after all. And he was fading out.

Piotr stepped toward the bed, and lifted his pistol to point directly where the beam of sunlight concentrated. Where the Count's torso slowly shifted.

"Count Tepsji," he said with a shaking voice. "Creature of death—"

The beam cut out.

47

Attack on the Palace, pt. 2

First came the light spray of sparks from the flint on Piotr's pistol, followed instantly by the sideways flash of powder at the flintlock. Then the shoooooffff-bang shot from the barrel, illuminating the room the way the light rays had done. But only for a fraction of a second. Then the light fell off, the sputtering, dying torches spinning into a neutral corner of the room. Kralov's men, who'd held those torches a moment ago, losing their forearms in the sound of screams, cracking bone and splitting sinew.

Whether Piotr's shot hit the Count didn't matter. The Count hadn't paused, but disarmed the intruders and then flew from the room with his customary jarring hum—which would have been paired with his black blur had there been any light to see by.

The whirr and hum and the press of air as the Count turned the room into a whirlwind had Amalina spinning. There was no more hand gripping her neck. That had gone. Long ago.

The darkness filled with moans and choking breaths. And soft, wet sounds from all around that Amalina could not assign images to. No one was talking. It sounded like they were all dying.

She thought to call to Piotr. But then she remembered Genadie had been by the Count's side and was probably still in the room. In case Piotr was still alive, she couldn't say anything to Genadie, either. These were Amalina's thoughts in the immediate aftermath; still slanted toward self-preservation. She felt shame. She wanted to lie down on the floor and go to sleep, welcoming oblivion over confusion. Why had the Count not killed her?

Without a light, she didn't know any route out of the room besides the way she'd come in. She held out an arm, and feeling the air with her hand and searching out with her toe, she made her way back to where she'd come from.

The Count hadn't re-erected any of the walls. Her return to the message center was slowed only by the darkness, her rattled memory of the path, and random debris. But when she arrived at her starting point, the message center, it was just as pitch black, with no sounds to be heard at all. She only felt the air of the room change, as the unseen walls widened out, and the ceiling lifted. She stumbled blindly through the bodies and kept going. Up the stairs, through to the study, and through the antechamber, until she reached the first light.

L'entrée grande was lit by ten torches and there was a great fire in the massive fireplace. It would have appeared as a normal, almost inviting setting, with the table laid out sumptuously to over-flowing for the eventual feast. But the large room was empty of humanity. Not even a child or animal was there. The only sounds were the discordant rings of steel and the cries of men floating in from the open front door.

She went there.

In the courtyard Kralov's cart was overturned. A handful of bedraggled rebels hunched over on this side of it. On the other side several of their band fought heatedly against a number of men wearing authentic soldierly dress: leggings, breastplates and helmets. Kralov was behind the cart, beet-faced but calmly loading a pistol. He glanced up at the sky, noted the sun's position and shook his head. Then he noticed Amalina.

"Here, here, here," he called to her.

She walked the distance, almost casually, but with a stunned expression. It felt like she was in a dream. On either side of the battle, and at a prudent distance, was a wall of Georg's people, staring at the contest with empty expressions—whether it was blank-faced stupidity, or solemn observance was unclear. She didn't think to wonder where Georg and Abraxa were.

"Damn, damn, damn," Kralov said at the end of his cursing. He was having a difficult time feeding the powder down the barrel. "The castle still stands, Mouse. Why? Piotr?"

"I … I think he died."

"Damn, damn, damn. Why did I come out here?" But then he grumbled in irritation at himself the answer to his own question: "Had to see what happened to the light. Should have just assumed the worst and set off the powder. What was I thinking? Reinforcements … of all things, Reinforcements! Come to the castle. Took down my boys in the courtyard— and our sun supply. Curse my stupid mind for not thinking! I told him vengeance was not our goal," he said, speaking of Piotr, "but justice, and prevention. Should have set off the petards right then and there."

Amalina stared at him, unsure what to say.

"Did you come from the secret rooms and through that vault?" he asked her, eyeing her hard.

"Yes, sir."

"The men?"

She shook her head: "It's all dark. Not even torches, sir. I think they're dead."

"Or they would've done their jobs. How are you still alive?"

She shook her head again, and admitted she didn't know. Then she explained how Piotr had shot the Count, then everyone was gone. She *really* didn't know much. Some might still be alive. But there was no light to tell.

Kralov grunted: "And no weapons." He nodded in a direction, and she saw a small pile of pistols and swords against the inside of the castle wall, as if they'd been thrown there. With a closer look, the weapons were broken down into halves and thirds. It could have only been the handiwork of the Count himself.

"So Piotr did not have his vengeance," Kralov noted under his breath. "And because I was soft-headed, the creature I came here to destroy, after months of preparation, will survive? No. No, it cannot be."

A rallying cry went up, and she saw that two of the armored soldiers had fallen to their white-shirted opponents. But arrows flew in and took one of Kralov's men in the shoulder. There also came the report of rifles. Three new men in armor rushed through the shattered threshold.

Amalina was going to ask who these men were, but Kralov grabbed her wrist and pulled her to him.

"Do you know what is going to destroy him, little Mouse, eh?" Kralov said as he secured the pistol he was trying to load in his belt. "His own soft head. He let you live. He does not kill you, little one, and so you are an asset."

She sensed she was going to be a hostage again.

He forced something into her hands.

"A flint and stone," he told her. "If you need it. But here:" and then he brought up a twist of slow-burning wick and added that carefully to the contents already given. "This should be all you need. Just don't make it obvious. The Count wouldn't suffer me a minute if I dashed through those doors, if I could even get there on my twisted ankle. But you just skip on down to that room with that lit wick and bury him inside this castle. You understand?"

He kept nodding at her until she returned it.

"It'll be a race," he said with a gallows grin, holding up his wick for her to see. "We'll see who gets there first. But you have to try, Mouse. You have to promise me that you will try, or this will have been all for nothing."

Kralov swallowed hard. It was the first time any sadness had broken through his craggy features, and his eyes seemed to droop. "You promise?"

Amalina nodded, feeling the warmth of the smoldering wick against the side of her forefinger and thumb.

"You ready?"

"Yes," she said, trying to picture herself touching off the powder on the first keg, wondering if she would feel the blast, or survive to feel the implosion of so much stone. Buried with the Count.

If such a thing would even kill him.

"Good girl. Let's—"

Riders on horses, wearing the same armor as the ones on foot, charged through the hole in the gate and over the rubble in the courtyard, and swirled around the cart, firing pistols at whoever was behind it, sending up howls of victory.

"Go, go, go, go!" Kralov said, shoving her through an opening between horses. "Go, go, go, go go! For heaven's sake, girl: Go!"

Amalina stumbled and ran, and ran for nothing less than her life, trying to avoid getting shot or trampled. She reached the safety of the entrance hall. Her momentum, and the sound of the pistols firing behind her, kept her moving, her legs cycling ever wider. They carried her to her commanded destination, the hidden rooms, the treasury, the vault, the message center. And somewhere along the way, she'd picked up a torch. She didn't even need the wick anymore, though she still held it.

She stopped.

The last she'd seen of her Commander, he was surrounded by a swarm of cavalry, all armed with pistols and lances. He was down to several men, knives, and maybe a ball shot. He wasn't going to survive.

She looked at the loose spray of gunpowder on the floor, and then at the towers of powder kegs piled at specific points within the large room. Would it really destroy the castle? Bring it down on top of the Count? Or fling him into the air to burn like Icarus as he flew past the sun?

Did she want to share the same fate?

Her body shivered.

She knew pretty well what would happen to *her* if she blew up the castle. But would it be worth it if the Count survived?

This wasn't *her* plan. This was Kralov's plan. Just as before, with Erik tying her to a chair and hanging her out a window, it had been Erik and Lady Flauna's plan to lure the Count into the tower, to enable their ill-conceived getaway. Not Amalina's plan. Never hers.

She had plans. She had plans to work against the Count. To stop him from continuing his crimes against the world. But she was always being pulled into other people's plots and schemes. Poorly designed ones. Ones that took her life for granted and were just as dubious, if not worse than her own.

Amalina closed her eyes and took a large breath. She would not set off the powder. Piotr had ruined Kralov's plans as badly by delaying the destruction of the castle, just as she was now going to. Kralov himself had failed to complete his own mission from a fit of fatal curiosity and error, running to the courtyard to see what had happened to the light instead of touching off the kegs. There was no ill-intention to it, for any of them. She just wasn't going to sacrifice herself—though for a cause she believed in—in a plan in which she did not have complete confidence.

She made sure not to hold the flame of the torch directly above any loose gunpowder on the floor, which meant she mostly held it over oddly shaped pools of blood and the headless bodies of Kralov's men. Their poses were awkward and unsettling. Especially because the bodies had only a jagged round of flesh between their shoulders. She tried not to look at their faces when she came across a head pointed in her direction.

She passed through the rooms, noting distantly that she wasn't afraid of the Count confronting her. Not more than she was of the Commander feeling the sting of disappointment and betrayal. Every minute that passed and the castle didn't detonate was for him confirmation that it wasn't ever going to. That he and his mission had failed. That the Count would live on. And maybe Amalina hadn't done what he'd asked, on purpose.

The trail of bodies led back to the skull room, and ended at what Amalina now assumed was the Count's sleeping chamber. The blood here was thick. She could hear her steps plop and squish as she plodded over the limp, splayed limbs.

She saw Piotr sitting up, leaned against the wall. The way his head was flopped to the side, and how his eyes were absently turned to his lap, and his white shirt, like so many of the others, now a mottled pink-red, she knew he was not alive. First Erik Kosche, now Piotr. These young, handsome, strong men, ending their lives when they rushed them against the permanent stone that is the Count. Only *he* ever survives.

The Count's cloak was centered on the bed, with the lump of his body underneath it. It stirred with a groan.

"This is the worst hour … on the worst possible day … to give me all this unending disturbance," he moaned irritably beneath the cloak, like the resident of an inn whining about the racket keeping him awake. "Mouse. That is *you* isn't it, Mouse?"

"Yes, sir."

"I went to the trouble of locking the door, but I suppose you came the other way," he griped. His hand came up and pointed to the hole leading from the skull room. "Why don't you just go find Genadie and tell him to make sure that one of them remains alive. I don't care which—but Kralov would be most useful. And, Mouse, on your way, please close and lock the doors. Make sure no one else disturbs me, and tell Georg I don't expect to rise until the evening."

Back in the message center Amalina shut the secret shelf door to the deeper chambers. It seemed her torchlight could now not help but reflect off of the metal letters: AXP. And it seemed that, knowing it was there, Amalina could not help but look to the book once again. And she felt the irresistible pull. The Count was trying to sleep. No one was nearby. And should anyone approach, she could put it away.

Opened, the AXP book was like all the rest she'd seen. Pages of gummed in strips of paper, with some written-in annotations in the margins. This book was larger than the others. For some reason, starting around the last third of the pages, the messages were loosely attached. Making them appear like little flags. They all seemed to have an inky smudge on their underside— evidence of the Count's grubby, inked fingers as he worked? When she flipped through the book toward its front, hoping to find some markings to indicate who in Korr these messages were from, or when the correspondence had begun, the movement dislodged a number of the strips. They were made of old, dry pig skin and goat skin, coarsely processed. A hair or two could be seen along the edges.

Amalina tried to fit the fallen strips back into place, but then saw the adhesive was, of course, dried and wouldn't hold. *Good enough*, she thought. She shook them loose from the page and pocketed one. Maybe one of the earlier ones would establish who this 'AXP' was. Then she went through the other pages, randomly pulling away strips, though not taking them. Just making it understood to anyone who might open the book—after she'd been through it—that such things happen, and notice many papers were free or missing. On the final page, which was still incomplete, Amalina detached two, and loosened a third. Then choosing one along the left margin, which she deemed the most inconspicuous, she took and pocketed it. Maybe one of these latest messages would let her know something timely and relevant.

She felt like a thief. And also felt taking these bits was rather pointless. She remembered a rat she'd once seen running off with a length of bootlace. To what purpose? she asked, both then and now.

As if in reward for asking, her eyes fell on the sheets lying on the small standing-desk at the bottom of the stairs. Kralov must have set them there. They were the Commander's unfolded copies of Piotr's maps detailing the rooms beyond the Count's treasury and archives. But she still felt like a pilfering rat as she greedily snatched these pages off the desk and tucked them into her dress for later consumption.

As she entered the upper counting house, she heard and saw the secret door inching shut, as someone in the Count's private study shoved the large cabinet to cover the entrance.

"Wait!" Amalina cried, running to the narrow opening. "Wait, don't close it! I'm here!"

"Ms. Dalca!" Genadie exclaimed, wide-eyed, trying to shield himself from the glare of the torch. "By Zeus, put that torch out! There's explosives everywhere! Send it through before you kill us!"

Amalina did. Then Genadie and she pushed the cabinet open so she could get through.

"What are you still doing in there?" he asked. "I thought you'd gone."

"I came back to check on you and the Count."

"What a trying day for Master," Genadie sighed. With Amalina in the study now, they both worked at getting the cabinet closed. "But no little successes are good enough for him, he must have them all at once. And so he tests himself as mightily as he can, or it shouldn't be worth it."

"Successes?" said Amalina.

"I know," he said, waving his hand, as if agreeing with her on a point that should, anyway, be dismissed. "But who are we to judge what Master decides is important? We can only agree."

"What successes?" she pressed.

"Well, the Princess Spaarvierlet and Kralov, of course. Love and hate. Peace and War. Harmony and Discord." He seesawed his gnarled hands, demonstrating the lifting and settling of scales.

"He didn't completely win this war on his own," said Amalina. "I just saw an army riding in."

"Nothing happens without Zeus' willing it so." Genadie made a face that matched hers, apparently also dissatisfied with his answer. "Besides, Master doesn't *need* them. And he did most of the work, anyway."

"He's back in his bed. I saw it."

"Exactly. He just wants his rest, and this expedient of a new army to fight this afternoon's battle suffices." Genadie shrugged. "What are you arguing about, Ms. Dalca?"

"He told me to tell you that he wants one left alive, preferably Kralov."

Genadie grimaced. "But it's too late. They've been executed."

. . .

Amalina didn't chide Genadie over his belief of Zeus' will *'always being done'* and yet his Zeus' inclination to have Kralov left alive being thwarted. It registered only as one distant, mean, sarcastic thought, sluggishly twirling inside her already exhausted, bewildered brain. Nothing felt humorous. The good guys had fallen, the Count still stood. And there were still pieces that she had to manage into their right place before she could rest.

Hadn't the day begun with her nearly dying in the teeth of that terrifying black wolf? And then her day carried on from there, with an attempted rescue of the princess—and where had *she* ended up?—and assisting Kralov's raid; and becoming a hostage; and witnessing Piotr, who had the Count at pistol point, fall to the creature. And finally, she'd been entrusted by Kralov to perform the final act that would—no, *might*—seal the Count's fate, only to then betray the rightful Commander, and instead be tasked by his enemy to make sure there was a remnant of the Commander's army to play with.

Oh, she wanted the day to end. To slink into her bed and throw the covers over herself and play as if she were the countess of the high castle: demanding this and that and getting her craved rest, as others did her bidding.

Georg, Abraxa and Genadie could do what needed to be done. Amalina would go to the woods and see if she could bring out Lisbet's people and her brother, and return them to the castle. If they hadn't already seen what had happened with the arrival of the new forces and returned on their own.

She kept her eyes down as she entered the courtyard, hoping to avoid seeing the dead bodies of all those men who had been so strong and formidable in the morning. The sun was still above the shoulder of the mountain. The sky was still a deep blue. But these men, she thought gloomily, had been separated from it just by bothering to climb the mountain and enter the castle.

"She's alive," sounded a voice of despair. "She's still alive!"

Amalina whipped her head up and saw who was weeping. It was one of those giant men with the fur caps, cannonball muscles and bushy black beards. He was tied to the cart, and the flames were already running up his chest and had turned his clothes black. Most of the other men tied to the cart were limp, heads dropped to their chests, or leaned backward to gawk at the sky. But three were still very much alive, though dying quickly. One now began to moan. And this first one continued to shout, then scream, with tears steaming in his eyes: "Still alive! She's still alive!"

And this one was staring right at Amalina. And she knew what he was saying, what he meant. It was clear from his abject despair: *She didn't do it!* is what he meant, what he was accusing her of. *She went inside, and she's still alive. She didn't blow the castle!*

She's a traitor!

Kralov made no sound. But his ice cold stare through the flames—aimed at Amalina alone—declared just the same.

48

Thank You

It was hard for Amalina to believe the last she would see of Princess Lisbet Spaarvierlet was on their brief walk from the castle to the princess' waiting carriage. The princess' delicate skin was a shade greyer, and her lips were tight, but her expression, over all, seemed wistful, even as she had to step over and around large chunks of broken walls, battlement and gate.

"Your Uncle hid Carila and I below his chambers," Lisbet was explaining in a light voice. "A secret place these awful men wouldn't have found us. I *told* everyone to trust in Count Tepsji's care. And I'm sure everyone would have preferred to await the conclusion of the assault in that comfortable space with me, attended by Georg and Abraxa, and with a table of nourishments and wine, instead of in the wild forest. The journey itself was quicker and more pleasurable, you have to admit."

"But-But I can't believe you are leaving," said Amalina. "So quickly. I thought you would be staying ... Well, staying forever."

"Forever?"

"You're married, aren't you? I mean, you're married. I mean ... you're getting married."

Lisbet looked surprised, and then smiled condescendingly to Amalina, who she still regarded as the little girl at her silky elbow. "My understanding is that I am to return when all this political tumult has passed. He said there is still more to come."

"Is that what he said?"

"And my parents would never countenance their daughter's daily peace disturbed by these terrible, unpredictable outbursts, no matter how safe *I* may feel."

They arrived at her carriage. Her footman opened the door and practically ordered her inside with his eyes. Astrell, Carila and her nameless maid were also pleading with their eyes for her to hurry up. Amalina was sure, too, that Aklan, who was stowed within his trunk atop the carriage, was also hoping to make this getaway a quick one.

"Abraxa said there's to be a ceremony this morning," said Amalina. "I thought ... Well, I thought that meant you had made your decision. About marrying."

Just as she would pat a silly, naïve child on the head, Lisbet hugged and kissed Amalina. "You can come visit me, if you like. Get free of whatever it is you have going on here. Bring Snowy with. I still see that shadow of something in your eye, which I never saw when you visited. Get free, then. Escape. Let me tell you, Katja, I found the light and escaped my gloom by making my choice. That is how the world works."

"Oh."

"Or, if not, I will return, when the time is right."

"Will you return? You will?"

"My father will insist."

"So then … did uncle show you … it?" whispered Amalina. "What you wanted to see?"

"Hm?" Lisbet twirled herself up into the carriage, but then leaned out the window. She whispered with a smile. "His true love? … or his treasury?"

"When you said your father would insist, I figured he showed you the treasury."

"He did," Lisbet said. "Tell me, have you ever been to the secret rooms *underneath* the Count's bed chamber?"

Amalina shook her head.

Lisbet sent a hand out and opened her palm, in it was a large golden block. Twice the size of the bricks in the counting room. "A present for papa. From the *real* treasury, Katty. Whatever he's showed you, your uncle has ten times more downstairs, the rascal. Don't let him cheat you."

. . .

Amalina wasn't allowed in the great hall. Ham and Gull didn't know who the morning's ceremony was for, or what it was about. Their orders were to keep the great hall closed "until uncle gives word to spring wide the doors."

She shrugged. There were other things to do.

She grabbed an apple off the dining table in *l'entrée grande* and went to the Great Library to think. With Lisbet barely out of the gate, the castle already felt empty and lonely. But somehow it was a relief. With all the other matters cleared by the previous day's storm, she wanted things to become as still and quiet as possible so she could think. So she could decide on what to do next.

"Our high lord instructs me to bring you to the great hall," Abraxa said with a sour note.

"For the ceremony?" Amalina asked, now wondering what this ceremony could be. Especially if the Count required her to be there.

"I should tell our High Lord what I know," said the old maid darkly. "He shouldn't continue to labor under the delusion that you are some innocent, blameless little girl."

"Leave me alone," She was too wrung out to care.

"How can I leave you alone, when you are *dangerous*? Georg told his family they would be safe here, and look what happened. We can't let threats linger ... fester ... become threatening. Better to cut them out."

"So why tell me? Why not just get it over with and report me to uncle?"

"The princess is gone, Mouse. You are no longer the niece. And I'd gladly cut you out today. But as long as His Eminence finds you worthy, I cannot bring myself to challenge his happiness. And as long as you do not challenge his happiness in regards to my Georg, I will remain quiet." Then she sneered. "... but remain always alert, Mouse. No stalemate lasts forever."

"Is this still about the books?" Amalina sighed.

Abraxa's sneer sharpened at one corner. "As I said, only if you bring it up first."

Amalina picked up the catalog and went to the wall. She placed her finger on the spine of a book there.

"What?" Abraxa said, her expression faltering.

"The book you accused me of losing. Here it is. See for yourself. Come. Come here and look and see if it isn't so."

Abraxa charged forward. She screwed her uncomprehending eyes at the title of the book. She took it down off the shelf and compared it to the entry in the catalog. Then she made sure it was placed correctly between the proper titles on the shelf.

"You replaced it," she hissed through gritted teeth.

"Come here," Amalina said.

Then she led Abraxa to the first set of shelves in the room, and drew her attention to spot where the other books were still missing.

"You threaten me—" Abraxa began, but Amalina stamped a foot and lifted a finger into the air.

At first she ducked down and acted like she was searching for something. But then, pulling out the books on the shelves below, she pointed to two sideways books that'd been hidden behind them. Amalina had hidden them there. Had relocated them there months ago, knowing that if she'd tried to hide them in her own bedroom or anywhere else—short of burying them in the forest—they would likely have been found by a snooping Abraxa. However, inside a room of books—things which intimidated Abraxa, things she was afraid to even touch—the missing books would never be found; as long as they were shielded from sight, protected by a front rank of even *larger* intimidating books. Now Amalina took the lost books from their hiding spot and returned them to their places, pushing with a bit of strength to make the proper space for them.

"Are those the books you said Georg misplaced?" Abraxa inquired, not sure if she should be angry or relieved.

"Yes."

"And you hid them there?" anger creeping into her voice, her eyebrows pinching together over her beak and round eyes.

"I don't know how it happened," Amalina lied with a pleasant smile. "But the same thing happened to mine. I simply looked for it thoroughly when I had the time and then found it. And now, with you present as my witness, I just did the same for Georg. And for you."

Before leaving the room, Amalina said: "We are not enemies. We've never been."

. . .

The man with the blocky head and wild mane of hair and dressed in a breastplate, with longsword at his side and helmet tucked under his arm, knelt before the Count. His hands quivered as he cupped them together in a strange display of prayer.

The great hall was mostly empty. There were ten soldiers sorted into two ranks, kneeling in the center of the room, who were similarly dressed as the man before the Count. Ham and Gull stood a distance behind them, with the same slack looks—the blank expression of Georg's entire clan—as when Kralov's rebellion had descended into the castle.

The Count was on the raised dais where the grand thronal chair sat. But he was standing, looking down with a mustache-rubbing complacence at the figure before him. Genadie was perched beside the throne, looking wary.

Amalina entered and walked around the sides of the room to get closer and hear what was being said.

"Oh, Great and Mighty Knight of Ardeel," the man with the blocky head and wild hair was saying, with drops of tears or snot or slobber, or all three, dripping from his face. "I devote my life, and the lives of all those who have sworn their service to me, to stand and protect you against all enemies. You are the sole savior of this land, Mighty One. Of the truest Ardeelian blood!"

"It is to me you make this promise, and me alone?" the Count asked in his ceaselessly self-referential way.

"By the blood of my brow!" The man took his dagger and slashed it across his forehead. Blood flowed freely onto the stone. He shook as if in ecstasy. Genadie held his nose and rolled his eyes, but then settled into looking jealous.

"I am glad of your coming," said the Count.

"Now that you have chosen to raise yourself, Your Eminence, it is time for all who are loyal to you, those who have signed their names to your cause, to declare their fealty. And to join your side."

"Have I risen from somewhere?" the Count asked himself, absently. "I have always *been*."

"Yes, your lordship. And you always shall be!"

"Of course." Then, as a side thought: "And all your soldiers believe as you do?"

"I swear to it. As they have sworn to me once before, they now swear to you."

"Not exactly though."

The ten soldiers were quick enough to understand, and drew their daggers and disfigured their faces in a fast and bloody manner. The Count stroked his mustache and murmured contentedly.

"You may rise," he said. "And see to it your entire army is of the same mind."

"Yes, Master of the Mountains," the man backed away until he was with his men. Then he stood proudly. The red X dripping down his face. "May you reign for eternity! And when the others come bent in supplication to your feet, remember that it was my family line who arrived first as your sword and shield. And believe that I shall never disappoint you in your service."

"I won't forget your flattering oath. But tell me, who are you?"

"Zsolt Marosh," he said, stirring his sword in the air.

• • •

The Count dismissed Zsolt with a brief wave of appreciation. Then he beckoned Amalina to his chair, onto which he curled himself, twirling his mustache vigorously. He waited with a glimmering eye for the others to exit. "Genadie, see everyone out," he said when he realized his servants had remained behind to serve him. Genadie did so. Then the two were alone.

He stared at her with his large, unmoving eyes. They felt like two weighted orbs before her, getting larger and larger. She redirected her eyes to the floor, and then stepped to the side to take her feet out of Zsolt's blood. The Count left his mustache alone now, his face a stone mask.

"Sir?"

"The Princess Lisbet Spaarvierlet," he whispered—more hummed—confidentially.

"Oh."

"Oh?"

Amalina glanced at him, confused. "I thought you—we—were going to talk about what happened."

"Yes," he said enthusiastically. Then he paused: "What do you mean? *What* happened?"

"The attack," she explained. "Yesterday. By Kralov."

"Kralov," he chuckled, as if remembering some long lost comrade whom he'd lost a bet to. "Yes, well, that Marosh fool didn't keep him alive as I wanted. So much for not disappointing me."

"I don't know if he knew he was supposed to spare the Commander," said Amalina. Then added quickly at the Count's frown: "The message didn't get to him in time."

"It matters little to me anyway, I suppose," the Count went on, rolling his eyes at the ceiling. "I know how the old circus tumbler did it. I can't tell you how long I've been waiting for someone to read that damned book and get ideas. I thought I'd managed to destroy all the extant copies. But it was too much to hope for. I might as well have had it published for all I kept worrying."

"Sir?"

"I have told you of my aversion to the sun, have I not? How my ever increasing sensitivity to its cleansing rays has made my exposure to it dangerous. My flesh is as dry wood to the flame, and the pain it exacts upon me ..." He shook his head with a look of displeasure. "*On Burning Glass*, is what it's called. A treatise by Dioclese on how mirrors and glass can be used to reflect the sun's rays, to transmit and intensify them, and use them for the express purpose of setting fire to objects. When I came across this *Greek*—" he emphasized the word for no apparent reason "—this *Greek* philosopher's work—translated into Latin, of course—I envisioned how it could be used against me. Oh, if I could ever be said to fear, Ms. Dalca, it is *that* theory I most feared: that someone would discover it and put it into practice against me. For the light is the only element in the world that can outrace me, and can convert my limbs to coal. I envisioned it ... and I was right, wasn't I?

"Kralov, that clever Muscovite," chortled the Count. "He either developed the theory on his own, or he was introduced to that book. An old, musclebound acrobat is no student of the sciences. And so he has read Dioclese somewhere; no matter the lengths I have gone to make sure that no other copy exists than the one I possess. A foolish waste of time on my part. Fortune does not favor the destruction of knowledge. And no matter how deeply and for how long I feared it, Kralov implemented its principles impeccably. And yet how little should I have feared, eh? It is too fragile a weapon. An overturned brazier, a smoked glass, or a cloud of steam can obscure it. An imprecise turn can foil it. An unexpected ally can ride in with his army and interrupt it ..." After silent reflection: "Even clothing can lessen the light's effect. What a waste of my time my fear was."

Amalina scratched at her raised eyebrows. He knew where the idea for the mirrors had come from, but he hadn't gone to his trunk to see if the book was still there? He was that convinced of its security? Or was he too fearful of the other items within the trunk that he thought it just as easy not to verify it was still there, and assume Kralov had found a copy of the text which he hadn't destroyed?

"Well, even if someone were to imagine a better way to implement the principle against me, I now have Marosh and his army as an added layer of defense. And that should be more than adequate to dispose of—or at least delay—even the largest forces to come against me. It is no longer a worry of mine, Ms. Dalca."

Amalina nodded, feeling relieved that he was not accusing her of being complicit in the attack, or Kralov's accomplice.

"You mentioned Princess Lisbet, sir?"

"Oh, yes, yes, yes," he stroked his mustache with renewed relish. He sat up in his chair, and leaned toward Amalina. "That is why you are here, isn't it?"

"About the Princess?"

"When you attempted to tell me about her, on your return from the western kingdoms, your best description was that the Flemish Princess Lisbet Spaarvierlet was 'Nice'."

"She was, wasn't she, sir?"

"You could have said, instead, that she was slender. And graceful in her movements. With skin as white, delicate and as smooth to the touch as porcelain."

"What's porcelain?"

"Never mind for the moment. Or that her hair was like a fountain of spun gold."

"It reminds me more of a great bale of hay," Amalina interjected. "But more yellow. Not gold, as such."

"A bale of hay is a giant, hulking stack. It is dead. A fountain pours and flows and has a vitality to it. You see what I mean? And her eyes are disks of a tantalizing hue, their color like the welcoming deep indigo waters of Lesbos."

"I've never seen Lesbos. And I thought her eyes more looked like blueberries."

"Will you be quiet?" said the Count, testily, but still with a toothful smile and sparkle in his eye. "I'm trying to teach you something here about serviceable, or adequate, if not elevated, description."

"But isn't that what Genadie's portraits are for?"

"Then let's tackle 'Nice', little Mouse. I would say, instead, that she is pleasant company; mannered; learned, though not precocious about it. Above all, she is considerate of others before herself, with acute sensitivity to their moods and desires, and accommodating, even at her own comfort's expense. I suppose that could all be wrapped up by 'pleasant company', but it is more specific. It would have been helpful to know, also, that she is more than simply devout in her religion. Short of taking to the habit, she is observant in her duties to faith and keenly punctual in partaking her services. Oh, yes, and observant in other manners, too. Those *blueberries* of hers are very keen, indeed. She misses very little."

"She is obedient to her parents," Amalina said helpfully.

"More so to her father, wouldn't you say?"

"And she is conflicted."

"Conflicted?" the Count drew back in surprise. "What an odd thing to say."

"But she is. She wants love. Her own love. Chosen by her heart. But her father wants her to match for money."

"Yes," his left nostril lifted disagreeably at a thought. "It did impede our speaking naturally. I wanted sparkling conversation, and a taste of civilization and society outside these mountains. Which was difficult with her constantly plumbing for the depth of my fortunes. Oh, you were right there, Ms. Dalca: how I had to practically provide her with a notarized manifest of my holdings to pry away her prejudices and misgivings.

"But it wasn't all that bad," he said with a bold grin and leaning in again. "Once she was sure that I wasn't a swindler, she revealed a passion that I must insist was more than accommodation. How she matched me, delight for delight. And as I savored the full measure of her skin—a doll of the finest china has never been imported; a netsuke for my own pleasure. She pressed her lips to mine, half-parted and panting, eager to taste my flesh."

The Count nearly gasped. He licked his lips, and where someone flying off on such a reverie might have closed their eyes and thrown their head back, his eyes grew wide and carnivorous, as he sought Amalina's attention. "And though she shut her eyes at other moments, those bilberries of hers stared into mine, as if seeking to connect our souls through them. I cannot convey to you precisely the joy of running my hands over her round tummy, or grasping her breasts, topped with the ripest of raspberries—"

It went on like this for a while. And for Amalina, the event he was sharing so descriptively made her feel embarrassed and awkward. She didn't know why he was telling her this, or why it seemed so important for him to do so. Only when he was near the conclusion, did she think of small children she had known who went on so eagerly about a subject—say, seeing a frog ride on a swan's back, for instance—and becoming only more impassioned with the passing moment, almost in frustration by how their listener wasn't being similarly swept away by the novelty and excitement. He wasn't confessing or confiding, so much as sharing the full feeling he had, hoping to relive it—reexperience it—by working inside Amalina the same degree of passion. Not knowing what to say, she patiently let him continue until he was done.

"And I let her dip her hands into my treasure, and even take a present of it back home." He was speaking of the gold brick he'd given Lisbet now. His smile slid into something a little more coldly cynical: "To beguile her father; the way we enthralled each other that night. I can't have my princesses coming here again with their minds diverted by apprehension about my finances. With that present, if her father does not speak of it, she will. And I won't again be beset by auditors in skirts, but ladies of genuine and open interests."

"Um, yes, sir," she said, trying to keep in mind that this man who was so raptly pulled up in his throne, was the man who had killed, with his own hands, Piotr, Erik Kosche, poor Lucinda Skeldar, and many, many, many, so many more.

"I'm delighted to have spotted you in your window," he said, his mind finding a similar track. "And that I spared you that night. Remember that night? While I just *knew* you would be of tremendous service to me, nobody could have guessed how intelligent, and talented, and helpful you would become. I'm so glad for you being there, Ms. Dalca, and overjoyed at my finding you. Such a surprising reward."

Though she didn't want to, she blushed. And in the companionability of the moment, thinking, *I might as well try*, she asked: "Sir, may I go home now?"

Epilogue

Eastern Princess

"**I**'m sorry what happened, Mr. Bronk."

Attila patted Hak on his big bronze shoulder. Though Attila's eyes were at their regular half-mast, he was obviously distracted after returning from the nearby town. "You don't have to keep apologizing, Sir Vogoneyevic. I've told you that already."

"I can't help it. I feel bad every time I see you." Hak rubbed at the dirty bandages on his head. When he did so he winced at all the other wounds distributed across his body. He didn't grimace or groan, but seemed to laugh a little, like the pain tickled him. Then he remembered how he got his wounds and commenced to grimace. He'd killed men.

"You just need to get better. And fast."

"You heard something, Mr. Bronk?"

"It's unbelievable, Sir Vogoneyevic."

"I think I told *you* you don't have to keep calling me that, Mr. Bronk."

"I need to," said Attila, turning to his wounded charge, who was laying on—dwarfing—a small cot inside a makeshift cabin of branches and leaves. "I need to call you by your proper title, now more than ever."

"How is that? Something's happened?"

"Beyond my wildest imaginings," the former low constable admitted. "This is nothing I ever would have thought of or considered with all logic at my disposal."

"Is Gug and the children all right?" Hak was suddenly concerned. He'd never seen anything get this small, strange man so unsettled.

"Perfectly safe," assured Attila. "Rest your mind about your family. Do you remember that carriage we saw passing along the road?"

"How'll I forget?" Hak gave another rueful laugh, touching his bandages.

"Not the governor's carriage. I mean the one we saw yesterday."

"The one with the pretty horses?"

"That's the one, sir. It carried a western princess. She'd just come from visiting Netz, and the Count's high castle there. She'd been staying there as a guest. As *his* guest."

"A princess, you say?"

"A princess from the west. Things have happened since I've been gone. The castle is now fully occupied. In fact, there was a battle."

"General Marosh? How did he do?"

"Amazing, Sir Vogoneyevic," only his voice didn't make it sound like a positive thing. "Astounding, Sir. Most incredible and unbelievable."

"I believe you," said Hak. "What is it? Did he win? Did he lose?"

"But it wasn't General Marosh at all. It was someone else altogether. As far as I can tell, it was Zsolt Marosh who came to the rescue. His army now occupies the castle, and has sworn to defend it and his patron against any force who would seek to attack him."

"Marosh is on the monster's side?" Hak whistled.

"Even more astounding, there's now another princess at the castle. Living there, they say. She's from Ardeel. I don't know who she is, but I can only assume she's related to the Count himself, somehow."

"An eastern princess." Hak whistled again. Attila's expression somehow flattened even more in annoyance.

"She could be just another hideous entity like him," Attila muttered. "Who knows? But that means the Count is coming out of hiding. And he now has an ally, a 'daughter', and a formidable army to act in his defense."

Hak whistled once more. Attila's expression couldn't flatten any further. His lips wriggled.

"And so why does all that stuff mean you have to call me by my title, again?" inquired Hak.

"Because that means you are the only hope that's left in this country, if it is to throw this monster off its back. You must rise as a hero, like never before, and lead your people against the Count and the treacherous scum like Zsolt who would choose to throw in with him." Attila's right hand grasped his shaking left. "And let me tell you, Sir Vogoneyevic, your job has just got a hundred times harder."

Hak seemed to swallow, and didn't whistle any more.

• • •

To bypass the doldrums and inactivity of winter, Amalina was sent away from the high castle before the first snow to make calls in Venice, Milan, and Rome. She declined Genadie's offer to take her to Korr to visit her father along the way as he'd done (somewhat) the previous outing. Witnessing her father and Jenna's precision teamwork in the bakery again, or chance encountering Dragomir and the Widow Lidsz as they canoodled in the street would only reinforce the bitter rage in her heart. Best to go without thinking about it. Before she left the castle, the only modification to the Count's previous instructions was that she should purchase more dresses, take more notes, and refer to the castle as *'the Palace of Pleasures'*; pleasure made plural, not singular. Plural pleasure seemed to matter to him, and he felt it would matter abroad, too. As a precaution, Amalina packed away all her secret materials (maps, ciphers, the Count's and AXP's pilfered private pigeon messages) and took them with. She had no intention of reading any of it. It felt pointless. In some moments she considered throwing the box containing them off a bridge, or burning the materials just to prevent their being found. Because the demands of that life was behind her now, despite the recurring dreams of Lucinda Skeldar skipping through the flax—no, remembering now, it was the barley—her head bouncing ever closer above their yellow crowns, demanding Amalina deliver justice for her; and the memory of Kralov's final glower as the flames ate him, accusing her of betrayal; even hearing again the protesting cries of White Snow at her abandoning the poor horse to the wolves (all for no purpose, to no end). Those visions might haunt her, and cause her to sit up in the middle of the night crying denials at their ghosts, but they did not rouse her enough to resume her work again against the Count. All that plotting felt like something old and dead; in the past. A more exciting future, one filled with life and promise, and free of lies and wanton carnage, lay just in front of her slaloming carriage. Liberty spreading ahead as far as … as far as eternity. With the freedom of escape there was no need to move backwards.

Much could be said of Princess Katarina Tepsji's experiences in Italy, as novel and colorful as they were, but they will be reserved for another time. The only relevant note here is that one of the many new friends she made— a clever friend—discovered a flaw in her. This friend observed and remarked on the faces Katarina made when reading, and the troublesome distance she held the page before her eyes when reading, and determined that the Ardeelian Princess could use some spectacles—pieces of glass done up in frames with armatures on either side—to help her read easier, and prevent the headaches she suffered. Maybe Princess Katarina's sudden and surprising response to this discovery was merely a way to fashion one more good excuse not to examine the materials she could use against the Count, as it required the use of her "tired" eyes. Or maybe it was in order to deny the weakness perceived in her; and as well, prevent the addition to her face a contraption so ridiculous looking. But she left Rome before this set of glasses could be made.

En route to Paris, after nearly three months of enjoying her first snow-free winter, and wearing the clothes and persona of someone who was not truly herself but someone she couldn't help but feel she was becoming, after so long playing the role, Amalina allowed for a moment to reflect on her life so far and how the past two years impacted it. As the solemn, brown, winter scenery passed outside her window, the leafless trees looking like blackened witches' hands grasping and fondling the low clouds, her thoughts took on melancholy colors. And she especially resented this past summer and fall, when she was forced to play one role on one side, and then play just as faithfully on the other. And then worse: having to play both at once when she was caught in between. And neither side represented what she truly wanted.

How fair was it that everyone in her life got to press their own demands on her? And why could they? Because they are older? Because they are stronger than her? Her father had raised her as a baker, a replacement for his wife, her mother. But as much as she longed to return home and to his comforting arms, did she want to *really* be a baker, and spend her life schilling loaves and muffins in the town of Korr? The Count used her as a charming liaison to the outside world, which was fascinating and exciting when she was in the courts of the foreign countries, but back in Ardeel, in his company, she was burdened with his crimes—crimes that outstripped the savagery of Genghis Khan. Did she really want to continue in the employ of a monster? And in their own turns, Erik Kosche, and then Kralov, had forced her into their service in order to combat the Count, ignoring her own plans and advice and simply *using* her because of her convenient placement next to their enemy. But did she really want to continue to be caught up in the centuries' long rivalry between humanity and the Count?

What do I really want? she asked herself.

She wanted to be herself, was the conclusion. No longer would she allow herself to be pushed and pulled by outside forces. When she wanted something, she would pursue it, using all the tools she'd been provided in these past years. She would no longer be anyone's spy, but she would be the spymaster; if spying was needed. She would be the monster killer; if killing a monster was needed.

When thinking of the Count, she no longer saw him as an existential threat to mankind. As much as he was nearly omnipotent, he believed he was caught within a cage. As long as he believed that way, he was. And though he had the ability to destroy every living creature within his boundaries, he would never do so. Look at the way he was enamored with life. How he waited on every word of her reports of culture and humanly doings. And how he lavished such immoderate care on his outside guests, in order to entice them, to share their existence with him. Look at the message center, that massive archive of intercourse he kept within his treasury. Communications from centuries ago are as valuable to him as the gold tucked away in the smaller room next to them. Why, the message center's contents dwarf the counting house's by the thousands at least. And look how painstakingly he preserves even the smallest communique.

The Count's real weakness was a simple one, never mind his physical vulnerabilities which might or might not be exploited. His secret was that he loved playing this game, this endless game with the ordinary people of

Ardeel. And he would continue it forever, because being trapped, he would never dare to kill everyone there in fear it would end. So he needed them to be there. Or else he would be lonely, and lost.

The monster was now only half, or a quarter of the one she'd imagined him to be. He was at the mercy of his own affliction—the need to consume human blood in order to exist. And he was doing what anyone—even someone as upstanding as the mayor of Korr—she was certain—would do if faced with that choice; maybe even—was it possible?—the minister's wife, Sadra, would do.

And so she would continue to serve the Count because he did have the power to wreak unimaginable destruction on her life and those she loved, and she did not want that to happen. But she would no longer fret about her circumstances, or feel compelled to seek out his destruction based on the belief that he was a threat to life itself. What had Genadie said once? Who knows why Zeus chooses that he should need blood to survive? Who knows why Zeus has decided to be weakened by certain substances? Who knows why Zeus keeps a wretched woman tied to a wheel in a room beneath his castle? *Who knows why the Count does what he does?* It was no matter anymore. He was the way he was, things were the way they were, and so Amalina would be what she would be. She would ride in his carriage, and meet with whom he instructed, and partake of an elevated life of society which she would never have experienced had she remained by her father's side at the oven. She made this choice. According to Lisbet it would get her free. She wondered, with a little anxiety, how life would react to her decision.

To celebrate her newfound independence in the world, such as it was, Amalina began buying silver trinkets and jewelry. She hid them from Genadie, but wore them in private. Or she would sneak them out to wear when Genadie—or any of their hired help—weren't around to see the effect it had on her newfound Frank friends.

. . .

Amalina insisted to Genadie they stay one more week in Paris, in order to attend the ball being held in honor of the opening of a newly completed bridge—which also coincided with the arrival of a number of battalions that had put down a revolt of some kind. (Amalina wasn't clear who was fighting, because her friends didn't know; or they were bored in discussing the matter). The ball promised to be the height of excitement, the talk of the year, as the noble daughters competed for the attention of the handsomest officers. From a secret fold in her dress, Amalina donned a silver necklace with five tear-drop cut rubies along its length. It didn't match her dress, but it did draw to her neck the eyes highest in demand that night.

It would be a personal triumph if she could cap off her stay in this magical city by ending it in the arms of a brilliant looking man in uniform. She would be talked about in important circles for weeks after she'd left.

"It's you!" said a high-pitched male voice. When she turned to the man at her shoulder who'd said this, he took her hand and grabbed her arm and said: "Yes, it is! It is!"

He had a thin face, a long, scooped nose, and wide eyes that were almost circular. His small, thin mouth was cut like a v, with lines of almost a smirk etched permanently on one side. He had a puffy brown wig atop his head, and wore finely crafted black clothes that were more of an eastern look than what was custom in the colorful France and Italy. But as much as he was looking at her and touching her and addressing her with the familiarity of a close friend, she didn't recognize him.

"I couldn't believe my eyes at first," he said. "Must be a trick of the light, I thought. But then, what light? It's her, indeed. The artisan princess. Who's been kidnapped from her father by a Strigoi, a monster from Hades, or what was it?"

"What?" she said, not able to focus on his face very well. She felt a hot blush spread across her cheeks. "Who? I don't know what you're talking about."

"I told my friend your story and he just found it so intriguing. He was thinking he should write it into a story."

"I don't know you." Amalina tried to pull away, but he held her to him.

"No, no, no. I was there. At the inn. That night you told your story. I saw you come in with that strange looking man. And you can't tell me it isn't you, because I just saw that very man on my way into the palace. And it was that same carriage, too. Those two details I will never forget. And I just knew when I saw them that I would find you here inside. And here you are!"

She didn't know what he wanted. His eyes and tone were somehow familiar and mocking at the same time.

"I am Princess Katarina Tepsji," she said, trying to make it sound important.

"Yes! That's the name you gave, wasn't it? Or was it the rodent-looking driver, when the tailor came to work on your dress? Oh, yes, I remember it all. And that was such an interesting night." His smile changed to a small, dissatisfied smirk. "But it's too bad, I think. Yours was such a heartbreaking story. But for someone being kept as a prisoner in a castle by a monster, you sure do get around. Kind of puts a stink to the tale a little."

When he laughed his grip loosened. She didn't see any of her friends nearby and was glad of it. They wouldn't have heard him. And she was free to pull her arm from him with a violent tug and wouldn't have to do any explaining later.

"Leave me alone," she growled as she fled from him, and pressed as hard as she could into the center of the crowds. She had to turn sideways, and nearly took two people off their feet with her wide skirt. But she had to get away from him. She almost regretted having insisted on staying for the ball, and thought to find a way to an exit and have Genadie speed them away.

But then she decided she couldn't just disappear like that. The thought of sharing a dance with her new friends, and showing off a lieutenant at her side was too much of an intoxicant to give up so easily. She just shoved forward harder, hoping for forgiveness from everyone because she was a stranger and younger than most of the other girls. She looked back to see if the man was in pursuit.

She ran into a blood-red uniform with a wide-shouldered back. At her speed, and with the surprise, she should have pitched him forward. But this soldier was sturdy, with thick legs like two trunks of a tree, and was well-grounded. It was like slamming into a stone wall with a thick crimson wool tapestry hung on it. She rebounded with a shout of surprise. And he must have shook a little because he spilled the drink he was holding.

The soldier turned in place as best he could in the crowd, and looked down upon her with his flashing hazel eyes. Not with anger but a smile of curiosity. But then his face changed suddenly, his expression quaking under the strain of so many emotions.

"A-Amalina?" he stuttered in astonishment. "Amalina Dalca? It's you, isn't it? But it couldn't be. It couldn't. It just *couldn't*."

And that was what she was thinking: It couldn't be … *It just couldn't*.

Here he was, after so many years, Ivanti Ion Vokent. The love of her life.

He took Amalina in his arms, scooping her off the floor, and with a whoop he threw her into the air. She felt like she was flying.

AMALINA'S DARK ADVENTURE

THROUGH IMPOSSIBLE CHALLENGES ...

... AND EVER GREATER DANGERS ...

FOLLOW AMALINA DALCA ...
AS SHE BATTLES HER WAY OUT!

www.badhoundpress.com